A Lamentation of Swans

by

Kerry Blaisdell

Wicked Portland #1

A Lamentation of Swans (Wicked Portland #1)

Lello Ball Enterprises
P.O. Box 331, Beaverton, OR 97075

Publishing History: First Edition, 2025
Print ISBN 978-1-951141-13-4
Digital ISBN 978-1-951141-12-7

Published in the United States of America

Dedication

For the Omicron Group: Joyce, Julie & Kevin.
Your faith in me and this book kept me going.
You're the best!

THE SWAN
Frank Stuart Flint (1885–1960)

Under the lily shadow
and the gold
and the blue and mauve
that the whin and the lilac
pour down on the water,
the fishes quiver.

Over the green cold leaves
and the rippled silver
and the tarnished copper
of its neck and beak,
toward the deep black water
beneath the arches,
the swan floats slowly.

Into the dark of the arch the swan floats
and into the black depth of my sorrow
it bears a white rose of flame.

Chapter One

Summer 1904 – Portland, Oregon

"TO PROTECT FAIR GUESTS – Many girls
are lured to the city at times of expositions.
The Traveler's Aid committee is in a great
measure preventing a repetition of the awful
record of the Chicago World's Fair in 1893,
when 693 girls left home and were never heard
from again…" —*The Morning Oregonian*

The pretty girl with the blonde ringlets stood on the busy corner, glancing from side to side. She wasn't quite his type, a little green, but beggars couldn't be choosers. He shifted his weight and scanned the crowd: men, women, children, hurrying about their business in the fading light, rushing to make it home in time for supper.

The musk of horse dung and the salty tang of human sweat filled his nostrils, and he withdrew a handkerchief and held it over his nose. No one paid him any heed, and he wiped the perspiration from his brow before replacing the linen square in his breast pocket.

It had been smart to save his uniform all these months. The dark wool trousers scratched his raw skin mercilessly, and the matching coat and cap were heavy for this heat, but the air of respectability they provided outweighed any discomfort. His collar pressed into the open sores on his neck, and he tugged it aside, relishing the moment of relief as he refocused on the girl. The crowd swirled around her like smoke from the fires of Hell, making her appear and disappear, again and again.

God had revealed her to him, and she *would* be his.

The power and the lust and the rage throbbed in his loins, and he clenched his fists. He must not seek his release now under cover of his coat. He *must* expel his excess fluids not into his hand, but into the young, sweet vessels God provided him. The Gospel was absolute and unyielding: It was his *duty* to purify the unclean.

The girl turned expectantly, as though someone had called her name, but then her face fell. She was in her late teens or perhaps just cresting twenty. Young, but not overly so. He had no truck with those who defiled children, the True Innocents. But this one, her full breasts mounded like the ripe, sweet fruit of Eden under the fine lawn of her blouse, *she* needed saving.

He caressed her with his eyes, admiring the cut of her jacket and skirt. Even her straw bonnet was well-made, the weave tight and uniform, its blue ribbon tied jauntily. It must have cost a pretty penny.

He frowned. Could that be a complication?

The advantage to whores was that hardly anyone ever missed them, and their procurers, if they had one, could be bribed into silence or coerced into acceptance. But this girl was surely not alone in the world, however solitary she might be at this moment. If she went missing, would a brace of angry males—father, brothers, uncles, perhaps a sweetheart—seek retribution?

He examined her again more critically, comparing her to the other ladies on the busy sidewalk. Her attire, while modish, seemed less sophisticated than that of her peers: more countrified, as though she were new to the city. Perhaps she had come to Portland seeking employment, like so many young women these days. Perhaps her family was far from here after all.

It was such a shame when one, or two, or…more…of these girls went missing. But not unexpected. The world was a dangerous place, seething with corruption and sin.

Fortunately, he was here to combat both.

He stepped into the dusty street, heedless of the horses, wagons, automobiles and bicycles, the masses that surged and clawed and fought to swallow him.

Yes. Their loss was *such* a shame. But not as shameful as wasting God's gifts. For he had been filled—*filled*—with a purpose that he *must* share, to bring the Truth of the Word to all sinners, everywhere. *God's* Word. God had chosen *him*, and through him, *her*.

He reached the corner and climbed onto the wood sidewalk in front of her. Up close, her scent of lavender water wafted over him, and he saw she had rouged her cheeks and lips, altering the gifts bestowed upon her by God. The rage seethed, feeding his shameful lust. His duty was not enjoyment; his duty was purification and returning the little lost birds to their Heavenly nest.

He swept off his hat and bowed. "Good afternoon, miss. I wonder if you might need some assistance?"

She regarded him curiously, no doubt judging the poor condition of his leather boots, the simple cut of his cheaply-made uniform. But in the end, it was this which decided her: The authority of his profession prevented her shying away and demanded politeness.

She smiled gratefully. "Oh, thank you! You are too kind!"

"Not at all, my dear. Not at all…"

Chapter Two

Saturday July 23

"WOMAN CRAZED BY INTENSE HEAT –
Loses Her Reason While En Route to
Jacksonville with Her Four Children – Her
actions became so annoying that the conductor
thought it unsafe for her to continue the
journey alone. Her husband has been
communicated with." —*The East Oregonian*

Solace Grey sat back on her booted heels in the bone-dry dirt and admired her handiwork. She needed to water, and the quarter-height garden fence wanted painting. Perhaps Allen could do that when he returned from the library. But in all, a good day's work. The little garden was now bursting with color and scent: upright fuchsias contrasted with low stonecrop; sweet alyssum lay at the feet of black-eyed-Susans; delphiniums, hostas, and foxgloves prepared to tower over their neighbors; and vinca and lobelia were poised to fall gracefully over the stone border she'd built yesterday.

To the left of the house lay the vegetable garden, planted by the previous tenants with neat rows of lettuce, cabbages, and peas, plus tomatoes in the center, and "sprawlies" like summer squash and pumpkins on the edges where they could roam to their hearts' content. To these Solace had added beneficials, such as wild carrot to boost tomato fruiting, and dill and fennel to repel aphids, slugs, cabbage loopers, and squash bugs. But otherwise, a bit of weeding and pruning, and one would hardly know it had been neglected half the summer.

Not so the flower beds, which after two days' hard labor were barely domesticated.

She glanced at the sky from under her straw bonnet. Whoever said it "always" rained in Oregon had never summered here. Nothing but relentless blue above, and an orange-hot sun hovering over the West Hills. Her poor plants would be dead tomorrow if she didn't get back to work. But there wasn't much she *could* do until the mulch arrived. Surely it should have come by now. Hadn't Mr. Fisher said all deliveries were made by six on Saturdays?

It must be well past that. Allen would be home soon, expecting to be fed, but cooking had quite slipped her mind. She'd have to improvise a cold supper and finish the garden tomorrow.

A quiet footfall in the rutted lane behind her made her rise and turn sharply. A man loomed, closer than expected, and she stepped back. He was middle-aged and stocky, only a few inches taller than she, with brown hair and long mustaches. He wore a navy single-breasted wool coat, matching trousers, and a helmet, which he tipped deferentially.

"Deeply sorry, ma'am. Didn't mean to frighten you."

His ingratiating manner touched a nerve. Or perhaps it was the heat and irritation over the delayed delivery. She put on a polite smile, using her apron to scrub ineffectually at the dirt on her hands and forearms. "Think nothing of it. May I help you?"

He glanced up the deserted block at the quiet houses,

shuttered against the late afternoon sun, before meeting her gaze again. "Mrs. Grey, is it?"

She also glanced around the empty lane. The mix of maples, oaks, and evergreens cast long, obscuring shadows. Even the neighbors' children, who had earlier been playing bats noisily in the road, were long gone. "Forgive me. I don't believe we have met. You are…?"

He bowed, indicating the brass badge on his left breast, which she had previously missed. "Detective Jenkins, ma'am, of the Portland Police."

"Of course! I should have recognized the uniform. But…did you say you are a detective, not a patrolman?"

"Yes. We are visiting the neighborhood as a service to our citizens. I believe you are new to Portland, and may not have heard of Joshua Creffield and his Holy Rollers?"

"I don't think so…"

"I thought not. He has committed a number of heinous crimes. You needn't worry your pretty little self over *what* he's done, but there is a statewide manhunt to locate him."

"I see," Solace murmured. *Pretty little self, indeed!* "How long has he been missing?"

She had not meant it as a barb, but he flushed. "Not long. He and his second, a Major Brooks, left Corvallis—that's south of here—three months ago after they were tarred and feathered. We believe Brooks died from his wounds, but Creffield could be anywhere."

He peered at the house's foundation as though the fugitive might pop out from under it. Surely Creffield was not so brazen as to hide in Portland, with its large police force searching for him? Still, for once Solace was glad they had no cellar nor even a crawl space.

As though reading her thoughts, the detective said, "Have you a shed, Mrs. Grey?"

"Yes, but it is not big enough for a man to hide in. Only a few shelves, no floor space."

"Pity. I see you are an avid gardener."

He stepped over the small fence and moved to inspect the side yard vegetable beds. "You've put weeds in the borders. Why?" Seeing her puzzled frown, he added, "I am from New York City and now have my first garden. I only wondered why you would plant them."

It seemed a strange topic given his stated errand, but perhaps he was being polite. "The wild carrot has beneficial effects, such as increasing production. The others are edible and repel pests, or in the case of the marigolds, attract bees, which aid in pollination."

"Ah. Did your *husband* teach you all that?"

Dear God, was he fishing for information about Allen? He *was* a detective. And there were those incidents, first in Wichita, then later in Berkeley…

But those had nothing to do with Allen. Merely coincidence. All cities were susceptible to the criminal element, and if she looked for patterns, she would find them. Jenkins was only being condescending. But either way, she must not act as if his words had affected her.

"My apologies, detective. I really must go in and make supper. Was there anything else?"

He returned to her side. "Yes, since you mention cooking. Perhaps you have not heard the other news making headlines, about the packers' strike in Chicago?"

Was he a cop—or a newspaperman? "I'm afraid not. What has that to do with Portland?"

"Most of our meat ships from the Midwest. If you have a large ice box, you may want to stock up before the butcher shops run out. I bought a whole side of beef last week, and they were already low."

Just then, a wagon creaked around the corner from Lownsdale Avenue. The driver spied her by the only tilled garden on the shabby, rundown lane and aimed the horse toward her.

Detective Jenkins pursed his lips, then bowed. "I'll be going now. I only wanted to warn you about Creffield. If you see anything unusual, report it immediately."

"Of course," she said, but he had already moved down the block, away from the wagon.

She unrolled her sleeves, soiling them further. She must look a sight. All day, sweat had trickled from under her hat, and she had wiped it away, never considering the smudges she made. Her low bun was nearly undone, and she couldn't bear to think what state her blouse and brown wool work skirt were in. Detective Jenkins must be accustomed to seeing people at their worst. But here she stood, covered in dirt, about to receive her second caller of the day. Fortunately, Fisher's delivery man was his elderly father, presumably with eyesight to match.

Except it *wasn't* white-haired Mr. Fisher senior at the reins. The man driving looked to be only a little older than she, perhaps nearing thirty, with a shock of auburn hair under his wide-brimmed hat. The stubble on his jaw glinted red-gold in the sunset, giving him a fierce, bandit-like appearance, and he sat tall, gaze unwavering, like a man who knew what he wanted and took it.

Solace untied her filthy apron and tossed it over the fence. She twitched her skirts into place and patted her hair for any loose pins. Then she stopped herself. What on earth was she doing? He had no business looking at her hair, and she had no business caring if he did.

For shame! And you a married woman, whose loyal and loving husband will be home any minute, expecting his wife to care for him, as he cares for her.

The devil on her shoulder protested the strict veracity of this, but she squelched it.

Married is married, no matter the circumstances. You chose this life and the man that goes with it, for better or for worse. Moved all the way to Portland to make it better, even!

Still, acquiring a reputation as a slattern would help nothing. A policeman could hopefully hold his tongue, but deliverymen visited many houses, and gossip was good for business. The neighbors must already think them eccentric, but they couldn't move *again*.

If only Allen—

Well, if wishes were horses and all that.

The wagon came to a groaning stop, and the driver stared down at her, his eyes a startling blue in his tanned face. Shouldn't he greet her? Or was Portland still so untamed that its residents eschewed civilized manners? It certainly no longer resembled a frontier town, with its wagons, buggies, bicycles, and automobiles crowding the streets, its multi-storied buildings sprouting on both sides of the river, and electric light poles and telegraph wires on every corner.

But perhaps the residents' attitudes lagged behind the sophistication of the city. If so, she might as well respond in kind. She stared boldly back, which only made her realize that he was too handsome by half, whereas she…was not. She had no illusions; she was neither classically beautiful nor commonly pretty. But looking one's best led to being one's best, and sadly, that ship had sailed hours ago.

At least the man's frayed work clothes made her feel better. She lifted her chin at the wagon, which smelled strongly of Fisher's Finest Mulch and Manure. "That my delivery?"

"Depends."

"On what?"

"Who you are, and if this is what you ordered." His words, while abrupt, were spoken clearly, like an educated man, but with a slight accent she couldn't place. Russian, perhaps?

Without thinking, she blurted, "Where are you from?"

He blinked, but only chewed his lip before answering. "Chicago. What's it to you?"

"No, not there."

His jaw worked, but he couldn't seem to form a response to her admittedly rude assertion. But then, he'd been rude first, and anyway, who needed a reputation as a polite, demure woman? Men valued intelligence and confidence, did they not?

In each other, not their women, whispered that little voice, but she ignored it. Despite its absurdity, Detective Jenkins's claim that weak-minded females were too stupid for details only the Big Strong Men could know had stung. Men could be so—so—*pigheaded!*

She tapped a finger against her lips. "You may have lived in Chicago, but you were not born there. Let me see. Somewhere in the Russian Empire? Or one of its neighbors?"

His gaze flicked to her mouth, and she dropped her hand. With sudden clarity, she saw how she must appear to him, covered in dirt, rudely discussing his parentage, and generally making a fool of herself. What would he say at his next stop? Or to Mr. Fisher? Their reputation, so recently re-knit, would unravel faster than a pair of Allen's socks, and all this—moving north, renting this tiny cottage in wretchedly poor Goose Hollow, trying to make things better for Allen—would be for naught. All because she *still* could not suppress her true nature.

See what you've done? the little voice prompted, and this time, she listened.

"I'm very sorry," she said quietly. "I am overtired. Forgive me. I placed an order for a wagonload of mulch, for Allen Grey. My husband."

"I see," he said, expression unreadable.

She forced herself to stand tall. She might owe him the apology, but she would not cringe. If only he wouldn't scrutinize her so, weighing her words, *judging* her, though she'd no doubt earned it. The heat rose in her cheeks, but she kept her mouth shut. For once.

He glanced at the new plants in the garden, examined the border outside the fence, and finally, peered at the vegetables along the south side of the house. "I see," he repeated, then cleared his throat. "Mrs. Grey, I'm from Fisher's, and I believe this is the mulch you ordered."

He knotted the reins and jumped from the bench. His heavy boots *thunked* in the lane, raising clouds of dust that further sullied her skirt. She coughed, waving her hands before her face, while he detached a shovel from its fasteners on the wagon's side.

"What are you doing?" she managed between gasps.

He unhooked the wagon's gate and nodded at the garden. "Spreading your mulch."

"But…" Heat burned her cheeks again. How to explain that she had paid only for delivery? That, with such a small advance on Allen's salary to draw from, they could barely afford fertilizer, let alone the labor to spread it? Even the flowers were a luxury, but she'd been desperate for something to liven up the dismal yard.

Now this tall young man reflected her folly back at her. As Allen would say, *Vegetables can be eaten, the seeds harvested for next year. But flowers? What good are they?*

True, he said it without rancor and smiled indulgently when he found specimens drying all over the house or perfuming the insides of his books. But he was right all the same. They hadn't the money for frivolous things, and wasn't beauty the most frivolous of all?

"I'm sorry," she said again, hating that this was her second apology in as many minutes to this aggravatingly unflappable man. "I—we—please put the shovel away."

The man ignored her. Instead, he expertly balanced a shovelful of mulch, brought it to her newly planted border, and let it slide gently into place around a purple pansy. His flannel shirt strained over his broad back, proving he could make short work of the task if she left him to it.

With a sigh, she sped that happy thought on its way and planted herself firmly in his path as he turned back to the wagon. "Excuse me, Mister…?"

He eyed her up and down. Then with a sigh of his own, he struck the shovel into the ground amid another cloud of dust and leaned on the handle. This time she managed not to flap like a goose, but her efforts only resulted in a loud and unladylike sneeze.

"*Į sveikatą.* Bless you. The name's Jacobs. Lucky Jacobs."

It was an effort, but she refused to be distracted by whatever language he'd spoken. From the challenge in his eyes, he'd done it apurpose to tempt her.

She said primly, "Very glad to meet you, Mr. Jacobs. If you please, you may back the wagon up over there by the side of the house and deposit the mulch. Then you may go home to your supper. I—*we* have paid for delivery, which you have provided. We"—thank Heaven, she'd remembered this time!—"are perfectly capable of mulching our own garden."

The sun was low, and Allen would return any minute. All else being equal, he wouldn't notice the transformed garden. But if the wagon and its tall, muscled driver were here, surely even Allen would notice a disruption *that* obvious in his tidy, flowerless world.

"Spreading is included in the delivery charge."

The obdurate man moved to go around her, and she stepped quickly to block him again. "Mr. Jacobs, *please!* It's past six. I would not wish to make you late in returning the wagon."

He gripped the shovel tighter. "Mrs. Grey—"

"You may tell Mr. Fisher I am very appreciative, but I do *not* need my mulch spread for me." There. If nothing else, her interruption had shocked him into silence.

He watched her a moment, then said, very deliberately, "*Us.*"

"I beg your pardon?"

"You meant to say, for *us. We* are appreciative, *we* don't need *my* help for *our* garden."

Oh, for the love of... What deliveryman noticed pronouns? Weren't they all like Mr. Fisher senior, who could barely see his customers, let alone hear them?

"I—we—oh, *blast it all to hell!*" She clapped a hand to her mouth. *What had she done?*

Mr. Jacobs's brows shot up. "I must say, *Mrs.* Grey,

I begin to wonder at this supposed spouse of yours, who allows his wife to use such language. Perhaps he is a figment of your imagination, or…" He became thoughtful. "Or he is real, but you have failed to tell him how you spend his money. Is that it? For shame, Mrs. Grey. A man deserves better in a wife."

~:~:~

The moment he spoke the words, Lucky wished them back. The flash of hurt in Mrs. Grey's eyes before she lowered them made him feel every inch the ass he was.

Hurt, and something else. Fear? Of him? Or her husband?

She obviously had not meant to swear, but he'd driven her to it. Blame the heat, or the long day, or that he'd been forced to work for Fisher's at all. Six days a week for Jones Lumber Company barely covered his living expenses, even when the creeks and machinery were in top form. When they weren't, and he had to take lower-wage jobs to make up some—but not all—his missed pay, it left him out of sorts. None of which was Mrs. Grey's fault.

Before he could apologize, she said softly, "My *husband* has given me leave to make our house into a home, whatever the cost. Lord knows, it needs it."

She spoke the truth. Like most of Goose Hollow, this lane consisted of small, cheap houses, haphazardly constructed on sad, untended lots to accommodate Portland's population boom. It was nothing like the slums of Chicago, but for Portland, it was close. Mrs. Grey had done an admirable job remaking the overgrown, half-dead garden of this particular cottage into a thing of nascent beauty, its honeyed scents alluring and homey at the same time.

Yet here he was, figuratively if not actually trampling her hard work into the ground. Apologies were not his specialty, but he knew when one was owed.

"Forgive me, Mrs. Grey. I was out of line. I'll spread this for you and be gone in no time. You won't have to lift a finger and can get on with your womanly pursuits."

There. That should restore her spirits. He waited, but her head still hung low, hiding her tears. Damn it, he'd have to do better. He didn't have time for this. He—

She lifted her head and a bolt of awareness shot through him. Far from being cowed, she'd found an inner fury. Hazel eyes blazed from her dirt-streaked face, her sweat-dark hair slipping from the prim confines of her straw bonnet. She jabbed a finger in the air, advancing on him, and he held the shovel sideways like a shield.

"You listen to me, Mr. Jacobs. Your job is to deliver *for* Mr. Fisher *to* his customers. If you would like to keep that job, and would prefer I *not* tell him how you insulted me, I suggest you take this shovel—" She wrenched it from his grasp and brandished it at him. "—and unload my mulch, quick as may be. Then you may leave my property and never return."

She paused for breath, then froze, shovel aloft, staring wide-eyed over Lucky's shoulder at something behind him.

"Solace?" said a man's voice, but Lucky couldn't drag his gaze from the woman before him. Her wrath had been so absolute, her color so high, but now she blanched and swayed. Instinctively, Lucky reached out, but she only lowered the shovel and steadied herself with it.

"Allen."

She met Lucky's gaze again, pleading this time. But for what? Was her husband such a monster? A violent terror from whom she feared a beating?

Lucky's hands fisted and he turned, only to find a slight man with gray, tufted hair standing in the lane. His wrinkled coat hung open, vest buttons askew, and his trousers were dusty, as though he, too, had been working in the dirt, although he carried a stack of books.

Lucky checked himself. Mrs. Grey did not seem precisely afraid. And yet…there was that flash of anguish in her clear eyes.

You're a fool, Lucky, plain and simple.

Mr. Grey moved to his wife's side, set his books on the ground, and gently pried the shovel from her white-knuckled grip. "Solace, what is happening here?" He stared at the shovel as though he'd never seen one before, then leaned it against the wagon.

"Nothing," Mrs. Grey replied calmly. "I was just…" Her gaze traveled over the mulch-filled wagon, then to the garden, and finally landed on Lucky. Her expression soured, like he was a stinkbug she'd found in her kitchen. She took a deep breath. "Mr. Jacobs, allow me to present my husband. Allen, Mr. Jacobs is from Fisher's. He has brought mulch for the garden."

Grey blinked and offered Lucky his hand, his grip surprisingly strong for one so thin. Up close, his hair showed brown amid the gray, and his pale eyes were framed with crow's feet. He smelled of musty books, and Lucky put him north of fifty, decades older than his wife.

"Very glad to meet you, sir," Grey said.

Lucky released his hand. "Pleasure's mine. Mrs. Grey and I were just discussing whether I should spread the mulch for you, or whether you would prefer to do it yourself."

"Ah, yes, I see," Grey said. "Are you one of the

neighbors?"

Lucky's confusion must have been evident, but Mrs. Grey's only reaction was a slight reddening of the cheeks. "No, my dear." Taking her husband's arm, she gently turned him toward the sign painted on the wagon, then gestured at the side garden. "He is from Fisher's. He brought mulch for the vegetables."

Why had she drawn Grey's attention away from the gay front borders to the more practical food garden? Mulch was a common commodity. Why fear her husband's reaction to it?

Perhaps Lola Baldwin and her do-gooder crowd had gotten under Lucky's skin. According to his landlady, those women could make anyone out as a "poor soul in need," but especially females who were new to Portland and ignorant of its Big City dangers. Yet…what if Mrs. Grey's danger lurked not *outside* her home but *in* it?

"Of course, my dear," Grey said, blinking at the wagon. "You know best."

He did not sound angry, and Lucky tried to relax. His instincts were off today, although Grey's demeanor *was* strange. He now stared blankly at the tomato plants in the side yard, as though unsure what to do. Mrs. Grey retrieved his dropped books.

"Did the library stay open late for you today? That was nice of Mrs. Ellesmere."

Grey took the proffered books. "Ah, yes. Yes, of course." He smiled vaguely at Lucky and let himself through the gate, then paused. "Solace, I believe my…uniform…will need repairs before school starts. I noticed a tear in one of the cuffs when I…when…"

"When you last wore it? Of course. I will mend it."

He beamed at her and continued up the walk, and

Lucky's gut did another reversal. The man hardly seemed dangerous. But what of his hesitation when revealing how his "uniform" had been damaged? Was there an unpleasant history there between man and wife?

Lucky gave himself a mental shake. *Forget Grey. What the hell is the matter with* me?

Mrs. Grey watched her husband go inside the house, then faced Lucky, a determined set to her chin. Before she reiterated her claim of not needing his help—a lie if he'd ever heard one—he retrieved the shovel and stepped around her. "I'll just spread this for you now, Mrs. Grey, and be out of your hair in no time. Fisher's appreciates your business."

He set to work, moving the mulch carefully from the wagon to its new home, protecting the roots of her tender young flowers. All the while, her anxious indecision pulsed at his periphery, a physical thing, like a deer at the edge of a meadow.

At last she murmured, "Thank you. It's very kind of…Fisher's."

He heard the swish of her skirts as she followed her husband inside. The door closed with a muted *clunk*, and then Lucky was alone with a wagonload of mulch to spread in the two hours before nightfall. He risked a glance at the house but could see nothing through the lace curtains concealing the windows.

A damn fool, that's for sure.

Still, perhaps Mrs. Baldwin or one of her cronies could look in on the Greys. Something about the business had got under his skin, and with a sense of foreboding, he knew he'd pick at it until it either went away or he rooted out the infection.

Chapter Three

Mrs. Aurora Greene Baldwin, known to her friends as Lola, saw the last of the Young Women's Christian Association committee members to the door. Mrs. Jessie Honeyman had stayed after the general meeting to discuss matters dear to Lola's heart: the plight of young women and girls everywhere, but especially here in Lola's new "hometown" of Portland, and especially with the Lewis and Clark Exposition arriving next year.

Not only to discuss, but to entice Lola to do something about the situation in advance. Many unchaperoned females would flood the Northwest in the coming months, seeking both employment and entertainment. If no safe, moral avenues were provided to them, they would follow *un*safe and *immoral* ones. Therefore, the new Portland chapter of the YWCA-sponsored Traveler's Aid Society, which Lola had immediately joined, now wished her to expand her role and supervise their "female-protective and vice-preventive" work for the fair.

Mrs. Honeyman's salary offer was generous, and Lola was flattered that Dr. Kate Waller Barrett, national head of the Florence Crittenton homes for "rescued prostitutes" and unwed mothers, for which Lola had been a staunch volunteer since she was a young woman living in Vermont, had facilitated their introduction. Though she had yet to meet Dr. Barrett in person, their paths had crossed remotely over the years, through letters and other means, and it was clear they had a shared vision of how best to help the country's growing population of "rudderless" young females.

But if Lola accepted the position, it would mean cutting back elsewhere, and how was she to do that? Still, the pull of such meaningful work was difficult to resist, and she continued to mull it over as she went to the kitchen to check the roast she had started for dinner.

Her husband, LeGrand, found her at the oven and leaned over her shoulder, inhaling deeply. "Delicious!"

Lola frowned and used a dish towel to push the pan back into the oven before shutting the door. "It's underdone. This stove is not as reliable as our last one."

"Did I say I meant the roast?"

She peered up at him over her spectacles. "After twenty years of marriage, I know very well what you meant. I also know that to keep you happy for the next twenty years, I must refrain from serving you raw meat."

LeGrand laughed and kissed her forehead, tucking back a strand of her dark hair that had escaped her top-knot. His own hair was beginning to gray, but the twinkle in his eye was that of the young man she'd married so long ago. In fact, he looked quite dashing in his tailored gray suit. Two sons and two decades together hadn't dulled their mutual affection, and she found herself smoothing her brown wool skirt and ruffled blouse, trying to tidy herself up after a day's hard work at home.

He said, "Perhaps it isn't the oven. Perhaps it's that the cook was distracted and forgot to turn the oven on."

Lola stared at him, aghast. "Oh dear—did I do that?"

"I'm afraid so. But I noticed it halfway through your meeting, so all is well. Dinner will be only a little delayed. How did it go, by the way? Will travelers to

Portland be safely delivered, thanks to your efforts?"

She grimaced. "Thank you. I don't know what is wrong with me, forgetting something like that. But yes, the Aid Society business is moving along well. They wish me to become more involved and have made an offer that will more than make up for my leaving the bookkeeping position at the store."

"Charlton's can find another bookkeeper, although I have enjoyed us working together. Will you accept?"

"I need to think about it. But yes, I'm considering it."

"Good," LeGrand said decisively, and Lola thought again how lucky she was to have married a man who shared her social welfare concerns. Not only shared them, but supported her efforts, even when it meant his dinner would be late.

She lit the burner under a large pot of preheated water on the stove, then retrieved the butter and cream from the icebox, placing them on the worktable in the kitchen's center. At the sink, she picked up her paring knife and one of the potatoes waiting in a bowl on the counter.

"LeGrand, I have been thinking. We are facing an uphill battle to draw attention to the plight of the friendless women and girls in Portland. General sentiment is that these poor females have brought their fates upon themselves, which is simply not true. Poverty is not their fault, and the men who seduce them…"

She glanced up from peeling the potatoes to find him watching her indulgently. Proselytizing was one of her worst habits, and she knew it gave her the appearance and reputation of a stern and unyielding woman. But LeGrand didn't need "converting," and would no doubt appreciate her getting to the point more quickly.

"Never mind. You know this, and that prison is not

the solution, for once released, they must return to illegal activities in order to survive. Worse, if a baby results, and the mother later returns to jail, the child is left to fend for itself. Look at that poor girl we found yesterday."

LeGrand's expression turned grim. He, like her, was most angered when innocent children suffered for the sins of their parents. "Have you found a place for her?"

"I think so. No one knows where her mother is, but most of the boarding houses can use extra hands in exchange for a room and meals. But that is merely responding to the symptoms of the issue. My idea is to fix its root cause—I intend to find gainful employment for every downtrodden female in Portland who is willing to work to turn her life around."

"Excellent. How?"

Lola let out a breath and dropped the last of the peeled potatoes into the now-bubbling pot. He had not questioned her logic nor told her the plan would not work. Not that she had thought he would. But by asking for more details, he showed he believed she could do it, and his only curiosity was about how, not if.

"In the months since we moved here, we have made important connections, many of whom are far wealthier than we are. Enough that they can afford hired help."

Another reason LeGrand was a good match for her was his quick understanding. "You are going to find the women positions as maids."

"Yes."

"What if they have no experience?"

"I—or we, for I intend to enlist the help of the Florence Crittenton people—will train them. I am on their board; surely they will listen to me."

"And if the women have children or are expecting?"

"We will provide childcare where we can."

"Excellent," he repeated. He stepped around the worktable to meet her at the stove and took her hands in his. "I'll look for your first candidate to arrive shortly."

"But… That is, I wasn't hinting…"

LeGrand grinned and kissed her. "We can afford it, too. And you need the help, especially if you become 'more involved' with the Aid Society. So it will benefit you, Portland, and me. I won't have my dinners late all the time, when there is such a simple solution."

He squeezed her hands and went through the door to the dining room. Lola turned back to the potatoes and smiled. Of course it made sense that she test her hypothesis before asking Portland's High Society matrons to take former prostitutes and opium users into their homes. But it truly had not been her intent to ask LeGrand to go all in with her plan in such a way.

Yes, he was a remarkable man, and she was remarkably fortunate to have found him. Furthermore, their sons could begin helping more at the store. Why, Pierre was eighteen, Myron fifteen. They could increase their participation, and she could focus on cleansing the city.

Now, if she could just get Portland's mayor and police chief to comprehend the depth of the problems these women faced, and agree to send them to Lola instead of incarcerating them…

But that was a task for another day, and first, she had to get dinner on the table.

~:~:~

Chief Charles Hunt stood at the window of his office in the Portland Metropolitan Police Force building, surveying the busy corner of Oak and Second below.

This was his hard-won kingdom, and he had the white hair to prove it.

A year and a half into his second term and he had accomplished much. He'd committed to cleaning the city of gaming and other vices before next summer's Lewis and Clark Exposition, even meeting with Mrs. Jessie Honeyman of the Traveler's Aid Society *and* Mrs. Mary Stillwell of the Salvation Army, to hear their womanly theories on the matter. And he'd redesigned the official police badge from that god-awful seven-pointed star to something more simple and authoritative.

But would he be remembered for any of that? *No*. He would go down in history as chief of the bumbling police force that couldn't find one small, charismatic man whose penchant for living with two dozen women had gone from the merely immoral to the possibly deadly.

Murdered girls—that happened elsewhere, not here. Only last month, a prostitute had been killed in Berkeley near the university. Perhaps it gave this Creffield the idea. Or perhaps he couldn't find another way to rid himself of his extra wives. Odd how he'd started with the Salvation Army, converting reprobates to Christianity, then swung so far away, he'd had to create his *own* religion. If only the Stillwell woman could say where he was, Hunt would let her march anywhere she wanted and set up red-kettle collection sites all over Portland.

At least Brooks, Creffield's even more fanatical second, had gone for good after the pair were tarred and feathered in Corvallis last January. Wandered off into the woods and died, or was eaten by wild animals. Likely both. A few other male Holy Rollers had left the group, and many of the females had been returned to their families or committed to the Oregon Asylum on grounds that their minds were "unhinged by religious mania."

But not Creffield. No, he couldn't take a hint if it stabbed him in the eye. Before the tar cooled, he'd returned to his so-called Bride of Christ church and married one of his followers, then bolted again in March when the woman's aunt, who he'd also tupped, swore out a warrant against him for adultery. At least that was a charge he could be arrested for. If they found him.

Hunt clenched his fists behind his back, staring out at the city. *Where are you, you rutting bastard? By God, I'll arrest you if it's the last thing I do in office.*

There was a tap on the open door behind him. He knew who it was, even before Detective Jenkins said "Sir?" in that obsequious tone Hunt loathed.

"Come!" he barked without turning, then waited a full minute, stroking his trimmed mustache and continuing to stare out the glass before facing his visitor.

Walter Jenkins stood ramrod straight in the center of the office, not a wrinkle on his pressed shirt, dark blue coat, or matching trousers. He'd been on the job a year, arriving with excellent references from the force in New York City, not to mention the "recommendation" of his wife's wealthy family. But as everyone knew he'd not been hired solely on his merits, he overcompensated by promoting new-fangled detection techniques from back East, such as this so-called "fingerprinting" nonsense.

Still, old money was difficult to ignore, and Hunt had ambitions of his own which Jenkins might assist with, if their mutually greased hands could stick together long enough. He sat behind the desk and gestured at the chair in front of it. However annoying Jenkins might be, he was a good detective, and it wasn't his fault Creffield still eluded them.

"Go on, sit. What's kept you here so late on a Saturday? Don't you have a pretty young wife at home?"

Jenkins tugged his collar with a gloved hand, a rare display of nerves which spiked Hunt's temper again.

"Well, get on with it. I have my own wife waiting for me. What is it?"

Jenkins glanced out the door, but while officers conducted the business of policing downstairs, the upper floors were empty this late in the day. He approached the desk, a glint in his eye, and Hunt understood his errand.

"Sir, I wonder if we might discuss the *extra* duties I have been managing for you."

Hunt glared at him. "Want to stop, do you? I'm sure any other officer would be happy to take over for you. Or put Patrolman Peters on it. He's an eager young pup."

Jenkins reddened. "I'm not dissatisfied with my responsibilities, sir. It's just that we—anyone on the force—are too recognizable. The newspapers are threatening to report on our system of collecting the, er, *business taxes*."

Damn. Hunt sat back, considering. A cleaner, more moral Portland was necessary to attract visitors to the exposition next May, but he couldn't fully shut down the bars and gaming halls. Their owners were too wealthy and influential. Yet public outrage would be high if the papers revealed his and Mayor Williams's scheme of "taxing" the clubs to keep them open.

Jenkins continued, "The last few times our men tried to collect, there were reporters waiting inside. The owners got spooked, and the officers had to leave. It's only been a week or two, but..."

He shrugged expressively. Theirs was a dicey relationship, for Jenkins could expose Hunt if he wanted to. But Hunt could fire him first, making him appear merely a disgruntled former employee. Besides, Hunt needed every available man on the Creffield case.

"Fine. Get someone less visible. But don't discuss it with anyone else in the department. Officers can't blab what they don't know. Is there anything else?"

Jenkins coughed delicately. "Well, sir, I have been coordinating these services for a whole year, at great risk to my own reputation, and without extra pay."

"I'm a man of my word. You'll get your promotion to captain. *After* we catch Creffield."

Jenkins looked thoughtful. "Of course he must be found and arrested, sir. But have you considered, what happens if we get him, and the killings…don't stop?"

Hunt beetled his brows at the detective. "Think it's someone else, do you? Because you're from the Big City and know better than we do here in little old Stumptown? He has no respect for females of any kind. It's him; I feel it in my bones. Now go and *find* him for Christ's sake, and when the killings stop, you'll see I'm right."

Jenkins stood. Whatever assurance he'd wanted, he appeared to have gotten it. "Yes, sir. Thank you, sir. Have a good night, sir."

"Go home," Hunt said irritably. "Go work in that garden you're always talking about. Clear your head. Or better yet, spend some time with your wife."

He turned his chair around and gazed back out the window, sitting there long after the detective had left.

Jenkins was ambitious and tenacious. Just what Hunt needed—a man who would leave no stone unturned in the search for a religious fanatic who was not only living in sin with his dozens of followers, but now appeared to be murdering them.

Chapter Four

Sunday July 24

"AMERICA'S MEAT INDUSTRY WILL BE
AT A STANDSTILL – The great sympathetic
meat strike, involving 100,000 men, will
effectually tie up the meat industry of the
United States." —*The Sunday Oregonian*

On Sunday, Lucky rose at dawn to go to confession. He hadn't slept well, but today, especially, he felt the need for absolution. It was one thing to lust after a pretty barmaid or the buxom woman who cleaned the boarding house. It was quite another to feel those base instincts toward a properly married, intelligent woman who, even covered in dirt, set his blood on fire with her soft curves, snapping hazel eyes, and sweetly curling brown hair.

Disgusted, he stared into the cloudy mirror above the dresser. "You're a damn fool," he said quietly, wary of disturbing his roommate, Samuel, snoring in the upper bunk. "A damned-to-hell idiot. Sweet hair, my ass."

A trip to the water closet, followed by a dry shave with a dull blade, restored his equanimity, until he dressed for church and found a tear in his "good" trousers. He set to work with a needle and thread, but even so, the money he'd earned yesterday would have to go for clothing. Besides a new Sunday suit, he needed another work shirt, heavier trousers, and thicker socks to cushion his boots. At least it was summer, and a winter coat could wait.

Still, at this rate, he'd never save enough for passage to the District of Alaska. That was the plan: a short stopover in Portland to replenish his cash, then north to join the gold rush or try his hand at fur trapping. A "stopover" that had lasted more than a year. Perhaps he'd lost the urge to wander and should settle here for good. And do what? Work for Jones Lumber the rest of his life? Or worse, Fisher's?

He took yesterday's earnings from his coat and added them to the hollowed-out Bible he kept in his satchel. Not many would be fooled by that trick, but on first sight, it did resemble a well-read book with a hasp to hold it closed. Besides, most thieves would think him not worth robbing, if they dared approach him in the first place.

Lucky was big, tall and broad-shouldered like his father had been, and hard labor six days a week kept his muscles strong. Many a pretty lass had said she felt safe on his arm, though some feared his bulk at first. But after he'd sweet-talked them, or furnished the liquor they desired, they warmed up. If not, he moved on. In contrast to his father, Lucky believed a woman who rejected his attentions still deserved his respect.

Which made it all the more frustrating during the long, sleepless night that he couldn't get Mrs. Grey out of his head. Was it her soft lips and wide eyes? The swell of her bosom under the sweat-damp shirtwaist? The sudden fire that lit her from within and made her *glow?* Or was it his unshakeable conviction that she needed his help, but because of that fire, she'd never admit it?

Solace. Even her name niggled, like a cool, life-giving rain on a hot, parched day. A promise of peace after years of strife. A woman who'd work hard, making a shack into a home. A home to share *with her husband.*

At first, he'd suspected her of flirting when she claimed to be fascinated by his accent, of all things. An accent he'd worked hard to lose. He'd left Lithuania when in short pants. But though his parents refused to learn English, he'd been proud he spoke like an American, until Mrs. Grey disabused him of that notion.

So, disgruntled, he'd hurt her with his thoughtless nosiness. Mrs. Baldwin's crowd and their causes: they had him seeing damsels in distress at every cottage. Probably happy, well-kept damsels the lot of them, Solace—*Mrs. Grey*—included.

But then she'd unleashed her fury, and suddenly he could think of nothing but having all that passion, intelligence, and beauty beneath him in a bed. Or against a wall with her skirts around his hips. Or, hell, right there in her yard, in plain view of the neighbors.

What in God's name was the matter with him? Had it been that long since he'd tumbled a woman? After ten- or eleven-hour days, pushing heavy logs at a pair of circular saws, he had little energy for nocturnal pursuits. But that didn't excuse lusting after a woman who was as unsuitable and unwilling as they came.

"You gonna stare at that Bible all day?"

Startled, Lucky squinted up at Samuel, leaning over the bunk rail above. "Sorry. Go back to sleep." He glanced down; yes, he'd closed the book's hasp before going off into lustful daydreams of Mrs. Grey. He tucked the Bible back in his satchel, then shrugged his coat on.

Sam grinned. "Fun night? Why not confess it all to me and save yourself a trip?"

"Sure. When Hell freezes over. Which around here

won't be until October."

"Speaking of Hell, Jones sent a man around yesterday while you was out. There's a problem with Chicken Creek. No logs gettin' through, so the mill's shut down. Looks like you get another day off tomorrow." Lucky said a very bad word for a Sunday, and Sam guffawed. "Aw, it won't be so rough. Wish I had a day to sleep in."

"I don't need sleep. I need cash."

"Nothing you can do. It'll be clear in a day or two, and the logs'll come through agin. Enjoy yourself. Go find a woman, or better yet, two. Then you'll have twice as much to confess."

Lucky swore again and stalked out, Sam's laughter following him into the hall. However, Sam was right. If the creek was blocked, there was nothing to be done until it was unblocked. With the recently-formed builders' unions, the lumber companies couldn't force the repairmen to work on a Sunday. But surely it would be cleared by Monday afternoon.

Heartened, Lucky took the stairs two at a time down to the main floor. Widow Sadie Smith would be in her kitchen, and a few other tenants would be up early like him, going to church or breaking the Sabbath to work odd jobs. Lucky hadn't come to that yet. His mother would turn in her grave if he worked Sundays, too.

Mrs. Sadie smiled as he entered the kitchen. She was the picture of a boarding house "mother hen": gray hair pulled into a straggly bun, complexion reddened from spending half the day cooking at a hot stove, the other half boiling laundry, and a vast bosom over an even vaster waistline. Half the tenants called her "Ma," and she encouraged it. Most were men younger than Lucky, far from home, with little prospect of reuniting with their families any time soon. Childless herself, she adopted them, and they adored her.

"Mornin'." Sadie wiped hands covered in flour on her flannel apron and waved at a tray of fresh baked goods. "Sure you won't take a roll or sumpin' wit' you?"

They smelled heavenly. As he opened his mouth to refuse, she took a linen dish towel, embroidered by her own hand with her initials, *SS*, and wrapped two cheese pastries and an apple tart in it. "Now, now, I meant for later. Why you Cath-o-lics cain't have breakfast on a Sunday is beyond me. But you gotta eat some time. Might as well be sumpin's included in your rent."

She held the bundle out, and he took it, then set it back down on the table. "I'll eat whatever you want for dinner, and that's a promise. But if I take this with me to church, it will smell so good, it wouldn't be fair to the other starving 'Cath-o-lics,' now would it?"

Her plump cheeks reddened further, and she reached for a large mixing bowl. "Oh, go on wi' you! You'll be home after church, then? And you'll set a spell? Sunday should be a day of rest. You work too hard." She began cracking eggs into the bowl, oblivious to the irony that she was already hard at work on the Lord's Day.

Lucky winked at her. "But I play hard, too. That's why I have to go to church so much."

She blinked, then hooted with laughter. "Git on, then. But be careful out there. That man is still on the loose, and the papers say they found another girl, this one in Tanner Creek."

"Another? And they think it's Creffield?"

She nodded. "I sure wish they'd catch 'im. They shoulda hung 'im when's they had the chance. Livin' wit more'n twenty women, just him and his *apostles*."

She said it like a dirty word, and Lucky hid a grin. Though in truth, it wasn't funny.

Sadie continued, "What I say is, who's worse? The man hisself, or them as follows 'im? Doin' all them crazy dances, havin' fits all o'er the floor. Why, my sister in Kansas tol' me about a killer they had running amok. She was so skairt, she tried to git her husband to move out west. And now it's happening here! We'll all be kilt in our beds afore this is done, you'll see."

Ordinarily a sensible woman, Sadie reacted with terror to every salacious story the papers printed or her sister relayed. On the other hand, this was the second girl found in as many weeks.

"Drowned?"

"In the creek, but din't say what kilt her. Also din't say if she was immoral or not."

Now this was interesting. When an "immoral" woman, usually a prostitute or opium user, got her "just deserts," the papers had a field day. With the previous victim, they'd made more of her vices than her murder. Did their silence here mean the new girl was not a prostitute?

Sadie kept cracking eggs in neat, practiced motions, with no wasted effort or dropped shells. "Anyways, be careful. Mebbe Creffield ain't the killer. But *somebody* is. I knows you kin take care o' yourself. But even so, don' go off an' do sumpin' stupid."

"I'll be careful," he promised, and she seemed satisfied.

"Speakin' o' girls, Mrs. Baldwin's comin' today. Got a new 'un for us. Mary, I think she said." Sadie's face darkened, black eyes snapping. "About ten she says.

Hard t' tell, the girl's so starved, she says."

Lucky stilled. A timely reminder that Mrs. Baldwin and her "busybody" friends did good, important work more often than not. "Massage parlor?"

"Din't say. Just asked if we had a place for her. I said o' course. Can allays find sumpin' for her to do. 'Sides, I think Bess's boy's gonna man up an' propose. Mary can take her place."

Lucky crossed the kitchen in two strides, spun Sadie around, and kissed her soundly on both cheeks. "You're a good woman, Mrs. Sadie. Why you haven't got a husband, I'll never understand. One of these days, I'll have to 'man up' and marry you myself."

Grinning at her flustered expression, he grabbed the bundle of pastries after all, stuffing it in his coat pocket, then ran out to the street before she found her voice.

Sadie's was at the north end of Portland proper, near Chinatown, ten blocks from St. Mary's Cathedral. This early on a Sunday, no one was about except a few drunks stumbling home, and a fancy lady or two, working late or starting early. Four blocks from home, he came upon one of these lounging against a lamppost. Her pink-striped skirts were grimy and her bodice was torn, and he put her age at about twenty. Her light brown hair was done in girlish ringlets, her pale eyes lined with charcoal, and her mouth rouged red.

After talking with Sadie, the thought of how this woman—barely more than a girl—came to be selling her body to strangers made Lucky angrier than usual at life's injustices. With Creffield "running amok," as Sadie called it, there was a real possibility she could die just trying to earn a living.

Unconsciously, he slowed, which she took as an

invitation, leaving the streetlight to totter closer on her high, wooden heels. She leaned forward, offering an unimpeded view of her ripe bosom, pushed up by her boned corset, as she batted her eyes at him.

"*Sveiki gražuoli.* Hel-*lo*, gorgeous. What you all dolled up for?"

He was about to push past when her words registered. She was Lithuanian? There were a few communities in this area, but not like Chicago. Not enough that running into each other was common. Still, he was very late, so he only said, "*Bažnyčia,*" and motioned her aside.

She fluttered her lashes again. "Church? Why you need—" Suddenly, her seductive air vanished, and she peered intently at him. "Lukas Jacobonis, is that you?"

Lucky blinked, realizing he knew her. Take away the tattered clothes and the cosmetics, and it left a pretty young woman, met by chance last year at a dance hall on Second Avenue. They had spoken the mother tongue, danced until dawn, and then... From her expression, she remembered what had happened *then*, too.

He pulled her name from the far reaches of memory. "Elzbieta? Ellie? What are you doing here? It's been a year since we—that is—"

His face heated, and she smiled sadly. "Do not fret yourself. Is what happens to *kekše*, to whores, like me."

"But the saloon—surely you earned enough—"

Her smile widened. "My purity did not worry you so much the last time we met."

"You weren't—that is, we—" He balled his fists. "Damn it! I didn't force you, and I wasn't your first. Unless...I wasn't, was I? Please, if I did this to you—"

Her sudden laughter echoed crazily in the deserted street. "Goodness! Lukas Jacobonis, get off high horse.

Sun and moon do not revolve around your *mielas užpakalis*." She teasingly admired his rear before sobering. "Truly. You are responsible for nothing, least of all me."

The sun was rising quickly, giving him a better look at her. There were circles under her eyes, and her skin was an unhealthy pallor beneath her falsely pink cheeks. Her hands shook as she smoothed her skirts, and the corset, which initially had seemed to be pulled too tight, he now saw was in fact too loose. It was her body that was too thin under her ill-fitting garments.

"What was it, then? Opium?"

Her gaze slid away, and she backed up a step, but he grabbed her arm. It was frail and bony, not the plump flesh she'd had before, and her eyes were bloodshot.

"*Atstokite!* Leave me alone. I should not have spoken to you." She glanced into the nearby alley as though afraid of something. Or someone.

"Who did this to you?"

"No one. Not his fault. I am to blame, no one else!"

She tried to pull away, but Lucky gripped her tighter. Countless women were in a similar plight, but this one he knew. She came from his homeland, and they had shared the physical act that had bonded man to woman throughout the ages. Perhaps it was the two dead girls, or the child Mrs. Baldwin was bringing to Sadie, or his instincts about Solace Grey. For whatever reason, Lucky wanted to punch the man who'd done this to Ellie.

"Who? Whose fault is it 'not'?"

She frowned and pushed at him. "What you care? Have not seen in a year and think you know me? You can fix me? Not even great Lukas Jacobonis can fix this. Not so *lucky*, at that."

She wrenched free and would have walked away, but he caught her again and forced himself to calm down. He couldn't help everyone, but he might be able to help her.

"Wait, just listen a moment. I'm staying at Sadie Smith's place. You know it?"

She nodded reluctantly. "Near Stark Street?"

"That's the one. Come by around midday. A lady will be there who can help you."

Ellie's eyes narrowed. "Most *ladies* pretend I do not exist."

"Not this one. Just come. She can help you dry out."

She looked uncertain. "You are not funning me? I have tried before, but…"

Her shrug encompassed the lure of the opium dens, her profession, and all the evils that made it so hard to get out once a woman got in. Lucky had never tried opium and rarely even drank liquor. In fact, his main purpose when visiting bars or dance halls was…to find female companionship.

Was he part of the problem? Was it hypocritical to tumble a willing woman, never thinking it might prevent her leading a respectable life later? There *were* men who, like him, didn't judge a prostitute for her choices. Women, too. Mrs. Baldwin being a prime example. From what Lucky had heard, she might have moral objections to Ellie's profession, but instead of turning her back, she found ways to combat the infections of poverty and despair, replacing them with decency and a dose of hope.

He pulled Sadie's pastries from his coat, then fished in his pocket for a handful of change. It wasn't much, a half dollar, a nickel, some pennies, but he added them to the dishcloth and re-tied it, pushing it into Ellie's hand.

She tried to refuse, but he closed her fingers over it,

putting on his most charming smile. "There's more where that came from. Come to Sadie's. If nothing else, you can eat a good meal and return the towel. It's one of her best, and I know she'd like it back."

His cajoling worked, and she accepted the offering. "*Taip*. Yes, I will come."

A sound came from the alley, and Ellie glanced fearfully over her shoulder. Probably an animal rooting through garbage on the street, but in a flash, Lucky realized that midday was hours away—plenty of time for her to reconsider.

Impulsively, he said, "I'm late for church. Would you care to join me?"

Her smile was wan but genuine. "*Ne*. But I will not hook up with anyone, if that is your fear. I will go home to sleep and clean up before I meet this *lady* of yours."

"Thank you. For trusting me."

A heavy footfall echoed up the block, and a uniformed policeman rounded the corner. While not always enforced, Portland's anti-prostitution laws could cause problems for a woman without the means to post bail. Ellie gave Lucky an apologetic look, then scooped up her skirts one-handed and tottered into the alley, the dishcloth clutched in her other hand.

The policeman came abreast of Lucky and looked into the alley. "Talking with someone?"

His brown hair, sideburns, and neat mustache seemed familiar. Was he the patrolman at the Greys' home? Or was it only that Portland's police officers were nearly interchangeable in their helmets and brass-buttoned blue-wool coats and trousers?

Lucky said, "What of it? She's gone now."

The man sniffed. "She got away this time. But we'll

catch her yet!"

Lucky merely tipped his hat and hurried past, thankful Ellie had escaped. He should have asked for her address in case she changed her mind after all.

But she had promised…

In the old country, that meant something. If he recalled correctly, Ellie was ten when she came over with her father, who had died shortly thereafter. When the cousin she lived with in New York also died, she'd spent her savings on a train ticket as far away as possible, to the West Coast.

Lucky's own story was not much different, although his mother had lived until he was an adult. But once she was gone, he had no ties to Chicago, besides a sister he wasn't close to. So, he'd set his sights on Alaska as the place for a strong, capable man to make his fortune. That is, until he stopped in Portland and never left.

Fool, he told himself and broke into a run as the bells of St. Mary's pealed, still several blocks away. *Mass will be starting, and you need to confess first.*

He could stay here and work for the lumber companies. Plenty of men did just that. Or he could join the gold rush after all, or become a trapper, or any of a dozen other possibilities.

He didn't have to decide today, or even tomorrow. He was not yet thirty. He had time.

He was still thinking about it all—Ellie, Mrs. Baldwin, and the new girl coming to Sadie's—when he arrived, breathless, at the church. Solace also occupied his thoughts. What would it be like to come home to her, greeting him with a kiss and supper on the table? He'd never imagined himself a family man, but with her there… Well, the idea held more appeal.

Lucky cursed himself again and entered the quiet church. He dipped his fingers into the basin, crossed himself, and stepped into the sanctuary. Parishioners knelt in the darkened pews, heads bent in prayer, and a handful of candles burned by the altar. The air was cool and redolent of incense. Peaceful, as though he'd come home. Which some might think odd, given his less than holy life. But church reminded him of his mother, and gave him the chance to be cleansed of his less moral acts, including his impure thoughts of the past day.

He hurried toward the confessional, but it was occupied, so he sat in a nearby pew, taking the time to slow his breathing and settle his thoughts. Moments later the confessional opened, and he politely averted his gaze. A light footfall on the marble church floor, then another next to him, and then a sharp gasp.

He looked up automatically—into the startled-doe eyes of Solace Grey.

Chapter Five

It was too late to turn away. Mr. Jacobs had recognized her, probably took great pleasure in her discomfort. Clearly God had it in for Solace, and making Mr. Jacobs Catholic seemed about right. Not only Catholic, but *in the same parish.*

Today, he'd exchanged his work clothes for what must be his Sunday best, although these garments needed mending as badly as those he'd worn yesterday. His hair was neatly combed, and the red-gold bandit's stubble was gone, exposing a smooth, hard jaw.

Which was worse? That she'd noticed he'd shaved…or that she missed the stubble?

Smothering her irritation at her own folly, she started down the aisle, but he rose and blocked her path, speaking in a low, hushed voice. "Mrs. Grey, please. I owe you an apology. There is no excuse for my rudeness yesterday. I had no right to pry, and I hope you can forgive me."

He was only respecting this holy day and place, but the effect of his tone was intimate, as though he whispered his secrets and invited her own. It was the sort of intimacy shared between married folk.

Or at least, between *normal* married folk.

"Please don't give it another thought," she managed, trying to pass by, but he put a hand on her coat sleeve. Despite the heavy material, she winced, and he frowned.

"It's nothing," she said hurriedly. "A little sore.

From—from the work yesterday."

He released her arm. "Was your husband pleased? With the mulch and your garden?"

"Yes, he was most pleased. I am sorry if you thought he might be dissatisfied with your work. Or—or with mine. He admired the flowers greatly and said just now, on the walk to church, how much prettier the garden is."

Oh, why couldn't Mr. Jacobs leave well enough alone? She was babbling worse than a brook. She had to get away from this man who had seen Allen's confusion, and her embarrassment, and instead of minding his own business, had detained her in church of all places to discuss *hers*.

"Please, I must return to my husband."

"Of course."

He stepped aside, but she felt his gaze burning her back as she walked down the aisle. And when she knelt beside Allen, her prayers were jumbled and incoherent, having more to do with *not* thinking about a pair of piercing blue eyes than anything more pious.

To make matters worse, the gospel was Matthew on adultery. Of course Father Henderson wasn't speaking to her directly, but when he quoted, "Anyone who looks at a woman lustfully has already committed adultery with her in his heart," she hung her head in shame.

When the Mass ended and she followed Allen up the aisle, the discovery that Mr. Jacobs had already slipped out was oddly disappointing. She dipped her fingers in the baptistery and crossed herself, so lost in thought that she bumped into Allen when he stopped outside.

"My dear, are you quite well?" He steadied her, and she forced a smile.

"Yes. I expect I spent too much time in the sun

yesterday."

The priest, a small, thin man with graying hair, beady eyes, and a beak of a nose, nodded sagely. "It is good to work in the earth, but you must not overtire yourself. And were you able to understand the readings today?"

Was there *no* man who saw the female intellect as comparable to a male's? Gritting her teeth, she murmured, "Yes. They have given me much to think on."

Father Henderson beamed and said to Allen, "And what of you? If you were not to teach at our little school, would you prefer the priest at St. Lawrence's?"

Allen demurred. "I wouldn't attend anywhere else if it cost me my immortal soul."

It was the party line, but Father Henderson knew he was sincere and appeared satisfied. To Solace he said, "You will rest today, my child." Then he blessed them both and stepped away.

How simple to be a priest, she thought impiously, *with nuns and laymen to do all the work.* A home didn't run itself, and Allen… Well, she could never rest while he needed her.

He said now, "Will you excuse me, my dear? I must speak with Sister Margaret about my class."

"Of course. I'll wait across the street by those children playing in front of the fire station."

He followed her gaze to where several young boys and girls caroused, their parents socializing nearby, and his face clouded. "Do you ever wish we had a child?"

"I…we…" A sudden lump rose in her throat, and she couldn't force it back down.

"I sometimes do." His voice held such longing. "A little boy, to whom I could pass on my name and my love of learning. And a little girl, to whom you could pass on yours. I haven't forgotten what you gave up for me, when first we left Kansas, and now Berkeley."

"Oh, Allen…"

It was so long since he'd focused on her with such clarity. He could be so sweet, a man who would not knowingly hurt a fly. But then, a lot of damage could be caused unknowingly.

Without thinking, she rubbed her wrist, and before she could stop him, Allen pushed up her sleeve, exposing the ugly purple bruise that had made her wince at Mr. Jacobs's touch.

"*Solace*…Did—did I do this?"

She shook her head firmly. "Of course not. I hurt myself gardening."

What good would it do, his knowing the truth? He hadn't known what he did. He was clear-headed in this moment, but for how long? How soon before the darkness reclaimed him? If only she understood the pattern and could predict when he would be lucid, or plan for when he was not. *If only this purgatory would end, one way or another.*

No. She did *not* want Allen to die. And yet sometimes, her life was a Hell on Earth.

The little voice whispered, *What if yours is not the only life he crushes? Whether he is aware of his actions or not, the result is the same. You cannot outrun your past—or his.*

She shuddered and Allen misinterpreted the reason. He replaced her sleeve, then kissed her gloved hand. "You are tired. I said you shouldn't work so hard. Didn't I say that very thing?"

"Yes." She swallowed. "I—I should have listened."

Whatever caused his illness, he was a *good* man, who

cared for her, and she loved him. They were well-suited, both scholars, alone in the world, each happy to find a kindred soul in the other. Unlike other men, he had initially valued her intellect as much as her housekeeping, a helpmeet with wits to match his own. Which made their current situation even more pitiable.

"That man," he said suddenly. "The one who came last night with the wagon."

She stilled. "You—you remember that?"

He frowned as though she were a ninny. "Of course. What was his name?"

"Jacobs. I—it was Jacobs. From Fisher's."

"Yes, yes." Something across the street caught his eye, and he stared vacantly.

Solace saw nothing of note, only a poorly dressed woman hovering near a group of stern male parishioners by the church steps. On the near corner, a Salvation Army man had set up his kettle and vigorously rang his bell, but the passersby ignored him. Then a policeman came from the opposite direction, and the woman turned and bumped into a short man in black, who glared at her before joining his cronies. She hung her head in shame and fled, and Solace's heart ached for her. At least Solace had enough money for food and decent clothing.

In any case, Allen might not have been watching her or any of them, merely staring into space. It happened sometimes: Instead of whatever was before him, he saw something else in his mind for a few moments, before snapping out of it. So far, it had only happened at home. But if he started doing it in public…

She shoved the anxiety down and said gently, "Allen…?"

He gave a start, clearly having forgotten her

presence. But then his expression firmed, as if he were determined to finish his thought. "You must go to him. To that man, Jacobs."

She forced a calming breath. "Whatever do you mean, my dear?"

"For help. With the work. He was strong." Abruptly, he grabbed her hands with a fierceness that made her cry out. "And if I hurt you again, you must leave. Do you understand me? Go to one of the neighbors, or come here to the sisters. *Promise me!*"

A few bystanders had turned at her cry. She must placate him before they drew more attention. "Of course. If necessary—which it will *not* be—I will protect myself."

"Yes…" He released her and looked around uncertainly. "Now, what was I doing? Oh, yes. Sister…Margaret. I must find Sister *Margaret,* and…"

He trailed off, and she touched his arm. "Your class at the school is so important. I am sure you have lots of business to discuss with her."

His expression cleared. "My class. Of course. I must speak with Sister Margaret about it. You'll wait for me here, my dear?"

She fought down the despair. "Here, or—or perhaps over there, where the children are playing."

But he'd already moved up the sidewalk, toward Sister Margaret, who stood by the church steps with a second group of black-clad men. Solace swiped her eyes with her sleeve, then crossed to the fire station.

A few women chatted nearby, and she caught bits of their conversation.

"If you take the seeds mid-month, it will prevent any unwanted occurrences…"

"When you turn the stitch just so, it will be invisible on the outside…"

"And then it *burned to the pan*. Frederick's mother will *never* let me forget it…"

Solace pretended not to hear. Not that they noticed her. Doubtless, they knew she wasn't One of Them. Her clothes were too well-made for the poorness of her neighborhood, but not fashionable enough for Society. If not for her gloves, her hands would also give her away: too rough for a woman of the upper echelons, they were not calloused enough to be working class.

This was always the way, no matter where they lived. Though she was more comfortable around learned men, they mostly shunned her as an "abnormal female." Even in these advanced times, they preferred their women docile, quiet, and unconcerned with anything outside the home. Detective Jenkins's attitude being a perfect example of this.

But perversely, she was also shunned by the "normal females" she was expected to emulate. She could have laughed at the irony: The women feared their menfolk would find her a more interesting companion than they, but the men wished her to be more like their wives, with the result that Solace was excluded from social circles both rich and poor, male *or* female.

She had nearly skirted the group when a middle-aged woman in a black bonnet and a steel gray dress said excitedly, "That poor, poor girl. And the papers say he has been seen in Portland! We had all better lock our doors or be killed in our beds—or worse!"

Interest piqued despite herself, Solace glanced up. The speaker's audience, a woman of about Solace's age, widened her eyes, appropriately shocked at the possibility of a fate worse than death. Her yellow-ribboned bonnet was jaunty, and her matching jacket and skirt dazzled brightly against the somber tones of her companion. Her golden hair was elegantly styled, and a string of pearls circled her throat. Probably she *was* Society, if attire alone meant anything.

The younger woman noticed Solace and smiled warmly, holding out a gloved hand. "You must be Mrs. Grey. I am Mrs. Adina Donner, and this is Mrs. Jane Howard."

Too late to escape; she was caught, fair and square. Solace accepted the proffered hand. "I am pleased to meet you. My husband is there, talking with Sister Margaret."

Mrs. Donner smiled. "He is our new teacher, yes? Mrs. Howard's husband owns the butcher shop on Seventh. Perhaps you have shopped there? It is near the corner of Kooch Street."

Solace frowned. "I live near Seventh Avenue, but I'm afraid I don't know that street."

"Ah. You are not from around here, then."

"We arrived from San Francisco mere weeks ago."

Mrs. Donner's smile widened. "One of Portland's many oddities. You may have seen the sign: it reads c-o-u-c-h but is pronounced *kooch*, after John Couch, one of our founders."

"Of course!" Solace exclaimed. To Mrs. Howard she said, "I know your shop well. The best prices and cuts of meat, and the wrapping never tears or loosens."

Mrs. Howard beamed. "You are too kind! Our little shop has grown quite busy, and we are expanding next door. Hiram even purchased a new electrical freezer. It is most exciting!"

Mrs. Donner frowned. "To make ice cream? In a butcher shop? Whatever for, Jane?"

"Oh, goodness, no!" Mrs. Howard exclaimed. "It is the *latest* in food storage, like they use in boxcars, but for a shop! The touch of a button and the air drops *right* down to freezing. Can you *imagine?* It was *so* expensive—more than your car, Adina. But who *knows* when we can stock it, for the packers are no closer to ending the strike. *What* are we to do if they will ship us nothing? I say, buy your meat *now*, before we run out."

She paused as though expecting a response.

Solace said politely, "That is good advice. But our ice box is very small, barely large enough for one- or two-days' supply."

"Well, and that is the problem, isn't it? *No one* has an ice box that large. Which is why I told Hiram we should offer the freezer to let, until the strike is ended."

Mrs. Donner looked amused. "That is very enterprising, Jane. What will you charge?"

"Oh, I don't know. I leave all that to Hiram. But when the freezer is stocked, our custom will increase, and we will hire a clerk *and* a shop girl. It is *most* exciting!" Her expression changed to one of avid curiosity. "Mrs. Grey, why on earth did you move here from California, where the winters are *so* much better?"

"We were in Kansas before. I believe the winters in Portland are milder than in the Midwest, at least."

"Still, you must have had a *very* good reason to leave. What made you do such an uprooting sort of thing? Although I did hear your husband performed missionary work for a time, so he must be accustomed to moving around. In Africa, was it? Did you go with him?"

Mrs. Donner cut in coolly, "If you will excuse us,

Jane, I see someone Mrs. Grey may wish to meet." She pulled Solace neatly aside, saying in an undertone, "I must apologize for stealing you away. Jane is a terrible gossip. Whatever you say, she will spread it faster than melted butter. With little fidelity to your actual words, I might add."

She smiled good-naturedly, and Solace found herself smiling back. "Thank you for the warning. And the introductions. We have been busy unpacking these last three weeks and have had no time for socializing." It was only half a lie, and Mrs. Donner seemed to accept it. But Solace's curiosity had already done her in, so she added, "Nor for the news…?"

Mrs. Donner's eyes twinkled. "I see you are not completely closed-eared and tight-lipped. Is it the meat strike which has caught your interest? Or—no, it must be our local terror, Edmund Creffield." At Solace's blank look, she added, "The Holy Rollers? No?"

"The name is familiar, but I'm afraid we haven't yet subscribed to any of the papers."

"And I suppose the neighbors have nodded politely in the street, and stared *impolitely* from behind their curtains, but never bothered to give you a real welcome or any useful information about this foreign land into which you have been dropped."

They had stopped on the far side of the fire station, away from the adults, but near enough to the children that Allen could still find Solace. Assuming he did not forget her entirely and leave without her. She glanced across at the church. Sister Margaret and her group still stood near the doors, but Allen was nowhere to be seen. Perhaps he had gone inside with Father Henderson.

Solace turned to Mrs. Donner. "The blame is not

entirely theirs. I admit I have made little effort to meet them, or to acquire needed information."

Mrs. Donner nodded sagely. "A woman who knows her own foibles. I believe we will be fast friends. You must call me Adina."

She waited, and Solace responded automatically, "And you must call me Solace."

"Thank you. But what an unusual name!"

"My mother died giving birth to me, and my father chose it."

"Ah. And might I infer that you were his 'solace' for losing his beloved wife?"

"Something like that."

Adina seemed to sense this was territory best left unexplored and gracefully retreated. "In any case, Edmund Creffield was a Salvation Army officer, but he broke away and created his own church, the Bride of Christ. He has two dozen female followers with whom he practices 'free love,' and who fall all over the floor in bizarre dances. It's why we call them the Holy Rollers. He and his second, a Major Brooks, also of God's Army, were run out of Corvallis, but Creffield returned and married one of his followers, then sinned with her aunt."

"That explains the sermon on adultery."

Adina laughed. "Yes. *That's* what brought about the warrant, not his living with so many women. Brooks, who was not charged, likely died from the tar burns. He has not been seen since, but Creffield went on the run, and the authorities have been hunting him for weeks."

"Wait, I've just recalled, I *have* heard of him. A police detective came by our house and mentioned the search. But isn't he called Joshua, not Edmund?"

"He changed it. He has other aliases, too, but no

doubt he settled on Joshua for its biblical significance, and to acquire the initials of our Lord. The papers love to blame him for any evil. But they only stir up the fears of ordinary folk rather than helping the investigation."

"And you believe there is nothing to fear?"

"He is a religious fanatic with a penchant for gullible women. It seems a simple matter to avoid him. However, two women were killed and thrown into nearby waterways. Creffield ran away months ago, and the murders occurred within the last two weeks, but still. I will feel safer when he is captured, and we can all find something else to worry about."

Two weeks…when Solace and Allen had been here for barely three.

She tamped down the anxiety. A coincidence. There must have been murders in Portland before their arrival, and would continue to be long after they had gone. But perhaps they should have chosen Seattle. Though rougher than Portland, it was smaller, and seemed somehow safer.

"Could the women have drowned accidentally?"

"Possibly. The papers did not say what killed them, only that they were found in the water. The first was of a certain profession and a regular at the opium dens. She could have fallen in by mistake. But the second… Well, no one has said much about her, perhaps because they don't *know* much. But either way, it is disturbing that the women of our city are not safe."

A man of medium build, wearing a brown suit and a straw boater, detached himself from the parishioners outside the church and crossed the street to them.

"Please excuse the interruption." He tipped his hat to Solace before facing Adina. "My dear, we must be going.

Mrs. Baldwin will arrive soon, and I believe she has a, ah, delivery later. She will not like to be kept waiting."

"Of course, my love. But first, may I introduce Mrs. Grey? Solace, my husband, Robert."

The love shining in Adina's eyes as she gazed at her husband twisted Solace's heart with a sudden, fierce envy. Mr. Donner extended his hand, and with an effort at normalcy—the imperfections of her own marriage were hardly the Donners' fault—she allowed him to shake her hand warmly, as though they were old friends.

"I am so sorry," Adina was saying. "We have a prior appointment. But perhaps I may call on you this week? I feel sure we will get on famously."

Her husband laughed. "No doubt you shall. Once Adina makes up her mind, all is settled. I had no idea of marrying her. None! And then one day she said the same to me, that we would 'get on famously.' I am honestly not certain if it were she or I who proposed. Either way, I *had* to marry her, completely against my will."

"*Robert!*"

Adina blushed, and Solace's envy dissipated. Who could feel anything but joy at two people so clearly in love? She hesitated, then took herself firmly in hand. Either it mattered or it did not.

"I would be happy to receive you any day this week. We are in Goose Hollow, on Myrtlewood."

Adina showed no negative reaction to learning Solace's address, only smiled again and inclined her head, while Mr. Donner bowed in a friendly manner. Then they moved away, leaving Solace alone by the children, lost in thoughts of murder and adultery and marriage, waiting for Allen to return.

Chapter Six

The midday Sunday meal at Sadie's was a loud affair. Even the graveyard shift roused itself to participate, crowding the enormous dining table that groaned under platters of meat, potatoes, and bread, and bowls of beans and gravy. If any of the men had visitors, Sadie set up folding tables in the parlor and found extra chairs. No one was denied, and all ate their fill.

This was also Sadie's preferred time for Mrs. Baldwin's "deliveries." In such a boisterous crowd, a shy girl could remain anonymous, while an outgoing one would fit right in. Either way, the men knew to keep their hands off "Ma's strays" or find lodging elsewhere. As no one who'd experienced Sadie's cooking ever wanted to lose the privilege, this rule was strictly observed.

But Lucky doubted Mrs. Baldwin appreciated the nuances of Sadie's machinations. Her expression when she arrived that Sunday was stern. A petite woman in her mid-forties, with a long nose and hooded eyes, her downturned mouth gave the impression she was a serious thinker who rarely smiled. However, her hair was still dark and glossy, and she was what most would call "handsome." She wore a plain navy dress, its severity relieved only by the white lace edging the sleeves.

As she passed the open dining room doors, she surveyed the unruly crowd, eating the way men eat, and talking the way men talk, when no ladies are present to curb them. Behind her trailed a waif of a girl in a too-large dress, her hair, skin, and eyes the dull pallor of the severely malnourished. Mary, no doubt. She glanced neither left nor right, seemingly disinterested in her fate, and anger stabbed Lucky's gut at what could have brought her here.

Mrs. Baldwin looked up then, intercepting his glare and likely misinterpreting its cause. She stared back calmly for a moment, then took Mary by the hand and led her down the hall and out of sight.

Lucky forced his attention back to his dinner. Ten minutes should be enough for the efficient Sadie to whisk into the parlor, assure Mrs. Baldwin that Mary would be well cared for, and then sweep the child into her wake and out again. When the allotted time was up, he hurried to the parlor, arriving just as Mrs. Baldwin was gathering her belongings.

"Ma'am, I wonder if I might have a word."

She eyed him up and down. "Mr. Jacobs, is it?"

Of course she knew his name—Portland had to be the smallest Big City in the States. "Yes, ma'am."

The ornate clock on the mantel struck one. She pursed her lips, then sat on the edge of a wing chair, back straight, gloved hands folded in her lap. "Very well. But I am meeting the directors of the exposition at two, and I do not intend to be late. When the Lord decreed Sunday should be a day of rest, He forgot to notify the politicians."

"Yes, ma'am."

Sadie had described Mrs. Baldwin as "civic-minded" for her involvement with the YWCA committee working to ensure the safety of the unchaperoned females expected to flood the city next year during the fair. However, rather than chatting about women's safety in general, Lucky needed to discuss one woman in particular. He checked the clock. Ellie should have arrived an hour ago. How could he help her if she wasn't even here?

Mrs. Baldwin remained perfectly still, but her lowered brows and haughty expression conveyed a woman tapping a mental foot with impatience. He cleared his throat.

"Ma'am, I met up with an old, er, friend on the way to church this morning. She agreed to meet with you. She needs help. I wondered if you might, ah, take her on."

Mrs. Baldwin compressed her lips. "I see. And with what, precisely, is she afflicted?"

"She…that is…"

Now it came down to it, Lucky found he didn't want to voice Ellie's troubles aloud, as if doing so made them more real. Yet they *were* real, and refusing to acknowledge them did her no service. He rechecked the clock. Had she changed her mind? Returned to her opium den instead of her home? Or perhaps the den *was* her home.

He sighed and shoved a hand through his hair. "Opium addiction and…prostitution."

Mrs. Baldwin remained unflappable. "I take it she is not here?"

"No, ma'am."

"Then there is little I can do for her."

She rose, straightening her skirts, and he stood hastily as well. "Mrs. Baldwin—"

"I am very sorry, Mr. Jacobs. Truly. As you may know, I have an appointed mission to help the immoral and abused women of this city. However, the first step to salvation must be made by the sinner herself. I cannot force her."

Strictly speaking, this was untrue. Lucky had heard tales of upstanding citizens badgering the police to jail a drug-addled prostitute, thereby sobering her up against her will. But it was true that the woman must be present in order to be thrown in the cell.

"Of course. But may I give her your address? And if she comes, will you help her?"

"I will never deny a soul who genuinely seeks to follow a better path. If all goes according to plan, I will shortly be moving into an office in the Young Women's Christian Association building, but until then, she may come to me at Charlton's. You know it?"

"Yes. Thank you. Her name is Ellie—Elzbieta." Shamefully, he did not even know her surname. "I will send her to you straightaway."

Mrs. Baldwin's expression softened. "Mr. Jacobs. Your heart is good. But you must realize it is likely your Ellie has decided she prefers an immoral life after all."

"I know. But I truly believe she meant it when she agreed to seek your aid."

Ellie probably *had* spent his coins on opium, ignoring his half-joking plea to return Sadie's towel. But due to the recent murders, the fear lingered that her absence was involuntary.

Mrs. Baldwin nodded sympathetically. "Very well. I shall expect her shortly."

She moved to the door, and Lucky cursed himself nine times a fool. "One more thing—there's a couple on Myrtlewood Lane, over by Tanner Creek Gulch."

She stopped and raised her eyebrows. "What of them?"

Now he'd begun, how to continue? Mrs. Grey had

shown no signs of a troubled marriage other than possible worry over spending her husband's money. And Mr. Grey was certainly odd, but Lucky couldn't pinpoint what made him so, beyond his vague demeanor.

He couldn't tell Mrs. Baldwin that Mrs. Grey *might* be being abused by her husband, simply because she had winced at Lucky's touch. Mrs. Baldwin would only point out that it *was* his touch, and perhaps revulsion, not pain, which caused the reaction. And she could be right. Yet…

Lucky's own mother had been adept at hiding the effects of his father's private beatings from public view. Lucky might be mistaken about the Greys. Or Mrs. Grey might be as good at concealment as his mother had been.

Mrs. Baldwin made an impatient gesture. "Mr. Jacobs, as I said, I have another appointment. Either speak your piece, or say good-bye and I will go."

"Yes, ma'am." Lucky blew out a breath. "It's just that they're new, and I don't think the wife knows the neighbors yet. I thought maybe you could send someone to—to drop in. To see if she needs, well, anything."

She was silent a moment, studying him with great intensity. Her erect posture and confident carriage made him itch to twist his hat in his hands or tug his forelock and bow. She was a woman who got things done, and damn all who got in her way. Wasn't that why he'd approached her in the first place?

"Hmph," she said at last. "I see Mrs. Smith is not the only one here who collects strays. I seem to be in the business of finding them myself, so I suppose I can take on two of yours. But Mr. Jacobs, there may come a time when I need a favor. If you can provide it, you will."

"Yes, ma'am. Anything you need, I'm your man."

Giving him another cursory once over, she *hmphed*

again and left the parlor.

Lucky sank onto the sofa. To say she was a "force of nature" was akin to saying a lightning bolt gave off a "little spark." God help Ellie or Solace if Mrs. Baldwin did take either of them under her wing.

~:~:~

The room was cold and flickered with shadows. Dirt floor, poorly framed wooden walls, smells of dying plants and mold. How had she gotten here? Ellie shivered and hugged herself. Her eyes wouldn't stay open, but inside her lids or out, everything swam and shifted. Something tickled her consciousness, a memory. A *good* memory. Something had happened, something that gave her hope. She was supposed to be somewhere, or—or meet someone. Or…something.

A steady drumbeat throbbed in her skull, making it hard to think. Or maybe it was the sickly-sweet smell. She knew that smell. It pulsed in her veins with a need stronger than anything. Stronger even than the thread of life reaching out from her womb.

"*Kūdikis*," she whispered through dry, cracked lips.

A man loomed over her, dressed in a dark coat and trousers, and she recognized him as he caught her wrist. "Stay still and this will be over soon."

He held a syringe and memory flooded back. She had gone to the church after all, then lost her nerve and stayed outside, across the street. When the Mass ended, she had watched as Lucky hurried out, expression tight. He hadn't noticed her, just jogged away as though escaping something unpleasant. She knew that impulse well.

Other parishioners trickled out, and she'd watched them wistfully. If Lucky was right about the lady he'd mentioned, Ellie might join them one day. The hope was almost unbearable, and eventually she'd left. But a block later, *he* had grabbed her from behind. She'd struggled, then felt the stinging pinch in her neck, the sweet drug entering her veins, then blessed blackness.

"No," she whispered. Her heavy body wouldn't move, and besides, where would she go? Tears burned her eyes and the life in her womb fluttered then stilled. "*Kūdikis*…baby…"

"Baby," he agreed, then shook his head with mock regret. "*No* baby. If you took your medicine, we wouldn't be in this mess. So, you'll take it now, or…"

The baby was the good thing. But she had no choice. Either she took the medicine, or he would force it down her throat. Somehow, he'd found her out. There would be no escape, not for her, and not for the baby.

She tried anyway. "I have not told. No one. I—I will leave, go to Seattle. Please, let me go…"

"And have the brat turn up later? Children are curious—the police might take an interest. I didn't come this far west just to have my life ruined. Eventually, you'll spill your guts. People always do. So, I'll spill them for you, and then even if you tattle, who will believe you? A man in *my* respected position, and a whore with no baby as proof? No one, that's who."

He held the syringe aloft, and she wept in earnest.

"I—I'll take it," she managed at last, and his grin was an evil gash of teeth across the face she had thought she loved. *Baisūna. Monster*…

"Good girl." He set the syringe aside and reached for a steaming mug. He brought it close, and she recoiled from the smell.

"*Ne—blogas*—bad. Something is wrong, like dead mice… Please, give me seeds to make tea myself."

"I think not. We tried that, and look where it got us."

"Here. I will make it here, while you watch…"

"*Enough!*"

He held the mug to her lips, pinching her nose and forcing her head back, tipping the hot liquid into her mouth and down her throat. It tasted like carrots, or parsnips, or some other root, and she choked, but he was inexorable, and most of it went down.

"Now, we wait. I have heard it can take a while, so perhaps I will leave you here. Would you like something to pass the time?" He bent his head toward the syringe, but she gagged, the drink's stench watering her eyes and roiling her stomach. "Very well, have it your way. I had better clean up. But first, a little insurance."

He tied her wrists with thick ropes, securing them to a heavy chest in one corner of the room, then eyed her objectively. "We had such fun until you ruined it. Perhaps a little fun now? At least you can't get knocked up again with this brat still in you."

He reached for his belt, and she would have cringed, but something wasn't right. The drink burned her throat, and the opium swam in her veins, but even so, she should be able to move. Her breath came in gasps—*no air—she had no air*. Her gaze flew to his, her mouth working— *no sound—no sound—no air…*

He frowned. "Why are you doing that? Never mind. Lie back, let the medicine kill the brat. And if it doesn't, well, we'll dig it out some other way…"

She couldn't lift her head, but she heard scraping, metal on stone, the sharpening of a knife. Her limbs ached; she was dizzy. He hummed as he worked, a child's lullaby. She wanted to weep but she couldn't, there was nothing she could do, she could barely think.

Are you sleeping, are you sleeping?
Brother John, Brother John!
Morning bells are ringing, morning bells
*   are ringing,*
Ding-dang-dong! Ding-dang-dong!

The drums throbbed. She smelled opium and the mouse-stink of the empty mug on the floor by her head. She was so confused.

Are you sleeping, Brother John? No, you are drugged. You are dying. You will die, and the morning bells will ring, but you will never hear them…

She should have gone with Lucky, gone *inside* the church and endured the stares. Or called to him as he left. He would have kept her safe.

But she had not. And now she would die in this place, far from home, far from love.

Are you sleeping, are you sleeping?

Her chest barely moved. The room was gray; her sight dimmed. Could she move anything—her fingers or toes? She couldn't, not anymore. Something wasn't right, it just wasn't right…

Ding-dang-dong rang the death knell, and everything went dark.

Chapter Seven

Monday July 25

"GAMBLERS QUIT TOWN – MAYOR
WON'T TALK – Poker and keno may be
conducted in private clubs, but sheriff says he
could only stop them by descending to
methods beneath his dignity as a man as well
as an official. When asked, Mayor Williams
said, 'I cannot tell what the future will bring.'"
—*The Oregon Daily Journal*

Allen left early Monday for the library, though Solace couldn't think what he might need to research. His position at St. Mary's wouldn't start for several weeks, when school reconvened in September. But on Sunday, after the Donners left her, Allen had sent Solace home alone, while he stayed with Sister Margaret until well past supper time. So he must have more to do.

In fact, he'd stayed so late at the church that Solace had begun to be very worried, until a wagon let him out at the garden gate just past sunset. He'd been agitated, muttering about a mistake he needed to correct, but when she queried him, he calmed himself.

"Nothing to be concerned about, my dear. God willing, I'll set it right in a week or two."

He'd smiled at her then, sweet and innocent like a child, and she'd tried to set aside her misgivings. But preparations for his classes kept him busy, so though he'd still seemed distracted this morning, she'd merely accepted his kiss on her cheek and extracted promises that he would eat his lunch and return in time for supper.

Though the sun had not been up an hour when he left, the heat was oppressive, unlike the cool fog that rolled across San Francisco Bay year-round. Still, it was better than the humidity of the Midwest, which she did *not* miss.

She cleared the breakfast dishes, then surveyed the little house's disarray. *No hope for it. The heat won't abate from me standing here while there's work to do.*

Hard work and lots of it, for they had not truly unpacked yet. Not that they had many possessions; their frequent moves saw to that. But Allen had shipped his books up instead of donating them to the University of California library, and now dozens of boxes crowded the floors. Though to be fair, several boxes contained her books. They weren't *all* Allen's.

She faced the living room. Two half-height, built-in bookcases flanked the fireplace. That would empty a few boxes; perhaps her books, separated from Allen's. But for the rest, she would have to buy lumber for shelves. Daunting, as their ready cash had gone to Fisher's. Perhaps Mr. Fisher would extend them credit, seeing as they were such newly loyal customers. Rough wood and cinder blocks couldn't be very expensive.

A frisson of something—unease? anticipation?— shivered up her spine. If she went to Fisher's, she might see their erstwhile deliveryman. But no, of course she wouldn't. He would be out, *making deliveries.* That's what delivery men did. They didn't sit about, twiddling their thumbs, waiting to accost hapless customers with legitimate hardware needs.

On the heels of that comforting thought came the abrupt realization that if she walked to Fisher's—for they had no cart nor pony, let alone an automobile—her purchases would need to be delivered later. She could hardly drag them home herself, even one brick or board at a time.

But would Mr. Fisher think it odd if she requested his father be the delivery man? Despite her threats, she had no real wish to see Mr. Jacobs fired. He'd apologized for his rudeness, and in all fairness, she had not been in the best temper. Worry over Allen's reaction to anything new tended to make her overly sensitive, and Detective Jenkins's patronizing hadn't helped.

She squared her shoulders. "Fisher's it is." She retrieved her hat, jacket, gloves, and pocketbook from their places in the entryway and stepped out into the heat.

Unfortunately, her resolve was for naught. After the two-mile walk, during which sweat pasted the fine lawn of her shirt to her skin, her feet swelled in her leather boots, and strands of hair once more escaped from her bun, she discovered the only boards Fisher's had were of the finished, and therefore costly, variety. At least the yard was wagon-less, so she needn't fear Mr. Jacobs's witnessing this latest debacle.

"You're certain there's nothing I can use?" she asked, hiding her disappointment.

Mr. Fisher squinted through his spectacles at an order sheet on the counter. "'Less you want two-by-fours, I'm fresh out."

"No, I need flat boards. To make shelves."

He frowned. "Shelves? The furniture store on—"

"Mr. Fisher." She hated to interrupt, for he seemed a

nice man, his thin hair combed over a balding head, bushy gray brows perpetually furrowed in concentration. In fact, he reminded her of her father. "I appreciate the suggestion, but I would prefer a more…rustic style."

He frowned some more, and the heat rose in her cheeks. Then his expression cleared, and he said in an overly jocular tone, "Of course, that is all the rage now, isn't it? So econ—er, fashionable!"

Before she could agree with his claim that it was an aesthetic rather than financial preference—in other words, lie—he scribbled on a notepad, then tore the sheet off and held it out. "Jones Lumber is on Macadam, but they have an office at Sixth and Yamhill. Sometimes they have boards that are uneven. Nothing you'd notice in a shelf, but not good for floors or framing. Tell 'em I sent you. They'll deal fairly with you."

There was nothing for it but to take the paper and thank him, before departing the store with her head high. He had been helpful and generous, but it was beyond humiliating to be begging favors at every turn. Pray God she could stretch their funds until summer's end, when Allen would receive his first real wages from St. Mary's.

She grimaced as she headed downhill toward the north end of town. Never mind his first month's earnings—pray God Allen could *keep* his job.

So far, his spells hadn't affected his academic abilities. He clearly recalled events from years ago, when he was a boy in school himself, or starting out as a teacher. But he forgot recent things, such as what he ate for breakfast, or where he went of an afternoon. It was most puzzling. And increasingly difficult to conceal.

Whenever she met Sister Margaret or anyone from St. Mary's, Solace was careful not to show concern for

Allen's behavior or indicate he might be ill. But…what of this "mistake" he'd made, which must relate to his work? If his mood swings were more frequent at home, they would surely begin to occur in public soon.

If they did, and Allen became violent in front of—or God forbid, *against*—his students, he would lose his place, and they their sole income, for he was set against her finding a job. *No wife of mine will work for a living*, he had said in one of his lucid moments. If only he could be *un*-lucid at times like these, when it would be helpful.

They had come from the Midwest to California on the doctor's recommendation that a coastal climate would improve him, then moved to Oregon when the University of California did not renew his position. He had never clearly explained what brought that on. Had he been violent to a student? At least there he had taught adults, but here he would be in charge of children.

Yet what could Solace do? Follow him around and try to stop the behaviors he couldn't control himself? Her presence would only raise eyebrows and get him fired for different reasons.

She crossed the cobbled road and turned onto Stark Street near the library. Perhaps after her errand she would check on him. He often got involved in his work and forgot to eat, a result of nothing more troubling than his academic nature. Her father had been the same. It must be the provenance of men, for though she was an academic, she had never once forgotten a meal.

Or she *had* been an academic once upon a time, in another life. Impatiently, she shrugged. She had chosen this path and would not regret it.

Jones Lumber came into view, and she hurried forward. This misguided mission had already taken too long. At this rate, she wouldn't need to remind Allen to eat; she could lunch *with* him. She reached for the door as a man in a worse hurry than she barreled out, knocking her across the wood sidewalk so that she nearly fell into the street below. If not for the quick hand of a man behind her, she would have twisted her ankle or worse.

Of course the lout who'd pushed her glared as though it were her fault. Before she could react, he turned rudely away and vanished into the crowd.

"Insufferable!" she muttered, then raised her most winsome smile to her savior, only to find herself gazing up—and *up*—into the inscrutable blue eyes of Mr. Jacobs.

"I was only aiming to help, ma'am," he said blandly. "Or should I have let you fall?"

In recent days, Solace—*Mrs. Grey*—was popping up more often than a bad penny. Lucky watched the play of emotions cross her expressive features, changing from a pretty smile to dismay, then confusion, and finally, embarrassment. The smile should definitely return. It shone from within and erased the lines of care carved into her face.

He still held her arm, though she no longer needed his support. But his hand couldn't seem to let go, and his body certainly enjoyed her nearness. Yessir, having all those soft curves so close to his own work-hardened muscles was Heaven blended with Hell, a sweet torture he both couldn't stand, and couldn't stand to end.

"Mr. Jacobs," she said faintly, sounding anything but enthused, "please release my arm."

"Of course, ma'am. My apologies."

He let go, and she drew in a deep breath, regaining

some of her color. "No, it's I who should apologize and offer my sincere gratitude. Without your aid, I would have fallen into the street. I did not mean to be ungrateful. I was only surprised to see you here."

It was an unspoken question, so he answered it. "I work for Jones Lumber at the mill on Macadam, but it's a fickle business. When there's a shutdown—machinery broken, waterways blocked, or something similar—I take odd jobs. Like Fisher's."

"I see. So you are actually an employee of...*this* company?"

She sounded alarmed, her body tense and poised for flight. Before she could claim to be headed elsewhere, he opened the door and held it for her. "Yes, ma'am. Can I help you with your lumber needs today, Mrs. Grey? Are you perhaps planning for a new addition?"

As soon as he spoke, he realized the implication of his words. Mrs. Grey reddened, and he cursed himself. He hadn't meant to pry into her business again, and he certainly didn't want to know if she *was* expecting a new arrival. The blunder had left her so flustered, however, that she had no choice but to enter the cool office.

He followed, letting the door swing shut behind them. "What I meant to say is, what brings you to Jones Lumber today?"

She paused, gaze traveling around the room, taking in every detail. She was that kind of woman, her intellect underused as a housewife, so that it must find other outlets, such as home projects, or noticing his accent.

He'd been here often himself. Today he needed to speak with the foreman, who was taking advantage of the shutdown to review the accounts with the clerk. But now he tried to see the office through her eyes.

It was small, an offshoot of the main lumberyard south of town by the river. A heavy roll-top desk stuffed with papers and ledgers stood against one wall, across from a counter separating customers from staff. Behind this, an open door led to the back rooms where most of the business operations were conducted.

She finished her perusal and turned sharp eyes on him, taking in his wool coat, flannel shirt, homespun pants, and heavy, crimp-soled boots. "Mr. Jacobs, I am grateful for your offer of help. But I can see you do not normally work in an office."

Her tone was not condescending, and she spoke no more than the truth. Most men garbed as he was held hard-labor positions. But something about her assumption got his hackles up, and he jutted his chin out. "Is that so?"

"Yes." She sounded mildly exasperated. "I mean no insult. I only thought you might direct me to whomever runs this office, so you may return to your own work. I need boards. Nothing finished or—or fancy." Her color rose and she dropped her head. Then she straightened, hazel eyes snapping. "That is, I wish to construct cheap shelving. Mr. Fisher suggested I might find decent wood here at a good price. And perhaps bricks for the sides? My husband has a lot of books."

"I see," he said, absurdly relieved that she wasn't outfitting a nursery after all. "How many shelves?"

She thought a moment, then gestured helplessly. "I'm not certain. We have books piled on the floor and two dozen boxes yet to unpack. Allen is a teacher."

"I suspected as much. I certainly didn't think he worked in *outdoor physical labor*."

For once, she returned his smile. "Yes, I suppose

appearances go both ways." She hesitated, as though unaccustomed to chit-chat. After a moment she spoke carefully, like she feared revealing too much. "He will be at St. Mary's Academy this fall."

"The Cathedral school? And…are you parishioners there?"

Her cheeks pinkened. "We've been busy unpacking. Yesterday is the first Mass we've attended."

"I see." The color did wonders for her complexion. He cleared his throat. "Please, will you wait here a moment? I'll see what is available for your shelves."

Before she could refuse, he went to the back room to make the arrangements. When he returned minutes later, she stood at the counter, examining a roll of building plans someone had left out. She hadn't heard him, and he took the opportunity to observe her. On the surface, she looked like any other woman. Lucky knew nothing of fashion, but her gray hat, jacket, and skirt were neat and clean, if rather dull, and her figure was trim, yet rounded in the right places.

But on closer examination, her differences showed like light breaking through the chinks in a painted-over window. Where most women would have disinterestedly awaited his return, she had found something to occupy her mind. She bent over the plans, frowning in concentration, her lips moving as she read the architect's notes. She tilted her head for a better view, and Lucky glimpsed the pale column of her throat above the lace collar of her blouse.

He swallowed, tugging at his own collar. "Are you interested in architecture, Mrs. Grey?"

She jumped and stepped away. "No. That is, yes, but I didn't mean to snoop. I noticed these are for the exposition. Is Jones Lumber contracted for that?"

He shrugged. "Many structures are needed, and the lumberyards will all compete for bids. As you pointed out, it is not my job to oversee official matters like this."

She grimaced, then nodded toward the back room. "Point taken. Were you successful?"

"Yes. A selection of boards and bricks are being loaded onto a wagon as we speak."

She stared at him blankly. "Here? But this is just an office, is it not?"

"And a small warehouse. Jones Lumber will be happy to offer what we have, and once you have determined your needs, will send you a bill." Her expressive eyes flickered with concern, and he hastened to add, "A fair bill. In fact, these boards are so discounted, you may object to their quality. In which case, we will take them all back at no charge."

The concern was replaced by a glint of amusement, and his heart gave an odd thump.

"Very well, Mr. Jacobs. Thank you for your aid. Again."

He moved past her and opened the door. "The wagon will be loaded by now, and the bench seats two. I would be happy to give you a lift home and unload your shelves for you."

"But don't you have work to do?"

"Unfortunately, no. The mill is closed for the day while the men are out trying to unblock the local creeks, and I am at your service."

Her dismayed expression was almost comical, but someone had raised her right. She managed a polite, "Thank you," before preceding him out the door.

Lucky allowed himself a moment to enjoy the view

from behind before following her.

You need to find a woman. And not this woman.

Someone available, like Fisher's widowed daughter, who regarded Lucky with wide-eyed admiration, whereas Mrs. Grey treated him like a snake in her garden. She was so stiff as he helped her onto the wagon that he feared she'd break in two if she fell off. He climbed up beside her, and she held her head high, which only made him want to run his fingers through her silky hair and then his mouth along her slender throat.

With a mental groan, he tore his mind from the thought, and carefully kept his thigh from touching hers, an effort that was wasted once they reached the street. The wagon bounced and jostled over deep ruts, throwing her repeatedly against him, despite her death-grip on the bench. When they hit a particularly rough patch, his whole body slammed into hers, and she gasped and grabbed his arm to keep from sliding off the seat.

"Sorry," he muttered once they'd righted themselves and she'd let go. The memory of her touch burned his skin, even through the flannel shirt and wool coat.

"Think nothing of it," she said.

If only he *could* think nothing of it. It was going to be a long ride and an even longer afternoon. For once he unloaded her shelves, only a lout would leave them in a pile for her to deal with. No, he'd be offering, probably *insisting*, on helping her build the damn things into bookcases. Dozens of them, from what she'd said of her husband's library.

A new thought occurred, and he brightened. "Is your husband at home today, Mrs. Grey?"

If so, he could build the bookcases. And even if Lucky felt honor-bound to help, at least he wouldn't lose himself in lustful daydreams of Grey's wife with the man himself at his side.

"No," Mrs. Grey answered abstractedly. "He is at the library. I intended to check on him later, but…" Her cheeks colored, and she stopped short of blaming Lucky yet again for her changed plans.

"Excellent."

"Excuse me?"

"Nothing." Lucky snapped the reins, wishing fervently that Mr. Grey would come home early to look after his wife. Somebody needed to, in order to protect her from, well, *him*.

Yes, it was going to be a long day.

Chapter Eight

Lola Baldwin strode into the crowded, poorly-lit police station and aimed for the stairs that led up to Chief Hunt's office on the second floor. Before she reached them, a man's voice called out to her from behind.

"Mrs. Baldwin—may I help you with something?"

She considered feigning deafness, but it might spur the speaker to chase after her, and she must maintain her dignity. She turned and found one of Hunt's detectives hurrying to intercept her. They all looked the same to her, especially the younger ones, even without the blue uniforms worn by Hunt's patrolmen. Still, the detectives all chose dark suits instead, making them equally interchangeable in her eyes.

However, now she thought about it, this one did seem familiar. He was marginally older than many on the force, perhaps in his mid-thirties, stocky and very buttoned-down. He even still wore his hat, despite the sweltering heat of the unairconditioned building, so he must have just arrived, perhaps following her in. This supposition was supported by the sweat dampening his face, as though he had just come from the worse heat outside.

He caught the direction of her gaze and quickly removed the hat and wiped his brow with a gloved hand. "May I help you?"

"I wish to speak with Chief Hunt." She turned back to the stairs, but he moved to block her access. Sighing inwardly, she acceded to the inevitable. "Detective…?"

"Jenkins, ma'am."

"Detective Jenkins, is Chief Hunt in his office?"

"Yes, ma'am. But his schedule is very busy this afternoon. I'll be happy to relay your message, and if necessary, he'll get back to you."

If necessary, indeed! Why were men always so difficult? Women were so much easier to work with and managed to get things done without all this rigamarole. Which was in part what had brought her here today.

Lola inhaled and exhaled. "Very well. Please remind him of the urgent need to shut down the gaming halls in Portland, not just because of the exposition coming next year, but because it's the right and moral thing to do."

"Of course," he said, and made as if to show her out.

"I am not finished. Gambling is a blight on our city. If we are to attract visitors to the fair—good, honest folk who will bring trade and industry to our economy—we *must* clean up our town. Look at these recent murders. If criminal activities were not so openly practiced in Portland, perhaps Creffield and his Holy Rollers—or whoever the killer is—would have gone elsewhere."

The detective's expression soured. "Think it's not Creffield, do you? That you know more about it than we do? Next you'll be angling for my job."

Lola paused, frowning. "My apologies, detective. I didn't mean to offend you. I am sure everyone on the force is working hard to capture the killer. I only meant that there is good evidence that open gaming in a city attracts a certain crowd, which in turn, creates opportunities for yet more immoral behaviors."

Jenkins took a handkerchief from his pocket and more thoroughly wiped the sweat from his face. "I am afraid I owe *you* an apology, Mrs. Baldwin. I am not myself this morning. I will share your concerns with Chief Hunt, and impress upon him the urgency of ensuring fair-goers feel safe enough to come here. Now, is there anything else I can help you with?"

He seemed in a tearing hurry to rid himself of her. Whatever errand had made him late must be weighing on him. But in truth, she had other places to be, as well.

"Just one more thing. I have asked in the past that when a patrolman encounters a prostitute in the act of solicitation, or who has over-imbibed or taken drugs, that instead of bringing her to the jail, I should be called first. These women need help, not incarceration, and the organizations I work with can provide it to them if we are given the chance."

Jenkins regarded her thoughtfully. He was an odd one, and difficult to read. He seemed highly intelligent, but perhaps not very empathetic. And his ego was touchy.

He wrinkled his nose at her. "So you do want a job on the Force, just not as a detective."

"No," she said with as much patience as she could muster. "I have no desire to be on Chief Hunt's staff. I only want to help the women of our city, who are currently unable to help themselves. All I ask is for a phone call before an arrest is made, so there is more room in the jail for the real criminals to be locked up."

He watched her again, then nodded slowly. "Okay, I'll ask the chief about it for you. But keep in mind, any calls will likely come in the middle of the night, when whores are most active."

She half wondered if he'd used the vulgar language to try and shock her. The canny look in his eyes said as much, but she refused to rise to the bait.

"Thank you, detective. I know when 'ladies of the night' work, and will appreciate being notified *whenever* one needs assistance."

He bowed as she moved past him toward the doors, and she felt his gaze boring into her until she was outside. Probably it was just his naturally suspicious nature as a detective. But either way, he represented yet another male roadblock in a seemingly endless line of barriers, stopping her from making any progress toward helping the downtrodden women and girls of Portland.

To be fair, he had agreed to speak to Hunt on her behalf. And though he'd no doubt meant to deter her, his comment about "angling" for a job on the Force had got her thinking: Why *should* the policing of women fall solely to male officers? Not female detectives, investigating crimes such as murder or theft. But female patrol officers? *That* had potential.

She moved up the block. The more she considered it, the more it seemed she must accept the Traveler's Aid position. Whatever came later, it was at least a step in the right direction.

~:~:~

When Chief Hunt stepped into the hall outside his office on Monday afternoon, he found Detective Jenkins coming up the stairs, sweating. In this old building, with no cooling system, who could blame him? But Hunt happened to know Jenkins had been late to work this morning. Not much, but enough to set him behind for the day. And so both his hurry and his overheating were his own fault. Jenkins was no slacker, but once something was allowed, others would follow suit, and then where would the department be?

"Well, what is it? I'm needed at the mayor's office."

He moved to the stairs, and Jenkins fell into step beside him. "Yes, sir. It's only that Mrs. Baldwin was here again, demanding that the gaming halls be shut down once and for all."

Hunt made a noise in the back of his throat which Jenkins must have correctly interpreted as, *She knows that will never happen, so tell me her real objective*, because he responded, "Yes, sir. She also requested again that we notify her when prostitutes are arrested."

Hunt grunted again. "That, at least, would save manpower. I'll consider it."

They left the police building and were blasted by the more than one-hundred-degree heat. Within a block, sweat soaked Jenkins's collar, and he tugged at his gloves as though removing them might provide relief. Hunt's situation wasn't any better, and they had ten blocks yet to go. Damn the council for moving City Hall so far south, and for refusing to add a patrol car to Hunt's budget.

Jenkins was saying something that Hunt hadn't been listening to. The man seemed distracted, probably by whatever business had caused his lateness. Or maybe Hunt was distracted, and Jenkins was his usual meticulous self. The thought irritated Hunt even more.

"What's that?"

"I said I spoke with one of our business friends. He's found a solution to the *problem* we discussed." Jenkins glanced at the passersby and lowered his voice. "A new collections man."

Hunt also looked around, but for once no reporters lurked close by, hoping for a scoop. He quickened his pace. "Hmph. That why you were so late this morning?"

Jenkins matched his stride to Hunt's. "My apologies, sir. I was at the Gem on a business matter."

Hunt scowled. "The point was to find a collections man who *doesn't* wear the badge."

Jenkins reddened. "Yes, sir. I mean, no, sir. I wasn't making a collection. I merely wanted to inform them that a new man would be coming soon."

"Good. I don't need to know the details." Anyone else would have taken this as the dismissal it clearly was, but not Jenkins. Hunt sighed inwardly. The man was good at his job, but just now, Hunt would have given his eyeteeth to have the conversation over with, so he could walk the rest of the way to Mayor Williams's office in peace. "Well? What else, then?"

"I have been thinking, sir. There are fresh reports that Creffield was seen in Portland."

"So? Every Tom, Dick and Harriet has 'seen' him twice a day for the last four months. Not only here—all over the damn state, which is obviously nonsense."

"Of course those reports are unreliable. But I visited Goose Hollow a few days ago, near St. Mary's. A small man with wispy hair was seen near a butcher's on Seventh Avenue, and also in Tanner Creek Gulch, below the Chinese gardens. The butcher is a good sort, not prone to hysterics. And it was the lumbermen clearing the creek who spotted Creffield in the canyon."

Hunt stopped. "How long ago? For the gulch?"

"Last week, before we found the latest victim, and again late Sunday or early this morning." He started to pick at his gloves again, then stopped himself, folding his hands at his back despite his obvious discomfort.

Hunt blew out a breath, considering. "Returning to the scene of the crime, perhaps." He frowned. "Hair, you say? Creffield was bald the last anyone saw of him.”

Jenkins nodded. “Yes, sir. I thought of that, sir. He could be wearing a wig, or he could have shaved his head before. Maybe he’s not naturally bald.”

Hunt grunted and resumed walking, Jenkins trailing a few steps behind. It wasn’t much, but it was more than they’d had previously. *Almost* confirmation that the little bugger was in town, not out in the desert or the mountains where they’d never find him. Then again, Portland was large, and easy to get lost in.

Hunt glared over his shoulder at Jenkins. “Why didn’t you tell me this immediately, instead of starting with that drivel about the clubs and Mrs. Baldwin?”

“I was hoping, sir, that you might consider putting me in charge of local operations, vis à vis Creffield. A temporary advancement until you feel I am ready for my full promotion to captain. I have many ideas that could help the investigation. Things I learned in New York, which we could implement here.”

Oh-ho! So that’s *his game.* Hunt faced forward again, striding purposefully along the sidewalk. *Sidetrack me with inconsequentials before dropping the meat of his ambition before me, while reminding me he comes from a bigger department back East. Well, I knew he wouldn’t be satisfied with “wait and see” for long.*

“I’ll consider it,” he barked over his shoulder.

“Thank you, sir. That’s all I ask, sir.”

Hunt kept moving, and this time Jenkins’s footsteps ceased to follow.

~:~:~

Allen looked up from the book he was studying to find the room dim and unlit, with an elderly woman he didn’t recognize approaching apologetically.

"I'm very sorry, Mr. Grey, but I must close up now and get home to make supper."

Her face was kind, and she seemed to know him, so he asked, "Is this the library?"

She frowned, and then her face cleared. "Oh, how you do get involved in your research! And you've forgotten to eat again, after your wife went to so much trouble. It's no wonder you don't know where you are. Lack of food'll do that to a person."

"Yes," he said uncertainly. "I suppose so."

A small metal pail sat on the table in front of him, filled with mysterious lumps wrapped in translucent paper. Something round and shiny red lay on top, and he touched it hesitantly. It was hard and smooth, and he *should* know what it was called, but its name eluded him.

The woman watched him, so he stood hastily, then wondered, should he do something about the books on the table? Had he put them there? He couldn't remember, so he picked one up and slammed it shut angrily.

The woman jumped, then said soothingly, "Now, Mr. Grey, let me take care of those. It is my job, after all."

Gratefully, he handed her the book. Except…there were other items, things that might be his that he should take. But which ones? If only his wife were here. How silly—for a moment, he couldn't recall her name, either. Laura. That was it—Laura would know what to do. Or his mother. She always steered him in the right direction.

Unlike this strange woman, who glared at him from beady little eyes.

"Don't worry, I'm going!" he snapped, and she flinched.

"Mr. Grey, is anything amiss? You must be so tired. Would you like Thomas to drive you home in the cart?

It's no trouble."

"I am quite capable of getting home on my own," he said coldly, noticing an open satchel on the floor. Surely that was his, and the papers strewn across the table. He grabbed it and shoved the papers into it willy-nilly, then snatched the pail and prepared to leave, only then realizing he had no notion how to exit the building.

Tall shelves loomed on all sides, dark and shadowed, a maze of books from which he might never escape. He kicked his chair into the stacks. Books tumbled to the floor, and the she-devil gasped. A door opened off to the right, a warm yellow rectangle in a sea of black, and a boy's voice asked, "Everything okay, Ma?"

Allen dashed for the light, slamming his shoulder into the she-devil's spawn, shoving it aside as he escaped into the marbled foyer. The creature yelped, fangs glinting in the low sun slanting through the windows. Allen pushed the doors open—out onto the stoop—*heart pounding*—so close—*he'd made it!*

His soul was intact; they had not corrupted him with their filth and lies. He clutched his satchel, the pail's metal handle hard and slippery in his sweaty palm, an anchor as he got his bearings. He was on a street, the evening heat pressing down after the cool of the library. The sun had not yet set, which seemed wrong for winter. Iowa was cold and gray this time of year, not hot and light. *The she-devil*—she'd bewitched him to make him think he was in Hell.

All these people, they were her minions. He avoided eye contact. If they saw into his soul, they could steal it. He *must* find Laura and his mother, but carefully, to avoid attention.

Which way? On one side, the street sloped up toward

hills covered in evergreen trees. On the other, it fell away toward a river thick with boats. In the distance lay a pointy, white-capped mountain. Iowa had no mountains. Had he returned to Africa for more missionary work? That would explain both the mountain and the heathens crowding the street. He must save them, and himself. He twisted this way and that—at any moment the she-devil and her spawn would attack—he *must* get away!

And then he spied her, a beautiful girl in an alley across the way. Her golden hair was pulled up, loose ringlets caressing her throat, her complexion pink and unspoiled. She would lead him to salvation, and the she-devil's spawn would hold no more sway in this world.

Settling the satchel on his shoulder, he stepped down into the street and crossed to her, the light of her hair an angel's halo, guiding him through troubled waters.

She turned to him as he drew near, her light-blue eyes wide and innocent, then she bit her plump, rosy lower lip. "Good day to you, sir. Can I *help* you wi' sumpin'?"

His brain could not comprehend her meaning, but abruptly his vision cleared. He saw the shabbiness of her plunging bodice, the filth of her satin skirts, raked up to show indecent expanses of plump legs covered in coarse black hose. Too late—Beelzebub had gotten to her first.

Then he brightened. Perhaps she was not to be his salvation. But *he* would be *hers*…

Chapter Nine

Far from returning early, Mr. Grey seemed determined to stay out all day. By the time they reached the house on Myrtlewood and Lucky had unloaded the bricks and boards onto the wide porch, it was midafternoon. Mrs. Grey insisted on feeding him, her good manners overriding her obvious discomfort. She prepared a tray of sandwiches and lemonade, then sat with him in the shade of the long porch roof, making pitiful attempts at small talk. He wasn't much better. After *your garden is beautiful*, he was out of ideas.

Or rather, there was plenty he wanted to say and do, but none of it was appropriate on short acquaintance, even if she didn't so clearly dislike him. Not to mention she had a husband, wherever he was. The man should be home, not abandoning his wife to the whims of Fate—in other words, to Lucky or other men of his ilk.

He made an impatient gesture, trying to force his mind onto a higher moral ground than the one his body inhabited. He must have appeared angry, for Mrs. Grey excused herself stiffly and went into the sunny garden, leaving him to stew. When she returned, she bore a handful of flowers, long stalks topped by tiny white petals in clusters that resembled flat umbrellas.

Lucky leapt up and blocked her way. "Stop! Put those down before the poison sets in!"

Mrs. Grey frowned in obvious perplexity. "Mr. Jacobs, I assure you these are perfectly harmless. It's only wild carrot. Or you may know it as Queen Anne's lace. See the red heart?"

All at once, he did see it. Legend said the queen had pricked her finger while sewing lace, and from then on, one tiny red flower grew amidst the otherwise white clusters. "I'm sorry. It looked like…"

"Hemlock?" Her smile was the first genuine one he'd seen since they'd left the Jones Lumber office.

He said sheepishly, "They're so similar, and hemlock does grow here. I thought perhaps you were raised in a city and might not know the difference."

"I have lived in cities and in the country. And…I have studied botany for many years."

She said it defiantly, as though his opinion *mattered* to her. "Is that a fact?"

She pursed her lips, then held the stalks out for inspection. "Both plants are in the Umbelliferae family, but these stems are uniformly green and hairy, not smooth with hemlock's purple streaks. In addition, the leaves smell carroty and, as you can see, are parallel and feathered rather than pinnate in form. The umbels—the flower clusters—are similar, but these form a level plane, where hemlock's are more rounded. And while not poisonous, wild carrot does have pharmacological properties, such as—"

Abruptly, she seemed to realize she was lecturing him. She lowered the flowers and stepped back, dropping her gaze. "I should clean up now."

Lucky collected his plate and mug with one hand in time to open the door for her with the other, then followed her into the house. He hung his hat on a peg near her bonnet and a man's wool coat that must be her husband's, then joined her in the kitchen to the left of the entryway. It was small but filled with light from windows on two sides. It contained a modern gas range and oven, a square wooden table with four chairs, and a door in the far wall, leading to the side porch.

"May I ask where you studied?"

She stood at the sink, removing any dying flower heads that had curled in on themselves, forming brown tangles amid the lacy white "umbels." The activity hid her face, but she answered levelly. "At the University of California. Allen taught there for a time, and I would help with his research and…other things."

"You have many interests. Linguistics, architecture, botany. Is there anything you haven't studied?"

She met his gaze briefly, expression unreadable, then brought the flowers to a vase on the table which already displayed a pretty selection of dahlias, roses, and foxglove. She stared at them, then blew out a breath. When she raised her eyes again, the spark was back.

"Mr. Jacobs, you may as well say it—I am an unnatural female. I'm *learned*. I speak more than one language—more than three, in fact. If you don't care how well I speak, it's more like six or seven. I read and write Latin and some Greek. I *am* more interested in how a building is made than the color of its paint, and I *do* know the kingdom, order, family, and genus of the species *Daucus carota*, commonly known as wild carrot, Queen Anne's lace, and a host of other easier-on-the-female-brain names like that!"

With this last outburst, she stabbed the poor *Daucus carota* in question viciously into the midst of the other unsuspecting flora, then slumped, dropping her hands to the table and regarding them, shamefaced. "I'm afraid I must apologize to you yet again—"

"Not unnatural, no." She glanced up, surprised, and he held her gaze. "But perhaps a bit…abnormal. No, don't go off again. I only mean that, by some standards, your interests are 'abnormal' for a woman. But that does not make you unnatural. Normal and natural are not the same. Many things in nature are far out of the normal sphere. The Northern Lights, for example."

He'd surprised her again. "In the District of Alaska? You've heard of them?"

"I was on my way to see them when I stopped here. They are said to be the most beautiful phenomenon in the sky. Made by God and nature. But they are not *normal*. By definition, a phenomenon is something extra-ordinary—out of the ordinary. You are not unnatural. But you are…extraordinary."

She stared up at him, wide-eyed, lips parted, and his blood pulsed with the awareness that, if he kissed her, neither of them would need to make small talk for a very long time.

He stepped back. What in God's name was he doing? Far from keeping his distance, he was…*wooing* her. Worse, he knew he should leave immediately, but he couldn't. He'd promised to help her, and by God he would, whether she wanted him to or not.

He cleared his throat. "I'd best get to work, building your shelves for you, ma'am."

She attempted to demur, but she was too flustered from his ridiculous compliment and he easily overrode her. Reluctantly, she led him to her husband's study.

Their home was built in Portland's popular "Pyramid" style: four roughly equal-sized rooms with a hall down the middle. Kitchen and living room were at the front, two bedrooms and a water closet at the back.

The living room was cozy, with a fireplace flanked by built-in shelves already filled with books, in front of which sat a large horsehair sofa, a rocker, and a wing-back chair, plus an assortment of occasional tables bearing oil lamps. The street was on the electrical line, but perhaps the cost was prohibitive.

Both front rooms had big street-facing windows, with smaller ones overlooking narrow side yards. Lace curtains admitted the light while preserving privacy, and framed dried plants graced the walls. However unfeminine Solace thought herself, she had beautified her home.

And why should this surprise Lucky? Perhaps it was the age difference, or his continued conviction that something wasn't right in the Greys' marriage. Somehow, he'd pictured their dwelling as bare and masculine, not homey and…happy.

Little tables in the hall and living room even sported vases of flowers to match the larger one in the kitchen. For some reason, this irked him the most. She'd been so afraid of her husband's reaction to the mulch that Lucky had concluded Grey must be a monster. Or at least a spendthrift. But though the Greys were poor, nothing in the warm, friendly little place suggested Grey abused his wife or denied her attempts to pretty things up.

Grey's study, down the hall on the left, held a desk, a chair, and innumerable cardboard boxes, filled with the books that needed shelving. More boxes lined the hallway, so that Lucky had to squeeze by sideways, although Mrs. Grey navigated them gracefully.

It seemed he was in for a long afternoon of hard work. He returned to the porch, hefted a stack of cinder blocks, and traipsed back to the study. The boards were more difficult, as he had to maneuver them past the stacked boxes and through the doorway. But eventually, he was able to start on the shelves by placing two bricks flat on the floor and adding a board across them. From there it was a matter of stacking vertical bricks topped by cross-boards until he reached the ceiling.

He did his best to stabilize the shelves, but on balance, he agreed with Mrs. Grey when she commented, "At least Portland is less prone to earthquakes than San Francisco."

As soon as he'd built the second shelf, she began unloading boxes, starting with the ones in the hall. It took less time for him to construct the shelves than for her to fill them with books, so when he was finished, he helped with the unloading, despite her renewed protests.

By the time they were done, it was past supper time. They were covered in paperboard, and Lucky was sweating from head to toe, though Solace—after a futile hour, he'd given up referring to her as "Mrs. Grey" in his head—seemed bafflingly cool and unaffected. She hadn't even rolled up her sleeves, whereas he'd hung his coat next to her husband's and bared his forearms long ago, deciding propriety could go to hell in the face of hard labor and stifling heat.

As the boxes in the hallway dwindled, a number of framed photographs were revealed on the walls, showing stiffly-posed subjects reminiscent of his family in Chicago. To fill the time, he'd asked her about them, and then, even more strange, told her of his childhood. She was so self-conscious about her intelligence, he feared any topic related to her interests would spark a recurrence of her earlier outburst, and so focused on his own history and interests instead.

More, it seemed he *needed* to talk about his family. Looking at the photographs on her walls, it was as if he must speak of them, or they would vanish altogether.

"I don't even have a picture of my own mother," he admitted.

"How sad," she said quietly, gaze filled with compassion.

He shrugged, and pried open another box. "I was already a drifter by the time she died, moving from one place to another. My sister kept everything."

"But can't you write to her? Ask her for a miniature, perhaps?"

"I suppose. There aren't many to share around." He indicated the hallway, visible through the study door. "You have an exceptional number of photographs here."

She regarded the pictures curiously, as though reconsidering them. "Yes, I suppose so. My father was interested in photography. He photographed our family more than most would."

One thing Lucky had noticed was that none of the pictures showed Mr. Grey or his family. There was not even a wedding portrait of Solace and her husband. He studied her profile, then forced his attention back to the box before him. Their marriage was their concern, and Solace seemed fine now. Still… The way things seemed was not always how they *were*, and she had been so afraid on Saturday. But of what?

"I think this is the last box," she said suddenly, peering at the mess littering the floor.

"No. It can't be. We are going to be unloading boxes for all eternity. It's my just retribution for all the pranks I played on the poor nuns when I was a schoolboy."

She made a small choking noise, and he glanced up,

catching her in what could only be a burble of suppressed laughter. Her eyes sparkled above the filthy hand clapped to her mouth, and when she removed it, he choked on a laugh as well.

"What? Why are you laughing at me?"

He crammed the last of the books onto an overfull shelf. "You laughed at me."

"That's different. You made a joke."

"And you," he said, stepping toward her, close enough to see the gold flecks near the centers of her wide hazel eyes, "just smeared dirt on your mouth."

"No."

She shook her head, denying not his words but his presence. She backed up, but a bookcase was behind her, and she had nowhere to go. He took another step, reaching for her, not sure himself of his own intent. To caress her? Kiss her? Or merely wipe away the smudge?

He was pretty sure he was about to make the wrong choice, the one he couldn't take back, for which she'd never forgive him. She shook her head, but her gaze dropped to his mouth, and her lips parted. With only the barest awareness of what he did, what this would mean, for either of them, he allowed his hand to brush her cheek. She inhaled sharply but did not draw away, and he leaned closer, a mere breath from her lips. He couldn't help it—he trailed his fingers over the curve of her neck, his brown, work-rough skin against her smooth paleness.

"Solace…"

Abruptly there was a heavy pounding on her front door, and a boy's scared voice cried out, "Mrs. Grey! Are you home? Come quick! It's about your husband!"

~:~:~

Solace stared up at Lucky uncomprehendingly. He

towered over her, a near total stranger, and yet she felt…comfortable with him. Familiar.

Safe.

He'd spent the entire afternoon helping her build shelves and unpack boxes. All of his presumably rare and precious leisure time, since he evidently worked two or more jobs, six days a week. They had chatted easily, as she assumed old friends would, although she had never lived anywhere long enough to *have* an old friend, so she really had no idea.

More, he'd disagreed with her. A lot, in fact. But he didn't simply announce she was wrong. He *argued* with her about why, so he must think her ideas worth considering, which Allen had only rarely done, even before his spells. They'd spent a lot of time discussing *his* theories, but not her own. On the heels of Detective Jenkins's condescension toward her "pretty little self," Lucky's response warmed her to her core.

Sometimes he even changed his opinion to hers, as when she argued for ordering the books by subject, then author, rather than by author alone. And he'd shared stories of his family, gruffly at first. But once he began, he was an entertaining storyteller. She'd been right about his accent—he had emigrated from Lithuania to Chicago as a young boy, where he'd attended a parish school until he was thirteen. Beyond that, he was self-educated, which made it all the more intriguing that he was so well-read, and that his speech was more refined than a typical lumberman's.

Then again, she was incorrect when she assumed him to be a lumberjack. Rather, he was something called a "big-bench sawyer," a position just below the foreman, which explained much. Given his air of authority, it surprised her he *wasn't* the foreman. But as he planned to leave Portland for Alaska soon, perhaps the bosses wouldn't promote him.

She also discovered he had a dry sense of humor. She couldn't remember the last time she had laughed. With Allen, she never knew what to expect, as though she were on quicksand, and the slightest misstep would cause the world to drop out from under her. But Lucky's stories of his boyhood scrapes and the nuns tasked with disciplining him, not to mention his poor put-upon mother, were told with such self-deprecation, she couldn't help but join in the humor.

Then, just as the day was ending, he'd made fun of the smudges on her face and moved as though to wipe them off. Instead, he had touched her cheek, gently, in a way she had not been touched in a long time. Married at eighteen, with no close women friends or relations, she'd had no one to ask if Allen's behavior was normal for a man his age. Her girlish heart craved more in the beginning, but she had soon accepted that good companionship must suffice.

And it did, until at twenty-eight she'd considered herself a staid, married woman.

But as Lucky leaned in close, an image of the Donners reared. She had a sudden, violent certainty that, though married, they *did* feel passion. It was shocking to realize how distant those feelings were for herself, and even more shocking now as they came crashing back to life, and the world simply…stopped. Nothing existed but herself and the man before her. Even the room—her husband's study—faded to black, and all she saw, heard, smelled, and felt was *Lucky.*

She couldn't help it—she swayed toward him,

readying herself for his kiss, his strong fingers sliding down her cheek to her throat. She shivered, saw his quick in-drawn breath, the rough red-gold stubble on the hard planes of his jaw as he angled his head to the side. His warm breath brushed her lips, so close she could almost taste him. And now he was—he was—

He was stepping back, frowning, and a cacophony came from the front of the house. Someone shouted, but she couldn't move, couldn't focus, except on what had nearly happened—how shamefully, awfully, she was *disappointed* at the interruption.

Dear God, what if it were *Allen* at the door?

She fell back against the bookshelves, burying her face in her hands.

"Solace!"

Lucky's sharp tone penetrated her fog of despair, and she lifted her head. "What is it?"

He grasped her shoulders and gave her a good shake, which thankfully knocked some sense back into her. "There's someone at the door. He says it's about your husband."

"*Allen?*"

She pushed past Lucky and hurried to the door, yanking it open. A boy stood on the porch: Thomas, the librarian's son, his round, freckled face scrunched in concern.

"Come quick, ma'am! Ma sent me, and the police is there!"

"Police!"

She couldn't breathe. It had finally happened: Allen had done something so awful, the police were involved. She must get to him before anyone from the school found out. Behind her, Lucky made a grunt of determination, and she turned, but he spoke before she got a word out.

"If you think for one minute that I'll let you handle this by yourself—"

"I won't be by myself," she interrupted, indicating Tommy on the porch.

Lucky lifted an eyebrow. "I'm certain this young man is very capable. And I know *you're* capable and don't *need* my help, but I'm coming anyway."

This was too much—she couldn't bear it if he saw her shame. "Please…"

His expression softened, and he drew her gently back into the house, out of Tommy's earshot. "You may need help getting him home. You can trust me."

She drew in a shaky breath. "It's not that. I do trust you. It's only that—that—"

"What is once seen can never be unseen?" His blue gaze was serious. "I have seen many things, not all of them good. And I promise, I *swear* to you, on my mother's grave, that whatever is troubling your husband will not change our…friendship."

She noted the pause and nodded again, choking down a sob. For friendship was all it could ever be, and that almost-kiss tonight would be the last time she ever felt this close to another human being.

As long as Allen lives, the insidious voice whispered, but she shoved it down with her other emotions and retrieved her hat and gloves, pausing at the hall mirror to wipe the smudges from her face with a handkerchief. Such a long time since they had returned with the bricks and boards, and yet only a few hours. Half a day, no more, since Lucky had compared her to the Northern Lights. Quite literally, to a heavenly phenomenon. No man had complimented her intelligence before.

Including her father and Allen.

Lucky came to stand beside her, filling the hall with his oversized presence. He pulled his coat on, then took his hat from the peg next to Allen's spare. "We'll take the wagon."

With an odd mix of gratitude for his support, and horror at what he was about to see, she nodded, then faced Tommy. "Let's go."

Chapter Ten

The scene across from the library looked like something out of a farce Lucky had seen as a teener in Chicago. He and a friend had snuck into the theater after hearing the show featured nude women. It did not, but he'd enjoyed it anyway, as it involved a comical police chase, people being whacked on the head with various objects—always a favorite—and a pretty leading lady, even if her clothes did remain disappointingly on for the entire play.

By the time he pulled the wagon up, it was past eight o'clock and heading on to dusk. Barely waiting for the horses to slow, Solace leapt from the bench and ran across the busy street, weaving between the vehicles, people, and livestock, Tommy at her heels. Cursing their recklessness, Lucky yanked the horses to a stop, then jumped down and slung the leads over a post before running to catch up. A crowd hovered at the entrance to an alley between two brick buildings, and when Lucky pushed to the front, he was glad Solace was not alone.

Allen Grey sat on the sidewalk corner, head in his hands, his knuckles scraped and bleeding as though he'd been in a fistfight. A few yards up the alley stood a shabbily dressed prostitute, arguing loudly with a uniformed cop who waved his billy club at her, his mustache working overtime as he raised his voice to be heard over her screeching.

Behind them, a woman in a black dress, bonnet, and

lace gloves pulled at his sleeve ineffectually. In front of Grey, with her back to Lucky, stood another woman in black, arms folded as though preventing Grey's escape, or protecting him from the mob. Perhaps both.

One of Portland's ubiquitous Salvation Army officers stood on the corner, apart from the crowd, and Lucky wondered if the women were with him, and if so, what their connection was to whatever Allen had done. Or perhaps the Army had been trying to "save" the prostitute, and Allen merely got in their way.

Meanwhile, the librarian, Mrs. Ellesmere, attempted to shoo the mob away, an effort to which her son added his voice. But as crowds do, this one had a mind of its own, and every time it was pushed back, it surged forward again like the tide, coming relentlessly closer. In minutes, it would overrun Grey's tableau, and if Lucky couldn't protect her, Solace with them.

The color drained from her face as she took in the wreckage of her life played out on a public sidewalk. Lucky's hand lifted of its own accord to offer some small comfort, but he stopped himself. He would only make things worse, and she wouldn't thank him for it. She had been clear about that after their near kiss. Her tears of regret stated unequivocally that she did not welcome his advances and would not appreciate further contact.

An image of her sighing into him, lips parted, head tilting, intruded into his memory, but he shoved it away. She had been caught up in the moment, as had he. They were sensible adults. She was married, he was a drifter, leaving Portland soon. That was the plan. He seemed to have forgotten it in recent months, but now getting far, far away from Oregon and the intelligent, unattainable Solace Grey sounded like the best idea he'd ever had.

Not yet though. Not when he might lessen her pain first if he could only find a path through the carnage.

Mrs. Ellesmere's face lit with relief when she saw them. "Mrs. Grey and Mr. Jacobs! Thank the Lord!"

Solace knelt by her husband, but he refused to meet her gaze. She looked to the librarian. "What happened?"

"I wish I knew. He worked late like always, and when I tried to close up, he ran for the door. I heard shouting and came outside to find…this. Has he—has anything like this happened before?"

Lucky cut in smoothly, "Mrs. Ellesmere, I'm so sorry Mr. Grey startled you. Mrs. Grey was just saying he has been so overworked, preparing for his new position, that she feared he would make himself ill."

The librarian's face cleared. "Of course! He works too hard for such a thin man. And he forgot to eat again." She stepped closer and lowered her voice, although Solace was too preoccupied with soothing her husband to overhear. "Mr. Jacobs, before my husband passed, we were married a long time, as I'm sure you've guessed. Now, don't protest—Tommy is my youngest of six, all boys, and they do age a woman faster than girls. In any case, I know *men*, and I know they have…needs."

Her speaking glance at the prostitute was followed by a head tilt toward Mr. Grey.

Despite Lucky's own worldly experience, heat burned his cheeks. "Ma'am, this is hardly an appropriate—"

"Oh, hush! We haven't time. I don't believe Mrs. Grey has noticed the, ah, *lady* over there. And I'm sure I don't know what Mr. Grey wants with her in the first place, him having such a pretty young wife at home. But she's mixed up in this somehow, and I'm thinking you might be able to…soothe her feelings? Perhaps convince her it was a misunderstanding?"

Solace had risen and was now having a heated discussion with the woman in black guarding her husband. Or at least, Solace spoke heatedly. The diminutive, stern-backed form simply stood her ground and did not engage. Between the two conflicts, it seemed prudent to calm Solace before she made things worse.

"Excuse me," he said to Mrs. Ellesmere and left her to approach Solace. "Mrs. Grey? May I be of assistance?"

"Mr. Jacobs!" The relief in her expression was echoed in her voice. "This—this *busybody* won't let me take my husband home. She insists he is drunk, and that he attacked that harlot over there and must go to jail!"

So much for not noticing the streetwalker. Lucky drew a deep breath and faced the "busybody," then mouthed an *oh* of surprise.

"Mr. Jacobs," Mrs. Lola Baldwin said calmly. "Why am I not surprised to find you in the thick of this?" She inclined her head toward the prostitute. "Would she by any chance be the lady you referred to me?"

Solace gasped, staring at him, wide-eyed and hurt. "You…" She waved a hand at Mrs. Baldwin. "And she…" She glared at the prostitute. "And *her*…"

"It isn't like that," he began, but Mrs. Baldwin rapped her heavy parasol on the wood sidewalk, causing everyone, including Grey, to jump.

"Never mind that other matter for now. I see you are acquainted with these people and their situation. Therefore, I shall tell you that Mr. Grey was found accosting the, ah, lady over there." She indicated the prostitute, whose screeches, along with the cop's bellows, had subsided due to the calming effect of the second black-clad woman.

"Accosting?" Lucky asked cautiously.

Next to him, Solace fumed, but he recognized her anger for what it really was: fear. Of exposure, of what her husband had done and might still do, and of seeing her life unravel before her eyes. Perhaps this once he could stem the disaster. Besides, he wanted to know what the hell was wrong with Allen Grey. Obviously, it was something more complex than simply an older husband controlling his young wife.

Mrs. Baldwin elaborated. "With a book."

Lucky paused. "With a…book, you say?"

Solace's expression changed to sheer relief. "There must be some misunderstanding, then. Allen would never hurt anyone. Perhaps he was reading to her?"

Mrs. Baldwin sniffed. "Hardly. He attempted to beat her, although with limited success, I understand." She eyed Solace. "I believe he said something about saving her soul. Are you a religious family, Mrs. Grey?"

"Of course! My husband traveled to Africa as a missionary, and we go to Mass every week." Solace's cheeks pinkened and she avoided Lucky's gaze.

"I see." Mrs. Baldwin's expression did not alter, and Lucky wondered if she were suspicious of what Sadie called "that Cath-o-lic mumbo jumbo."

Solace evidently thought so and opened her mouth to, most likely, deliver a scathing retort, but her husband chose that moment to rise and look at her in puzzlement.

"Laura? You changed your hair…"

If possible, Solace's face went even whiter than before. Grey was obviously confused, and just as obviously, Mrs. Baldwin didn't know Solace's name wasn't Laura. But if Lucky didn't act quickly, this new wrinkle could cause more problems later.

"Allen!" he exclaimed jovially. "Good to see you again! Your wife was just saying we should meet up after church next Sunday."

"Laura…?" Allen asked petulantly, peering around as though expecting to see that lady, whoever she was.

Lucky leaned closer to Solace, murmuring, "Is your husband drunk by any chance?"

"No!"

He raised his palms. "My apologies. I had to ask."

Many men, including Lucky's father, could be pleasant on the surface, then go on a bender, beating their wives, children, or anyone else. Solace's denial proved nothing; Lucky's own mother had never acknowledged her husband's excesses, even when he came home on payday with empty pockets and whiskey on his breath.

Thinking of the man on the corner, Lucky added, "Or is he a member of the Salvation Army? Many in our parish support their mission of spreading Christianity."

"No," Solace said.

Too bad, for if Allen was a Soldier of Christ, it would give a reasonable explanation for his behavior. The Army was known for converting prostitutes, drunks, and opium addicts to their cause, in order to save their souls.

Mrs. Baldwin gestured impatiently with her black-gloved hand. "Mr. Jacobs, if I may cut in, I believe I have found one or both of those strays you mentioned." She tilted her head toward the prostitute again, but Lucky shook his head regretfully. She tilted instead toward Solace, who was absorbed with her husband, and this time, Lucky nodded.

"Very well." She faced Solace and extended her

hand. "Mrs. Grey, we have not been properly introduced. I am Mrs. Baldwin. How do you do?"

Looking dazed, Solace accepted the proffered hand.

Mrs. Baldwin continued, "I think we have things to discuss. But later. Now, you must take your husband home. He is not himself, and needs rest and recovery, but I believe an arrest is not necessary."

"Yes…thank you…"

"I will speak to the police officer on his behalf." She turned to Lucky. "You will see the Greys home?"

"Of course. But please, give me a moment. I would also like to speak with the, ah, officer for a minute."

"Very well. I will wait here with Mrs. Grey."

"I am perfectly fine—" Solace began, but Mrs. Baldwin interrupted her.

"Of course you are. But your husband is not. I would not leave you alone with him in this crowd."

For the first time, Solace appeared to notice the mob surging around them. The ones in front were losing interest, but as they left, their places were filled by those behind. Likely none of them had seen what actually transpired. They only wanted an evening's entertainment and gossip to share after church on Sunday.

Lucky hated to leave Solace, even for a moment, and even under Mrs. Baldwin's protection. But he needed to do this one thing while he had the chance, and so he headed up the alley.

Mrs. Baldwin's companion realized his intent and glanced over his shoulder. A moment later she stepped aside, clearly having received permission to let him pass. She was younger than Mrs. Baldwin, perhaps in her thirties, with honey-brown hair and a pretty, but serious, face. Lucky tipped his hat and moved into the dank alley.

The cop frowned at him. He was younger than expected, but he puffed himself up like a veteran of the force. "Yes? What is it? Here to defend the actions of that ruffian over there? Perhaps he's your drinking pal, and you can testify to his outstanding character?"

Lucky cleared his throat. "Actually, Officer…?"

"Peters. Vincent Peters."

"Thank you, Officer Peters. In point of fact, I'd like to talk to this, er, lady." He indicated the prostitute.

Taken aback, Peters opened and closed his mouth, then threw up his hands. "Women ordering me about, learned men running amok, workmen chatting with fancy ladies. What is the world coming to?"

Not having an answer to that, Lucky faced the woman. "What is your name?"

"Molly," she said sullenly. "What's it to you?"

"Molly, my name is Lucky. Lukas Jacobonis. Does that name mean anything to you?"

She shook her head, but something flickered in her expression. "Why? Did I…*meet* you somewheres?" She lowered her lashes, then swept them up, an obvious offer in the way she somehow thrust her breasts forward without altering her posture.

Lucky barely refrained from checking to see if Solace watched them. "No. That is, I wonder if you might know a friend of mine. Ellie—Elzbieta. She has light brown hair, worn in ringlets, and the last I saw her she wore a pink striped dress."

Molly straightened. "No! I don't knows anyone called Ellie." She faced Officer Peters. "Wasn't you arrestin' me? Cain't you git on w'it?"

"I *was*," Peters said irritably, indicating Mrs. Baldwin's associate, "until this fine woman interfered!"

She glared at him. "Incarceration is a bandage, not a cure. Molly needs decent employment, so she is not forced to do *this* anymore."

"Jail ain't so bad," Molly said desperately, glancing at the dirty alley and the restless mob. Anywhere but at Lucky. "I can sleep off my drunk. Public drunkenness is a serious offense, ain't it, officer?"

"It most certainly is!"

The other woman opened her mouth, but Lucky cut in quickly, "Miss…?"

She pressed her lips tight, then said, "Barnum."

"Miss Barnum, if you will allow me…? Thank you. Molly, please, I spoke with Ellie yesterday. She was to meet me and that lady over there"—he indicated Mrs. Baldwin, to the surprise of all three of his listeners—"but she never came. I think you know something that may help me to help her. Can you tell me? Anything at all?"

Molly shook her head, greasy blonde ringlets flying, her blouse slipping unnoticed off one plump shoulder. "No, sir, I don't know nothin'. Was jest mindin' my own business when that *gen'lman* there up an' attacks me. I ain't seen this Ellie, an' I don't know nothin' 'bout where no one spends their time but meself."

Lucky sighed inwardly. The mere mention of Ellie's name had frightened her and she wouldn't open up to him. Where could Ellie have gone? No hope for it; he'd best come back later and search for her, beginning with the corner she'd been on yesterday and working outward.

He thanked Molly, tipped his hat again to Miss Barnum, and nodded to Peters, who grabbed Molly's arm and led her away, apparently concluding that arresting her rather than Grey would cause fewer headaches later. If only Lucky's choices were so simple.

As they were not, he retraced his steps to the street. Solace murmured to her husband in soothing tones, while Mrs. Baldwin and Mrs. Ellesmere stood apart, chatting and glancing toward her periodically. The librarian did most of the talking, and Mrs. Baldwin's expression remained inscrutable. But she listened intently, and Lucky had no doubt she judged every word with careful consideration, both for the teller and the tale.

Tommy had found a smooth stone and attempted to juggle it with his feet. Either he finally got through to the mob, or they had grown bored and dispersed on their own. A few stragglers remained, but none were overtly threatening, and the tension left Lucky's body.

"Are we ready?" he asked with as much cheerfulness as he could muster.

Mrs. Baldwin asked sternly, "Did you accomplish your business with the *officer*, Mr. Jacobs?"

"Not precisely, no," he said, noting that his frankness startled her. Or perhaps it was merely that he no longer felt cowed by her, and she was used to cowing people.

To hell with it all. To hell with Portland, and barmaids-turned-opium-addicts, and moralistic do-gooder social hygienists. But especially to hell with smart, pretty women who were so un-*sensible, they married sick, elderly men and ruined their own damn lives as a result.*

This last was so patently unfair that he chuckled at his own stupidity. Mrs. Baldwin watched him, observing both his sudden flare of temper and subsequent idiotic grin, and therefore most certainly revising her opinion of him downward. He tipped his hat to her and the librarian.

"Evening, ladies. Tommy, thank you for your assistance. You were a big help tonight." The boy grinned and tugged his cap, and Lucky turned to the Greys. "Your chariot awaits, my good people."

Solace gave him a wan smile that could have meant anything, but that he hoped meant gratitude for his help, while lacking suspicion of his motives. Taking her husband by the arm, she led him toward the wagon, and Lucky fell into step behind them.

As they crossed the street, he heard Grey saying, in the tone of a petulant child, "Laura? Is that you? Are we going home to Mother's house?"

And Solace responding, "Yes, dear. I'm here. Don't worry, I won't leave you."

And to hell with that above all else, because how could Lucky leave her, when the life she was forced to live was apparently not even her own?

Chapter Eleven

Interfering bitches, the lot of them.

He turned onto his side, mindful of the woman sleeping beside him. It had been an exhausting evening, but after only a little sleep, he already felt better. Alive and clear-headed, able to reflect on this new bump in the road that was his ambition.

The crowd across from the library had dissipated at that Ellesmere woman's direction, and eventually, he'd had to leave as well. Between her, Officer Peters, and those two do-gooders, not to mention the Jacobs fellow and that *other* woman—the one who played the part of devoted wife, despite what he knew lay underneath—thanks to all of them, he'd been prevented from further communication with the whore, Molly.

But he'd find her again—she couldn't hide in a cell. In fact, jail made her a sitting duck, ripe for the picking, with no one the wiser. She knew too much, and not only that, had revealed too much, when Jacobs brought up that other whore, Ellie. Like all females, her mind was weak, and she couldn't be trusted not to blab.

He flopped onto his back, and the woman beside him stirred, mumbling something inquisitive before drifting back to sleep. He cast her a disdainful look. She had no idea who she'd married. None. She went about her day, performing her wifely duties, thinking him an adoring husband and yet oblivious to his true goals.

But he would have the last laugh. He would achieve

his desires, and no simple-minded female—do-gooder, whore, *or* wife—would stop him.

No man, either, though they presented more of a challenge. That Jacobs fellow was getting in the way, inserting himself where he didn't belong and was least wanted. And now it seemed he and the Baldwin woman were pals, though who knew what they had in common.

After seeing Jacobs at the church on Sunday, he'd asked around and discovered the man had barely achieved a seventh-grade education. Doubtless he couldn't read words longer than four letters—if he could read at all—so perhaps he wouldn't be a complication after all. A little misdirection, or maybe some new "evidence" could be brought to light, pointing Chief Hunt in the *right* direction.

Still, males were hard to get rid of. Whores, no one cared about. Young women were gullible, and it could be put about that they ran off with a fellow. But a man with a job and responsibilities, he wouldn't just up and leave for no reason. And the community was less inclined to turn against them. Women could be easily blamed for any crime. But a man, an upstanding citizen, with friends and character witnesses, that was different.

At the very least, Jacobs needed watching. And Molly needed to be taken care of.

His wife stirred, and he murmured, "Go back to sleep, my dear. You need rest after today's excitement."

Then he took his own advice and closed his eyes. A good night's sleep would further clear his head and show him the path he must take. He always found the solution, one way or another.

Chapter Twelve

Tuesday July 26

"WOMAN DISFIGURES ALLEGED
TATTLER – Mrs. A. Riggs threw a glass at
Mary Sutton, cutting her face frightfully. Mr.
and Mrs. Riggs have indulged in many
quarrels, and Miss Sutton thought it her duty
to tell her acquaintances of their domestic
troubles." —*The Oregon Daily Journal*

After a good night's sleep, Allen was much recovered. So much so that Solace began to hope he was, if not improving, at least not worsening. As she prepared their breakfast, she noticed herself smiling unabashedly. Except for her time with Lucky the previous afternoon, she couldn't remember when last she'd felt so unencumbered. Which produced a terrible suspicion about why she was so happy today.

Every time she entered the kitchen or passed its door, she noticed the vase holding the wild carrot blossoms, standing out in white relief against the deep red dahlias and blushing pink roses. They reminded her of Lucky and his absurd compliments, and she grinned—absurdly.

It was almost enough to drive out her shame over how their afternoon might have ended, and her anxiety over how it *had* ended. Almost, but not quite.

For once Allen ate a full breakfast before retiring to

the newly organized study. He was surprised and pleased when he saw it, but he also regarded her sadly.

"My dear, did you do this all on your own? I am so sorry I was not here to help."

"Don't fret about it. That man from Fisher's also works for the lumber company. He delivered the materials and built the shelves. I only unboxed the books."

There. She had spoken of Lucky—Mr. Jacobs—without a tremor or displaying any feeling beyond gratitude for services rendered. Which was all she *did* feel toward him. He was a true gentleman, who had helped a lady in need. It was nice to be taken care of for a change, instead of always doing the caring. But she had a good life, and a good husband, and truly only became overwhelmed on rare occasions, such as last night.

She smiled at Allen now, so childish in his delight at seeing his books again, as though they were old friends he'd dearly missed. He ran from shelf to shelf, pulling them out, flipping through them, replacing them.

"I'll leave you to your work," she said indulgently, but he stopped abruptly, staring at his hands.

"Solace! Did—did I cause you any pain last night? Physically, or—or emotionally?"

He turned, displaying his scabbed knuckles, and she crossed quickly to him. Running her thumbs over the wounds, she shook her head. "No, dear. Of course not. You scraped your knuckles on the curb when you fell. Do you remember?"

"No. I don't remember anything." His voice cracked. "I'm so ashamed. I'm not a good husband to you. Please, I've wanted to discuss this for some time. You must go to the church and seek an annulment on grounds that I was mentally incapacitated before our marriage. I asked Father Henderson about it on Sunday, and he said—"

Solace gripped his fingers so hard he cried out. "Please tell me you did not say to Father Henderson that there is anything wrong with you!"

"Of course not."

But he sounded uncertain, and the icy terror gripped low in her belly. "Allen, there is *nothing* the matter with you. Your spells are temporary, due to the stress of moving and to overwork. I'm sure of it. When you start teaching again, things will improve—you'll see."

"But if we were to get an annulment, or—or even a divorce. The church does allow them in extreme cases. And then you could remarry and live a normal life."

He was so wretched that she folded him in her arms, rocking him like a child. His shoulders were thin and insubstantial, the blades sharp even through his coat.

"Please, you must stop this nonsense. Of course I won't leave you. You are simply tired. Come, sit." She led him to the chair and moved the books he'd piled on the desk closer. "I see you have already chosen works for review. I'll make tea, and we'll sit together. I can read to you if you like, while you write out your notes."

"No," he said, but he sounded somewhat restored. "No, we will read and take notes together. You often find what I miss, and there is a difficult passage of Waring's mathematical theorems that I have been struggling with. You always were better at Latin than I."

He opened one of the books, and Solace retreated to the hall, letting her warm, confident smile slip only when out of his sight. He had been—*still was*—a brilliant scholar. If only he remembered important details of his own life. Such as that they had finished studying Waring more than five years ago, back in Kansas.

A knock came at the front door, and Solace paused at the mirror in the hall to check her appearance. Not that the neighbors would care if one—or twenty—of her hairpins were out of place. But after Saturday, when both Detective Jenkins and Mr. Jacobs had caught her at her worst, it seemed prudent to spend a moment straightening her apron and tidying the hairs that had strayed from her French knot. Upon opening the door, she was very glad she'd done both.

On the tiny porch stood Mrs. Baldwin. She was dressed in the same dark colors of the previous evening, but today a pair of wire-rimmed spectacles perched on her substantial nose. In the daylight, fine lines were visible in the corners of her eyes, indicating she must be in her forties at least, and that she must smile *sometimes*.

"Mrs. Grey," Mrs. Baldwin said in her cultured, clipped tones, making Solace think she had recently come from somewhere back East. "I apologize for calling so early, but I wondered if I might have a word."

This being delivered as a statement, not an inquiry, Solace opened the door wider and moved aside. Mrs. Baldwin crossed the threshold and placed her parasol against the wall, looking around the house's interior. Without waiting for an invitation, she passed through the arched doorway on the right into the living room.

Solace trailed behind, feeling bemused. She did, at least, recall her manners enough to say, "May I offer you some tea? Or coffee?"

"No, thank you. I won't be long. May I sit?"

"Of course." Solace didn't know why she should blush at this. Mrs. Baldwin had hardly given her time to be polite, and therefore could not blame her for the lapse.

Her guest sat, very dignified, on the black horsehair sofa, while Solace chose the wingback chair in which she sat most evenings. Mrs. Baldwin's astute gaze took in the tomes stacked on the small table at Solace's elbow: a selection of Greek language poetry; her best-loved and most scientifically inclined botanical; Balzac's *Le Père Goriot* in French; a *Canterbury Tales* that included the Middle English on the left pages, with a decent modern translation on the right; and several works on Russian history, geography, and politics that she had pulled from the study shelves last night, as Allen had nothing on Lithuania specifically.

The uppermost of these was a work in Russian, which she had been attempting to translate before admitting defeat at midnight. Mrs. Baldwin examined its title, which was set in the Cyrillic alphabet, before facing Solace. "Do you read Russian, Mrs. Grey?"

"A little. If the text is set in our alphabet."

"Do you speak it?"

"Barely."

"Pity. Italian?"

Where was this going? Pray God Allen would remain so engrossed in Waring that he stayed put in the study.

Curbing her irritation, she said, "Yes. And French, German, and some Chinese and Japanese." There. Let Mrs. Baldwin make of *that* what she would.

But Mrs. Baldwin's expression revealed nothing, and Solace fought the urge to squirm. This must be how Lucky had felt when interviewed by the nuns, just before they applied a ruler to his knuckles or paddled his behind. Apparently, nuns were more violent than Solace had realized, not having attended a parish school herself.

Showing no signs of imminent knuckle-rapping, her

visitor merely nodded. "How interesting. It appears Mrs. Ellesmere did not exaggerate your linguistic talents."

"Mrs....Ellesmere?" Solace shook her head to clear it. "Mrs. Baldwin, forgive me. I am quite certain you are not here to chat about the various languages I do or do not speak."

Pray God she doesn't want to discuss Allen. But that must *be why she's here. Perhaps I should bring the subject up myself...?*

"On the contrary. That is precisely why I have come—to offer you a job."

Solace stopped her planned retort just in time, then couldn't form a coherent response to this new intelligence. "You—I beg your pardon, but...what did you say?"

"As you may have inferred from my actions last night, I am concerned by the plight of misused women in our city. I work with various civic organizations whose aim is to remove these women from bad situations and instead find them respectable employment. Recently, I was asked by the Young Women's Christian Association to be the director of our new local Traveler's Aid Society. Perhaps you have heard of it?"

Solace nodded, feeling dazed. "A worthy organization, whose purpose is to prevent inexperienced females, alone in large cities, from falling prey to white slavery and other vices."

"Precisely."

Mrs. Baldwin had remained iron-rod straight on the edge of the sofa, but now she leaned forward earnestly, her enthusiasm softening the harsh lines of her face and lending a spark to her cool eyes. "Mrs. Grey, these poor girls come from all over the world, friendless and innocent. Without proper supervision, they may fall victim to the machinations of unscrupulous men or immoral women."

"I understand. It was the same in San Francisco."

"Ah, that explains your knowledge of Far Eastern languages." Mrs. Baldwin sat back. "You see, when the girls speak no English, they *cannot* know they are being led into immorality. And when we find them, we are unable to communicate or discover who corrupted them, making even more girls vulnerable. We must converse with them, both to give and receive information. A person with your abilities could be very helpful."

"Surely the police have a translator? Or the University of Portland?"

Mrs. Baldwin sniffed. "Only men. These girls have been mistreated by males for months or years. Our questions and the aid we offer are better received from the female sector. To be blunt, Mrs. Grey, I need a woman translator, and you are the first I have met with so many languages at her disposal. As well, I would prefer one woman who speaks many languages to seeking a new translator for each foreign girl."

A tiny ray of hope bloomed in Solace's heart. Her worry for Allen, her fears for their livelihood should he worsen, the ice that had gripped her belly for so long, all began to melt, just a little.

Not just menial labor, sewing shirts for pennies a day. If I can earn a real income, using my God-given talents, it could mean our salvation.

Feeling like Alice, peeping down the rabbit hole, Solace asked, "This position is paid?"

Regret flashed in Mrs. Baldwin's eyes. "Not at this time, no. I wish it were, but most in our organization do not yet earn a salary. However, we are fundraising, and I hope to create a paid task force before the exposition opens next year."

She glanced around the living room, cluttered with the overflow of Allen's research from the study, then at the smaller pile of books by Solace's chair. "Mrs. Grey, I believe you are a woman who cannot be satisfied by housework alone, or by working as a shopgirl. When we met last night, I sensed you could only be fulfilled by working for a greater good, as part of the world at large."

This was so close to Solace's own feelings that she nodded unconsciously, and Mrs. Baldwin's eyes lit with the triumph of a hunter homing in on her prey. "I am also new to Portland and understand it can be daunting to find one's place. You have an active mind and a gift for languages. Please consider joining us. It will be erratic work, as we find women at all hours. I cannot promise steady employment, but I can offer the reward of serving the needs of women who have been severely wronged."

It was an impassioned speech, and Solace wanted to respond in kind. So it was with genuine regret that she said, "I'm very sorry, Mrs. Baldwin. It sounds worthwhile and rewarding. But my husband does not wish me to work and would not like my leaving at night, making it impossible for me to come when needed."

"I see." The words were simple, but Mrs. Baldwin had seen Allen at a low point and must realize that it was Solace who couldn't leave him, not he who wanted her to stay. "Very well, if you are certain. I had hoped… But no matter. We are all prisoners of circumstance. Thank you for your time. I will leave you to your work."

She rose, and Solace stood also. "Thank you for considering me. If—if my situation changes, perhaps I will come find you. If you still need someone."

Mrs. Baldwin's expression softened. "Mrs. Grey, your services are always welcome. I was sincere in my assessment of your value to the organizations with which I work. However, I do understand that circumstances make it difficult for you. But not impossible. You may be surprised to learn that I have worked outside the home for the duration of my marriage, including after the births of my sons. Of course, my husband is an unusual man, for which I am fortunate."

She moved into the hall and retrieved her parasol. "If your husband changes his mind, or if one day you need a job of your own, there is hardly a better position for someone with your skills. As I said, I cannot pay you at first. But when I have my task force, or—well, I have other plans that will allow me to hire paid staff. Please consider it. For your sake, as well as ours."

Mrs. Baldwin let herself out the door, and Solace collapsed weakly onto the boot bench. She doubted she had ever met a more forceful woman. Last night, Solace had hated her for witnessing Allen's pathetic state, and was incensed by her autocratic demeanor. Today, she'd been certain Mrs. Baldwin had come to gloat or ask nosy questions, or at best, to check on Allen's recovery. In which case her pity would be worse than her superiority.

Instead, Mrs. Baldwin had coolly questioned her, matching her responses with information provided by their mutual acquaintance, Mrs. Ellesmere. Then she had drawn her own conclusions and offered Solace truly challenging and meaningful work, for a good cause.

And Solace had been forced to refuse.

One of Allen's boots peeped innocuously from beneath the bench, and she grabbed it and hurled it into the kitchen. It slammed into the table, knocking the glass vase to the floor and shattering it. Blood-red dahlias and innocent pink roses flew everywhere, and a bedraggled, broken wild carrot umbel came to rest amid the carnage.

Solace dug the heels of her hands into her eyes. *I will not cry. I...will...not...cry...*

But the hot tears came anyway, and she gave up trying to stem them, instead focusing on keeping silent as the wracking sobs engulfed her.

Still, it was mere moments before Allen called peevishly from the study, "Laura? Is the tea made?"

Solace dropped her hands and wiped her face with her apron, then blew out a breath. "Not yet. Someone was at the door, but she's gone. I'll get it now."

Then she went into the kitchen and put the kettle on, before cleaning up the mess.

Chapter Thirteen

Lucky spent the hours before dawn on Tuesday combing the streets near St. Mary's for any sign of Ellie. Initially, his reaction to her non-appearance at Sadie's had been one of disgust, with himself as much as her. Obviously, she'd gone to an opium den after all. Worse, Lucky had supplied the funds. But on seeing Molly's distress, he'd begun to wonder. Ellie had seemed sincere about drying out. What could have happened in the five hours between their meeting and the midday meal at Sadie's? And where was she now?

As a "streetwalker" it was implied she would move around. But when Lucky went to work or to church, he followed the same routes, being like most men a creature of habit. Prostitutes were no different, and once they found a corner they liked, they worked it regularly. True, he hadn't seen Ellie on that corner before, but that could have been the timing, as he usually left for Mass earlier than he had on Sunday.

However, he found no sign of her, even when he branched out onto various cross streets. And each time he queried another prostitute, they clammed up just as Molly had. Some seemed to feel that *any* question was a bad one, but many were fearful, and one was terrified.

This girl couldn't have been past her late teens, but the expression in her eyes was much older. As he approached, she tottered forward on high platform heels, her gold-embroidered pink silk robe falling open to show her barely formed breasts. Her black hair was up in a knot on top of her head, and her white face paint and rouged lips only emphasized her Far East heritage. Even with the heels, she was tiny, the top of her head barely reaching his chest.

"Do you speak English?" he asked her.

She nodded enthusiastically. "Yes, yes! Little bit. You like come wi' me? Good time?"

"What's your name?"

She shot him a puzzled look. "Hua Shui. Mean 'water flower.' You like see my flower?"

She started to raise the hem of her robe, and Lucky said hastily, "I'm looking for someone. Maybe you know her—a woman named Ellie?"

Her smile vanished, and she stumbled back as though he'd struck her. "No. I no want good time wi' you! You go now. Someone else for you!"

She turned to run, and he grabbed her arm. It was bony under her slippery sleeves, but fear made her strong. She nearly wrenched free before he gained control of her other arm, gripping tightly as she twisted to and fro. "Stop it! I just want to talk with you."

She kicked his shin with her wooden heel, and he grunted with the pain.

"Please! He no like I talk wi' you. Ellie not good girl, not do what he say. She no take *yànwō*. I good girl—take *yànwō*. Please, you let me go."

"He? Who he?"

But she only shook her head and burst into tears, and he knew he wouldn't get anything sensible out of her, even if he dragged her back to Sadie's or to Mrs. Baldwin. "Shh, stop crying. I'll let you go in a moment. But first, tell me, what is *yànwō*?"

Whether she was beyond caring, or believed it no longer mattered, she answered promptly. But her words garnered him nothing that seemed relevant or useful.

"Bird's nest. I take bird's nest, for babies. Ellie no take bird's nest. Say make her sad."

What the hell?

He'd heard bizarre things before, but not like this. Was there some shady Chinatown business involving baby birds that Ellie had rejected? No laws prohibited hunting birds' nests or taking the eggs. Perhaps Ellie was too softhearted? He knew little of her, and yet…surely she wouldn't put a bird's safety above her own?

Hua Shui's sobs had subsided into wet sniffles, but she had also stopped supporting her own weight, slumping in his grasp like a rag doll. He suspected this was a trick to lull him into a false sense of security, or to make it more difficult to hold her up. Tiny though she was, as deadweight she was quite heavy, and his grip slipped on her silk robe.

"I'm going to let go of you," he said. "But you have to stand up—there, that's it. Now, if you ever need anything, come to Sadie's over on—"

But she was already gone, her wooden shoes clattering on the stones of the alley as she hobbled back to whatever hovel she called home.

You can't save everyone. Not her, maybe not Ellie, and certainly not Solace Grey.

It was well past dawn, and Lucky put aside thoughts of females in general, and one woman in particular, as he hurried for the docks. The lumber crew had discovered another blockage in Chicken Creek, so there was still no way to transport logs into Portland for processing, and he couldn't afford more lost wages.

Fortunately, shipping companies always needed men to load or unload their goods, and Lucky often found work on shut-down days. His reputation usually earned him the better jobs, but if he ran late, he'd be stuck mucking out the slaughter troughs or cleaning up fish guts.

Sure enough, by the time he arrived at the lineup, most of the men had dispersed to their positions. But one of the bosses, a man Lucky had worked for in the past, who dealt fairly but didn't take guff from anyone, beckoned him over. Miller was in his sixties, sunburned and weather-beaten from decades at sea, with thin hair that had once been yellow but was now mostly white. His eyes were a pale blue in his leathery face, and he clutched a so-called "board clip," rifling through the attached papers, then looking up and grinning as Lucky neared.

"Heard the creeks're blocked and Jones shut down again. Wondered where you were."

Lucky shrugged. "I had something to do. What have you got for me?"

"Early bird gets the worm. Or rather, late bird gets the guts." He gave Lucky a considering look. "Still, you're a big fella. But better educated than most."

The statement caught Lucky off guard. He didn't hide it, but knowing his letters was dicey in this crowd. Some might accuse him of taking a day's pay from one who needed it more, when he already had a permanent job. But the bosses had noticed and often sent him on special errands, such as those requiring written receipts or confirmation that a ledger was accurate.

Today, Miller's comment sounded deliberate, like a challenge.

"I've been around and picked things up."

When he didn't elaborate, Miller checked his papers again. "I do have something, if you're interested."

"What is it?"

"Cautious bastard, aren't you?"

"Like I said, I've been around."

"It's nothing illegal, if that's what you're worried about. The boss—my boss—the *company* boss—needs a man we can trust, to keep certain…functions…running."

"Functions?"

Miller jerked his head at a small shack which served as a shared office for several businesses. "Come away from all these stinking guts and I'll give you the scoop."

The little building didn't smell much better, but it did afford some privacy. Narrow and windowless, the only natural light came through the door, which Miller left open. Shelves lined the walls and a desk sat opposite the door, covered in papers, pens, an adding machine, and a typewriter. A wood chair was tucked under it, with two stools nearby. The room was ten feet long and not quite as wide—about the size of a jail cell. Shoving aside what his mother would have called a *priešiškumas blogiui*, an evil premonition, Lucky climbed onto a stool.

Miller set his board clip on a shelf and pulled up the other stool. He produced a double-walled flask from a satchel on the floor and uncorked it. "Coffee? Or…something stronger?"

His meaning was clear: If Lucky refused, the interview ended, and he'd be left shoveling guts, or maybe get no position at all today. Therefore, he should accept. But if his guess was correct, would it be smart to get involved in Portland's liquor wars, on either side?

He chewed his lip before making his decision. "A bit early for me. But if you give me a good day's work, I'll buy you a drink tonight."

Miller grinned and took a swig from the flask before recorking it. "A true diplomat. Just the man for the job."

"*What* job? If you don't tell me soon what the hell it is, I won't have time to do it."

"You know Chief Hunt and Mayor Williams are cleaning up the city before the exposition next year?"

"Yes. But everyone also knows that Hunt is on the take from the saloon owners, maybe Williams too."

Miller ignored this. "You also know that in June, Oregon passed the Local Option Liquor Law. Meaning in November, we vote to make Portland dry or not."

"That'll never pass. Too many rich owners of the wet establishments."

"I know it, and you know it. But Mr. Average Citizen doesn't know it. The levy passed more closely than Williams predicted. The prohibitionists think they have a real chance, and Williams wants them to keep thinking it. Feels it's better for the business end of the fair."

"But the election is in three months, and the fair won't open for a year."

"Yes, but Williams has work to do *now*, attracting vendors and guests. No one wants a repeat of the St. Louis riot, and right or not, folks blame liquor for that."

Miller had a point. The papers reported daily on the St. Louis World's Fair, Portland's model for next summer's exposition. Just before the June election, a bullfight was scheduled at St. Louis, despite Missouri laws forbidding them. The governor had it shut down but refused to refund the ticket monies already collected. Protesters had begun by throwing a stone at the box office, and ended with burning the entire arena down. While not mentioned as a factor, beer was served at the fair, and Portland's prohibitionists argued that their city *must* be entirely dry or no one at the Expo would be safe.

Miller leaned forward. "Hunt had a man greasing the gears at the clubs, but he was an officer and too well-known, even in plain clothes. Everyone may *know* the chief is on the take, but he doesn't want it advertised, not with so much—the fair, re-election, you name it—on the line. That's where you come in."

Lucky sat back, trying to get a read on Miller. "You said it wasn't illegal."

Miller shifted uncomfortably. "It's not. You'll just pick up some packages from the club owners and deliver them to another location. Nothing illegal about that."

"What's in the packages would be illegal."

"When you work for me, do you know what's in the crates you're lifting?"

Lucky paused. So much for being smarter than "Mr. Average Citizen." Whatever the bill of lading said, or the crate labels, anything could be inside. He was paid to load, not to ask questions. Would this be so different?

Besides, it could aid in his search for Ellie. Saloons were the very places where prostitutes, pimps, and johns were found. He could chat up the bartenders and nose around the customers, without attracting undue attention.

He asked, "How do you come into all this?"

"Shipping. The boss makes good money importing liquor for the clubs, and he gets a 'tax break' from the city. So he pays it back by providing a service."

Lucky blew out a breath. "How long and how much?"

"Knew you'd come around. I hear Jones is shut down for the rest of the week. On top of the blockages, a saw broke and they have to order the parts. So let's start with that. If you do good work, it's not a day-only job. You can do it on your off hours. As for how much…"

He named an amount that seemed too generous given the job's supposedly easy nature. Lucky countered with a higher amount, and they settled on the expected in-between number.

They shook hands, and Miller said, "One more thing. As part of the job, you may have to deliver a message here or there if the packages are…unavailable."

Lucky withdrew his hand. "Now wait a minute. I'm no thug."

Miller raised his palms. "Hold your horses! No one wants you to thrash anyone. But you're big, and you look meaner than you are. You just need to *suggest* that the packages aren't optional, if anyone thinks otherwise."

"So I don't have to hurt anyone, just act like I will?"

"Exactly."

His instincts shouted that this was a bad idea, but he *had* to find Ellie. "Fine. But I don't hit first, I only hit back. Understood?"

"Whatever you say. Glad you're on board." Miller produced a sealed envelope with Lucky's name on it, as if his acceptance was never in doubt. "Here's the clubs you need to start with. It's a bi-weekly rotation, but it's been a few days, so you have some catching up to do."

Reluctantly, Lucky took the envelope, and Miller retrieved his board clip and went to the door. "Advance on your first payment's in there too. Buy yourself a new coat and hat. Some of these places cater to a higher class. You'll want to fit in."

He went out the door, leaving Lucky with the envelope burning in his hand. Surely it wouldn't be so bad, and he could always quit after he'd found Ellie.

Except his instincts said it was too late. He didn't believe in the current fad for psychic mumbo-jumbo, but his gut told him something *very* bad had happened to her.

He put the envelope in his worn coat pocket, then left the shack and the docks, heading for the nearest tailor who wouldn't overcharge him. Miller might be right that he needed a new suit. But it wasn't Miller's crusty, sunburnt face he pictured, smiling appreciatively at the fine form he would cut in his new duds.

With a by now habitual growl of frustration, Lucky shoved thoughts of Solace away and began plotting how to use his new position to find Ellie once and for all.

~:~:~

Patrolman Vincent Peters, leaning against a wooden rail and chewing a wild carrot stem, frowned as Lucky Jacobs exited the shipping shack and headed away from the docks. Odd coincidence, seeing him again so soon after he'd inserted himself into that business at the library last night. Why, he'd even charmed Mrs. Baldwin, preventing Peters from arresting that madman, Grey. Mad or drunk, Peters still wasn't sure which. From what the prostitute Molly had said, maybe both.

Either way, Jacobs was connected somehow, not only to the Greys, but to Molly's prostitution ring. She'd been so relieved when Peters took her away that she'd let slip a few important morsels, prime among them that she did in fact know the woman Jacobs had asked after, and that she—Ellie—had not returned to their crib in two days.

Jacobs had called this Ellie a "friend," but in Peters's experience, men who "befriended" prostitutes were one of two sorts: johns or pimps. Yet even the most regular customer wouldn't care enough to search for a girl if she vanished, and Jacobs was no pimp—Peters would stake his badge on it. So why had he asked after her?

Jacobs disappeared from sight a block up the hill from the river, and Peters turned away in time to see Detective Jenkins emerging from the warehouse where he'd been conducting whatever errand had brought them to the docks in the first place.

Peters tossed the chewed root into the river and hurried to meet his superior. "Sir, remember that man Jacobs? The one who butted in with my arrest last night?"

Jenkins, meticulously dressed as always, regarded him disapprovingly. "Officer Peters—gloves! I would dislike having to report you to Chief Hunt for lack of professionalism."

Peters snatched the gloves from his coat pocket and quickly drew them on. "Sorry, sir. I took them off to pick a root. Didn't want to stain them."

"Hmm," Jenkins said noncommittally, but he seemed satisfied, and Peters fell into step beside him as they navigated the piers and boardwalks along the waterfront, heading back downriver toward headquarters. "Now, what's this you say about Jacobs? He's here?"

"Yes, sir. I saw him coming out of that shack back there. I thought it curious, especially since he was so involved last night, with the Greys and that prostitute."

Jenkins did not immediately respond, staring ahead as they walked. Ever since Peters had joined the force two months before, he had admired the detective's steel trap of a mind, which latched onto the smallest details that often proved the most significant. He also had brought many innovative techniques with him from back East that Peters was eager to learn, in hopes he might someday earn the rank of detective himself. It was why whenever the opportunity arose, Peters volunteered to join Jenkins in performing his duties, however inconsequential they seemed.

At last, Jenkins gave a decisive shake of his head. "I've seen Jacobs around. He's a lumberman, but Chicken Creek's blocked, and he comes here to pick up extra work."

"But sir, he was bent on defending Grey, who attacked a prostitute for no good reason."

"So you've said. But that doesn't make Jacobs a ne'er-do-well himself."

Peters bit back an impulsive response. Jenkins wouldn't argue the point without evidence, so Peters set his own mind to the problem, trying to understand the why of it all. Finally he said, "My instincts say Jacobs is up to something. He didn't just stop the arrest of Allen Grey, he also asked nosy questions of the prostitute, Molly. Seemed very interested in her."

Jenkins's eyes narrowed. "Questions, you say? Of a whore? What did he want to know?"

"Something about another prostitute, Ellie. Asked if Molly knew her whereabouts."

"And did she?"

"No, sir. Said she hadn't been home in two days."

"Hmm. Well, odd though his interest may be, I find Grey's actions more noteworthy. If Creffield is innocent, my money's on the man who attacked a whore and pretended amnesia, not the man openly asking about another whore. Who knows what might've happened to Molly if you hadn't shown up. Good work, that."

"Yes, sir. Thank you, sir."

"And perhaps you are partially correct, and Jacobs is

not all he seems. But mark my words, he won't hold up as a murder suspect. Allen Grey, on the other hand…"

He trailed off thoughtfully, and Peters held his tongue. If he played his cards right, the detective might let him tag along during the investigation, giving him what he wanted: the chance to prove he was right about Jacobs, and show both Jenkins and Chief Hunt what an asset he was to the department. But if Allen Grey turned out to be the worse criminal, it was all the same. Peters would be on record as the first to suspect either man, which had to count for something. It might even earn him a promotion to detective, perhaps as Jenkins's partner.

One way or another, Peters was going to learn everything he could from the experienced detective, before climbing the department ladder himself—all the way to the top.

Chapter Fourteen

Friday July 29

It was so early when Allen rose on the feast day of Saints Martha, Mary, and Lazarus that the house was dark, his wife still asleep in the bed he had just vacated.

Poor Laura. He gazed fondly at her supine form. She worked so hard for so little thanks. As did his mother. His two favorite women—the only two who had ever loved him, and who he would ever love. Sometimes, of course, they angered him. But that was natural. A man's brain was filled with many things that his women couldn't understand. Still, they took care of him, and he must show them his appreciation.

Soon. Today, he had other items on his agenda.

But when he finished dressing and left the bedroom, the house was unfamiliar. Where were the back stairs descending to the kitchen? Or the front ones leading to the wide hall between the parlor and the dining room?

This house had no stairs, and the hall was narrow and

cramped. He found his way to a tiny kitchen with the makings for a pot of coffee on the counter. Were he and Laura away visiting? That must be it. How silly to have forgotten. It must be Christmas, and they were in Minneapolis with his mother and her sister, Ruby, who moved a lot. That was why he didn't recognize this house; he'd never been here before.

Humming happily, he prepared the coffee, then found sweet rolls in the pantry. They were not very good, so Ruby must have baked them, as Laura and his mother were excellent cooks.

But as he ate, something else niggled. The house was warm for December in Minnesota. He set his plate in the sink and went to retrieve his greatcoat from the front entry, but found only his summer coat. Even more perplexing was that, when he stepped onto the porch, he found not snow and ice, but a more temperate climate.

He almost retreated inside, then stopped himself.

Of course! God was testing him again. In His wisdom, He had transported Allen from the safety of the home he shared with his wife to a strange land, fraught with danger and mystery. God would *have* to do so in order for Allen to cure the heathens, as he and Laura had done during their missionary work in Africa.

There were no heathens in Minnesota. Only good, simple folk, moral and upstanding.

No, God would not waste him on a people already saved. All good heroes journeyed afar, before finding treasure and returning, triumphant, to their homeland. Look at Jesus, who had spent most of his life away from the land of his birth, before returning to proclaim himself the son of God and save the people from themselves.

Now it was Allen's turn. He had suffered many trials;

he could survive this new one.

Carefully, he crossed the yard and entered the dirt lane. A man was exiting a nearby house and tipped his hat in a friendly way, but Allen was not deceived. The man was a serpent in disguise, and Allen hurried past, lest he be corrupted.

At the end of the lane, he hesitated. Which way? To the right a hill loomed, black and menacing, while to the left a paved road sloped down. In that direction the sky was lighter, so that must be east. The Wise Men had seen the star in the east, so he would follow their lead.

He set off briskly, passing the still, sleeping houses. The farther he walked, the more they seemed to draw closer together, an imposing, impenetrable army of buildings on either side. Meanwhile, the street widened, lit now by streetlights, and he knew he would be safe if only he stayed the course. Whenever he came to a side street, he peered down it, unsure for what he hunted, only knowing it would be revealed when the time came.

Just when he was about to give up—time was running out—the thin margin of light in the east had grown to an evil red glow—his patience was rewarded.

~:~:~

The water was cold, and he'd scrubbed his hands so raw, a fingernail had torn clean off.

Allen shook his head to clear it. He was in an empty lot next to a large brick building. A watering trough was in front of him, and he had evidently used the rusty pump to wash, for the draining waste was a reddish color. Pink splotches stained his upturned cuffs, and the knees of his trousers were dusty, as though he had knelt in the dirt.

Solace would be upset if his new clothes were ruined already. Worse, if the brown dirt was visible on his black trousers, it must be very late. Looking up, he saw it was full dawn, with sunlight filtering between the tall structures on either side of the yard, bathing him in warm gold. Very warm. It would be another scorcher today. Or perhaps it was nerves that made him sweat so.

Regardless, it must be six o'clock, and he had no idea where he was. The establishment near the yard was silent, its business likely nocturnal, but other distant sounds reached him as Portland woke to face the day.

Suddenly, he noticed a searing sensation on his hands and forearms. The cold water alone hadn't made them red—where the sunlight touched his skin, a violent hot rash was spreading. He poked one of the bumps, then yelped and pulled his finger away, only to find an angry welt forming on its tip. He rolled his sleeves down so he couldn't scratch and spread it further. Solace would know what to do; she always did. But how to find her?

He retrieved his coat from the edge of the trough, then inspected his surroundings. The yard was narrow, with refuse bins and piles of slabwood along the wall of the brick building. The ground was hard-packed, covered in tall, dead grass, and the whole was enclosed by a weathered wood fence, one side of which held a gate.

There was also…*something*…in the grass. His mind shied from it; it was both too familiar, and too obscene. But the smell—sickly sweet and putrid in the rising heat, it slid up his nose and nauseated his gut. He covered his mouth and ran for the gate, flinging it open.

But the street was as foreign as the yard. The building behind him occupied the entire block, its unlit, vacant windows glaring down. He shrank away, stepping hastily onto the wooden sidewalk. The gate swung closed with a *clunk,* and his heart leapt into his throat, his body shaking. He *must* get home. Solace would worry if he were gone when she woke at half past six. Surely he wasn't more than thirty minutes away.

But…where was he? How had he gotten here?

He must have risen early and gone for a walk. He used to do that with Solace. Was it now his habit to go alone? Or had he some errand in mind, and if so, what? Had he completed it, or was there some unfinished business that would later haunt him?

A deep *boom!* came from his right, as of something heavy shuddering onto the wood sidewalk. He jerked away, pulse racing, then saw the back of a man in a dark brown suit and bowler, who peered around the fence's far corner in the opposite direction. Quickly, Allen dropped down to the sound-muffling dirt of the street, walking fast, his heart thundering. Surely the man would sound the alarm!

But when he reached the end of the block and looked back, the man was gone. Could he be hiding in the shadows of the buildings across the street, waiting to trap Allen? No, he could have no interest in Allen, a law-abiding citizen out for a stroll. Unless the man was aware of what was in the yard…

Allen drew a ragged breath. If the man knew, he would have shouted for the police, so Allen must be safe.

He glanced around. This street was also small, but the next one over was a busy thoroughfare. When he reached it and looked downhill, he saw ships and heard sounds of the river industry. His home was not near the water; of this he was certain. So he headed uphill instead, away from the docks and the horror in the yard.

Carts and pedestrians filled the streets, but he ignored them, only lifting his head to check his location. At last he came to a familiar corner. To the right one block over was the butcher Solace frequented. Was it…Howard's? Yes, the wagon bearing their logo waited out front.

This must be Burnside Street. Yes, yes, if I turn at that tobacconist's, that's Seventh. A few blocks south and a few more east and I'd be at J.K. Gill's. Perhaps the book I ordered is in. Shall I pick it up while I'm out?

He shook his head. Of course they weren't open yet, not for hours. But Solace would rise soon. He *must* get home to her.

He peered up the dark canyon of tall buildings. Several blocks away were Washington Street and the West Hills, rising up to the sky. Bathed in the golden light of the low sun, they were exactly where they should be, and he broke into a jog, nearly crying with relief.

A short time later, he came to another intersection he knew. To his left, the high school loomed in its habitual location three blocks from home. To his right, St. Mary's Cathedral pealed the glorious call to morning Mass, which would start at half-past six. He should go and give thanks for safe deliverance from his misadventure. He took a step in that direction—

But no. He *must* be home before Solace woke.

The crowd parted before the church, revealing a patrolman strolling by. Allen couldn't recall why, but it seemed important to avoid the police, so he turned from the church and aimed for the high school. He had been traveling in the rutted street, but now he returned to the wooden sidewalk. Only when he climbed onto it, he discovered that one of his shoes was missing. How very strange. Where could it have gotten to?

Furthermore, the sock on that foot was ruined. His wife would have to mend it, and she would be angry, both for the extra work and for the expense of replacing the shoe. Unless he hid it from her. Yes, perhaps that was best. Hide the loss of his shoe from…

He frowned. How silly. For a moment, he couldn't recall his wife's name. But it was Laura. No—that was his first wife. This one was called…Solace.

Solace…his wife… He must get to her. He would make amends for the extra work he'd caused her by doing something special for her. Like prepare the coffee. He knew just how she liked it, with lots of cream but only a pinch of sugar. She would be so pleased, she would forget to be angry about the sock, and the shoe, and the…other things…that had transpired this morning.

Yes, a good strong cup of coffee was just what she needed. What they both needed.

He cut through the lot behind their home and slipped between the hedges into their backyard. The house still slept, which meant that, thank Heaven, so did Solace.

He moved through the side yard, past the vegetables and around to the front. He removed his remaining shoe and tossed it into the bushes by the steps, before tiptoeing onto the porch and slipping through the front door and entryway into the small kitchen. He paused. He had been upset, but…why? Something to do with…with his wife…

With…Solace.

That was it. He was not upset, but she might be. If only he could remember what it was she might be upset about…

No matter. If he could just recall the steps for making coffee, everything would be fine.

Chapter Fifteen

Solace woke later than usual on Friday, to find Allen dressed and in the kitchen, preparing a fresh pot of coffee. A pile of grounds lay in the sink, from which she surmised he had spilled the coffee she'd set out last night. The little hand broom leaning in the corner attested to this, as did the guilty start he gave when she entered.

She put on her brightest smile and kissed his cheek, but when she touched his arm, he winced, and she quickly withdrew her hand. "What is it, my dear?"

"It's nothing. I seem to have contracted a rash, but I don't know how."

"Let me see. I'm sure it's nothing we can't fix."

He hesitated, then pushed up his sleeves. Red bumps trailed from his rolled cuffs down to his palms, interspersed with pink streaks and puffy welts.

"Oh dear! You poor thing. They must itch terribly!"

He nodded miserably as she led him to a chair at the table. "I'm sorry. I don't know what I got into, or how."

"I do," she said decisively, and went to the cupboard where she kept her medicinal salves. "Did you spill the coffee grounds this morning?"

"Yes," he answered, surprised.

"And when you swept them up, did you also find some green leaves on the floor?"

His amazement was comical. "How did you know?"

"Because I dropped them when I arranged those flowers yesterday." She indicated the vase on the table, which she had refilled with fresh wild carrot stems. "Some trimmings fell on the floor, and I forgot about them."

Excitedly, he took up the tale. "There were quite a few. I carried them to the compost pile with the coffee grounds." His face fell. "Was that right? Should I have thrown them out instead? I didn't want to leave them in the sink for fear they would clog the drain."

"You did just right." She paused to ascertain that she had the correct jar, containing the last of her calendula cream. She would have to make more, particularly if Allen's sensitive skin was breaking out again. But she had none in the garden, and it was too late to plant any. Perhaps someone at the Chinese gardens across the gulch could recommend another local remedy.

She returned to the table, lifting Allen's left arm gingerly and applying the salve. "I think what happened is this. The leaves were wild carrot. They cause a rash in sensitive skin, and sunshine makes it worse, like a bad sunburn. Let me guess, you rolled up your sleeves before sweeping up the coffee? And left them up while you went out to the compost pile?"

"Yes!" He sounded so relieved to have the mystery solved. "That must be what happened. I woke early and wanted to surprise you. You do so much. The least I could do was make your coffee. But after I came downstairs, I must have been more tired than I thought."

She frowned at his reference to *coming downstairs* in their one-story home. But no doubt he'd meant *down the hall*. A simple slip. She switched to his right arm.

"Did you sit in a chair and doze off?" It would not be the first time. Even before his spells, he had been absentminded and prone to forgetfulness.

He nodded sheepishly. "I must have. And when I woke, I found the coffee pot cold on the stove. I tried to hurry, to make a new one before you came down, but I only made a mess. Forgive me. I have wasted a pot of coffee and made more work for you, not less."

"Never mind. I'll make the coffee when I'm done treating your rash. You would break out if you even came *near* poison ivy, let alone handled an irritant like wild carrot. We can eat the roots and harvest the seeds for medicinal purposes, but you, at least, should not touch the leaves."

She finished with his right arm, noting that his skin already appeared less irritated, then paused. "What on earth happened to your fingernail?"

Allen snatched his hand back, staring in confusion at his nail-less index finger. "I don't know. I must have scraped it on something, but I don't remember."

He was getting agitated again, so Solace stood briskly and put the empty calendula jar in the sink. "No matter. I only wondered. But here, we'll cover it to protect it while it grows back."

She found the sticking plaster and brought it to the table. In truth, he was overdue for a serious injury. Since they'd arrived in Portland, Solace had noted minor bruises or scrapes on him almost daily. But a fingernail completely ripped off—with no knowledge of how he'd done it—was worrisome. If only school would start. Surely he would be safer in a classroom, away from botanical irritants and mishaps of all sorts.

She looked up from her ministrations to find him regarding his fingertip with a troubled expression. Quickly she said, "Would you make the coffee after all? We really must start getting the papers again. I'll just step down to the store and be back before you know it.”

“Of course,” he said eagerly. And like a child, he readily forgot his own troubles in the pursuit of a new project. “I can cook some eggs, too, if you show me where the skillet is. I used to be good at it! But are you certain you wish to go out before you’ve eaten?”

“I’d better go now, before the heat worsens.” She retrieved her heaviest cast-iron skillet from a cupboard and set it on the counter. At least if he forgot what he was doing, the pan wouldn’t melt and could be scraped clean. “Do you remember how to light the stove?”

“Of course!” he said again, and she smiled at his indignation, then went into the pantry and brought out the eggs, setting them next to the skillet.

“Good. When I return, you can read the paper while we eat. I am sure there is lots of interesting news that we have missed while settling in.”

Detective Jenkins’s visit had reminded her of how ignorant of current events she and Allen had become. But she was also restless. Caring for Allen should not be a burden—she should *want* to do it—in sickness and in health, as the marriage vows said. But the events of the week, and especially this morning, were taking a toll, and if she didn’t get out of the house, she’d go more “bonkers” than the Mad Hatter in Lewis Carroll’s novel.

Allen was carefully measuring coffee grounds into the percolator and barely acknowledged her kiss. Surely he could cook eggs safely; he’d made them often enough before, and the iron skillet really was indestructible. She retrieved her straw bonnet from its peg and tied it snugly under her chin, then drew on her gloves, checked her pocketbook for money, and set forth from the little front door and up the lane to Lownsdale Avenue.

While not as big as San Francisco or the Midwest cities they'd resided in, Portland was quite the metropolis, and the streets were already busy. With Allen traveling mainly from home to the library, and Solace not much farther, it was easy to forget their urban setting. Or perhaps it was living in Goose Hollow, which felt very insular, thanks to defining boundaries such as Tanner Creek, Cable Car Canyon, and the Chinese gardens.

Whatever the reason, as she left their neighborhood and aimed for Portland proper, she was reminded that this was no longer a frontier town. Small enough to easily navigate, but large enough to remain anonymous should one wish to. Thinking along these lines reminded her of Mrs. Baldwin's concerns for the fallen of their fair city. It was easy for Solace to ignore their plight, as she had a home, and through Allen, an income.

For now…

Pushing that aside, she examined those she passed with new eyes. Most were dressed respectably and seemed like good, moral citizens. But appearances could be deceiving, and anyway, it was too late in the day for ladies of the night to be out. Still…should she be doing more to help those less fortunate? If only she could!

The walk cleared her head, but her thoughts circled back to Allen. Something had been teasing her consciousness, a detail she had half-noted while treating his ailments. Pink splotches had stained his cuffs, as though he'd been painting or picking berries. But it was too late for raspberries, too early for blackberries, and where would he have found red paint before dawn? Never mind what on earth he could have been painting.

But there was something else. When he stood to make the coffee, she had noticed he wore only socks.

Was this a new manifestation of his careless spells? That he forgot his shoes?

With growing despair, she tightened her grip on her pocketbook and hurried toward the closest general store. How would he last until St. Mary's Academy opened for fall term? Work always improved him. But what if he worsened before then? What would become of them, with no savings and no income? They would be destitute—or worse, for he could be arrested and committed to the Oregon Insane Asylum in Salem.

Solace shuddered. She could *not* let that happen—it would kill him. She would have to *make* him well, take better care of him, until he returned to work. If that did not improve him, she would think of something else. Whatever came to pass, she would simply work harder.

She rounded the final corner and saw a crowd in front of the dry goods store at Fourteenth and Washington, where the *Portland Gazette* newsboy usually stood. Through the mob, she heard him crying, "Hot off the press! Woman murdered! Police blame Creffield!"

Solace started to push into the crowd, when suddenly her arm was gripped and someone pulled her back out. Startled, she looked up into the friendly gaze of Adina Donner.

"Solace! I knew it was you. How fortuitous! I was just coming to call."

Of course Adina had chosen today of all days. Why could she not have come yesterday, when Allen had done nothing more concerning than read in his study?

"I'm afraid I only stepped out to buy a paper. My husband is waiting for me."

Adina pulled her farther from the crowded corner. "Even better, for I have bought a paper for you. It is the world's poorest housewarming gift, but I remember you said you had not subscribed yet, and I couldn't come empty handed."

Adina's smile was warm, and it was clear she would not give up unless Solace could bring herself to rudeness. And so, far from a solitary walk home with a chance to examine the paper on her own, Solace found her arm linked through Adina's, her person being propelled along, while Adina chatted as if they were old friends.

"I am so sorry I haven't called on you before. I have been a little…unwell this week." She blushed, leaving Solace in no doubt over what had caused her illness.

There was that flash of envy again, but it was brief, and in its wake came genuine pleasure at Adina's happiness. As Mr. Donner had said, one couldn't help but like her.

Adina continued, "Have you heard the news?"

Confused, Solace started to ask if she meant Adina's personal news, then realized she referred to the newsboy's cries. "I heard that something happened, but not the particulars."

"Another woman was found dead—murdered—not far from here!"

"How terrible," she murmured, then noticed Adina's raised eyebrow and added sheepishly, "I mean, of course it is awful news. Forgive me. I am distracted today."

"I do forgive you. After all, I led you to believe I disapprove of gossip, yet here I am, spreading it!" She unfolded the paper. "You see? The *Gazette* publishes later than the other papers and uses a linotype for speed. While *The Morning Oregonian* headline is on the meatpackers, the *Gazette* scooped them. Oh, but speaking of the strike ending, Jane Howard is over the moon. New deliveries of meat may arrive as soon as today, and Hiram will finally get to use his new freezer!"

"But what of the plan to rent it out?"

"That is the best part. A man who lives near the shop rented it Sunday evening. All of it, just for him, for he had bought meat in advance of the strike, and then his ice box broke. I hope his new one arrives before the Howards' meat does! But I should not poke fun, not when there is such other news."

"It's human nature. We need to laugh in our darkest hour so that we may soldier on."

"You are too kind. I am a worse gossip than Jane!" Adina sighed, then pointed to a hand-drawn map within the *Gazette* story. "The poor girl was found in an empty lot behind Erickson's Saloon on Third Avenue."

Solace shivered. Erickson's was not the closest saloon, but it was close enough. Could Allen have walked there and back in time?

No. It was not he. It couldn't be.

She said, "Did I hear the newsboy say it was Creffield? How can they know already?"

"They can't. But with such a madman on the loose, of course the papers will blame him."

"But previously he didn't harm his female disciples, did he? Beyond ruining them—he doesn't *kill* them?"

"Who can know? He believes himself the reincarnation of Jesus. Perhaps not every girl falls under his spell, and if they don't…" Adina shrugged. "But of the women who *are* crazy for him, many have now been returned to their families or committed for their own protection. Even his mother-in-law, Mrs. Hurt, was sent to the Insane Asylum two weeks ago."

Solace suppressed another shiver at the reminder of

that institution. "But isn't that so the girls can't harm themselves, not to prevent violence on Creffield's part?"

"True. Give me a moment, I will see what the paper says. Perhaps there is another suspect."

Apparently trusting that Solace would keep her from any misstep, Adina skimmed the article as she walked. "Found in the saloon yard, but possibly killed elsewhere. Lots of…blood…on the body, but not in the yard itself."

Solace nearly gasped with the relief. "She did not die this morning?"

"What…? No," Adina said, still reading. Abruptly she came up short, wrenching Solace to a stop. "*Oh dear. She was stabbed dozens of times—mutilated.*"

She paled, and Solace took the paper from her and guided her to the curb. "Here, sit. You should not be reading such upsetting things."

Adina rested her head on her knees. "I am fine, truly. I am not a 'fainting female.'" She glanced up. "You are a married woman. But…have you any children?"

Solace swallowed. "No. Allen and I have not been so blessed."

"Ah. I am sorry. But I trust you understand the way of things? The changes a woman's body experiences with pregnancy and such?"

Solace said cautiously, "I am not ignorant of the workings of the human form."

Adina smiled wanly. "Forgive me again. It is just that I am so sick every morning, it makes it difficult to think. I only meant to ask if I may speak frankly."

Solace felt her expression clear. "Of course. Some women are more affected than others. And you may be as frank as you like. I am not a 'fainting female,' either."

"Thank you. This will be our first child. But not my

first pregnancy." She stared at her fingers, laced and resting on her bent knees. "The other times—there were three—I was not this sick. I fear to believe this is a good sign, in case it may be a bad one."

Not having an answer to this, Solace said, "We are close to my home, and by now, Allen will have made the coffee. Or I can make some tea. Are you able to walk?"

"I think so." With Solace's aid, she stood, shakily at first, but gaining strength after a few deep breaths. "Yes, I am much improved."

Still, Solace folded the paper under her arm and supported Adina's elbow as they walked, steering her clear of the many ruts in the dry lane, until the house was in view. Adina made no comment about the shabby building itself, but looked with delight at the garden.

"How lovely! And such variety. Not for you only the 'simple' rose."

"I wasn't certain what would grow in this soil and climate," Solace said with embarrassment. "I asked at Fisher's and then took one of each plant they suggested."

Adina eyed her choices critically. "You were given sound advice. And you were smart to include flowers that bloom in the fall, but display pretty foliage now."

"Thank you. Would you like to sit on the porch while I bring out the coffee?"

"Yes, that would be lovely. The fresh air will do me good. Thank you."

Solace hurried inside. Allen sat at the table, drinking coffee and eating bread with jam. He had not changed his shirt nor put on his shoes, but he appeared restored.

"My dear, I was beginning to worry. The coffee is hot, and you see, I have made my own breakfast."

He sounded so proud of himself, but she saw the eggs

still on the counter, next to the unused iron skillet. Apparently, he'd forgotten his original plan. She cast a glance at the closed front door, then smiled at him.

"That was very resourceful. I am sorry I am late. Do you remember Mrs. Donner, who I met at church last week?" It was doubtful he would have remembered such a trivial thing even before his spells, so she hurried on. "I have just met her again and invited her to visit. I thought perhaps you would be at your work already."

She suppressed a pang for hinting he should leave her alone with their guest, but he beamed. "How wonderful! Of course you shall play hostess. When I have read the paper, I will retreat to my study so you may discuss your womanly interests to your heart's content."

"Thank you," Solace said sincerely and busied herself preparing a tray with the coffee, two cups, and a tin of cookies from the pantry. She added a pot of cream and a bowl of sugar, then brought it out to Adina on the porch, where they passed a pleasant half hour, getting acquainted. When Adina rose to leave, it was with genuine regret that Solace saw her to the gate, and with utmost sincerity that she promised a return visit at her earliest convenience.

Smiling to herself, she ran lightly up the walk, gathered the tray of used dishes and cookie crumbs, and balancing it on her hip, opened the screen and let herself in. She moved to the kitchen, but instead of finding it empty as expected, she saw Allen still at the table, the front page of the *Gazette* spread before him.

He looked up as she entered, and the horror in his eyes made her almost drop the tray.

"My God, Solace—what have I done?"

Chapter Sixteen

After three days of fruitless questioning, and a more thorough knowledge of Portland's seedier establishments than he had ever hoped to possess, Lucky was in a foul mood. He threw off the bed covers and sat up, then pitched back onto the mattress, waiting for the world—and his stomach—to stop churning.

He was also apparently suffering the worst hangover he'd experienced in a while. Not being a regular drinker, he had forgotten how awful the effects could be. For the first two days of his new position, he'd managed not to drink much in the establishments he'd visited. But on Thursday evening, he'd found himself in the Gem, a gambling hall near the foot of the Morrison Street Bridge, with a group of men he thought might know something about Ellie.

He'd begun gaming and drinking to earn their trust and loosen their tongues, and by the time he realized they knew nothing useful, it was too late. He was dead drunk and had lost most of what was in his pockets. Fortunately, this was not much. After buying his new suit, he had hidden what remained of his advance in the Bible in his room. He slid a hand under his pillow and found it reassuringly still there, the hasp secure. Maybe it was time to open a bank account and admit he was not leaving Portland.

He examined that thought. Along with drinking to gain the gamblers' trust, he'd craved oblivion from things he otherwise couldn't expel from his mind. Like a certain botanist and her erstwhile spouse.

Evidently it hadn't worked.

Though he hadn't set eyes on Solace since the night Allen had accosted the prostitute, Lucky's brain had no trouble tormenting him with images of her. Most often, he recalled the way she had leaned into him, lids half-closed over eyes dark with newfound desire. For *him*. Even that brief image was enough to send lust coursing through him. Then his brain helpfully added a memory of the heat of her body, so near he could have caressed her, explored the secrets of her soft, rounded femininity that was so different from his own hard planes.

He groaned and slammed his fist into the pillow.

The light leaking through the shutters indicated it was late. He squinted at Sam's bunk and found it empty. No doubt he'd risen at the usual time for his job at the docks. *That* was reliable work. No equipment to break down, just endless ships sailing up the Columbia into the Willamette, to offload in Portland. Maybe Lucky should leave the lumber business. Or at least return to the logging camps, where the only equipment needed was crimped boots and a big axe. Just now, hacking down a giant tree sounded like a really good idea.

No use lying in bed, stewing. Experimentally, he pushed up on one elbow. His head swam, and a pickaxe seemed to be stabbing his right eye from behind. But the contents of his stomach stayed down, so he continued to a sit and assessed the rest of him.

Everything appeared to be in working order. No bumps or bruises, so he hadn't gotten into a fight. He'd half-wondered, given the quantity of alcohol he must have consumed and how much money he'd lost. But unlike his father, Lucky had never been a mean drunk. Instead, everyone was his new best friend, resulting in fewer altercations but a higher degree of spending his hard-earned cash. Even when he didn't have any.

Abruptly, he remembered the "package" he was to collect at the Gem. He jumped out of bed, then clutched his head and swayed until the urge to topple like a felled tree passed.

Damn, shit, and—as Solace would say—*blast it all to hell!*

He'd forgotten all about it. What if he'd spent its contents on his own entertainments?

He grabbed his new coat off its peg and fumbled through the pockets. Empty. So were those of his trousers, which he still wore, along with one sock, having evidently given up undressing partway through the process. Further searching was equally fruitless; the cramped room showed no sign of the envelope.

Think, you goddamned bastard. Did you get it before you joined the gaming table?

No matter how he tried, he couldn't picture the Gem's proprietor or remember whether he'd approached that worthy for his civic contribution. If he hadn't, he could simply return for the envelope, then deliver it to his contact at police headquarters. But if he *had* remembered, and had spent or lost the money, he would have to repay it from his own meager savings. Who knew how much the bribes were, but any amount was more than he could afford.

Shit, shit, shit. He'd have to retrace his steps, go back to the Gem, and admit he was a fool who couldn't recall if he'd done his job or not.

He found his missing sock and rooted his shirt out

from under the bed. It wasn't too wrinkled, so he put it on, then sat to pull on his boots. It must be after ten o'clock. If the Gem wasn't yet open, at least someone should be inside, preparing for the day.

Lucky paused with one boot half-laced. *Hell and damnation!*

What guarantee did he have that the proprietor would tell him the truth? Why not lie and say he'd given Lucky the money, then keep it for himself, leaving Lucky to take the blame? Or was there honor among this group of thieves? Either way, he had to try. He finished lacing his boots and ran a comb through his hair—no time to shave. He pulled on his coat and hat, then heard a faint scratching at his door.

He flung it wide, growling "*What?*" at whoever dared disturb him.

It was Mary, the girl Mrs. Baldwin had brought. She was tiny and mouse-like, still half-starved, with blue-veined skin stretched thin over protruding bones. She was twelve but appeared much younger. Her blonde hair was limp and dull, her big eyes haunted. She shrank from him, tripping over her too-long skirts, and fell onto the hall carpet.

Lucky forced his expression back to something more genial, more avuncular, and not like the raging bear he must have seemed when bursting out of his room. "Mary! Are you hurt?" He knelt and offered her his hand, but she scrabbled away. "I'm so sorry I scared you. I wasn't frowning at you, I promise."

She only shook her head violently, then buried her face in her hands and burst into tears. What could he say to calm her? And was her errand important enough to delay his hunt for the missing envelope?

Since her arrival on Sunday, she had barely spoken to anyone but Sadie. She hid her face from the men she encountered in the dining hall and avoided coming upstairs at all costs. Her room was a closet off the pantry, near Sadie's own bedroom, so she rarely had cause to visit the men's quarters unless Sadie sent her on a specific errand.

Her sobs were easing into sniffles, so he pulled a handkerchief from his pocket and offered it to her. She took it hesitantly, then blew her nose loudly.

"There," he said gently. "I really didn't mean to scowl at you. Can you tell me now why you were sent to fetch me?"

She nodded and drew a bracing breath. "You're one o' the nice ones. 'S why I said I'd come. There's a lady to see you. She says it's very 'portant, and can you come right away?"

Lucky smiled at her compliment, then registered her message. "A lady?"

He stood too quickly and had to reach for the wall and cover his eyes while his head pounded and the nausea surged again. Had Ellie finally come? Or had she gone to Mrs. Baldwin, and that lady was his visitor, come to deliver the news?

Head and stomach mostly settled, he pushed off the wall, saying a hurried, "Thank you!" over his shoulder to Mary as he headed downstairs.

But upon opening the double doors to the parlor, he found neither Ellie nor Mrs. Baldwin waiting. Instead, the woman pacing by the window, who whirled as he entered, was Solace Grey.

"Mr. Jacobs—thank God you are here!"

"Solace! What has happened? Are you well?"

She nodded, then shook her head, then nodded again. "Yes—no—I hardly know. It's not me—it's Allen. I didn't know where else to go. You've seen him—you know something of our situation. I thought—I wondered if you could—oh, forgive me! I shouldn't have come!"

She sank onto the same sofa where Mrs. Baldwin had so recently sat and, as Mary had done, put her face in her hands, shoulders shaking. But when a moment later she raised her dry-eyed gaze, he realized she shook not with grief, but with terror.

"Good God, Solace, what is wrong?" He crossed the room in two strides and sat, taking her hands in his, past caring for the proprieties. "Is your husband hurt?"

God forgive him, but at the thought, a tiny ray of hope blossomed in his black, disgusting heart. He only prayed she wouldn't see it in his eyes.

She shook her head. "No. At least, not precisely."

In her agitation, she tried to withdraw her hands and rise from the sofa, but he pulled her firmly back down. "Perhaps you'd better start at the beginning. I will do anything I can to help you, but you must tell me what has happened first."

He had never seen her so upset and unable to master herself. Twice now he had used her given name—the feel of it on his tongue was bittersweet—and she had not noticed.

She had also left her hands in his. In her haste, she had forgotten her gloves, and despite being calloused from good, honest work, the feel of her bare skin beneath his fingers was unbearably soft. As one would soothe a frightened kitten, he stroked her palms with his thumbs and murmured, "All will be well. I'm here. Tell me what is wrong and I will fix it."

She gave a wan smile. "I don't know if anyone can fix this, but you have been so—so kind. I couldn't come to Adina—my friend, Mrs. Donner—for she is… Well, she has other concerns just now. I hope you don't mind—I asked Mr. Fisher for your address." She hesitated. "I am sure you have heard about—about the women. The two found in the river and the creek?"

Whatever he had expected, it was not this. "Yes. Anyone who lives in Portland couldn't fail to have heard about them."

Solace's choke of laughter held a note of hysteria. "Anyone who reads the papers, at any rate. Do you read the papers? Have you seen today's headlines?" When he shook his head cautiously—no sense upsetting his equilibrium again—she said, "They have found another dead girl. Not in a river this time, but stabbed and left behind a saloon."

Lucky's heart hammered in time to his skull's throbbing. "What has this to do with you?"

Her eyes were wide with fear, and she seemed to have trouble finding the words. But once they came, it was all in a rush, as though she must get them out before losing her nerve.

"Allen believes—he says—*he* killed her. That he went out early this morning and must have killed her before coming home to make coffee for me. He doesn't remember doing it, but when he read the paper, he says it all came back. He wants me to go to the police, and I told him I would. I gave my husband a sleeping draught and told him I would arrange to have him arrested. What sort of wife *does* that?"

Her voice shook, and it took all Lucky's resolve not to fold her in his arms and swear to protect her, from this or anything else. But he couldn't so dishonor her. At best, she'd wish he'd kept his distance. At worst, she'd hate him for taking advantage of her emotions.

She mastered herself and continued. "But instead of doing what he asked, I came here. What wife does *that*? Makes a promise to her husband, with no intention of keeping it?" She gripped Lucky's hand so hard, her nails cut into his skin. "Please help him. He is innocent—he could never hurt anyone. Not like that. He was a missionary, for pity's sake—he believed it his calling to save souls, not murder them! I can't go to the police—they'll arrest him for insanity, if not for the murder. He'll go to the asylum! Even if he is found innocent, it will ruin him. He'll lose his job and never get another. He is a scholar—his mind is all he has."

She released Lucky's hand, her touch still branding him, and lowered her eyes as though fearing his reaction to what she would say next. "There's more. This is not the first time we have had to move and start over. He has been having these spells for some time. It's why we left San Francisco, and before that, why we came west. The climate was supposed to be better. But it's not—his spells are getting worse. I don't know what to do. I can't help him—I've tried, and I can't."

She held something back, Lucky could feel it. "Solace, you must tell me all of it."

She avoided his gaze, then abruptly drew a deep breath. "I am sure it is only a coincidence. A facet of living in large cities that support a criminal element."

She paused, and he waited, not saying anything, allowing the silence to grow while she gathered the strength to finish what she had to say. Finally, she forced the words out.

"There have been similar…occurrences, in places we have lived before. Similar…deaths."

Something sharp stabbed his gut. No. Allen Grey was eccentric. But he was not a killer. Was he…? As Solace herself had said, murders happened all the time in large cities, especially among the "criminal element."

As though reading Lucky's doubts in his expression, she straightened, glaring fiercely. "I know it wasn't Allen. Do you hear me? He is innocent—I *know* it! And yet…that poor, poor girl…"

Her face crumpled, and he thought, *To hell with what she'll think later*. He took her in his arms and pressed her close, and in her abject misery, she let him rock her gently while she sobbed out her terror. And God damn him for the basest sinner that ever lived—he enjoyed holding her. *Enjoyed* the rose scent of her hair that brushed silkily against his jaw, the warmth of her soft, yielding curves that fit so perfectly against him.

More than that, he took pleasure in soothing her, caring for her, lending her his strength in what was certainly a rare moment of weakness. Tomorrow, she would hate him for seeing her break down, for being party to the ruin of her life, no matter that she had invited him to witness it. Today, he would help her and take what he could, however small and unknowingly given. Because tomorrow, he would punish himself for his weakness more than she ever could.

When, also like Mary, Solace's sobs subsided into sniffles, he allowed himself one more stroke of his hand on her back and one more brush of her hair against his lips. It was not much, but as he would never have the liberty again, he committed the feel of her to memory. Both touches were so light, he hoped she hadn't registered them, but they would have to do.

Then he set her aside and moved away on the sofa. He would have offered her his handkerchief, but he had left it with Mary. Fortunately, she had one of her own. She took it from her sleeve and dabbed her eyes, still too lost in the moment to be embarrassed.

As *he* was too lost in her to make the right choice and send her to someone—*anyone*—else who could be objective. Someone who didn't hope, on some level, that her husband *was* a killer, and would be sent to jail, or even executed, thereby setting her free. Someone who could think clearly and not feel a haze of blinding rage at the thought of her in pain.

But who else would fight for her if not Lucky? She had no one. Like him, she'd been uprooted so often as to have few connections anywhere, let alone here, where she'd lived but a few weeks. And how else to take the fear and pain from her, unless by helping her prove her husband's innocence?

Lucky drew in a deep breath and blew it out again. "Tell me what you need, Solace. Tell me, and I'll do it."

Chapter Seventeen

Allen was still asleep when Solace returned with Lucky in tow. She knew she was in shock, her mind seizing on inconsequential things rather than facing the fact that her husband—sweet, gentle Allen—might be a killer. For instance, she had a vague sense that she should be correcting herself and return to thinking of Lucky as "Mr. Jacobs." But somehow she couldn't make herself care about social mores or distancing herself from him.

If she was honest, she didn't want to.

The feel of his arms around her, the way her head fit under his auburn-stubbled chin, nestled in the crook of his strong shoulder and neck—she didn't want to let that go. For years, she had held Allen when he was scared or hurt, and was glad to do it. But today, it had dawned on her that no one held her when she needed it. Gradually, over the years, she had ceased wishing for it and hadn't realized how big the deficit was until Lucky filled it.

He'd only offered what any compassionate person would in the circumstances. She knew that. And she wanted nothing more. But it was a shared moment of companionship that she would cherish in the dark days ahead. For dark they *would* be. She knew that now, too.

"Please wait here," she said to Lucky, indicating the kitchen. It seemed important to leave him in the beating heart of her home rather than the more formal living room. "I'll go wake Allen, so you can hear all this—this nonsense—directly from him."

She went to the bedroom and touched Allen's shoulder. The sleeping draught was wearing off, and he stirred. "What is it, Solace? What has happened?"

Hope flared. Might he not even recall the morning's events? His recent memories were more affected by his condition than those of his youth. It would be better if he *had* forgotten; then they could all forget about telling the police of something he *hadn't* done.

Except she had already gone to Lucky. Would he let it go? Or would he, as she suspected, want to pursue it and uncover the truth, whatever that might be? And…could *she* forget that her husband had convinced himself, however briefly, that he was a brutal killer?

Then she saw his haunted expression and knew that today, at least, he remembered.

"I've brought someone to speak with you."

"The police?"

"Not yet. I wanted you to talk with someone else first, someone who can help you see that you couldn't have done this terrible thing."

"But I did. Solace, you must believe me, and you must have me arrested at once, before I do it again."

His voice had risen with his agitation, and the kitchen floorboards creaked as Lucky moved across them.

"Shh. There, there. We'll talk with Mr. Jacobs. He'll know what to do."

If nothing else, that was certain. Lucky exuded confidence. Of course, the most confident people often had the least idea what they were doing. Herself included. She suppressed a hysterical giggle. But even if Lucky did not know what to do, he was someone she could confide in. For that alone she'd be forever grateful.

She helped Allen up and smoothed the worst of the

wrinkles from his shirt and trousers. He was still in his socks, so she found an old pair of shoes for him, then led him to the kitchen. Lucky hovered near the doorway, confirming her suspicion that he'd been about to check on her. He glanced at Allen, then raised an eyebrow at her, which she interpreted to mean, *Everything well?*

She lifted a shoulder in response, hoping he would understand this as, *Not really, but he would never intentionally hurt anyone, so please help me prove he's not a killer, and then we can all go back to our mundane lives and forget this ever happened.*

Whether or not he got all that from the slight gesture was difficult to discern, but he offered Allen his hand. "Mr. Grey. A pleasure to see you again."

Allen regarded him in confusion. "Do I know you, sir? I sometimes forget people. I'm terribly sorry!"

Lucky smiled. "No matter. Until I've met someone a few times, I'm terrible with names and faces myself."

Solace suspected this was a bald-faced lie, but it soothed Allen, and her gratitude for Lucky's many kindnesses spread warmly through her. How could she ever repay him?

She said to Allen, "This is Mr. Jacobs. He…"

And all at once she came up short. How to explain who Lucky was and why she had involved him? *He's a delivery man for Fisher's* wouldn't quite cover it. *He's a delivery man who built your bookcases, then drove you home after you accosted a prostitute* was more correct, but still wouldn't explain his presence now.

The most accurate would be, *He's a delivery man who has helped me twice already when I didn't even know I needed it—three times, counting the mulch—and I trust him enough to ask for his help with this, the most difficult challenge of our lives*. But she could hardly say all that to Allen, much less in front of Lucky.

Fortunately, Lucky himself stepped into the breach with the one thing she had entirely forgotten, but which was guaranteed to soothe Allen further.

"I'm a parishioner at St. Mary's. I've met you and your wife on several occasions." He hesitated, then gave her an apologetic look before continuing to Allen, "I also have connections at the Police Force. Perhaps I can help you discover the truth of your actions, without directly involving the law."

He had "connections"? With the *police*? Was there *nothing* this man didn't dabble in?

"Mr. Jacobs…" She paused, the heat rising in her cheeks. "I—I hope you aren't obligated to tell them of this. That is, if I'd known, I would never have involved you. I wouldn't want to put you in an awkward position."

"That's why I didn't tell you. And it's a recent connection."

He said no more, and she wondered if that was why he had gone to talk with the officer and the prostitute on that terrible night in front of the library. Regardless, she had already involved him, so she plowed ahead.

"Please, won't you sit? I'll make fresh coffee. Allen, tell Mr. Jacobs what you told me, about—about the dead woman, and why you think you are involved."

"I *am* involved!"

He was so certain. For one insane moment, Solace considered taking him at his word and sending Lucky for the police after all. But no. He was just confused.

Lucky said, "Perhaps you could start from the beginning, so we can examine the facts before coming to any conclusions."

Allen nodded, instantly becoming calmer. He sat at the table, then paused, ordering his thoughts. "I went for a walk early this morning and—"

"How early?" Lucky interrupted, taking a seat across from him.

Like a hound dog, once he'd scented something interesting, he'd never give up until it was firmly in his teeth. And yet…that was precisely why Solace had gone to him—to get at the truth. And she must *let* him.

Trying to stay out of the way and to not think what any of this might mean for Allen, she busied herself with the coffeepot, emptying the old grounds from the top and cleaning the metal filter while Allen answered.

"Around four, I believe. It was full dark, so it couldn't have been later, as sunrise is before five now. I was searching for something. I don't remember what, but I think it must have been a—another victim."

This was too much; so much for staying out of the way. Solace whirled, interjecting, "Of course it wasn't! You had nothing to do with the first victims, and you most certainly had nothing to do with this one!"

Allen said sadly, "I am grateful you believe so. But I must tell Mr. Jacobs the rest." He faced Lucky again. "I remember turning the corner at the end of Lownsdale and going down to Fifth Avenue, or maybe Fourth. Something caught my eye, and I went to investigate. After that, I…can't recall. When I came to myself, I was in an empty lot behind a saloon. With—with the body."

Lucky's eyebrows rose. "You are certain? Forgive me, but it seems you were already confused. Perhaps what you saw wasn't a body but only your imagination."

"It was a body—I am positive. And it wasn't so much what I saw that stands out as…as the smell." Allen glanced at Solace in anguish. "My dear, perhaps you should leave us. There are things I did not tell you this morning. They will be upsetting for you."

"Of course they won't. I am not in the least missish!"

Lucky chewed his lip. "Your husband may be right. If he was near the victim, what he describes may be—"

Solace shook her head violently, sloshing water from the coffeepot. "He didn't see anything, because he wasn't near her. And even if he was, I am staying. I am not a conventional female, as you know. I have as much fortitude as any man. If you can stomach this, so can I."

Lucky regarded her consideringly. "You are certain? Because to be brutally honest, I am not certain I *can* stomach it. Whatever *it* is."

She set the percolator on the stove, lit the burner, and steadied herself before speaking. "Allen is my *husband*. I have sworn in front of God and the church to be his helpmeet, in good times and bad. I can't *not* help him now, when it is surely the worst time of all. Please understand—he is my *husband*."

Lucky's gaze was inscrutable, and she dropped her own, afraid he'd see too much and understand why she *had* to remind him she was Allen's wife. Not only because the church said so, but because of who she was. She could not desert Allen, no matter how terrified she was, nor how much she wished someone else would shoulder her burdens for a time.

Lucky was silent a long moment, but she kept her head down, unable to bear reading further compassion or realization, or anything else, in his eyes.

At last he said, "Very well. Grey, please continue."

Allen's voice was quiet but sure. "I stood by a water trough, washing my hands. I must have scrubbed them, for my skin was raw, and one of my fingernails had torn off." He held his hand out, displaying the sticking plaster Solace had attached. "And there's this."

He pushed up his coat sleeves to reveal his shirt cuffs. Clearly visible were the pink stains Solace had noticed. Most were mere droplets, but one was bigger, about an inch and a half long, and half an inch wide.

Lucky examined them, then saw the red bumps on Allen's hands. "What's this?"

"A rash," Solace answered. "From some wild carrot I picked in the yard yesterday."

The heat rose in her cheeks at the memory of why she had needed to replace the flowers in the kitchen, and why she had chosen wild carrot as the focus of the new arrangement. She hurried on. "I must have dropped the leaves on the floor, and Allen swept them up this morning with some spilled coffee grounds."

Lucky unbuttoned the cuffs and pushed Allen's sleeves up to expose his forearms. The ointment had helped, but there were still red streaks up to his elbows.

"All of this from a few leaves?"

"Yes. The roots and seeds are safe to consume—it's a known medicinal—but the leaves cause a rash on sensitive skin, made worse by exposure to the sun. Allen bared his arms to clean up the coffee, then carried the sweepings outside to our compost pile." A thought struck her. "Could the stains on his cuffs be from the coffee?"

Lucky unrolled Allen's sleeves again and examined them more closely. "It's possible. The small drops are a little pink, but that could be from scrubbing them."

Allen broke in, "The drops were there when I was at the trough, before I spilled the coffee. I'm certain of it." He withdrew his hands. "Please, I must finish. I turned from the trough and saw the—the body, on the ground."

Lucky said, "Can you describe exactly what you saw? Even the smallest detail may be important."

"She was on her back. Her eyes were closed like she was sleeping, but there was blood…so much blood…"

Solace swallowed the bile that rose in her throat, like the hot, sour coffee percolating behind her on the stove.

"Solace…" Lucky's voice held a note of desperation. "Please, you must reconsider."

She shook her head. "He told me most of it earlier. It can hardly be worse with new ears. Go on, Allen."

But Lucky interjected, "Wait. Tell me more about the blood. Was it fresh? Or…dried?"

Allen considered, then said, "Dried. I think. But it was all over her skirt and in her hair."

"What did she look like? Her face and hair, I mean."

"She had light brown hair, curled in ringlets. I could not see the color of her eyes, but her skin was fair. She wore pink and white satin skirts, and wooden heels."

Lucky's face went white, and he closed his eyes briefly, as though reeling from some unseen blow. "How old would you say she was?"

"I believe she was young. Maybe twenty?"

"Do you recall anything else? Anything at all?"

"I don't think so." Allen paused, then his expression changed to one of excitement. "Wait—there was something. Her skirts were up. Not all the way. Just enough to reveal her—her calves and a bit of her thighs."

He blushed furiously, keeping his gaze on Lucky, and Solace suppressed a fleeting irritation. How could it be that her husband of ten years felt more comfortable discussing the naked female form with a perfect stranger, who happened to be a man, than with his own wife?

"I tried not to look at her," Allen continued, "which is why I forgot until now. Her skin was red and bumpy. Like mine."

Solace stilled, and Lucky went motionless as well. This was damning. If Allen had not picked up the rash *after* his walk, but *during* it, and if he had transferred that rash to the poor, murdered girl—or she had transferred it to him—it meant he had touched her. And in a place that no man besides her husband should touch.

He knew too much.

About her condition, her appearance, her *death*.

Solace's husband, with whom she had lived from the end of her girlhood until now, and who often could not recall his own wife's name, spoke with clarity and confidence of the horrifying murder of a young woman.

A haze of silver dots clouded her vision, a rushing filled her ears, growing into a roar. She wasn't breathing—she couldn't make herself inhale.

"Solace?" Lucky's voice came from far away, across the thunder. "Are you well?"

Her lips were icy and wouldn't work properly, but she managed to whisper, "I…don't think so."

Her limbs were heavy, her palms sweaty, but her fingers were frozen, prickling painfully. She lost her grip on the counter and crumpled to the floor, too numb to care for anything but finding respite from the knowledge that her husband might be a *killer*, a man who could stab a woman to death, and then come home to make coffee for his wife—whose name he couldn't recall.

Someone pushed up her sleeve, chafing her wrist, but it was no good. Her vision grayed, and Lucky's shouts of *"Solace…!"* echoed farther and farther away, until her sight went black, and her hearing faded to naught.

Chapter Eighteen

Chief Hunt looked up from the *Gazette* to find the young pup Peters standing hesitantly at the doorway.

"You wanted to see me, sir?"

Hunt rose, brandishing the paper at him. "Explain to me how the *hell* this happened!"

Peters paled, but to his credit he stepped forward and took the paper, unfurling it and reading the headline about the latest murder victim. "I don't know, sir."

"The hell you don't! How could a reporter find out about this—any of it—*without* anyone noticing?" Hunt snatched the paper back and jabbed a finger at the article. "Details, about her death, the body, that she was murdered elsewhere and moved to Erickson's. *Someone* spoke to a reporter, and I want to know who it was!"

"Yes, sir," Peters managed. "I was there, sir."

"I know that! Why else would I send for you?"

"Sorry, sir. Of course, sir. I only meant that by the time I arrived, there was a crowd milling about, but I could swear none of them were reporters. Perhaps Detective Jenkins saw something? Being as how he's the one who discovered the body in the first place?"

"I'll talk to Jenkins in a minute! I'm talking to you now. What's your opinion—is Creffield the culprit? Or should we be looking elsewhere?"

The rapid-fire question had the desired effect of catching Peters off-guard. But as Hunt had suspected, the man thought a moment before answering. He was young and rash. But also observant, and by all accounts, determined to learn and improve himself.

"Well, sir," Peters said at last, "It would be a convenient resolution if Creffield is the murderer."

"And what would be the *inconvenient* resolution?"

"Detective Jenkins thinks—"

"Not Jenkins!" Hunt barked. "You!"

"Yes, sir. There's this man, Jacobs. He was interested in a missing prostitute. Likely the dead woman, based on his description. Asked after her during that incident at the library earlier this week, when that man, Grey, accosted that other prostitute. Jacobs has some connection to the Greys, so I thought he might be worth looking into, but—" His face reddened.

"Go on, spit it out."

"Yes, sir. Detective Jenkins dismissed the idea. Said he thought Grey was a better suspect. But while Grey *is* clearly insane, I doubt he's capable of murder."

So, the pup had teeth. Was he sincerely reluctant to criticize his superior, or only feigning loyalty? Either way, pitting the bureau's officers against each other produced results. Especially when Hunt gave them enough rope to hang themselves.

"You have my permission to put together a case against this Jacobs man, *if* you can find sufficient evidence. But make it quick! Three dead women is three too many, no matter their professions. You're dismissed! And send Jenkins up. I'll have that word with him now."

Jenkins appeared promptly but had no better explanation for how the reporter had sourced his story than Peters. Hunt grunted and eyed the detective, but unfortunately, not a thread was out of place on his dark brown suit.

"You *are* the one who found the body. What were you doing at Erickson's at that hour?"

"Following a lead, sir." Jenkins was stoic as ever, but a flush crept up his neck. Perhaps he'd overheard Peters's critique and saw his promotion vanishing.

"Which was…?"

"Allen Grey, sir. His behavior is odd, to say the least. He was a missionary for a time and now seems to have a religious mania focused on the salvation of whores."

"Creffield has religious mania in spades! So did Major Brooks and every goddamned woman or man who joined with them! It's why they started the damn Holy Rollers, because God's Army wasn't religious *enough*!"

The flush deepened. "Begging your pardon, sir, but Creffield seems to want to fornicate with the women, not reform them—or kill them. But Grey was caught in the act of beating a whore, and when I spoke with his wife, she seemed afraid, obviously of him."

"What about this Jacobs man? Peters likes him better than Grey."

Jenkins looked alarmed, glancing at the open door before stepping closer and lowering his voice. "Sir, Jacobs is an *honorable* man." He ran his thumb across his gloved fingertips, mimicking fanning paper money.

Hunt frowned. "*He's* our new collections man?"

"Yes, sir."

"Hmph. Well, that doesn't make him a murderer, but it also doesn't make him not one."

"No, sir. But why would he ask about a whore he killed, in front of Peters?"

Hunt grunted acknowledgment of the point. "Was she already dead when he asked? Is the reporter correct, and she died days ago, before turning up in the yard?"

"We don't know yet. Finley just started the autopsy."

"Well, find out, for Christ's sake! Now!"

"Yes, sir." Jenkins turned and went out the door.

Hunt sat back. It seemed more and more likely that Creffield was not the killer, if for no other reason than that he would have had to come out of hiding many times in recent weeks, instead of lying low. Fortunately, they had two new suspects. Surely one of them—Grey or Jacobs, he didn't care which—would be proven guilty, women and prostitutes everywhere would be safe again, and he could get that Baldwin woman off his back. Plus, he'd get credit for stopping a crazed killer.

He gave a satisfied grunt and opened the paper to the society section, looking for tidbits that might be useful later as his career advanced.

~:~:~

Along with Portland's dark underbelly, Lucky was now far too familiar with its criminal justice system. To date most of his "packages" had been delivered to a Detective Jenkins at Police Headquarters on the corner of Southwest Second and Oak. But a few went instead to City Hall, eleven blocks away at Fourth and Madison, so he had well-worn routes to either place.

Today, however, he detoured east around the one-block-square Hall toward the morgue. Two years ago, John Finley, a successful undertaker, had decided he'd like a paycheck from the county, too, and ran for coroner. He'd then opened adjacent offices for his private and government businesses inside a new building on Southwest Third.

Lucky entered the grand marble foyer, noting its contrast with the dark, old-fashioned Police building. When the new City Hall was first built, this area was all dirt roads and few structures. Today, the streets were still dirt, but the lots were built up, and now this was the center of government, whether the Police Force wanted to admit it or not.

And Finley's was hands down the most modern building, with heated air and water, gas and electric lights, and a telephone system. But it was also beautifully designed, with a steel ceiling, large chapel, funeral offices, and eight fireproof vaults to house the visiting bodies, which *The Morning Oregonian* had praised as the first innovation of its kind in the Northwest.

As it was midday, most employees were out at lunch, but Lucky found a clerk who directed him to the coroner's exam room, housed in the basement with the vaults. The clerk seemed neither curious nor suspicious of Lucky's motives, only telling him that Finley was out, but he could see if the policeman guarding the body would answer his questions.

Lucky descended into the dim hall below and rapped on the exam room's frosted glass window, then waited as a shadowy figure inside came to open the door.

"What is it?" the officer said irritably, and Lucky found himself confronted with the glaring countenance of Detective Jenkins, dressed today in plain clothes but just as starched and proper as ever.

He recognized Lucky, and his frown deepened. "Are you back again? Stop making deliveries every damn day. We're knee-deep in reporters, digging for stories about the new dead girl. When they don't find one, the last thing Hunt wants is them writing about the man 'helping' us instead. Come once a week if you have to, or better yet, twice a month."

He tried to shut the door, but Lucky managed the

age-old trick of getting his foot inside. "I don't have a delivery today."

In truth, he'd forgotten the Gem's envelope again, but for now, no one seemed to have missed it. He had enough to worry about, between Ellie, Allen Grey, and most of all, Solace. At the memory of how he'd left her, a bubble of rage, hot and seething, burned in his chest, and he fought the urge to slam his fist through the thick glass of the exam room door.

When Solace slid to the floor, he'd leapt to her side, pushing her sleeves up to chafe her wrists. But then he'd seen what should have been her unblemished skin bearing the yellow marks of days' old bruises, and his vision went red. Priming his fist for a murderous punch, he'd turned to Allen—and found him regarding the bruises with as much confusion as Lucky, if far less rage.

Lucky had forced a breath. Clearly, he didn't have all the facts. Yet. When he did, he *would* kill the man responsible, even if Solace begged him not to.

Her eyes had opened then, and she had sat up. Lucky was happy she was well, yet horribly envious when Allen insisted on making her tea, the forgotten coffee having burned beyond drinking. And then to see her gratitude for her husband's care. Care that, if God were just, Lucky would provide her instead.

But God was not just, and once Lucky was assured of her health and immediate safety, he reluctantly left her. On the one hand, Allen truly did not seem like a killer, even with his condition. On the other, he *had* been with the latest body, but couldn't remember how he'd found it, or what had transpired up to that point.

Lucky had considered asking about her bruises, but to what end? Like his mother, Solace was ever defensive of her husband, so to uncover the truth, Lucky would have to investigate the victim and her murder. Even if it meant leaving Solace alone with Allen for a short time.

Jenkins's expression changed from displeasure to suspicion. "Then what do you want? Can't you see I'm busy? The mayor is having fits. Can't attract exposition business to a city that's the murder capital of the west!"

"Actually, I'm here about the dead woman."

"Oh?" His eyes narrowed. "What about her?"

"I may be able to identify her, if no one else has."

Jenkins's brows rose. "How will you do that? Go whorin' a lot, do you? Know 'em all?"

"No, only a few. But thanks for confirming she *was* a prostitute."

The detective's mouth worked like the proverbial fish. Then he burst into loud guffaws that echoed crazily in the hushed basement. He wiped his eyes. "Clever bastard, aren't you? Well, come in, then. Coroner's out getting lunch, so you can gawk to your heart's content."

They moved into the exam room, and Lucky braced himself. The body lay on a table under a white sheet, which Jenkins removed. "We think we know her, but confirmation won't hurt. She ain't pretty, though. Killed elsewhere before being dumped in the yard in the heat."

He stepped aside, and Lucky fought down the sickening, sour bile. Ellie lay before him, her light brown hair loose around her shoulders, eyes closed in permanent sleep, her naked, abused, and bloody body a testament to the violence of her final hours.

Lucky scrubbed a hand over his face and shoved his emotions into a cold, still place, deep inside. To atone for failing Ellie, and to protect Solace now, he had to remain objective. Which meant he couldn't feel.

Jenkins watched him approach the table and examine the…corpse. Better. Seeing "Ellie" like this was too horrifying. But if he shut off the part of his mind that knew her, he might make it through the viewing without shaming himself.

She lay on her back, stripped, arms at her sides. Bruises darkened her face and wrists, and several stab wounds sliced into her torso on either side. An odd pattern, if the goal was to kill, but perhaps she had been on her stomach during the attack, and a wound from behind had penetrated her heart or lungs. Finally, Lucky noted many angry red bumps on her calves, so it seemed Allen *was* near the body, and had likely touched it.

He cleared his throat, forcing the revulsion down again. "You say she's been dead a while, killed at a different location. How do you know?"

Jenkins wrinkled his nose. "I don't know you from Adam. But you're Hunt's collections man, which could be good or bad, and I'm not saying which. So tell me what you know first, and we'll go from there."

Lucky considered. "Fair enough. Her name is Ellie—Elzbieta. I don't know her surname. She emigrated from Lithuania as a child. A year ago she was waiting tables at the Bridge Saloon. We had a…fling. I met her again last Sunday near St. Mary's. She was in bad shape, opium I think. I asked her to come to my boarding house, to meet a woman who could help."

"A woman?"

"Mrs. Baldwin, of the—"

Jenkins made a face. "Oh, we're familiar with Mrs. Baldwin's lot and their agenda. They're worse than the Salvationists. She know what you do for Hunt now?"

Lucky swallowed. Jenkins was right: She would

disapprove of Lucky collecting the bribes that allowed the vices she worked to eradicate to continue instead. Given Ellie's still, gray form, she had a point.

"Ellie never came, and I've been searching for her since. I suspect she went missing shortly after we met."

"What makes you say that?"

"Instinct. I gave her a little food and some money. I believe she really meant to meet me."

The detective chewed his lip. "You gave her money. How much?"

Heat burned Lucky's face. "Sixty cents. It was all I had in my pocket. I know how it sounds, but I swear I didn't pay for her services. It was a gift, nothing more."

Jenkins's expression was unreadable, but at last he said, "I'll tell you why we think she was moved. Or rather, I'll show you. Squeamish much?"

"No more than average," Lucky answered honestly.

"Give her belly a poke." When Lucky stared at him, he grinned. "Go on."

Lucky drew in a deep breath, then wished he hadn't, as the putrid smell wafting from the body filled his nostrils and slid down the back of his throat. He leaned in close and gave Ellie's abdomen a cautious poke with one finger, then drew his hand back in shock.

"It's hard under the skin, not soft and, ah, squishy."

Jenkins was clearly enjoying himself. "Do it again, longer, and tell me what you feel."

Only his desperate desire to discover Ellie's fate made him reach out again. This time, he forced himself not to draw away, but to note the sensation of his fingers pressing into her stomach.

"Her skin's warm, like the room. But inside, she's...*cold*. What the hell?"

"Good detective work, Jacobs. I'll tell you what Finley thinks. He says she's been dead a few days, but was kept on ice until last night."

"She was *frozen*? And now she's *thawing out*?"

"Like a side of beef. Thawed wrong and it gets all—what'd you say?—'squishy' on the outside, but still cold and hard inside. Unfortunately, makes time of death hard to pin down. But based on your timeline, maybe he killed her on Sunday, froze her, then moved her last night."

Lightheadedness threatened, and Lucky clenched his fists. "How long…" He cleared his throat. "How long would it take? To freeze her, in hot weather?"

Jenkins frowned. "Good question. He—the killer—would need an industrial freezer, not an ice room. But even that would take time. Probably have to head up to Union Meat Company and ask. Who knows? Maybe he used one of their boxcars."

"That's pretty far from Erickson's."

"Unlikely to find one closer. More common in meat shops back East, as all modern inventions are. My wife's family even purchased their own electrical refrigerator." He sniffed disdainfully. "Of course, that wouldn't freeze, just cool. They can't afford anything *that* fancy."

"How long would it take her to thaw this much?"

"How should I know? In this heat, when it's warm all night, I'd think not long. But it's not my job to figure it out, it's Finley's. And speaking of *my* job, it's not to satisfy your curiosity. I let you in as a favor. So unless you have anything else to share…?"

"One more thing. The papers are saying it's the same killer as the other two women."

Jenkins chewed the inside of his cheek, regarding Lucky thoughtfully, then shrugged. "The papers seize on any story they like, true or not."

"You don't think it's the same man?"

"Could be. Or not. What's your opinion, *detective*?"

Despite the jab, Lucky took his time, thinking it through. "Well, we have three dead women, all roughly the same age, fair-skinned, and wearing their hair in ringlets, although two were blonde and one a brunette."

"Plenty of girls wear their hair in ringlets and have light complexions."

"True. But only two were prostitutes. Unless the third was, also…?"

Jenkins's thick mustache twitched. Finally, he said, "I may as well tell you, as the papers will print it soon, regardless. No, she wasn't. Finley has ways of telling." He made a face, then his expression turned sly. "Here's something the papers don't know—the two found in the water were strangled, not drowned *or* stabbed. What do you make of that?"

Lucky couldn't hide his surprise. "It doesn't make sense. We either have one killer with no particular agenda, or we have multiple killers that all prefer women who look the same."

It was also damning for Allen Grey, who had accosted one prostitute and, at a minimum, been near the body of another. Perhaps the lack of "agenda" was due to his unclear mind? Solace had mentioned "similar" deaths in their previous hometowns.

Between those and her bruises…

Still, it would have been difficult for Allen to kill Ellie, especially if she'd died days ago. He would have had to black out—or pretend to—twice, first to kill and then to move her. And where could he have frozen her? But if not he, then how to explain his bloody cuffs, the red bumps, and how he came to be with the body?

The rash. "Did the other victims have the same rash as she?"

Jenkins's expression soured, and he tugged his gloves on more tightly, then adjusted his tie. "Coroner's almost back—time to leave. Why do you care, anyway? About any of them? Starting *another* job, are you, reporting for the papers?"

"Nothing like that," Lucky said hastily. "I—er—"

How to explain, without mentioning the Greys? If no one had recalled Allen and Molly's altercation, Lucky didn't want to remind them. He settled on a half-truth.

"She was sweet and young once, with dreams of a better life." He looked Jenkins in the eye, willing him to understand. "I failed her in life. But if I can bring her justice in death, I will."

Jenkins assessed him, then nodded slowly. "The other girls were, too. Sweet and young, with dreams. The first, Meg, had family back East. They were devastated by her death. The second, Emily, was from a farm in Idaho. She came seeking work ahead of the fair. This one..." His gaze travelled over Ellie's form. "Well, a good cop remembers who his victims are, not just what."

He went to the door and held it open, and Lucky thanked him and left.

Chapter Nineteen

Lola Baldwin sat erect in the wood chair across the massive oak desk from Mayor George Williams, who regarded her with obvious dislike. Spread between them was her copy of Thursday's *Oregon Daily Journal*, which he studiously ignored. A tall man with wide shoulders, he was imposing even when seated. His bushy white brows, mustache, and sideburns compensated for his thinning pate, and the veins marbling his nose and jowls attested to his preference for overindulgence.

"Mayor Williams," she began again, "you must take a clear and decisive position. The Municipal League—"

"Yes, yes," he said brusquely. "As you can see from the very article you brought, I have done exactly as you suggest. There can be no doubt about my position on gaming in Portland."

Lola pursed her lips. "What *I* see is that the mayor of our city, who hopes to attract a great deal of exposition industry and tourism over the coming year, is remaining noncommittal and saying nothing concrete." Without glancing at the paper, she quoted, "'I decline to make any statement regarding the matter, as to what action I may take in the future.'"

"Everyone knows I will abide by the law. The law chosen by our voters, I may add!"

She did not dignify this drivel with a response, instead quoting him further, "'I will not bind myself to any agreement regarding the gambling houses, one way or another, but shall reserve the right to act according to circumstances as they may arise in the future.'"

His own words thrown back at him did not impress the mayor, who put on an ingratiating smile. "Mrs. Baldwin, I have repeatedly assured you of my intent to clean up our fine city. I am aware of the evils associated with open gaming, and Chief Hunt and I are working to solve this terrible problem well in advance of the fair."

He sat back, evidently pleased with this little speech.

She sniffed. "I have no doubt you and Hunt are in each other's pockets. As to what you are doing there, I cannot say. The papers seem to think you both benefit handsomely from this system of bi-weekly 'fines' you have imposed on the gaming halls."

He went red in the face and beetled his brows at her. "I beg your pardon, but the *city* benefits from the fines, not I. Fines which, I may add, supplement programs such as your own YWCA and the Traveler's Aid Society. Without the generosity of the club owners, where would those noble societies be? Who would clean up our city?"

Lola thumped her parasol on the floor. "Mayor Williams, if you would simply *close the gaming halls*, our city would be cleaner, thereby reducing the need for either society, *and* the fines that supposedly fund them."

Seeing she would not be swayed, he changed tactics. "Of course we will close the gaming halls before the fair opens. But meanwhile, why not benefit from them? Nothing illegal about it, merely a business tax. Your husband pays taxes on his store, does he not?"

Lola ignored the insinuation, focusing instead on the mayor's earlier comment. "Nothing illegal about the fines? Is that your position?"

"Of course."

"Then why ask Hunt to stop sending a uniformed officer to collect them? If everything is aboveboard, why ask some poor private citizen to be your lackey?"

His jaw snapped shut, and he glared at her.

Unperturbed, she continued. "Whoever is now collecting the money may not be breaking the law. But none of this is aboveboard. You were to close the gaming halls this week, yet you did not. Consequently, we continue to attract the wrong people to Portland. Corruption and crime start at the top." She removed the *Journal* from his desk and replaced it with *The Portland Gazette*. "Have you seen today's headline?"

He had the grace to look abashed. "Of course. That poor girl." He withdrew a handkerchief from his pocket and wiped his brow, before folding the material carefully and tucking it away again. "I have authorized Chief Hunt to use every available resource to solve these crimes. He expects a resolution any day."

Lola kept her mouth shut lest she say something regrettable. Once certain that dignity could be maintained, she said, "And did you note where she was found? At Erickson's—an establishment that was raided for Twenty-One in April, but has remained open since."

"It was Faro," Williams said, as if that made a difference.

"I don't care what it was." She rose to her full height and put the weight of her past upbringing and current position in Portland Society behind her words. "Portland *will* close to gaming, and if you and Chief Hunt are unwilling to fulfill the obligations of your respective offices… Well, we shall see how long you retain them."

"Do you threaten me?" He also rose, putting her back at a disadvantage. "I, who have been a firm supporter of

Women's Suffrage? How dare you!"

"I am not threatening you," she said icily. "But I will not be cowed, nor will I be placated by empty words. The people will know the truth of your character soon enough. Oh, I believe you support women's rights, as far as that goes. I am certain *your wife* appreciates your efforts. Shall we say, what is good for the goose is good for the gander?"

She took satisfaction in watching his complexion go from angry red to ash white. He opened his mouth but found no intelligible outlet for his spluttering rage.

Lola nodded agreeably. "When they elected you, the voters chose to ignore your dismissal from the position of U.S. Attorney General. Accepting bribes is a nasty business. But that occurred far from here, and many years ago. And technically, it was your wife who took the bribe. Thirty thousand dollars, wasn't it? But now Portland will *not* ignore your repeated failure to perform the duties of the office to which you were elected."

Williams regarded her thoughtfully, then leaned across the desk. "You are new to Portland and perhaps not acquainted with how we do business. Speaking of which, how is your husband's store coming along? We were so pleased to welcome E.P. Charlton's five-and-dime stores to our town. I trust Mr. Baldwin found it easy to navigate the process, and that he will continue to make the *right* connections, for his future endeavors."

There was no mistaking the threat in *his* words.

She smiled serenely, hooking her parasol over her arm. "He has been most pleased with his reception. But he will not be intimidated any more than I. And it may surprise you to learn that the *connections* we have made fully support Portland closing to both gaming *and* liquor.

Whether you and Chief Hunt do remains to be seen. Good day, Mayor Williams."

Back straight and chin up, she marched from his office, past his startled secretary, and down the stairs. Once outside, she crossed Madison and walked a few yards up Fourth, before resting the tip of her parasol on the wooden sidewalk and leaning heavily on the handle.

"Insufferable man!" she said under her breath.

She needn't have bothered lowering her voice, as the Southern Pacific Railway's Fourth Avenue Westside Line chose that moment to thunder by, spewing smoke and clattering so loudly, she could barely hear herself think, let alone speak. She considered venting her feelings further under cover of the train, but in truth, the visit with Williams had gone just as expected.

He had admitted to, committed to, and resolved nothing. In fact, he gave every indication he was satisfied with the status quo. Whoever had been appointed as the new "fines" collector must be performing well. Perhaps if she could discover who this man was, she could use that to pressure the mayor and Chief Hunt.

Sudden tiredness overtook her. Forty-four was not so old—she was not even a grandmother yet. But when, like today, the work of cleansing the city stretched before her in an unending parade of battles with men like the mayor, she almost wished she could sit at home and knit or read a book. But she could not, and the work never ended.

Once it did, descent to the grave began, and she was not ready for *that* yet.

The caboose jolted by, revealing the figure of a tall man with auburn hair jogging across the tracks from the other side of the street.

And just like that, Lola's spirits lifted. *Precisely what*

I need—an emissary to aid in my quest!

She straightened her hat and jacket, secured her parasol on her arm, then hurried to meet him as he reached the sidewalk.

"Mr. Jacobs, I am so very glad to find you here."

"Mrs. Baldwin."

He doffed his hat and bowed, and when he straightened, his smile was pleasant. But she also detected an underlying urgency, as though he were expected elsewhere. He wore a new suit, although it was somewhat wrinkled, and at least a day's stubble glinted red on his jaw. Interesting. Whatever his business, it merited his Sunday best, but not the time to shave.

He fell into step with her and, replacing his hat, asked politely, "How may I help you?"

His keen gaze took in each pedestrian and vehicle, the residences lining the street, even the crows wheeling across the sky. And yet he also maintained the appearance that his focus was on her. Yes, he was just the man for the job. He missed nothing, was conscientious—the unanimous opinion of the lumber- and shipyard bosses she had quizzed—and possessed a not-so-secret soft spot for the underserved.

"Do you recall the favor I said I might ask of you?"

"Of course. Anything I can help with, consider it done. Do you need something delivered? Or removed? Or does your husband need help at the new Charlton's?"

Evidently, he had done his research as well. Good. Providence was looking out for her when it threw Mr. Jacobs into her path today.

"Nothing like that. I have just been to City Hall, to the mayor's office."

"Oh?" His tone and gaze sharpened, but he only

waited for her to continue, slowing his stride unobtrusively when he saw she was jogging to keep up.

"As I'm sure you know, the Municipal League and the Traveler's Aid Society both have an interest in seeing the local gaming houses closed, if not the saloons as well, before the exposition next year. It is the *right* thing to do. Gaming brings all sorts of evils, and to have it openly approved by both Mayor Williams and Chief Hunt—"

All at once she realized they had stopped altogether, and Mr. Jacobs was staring down at her in some consternation, no doubt surprised by her uncharacteristic outburst. She drew a steadying breath and continued up the sidewalk. "Forgive me."

"No matter. Please go on. What may I do for you, that has to do with the mayor and chief of police?"

Though his tone was polite, she sensed his tension. Perhaps to do with the errand she had interrupted? She had best hurry this along and let him go on his way.

"Perhaps you are aware of the so-called 'fines' the police have been collecting from the gambling clubs?"

He inhaled sharply, choking on the clouds of dust rising from the street, and had to clear his throat before speaking. "I'm…aware of the practice."

"Until recently, they were so flagrant that a *uniformed* officer collected the monies. But public opinion has swayed against them, forcing them to find some other lackey to do their dirty work. A regular citizen, duped into abetting them, the poor fool."

Mr. Jacobs stared studiously ahead, but his cheeks reddened. "Mrs. Baldwin, I'm very sorry, but I am late for a prior engagement. If you could let me know what it is you need?"

"Of course. I beg your pardon. The gist is that I need

to discover the identity of the new collections man."

Abruptly, he stumbled on a loose board in the sidewalk, righted himself, walked another few paces, and stopped. "You…what now?"

She stopped also and craned her neck to meet his gaze, for he was nearly as tall as Mayor Williams. "I need to know who their new errand boy is, and how they have coerced him. And I need him on my side, to testify when charges are brought against them."

Mr. Jacobs seemed to be fighting for control over some strong emotion. At last, he said in a strangled tone, "And you think *I* can help you find…whoever he is, this—what did you call him? This *foolish lackey*?"

"Mr. Jacobs. You are a man who gets things done. You are well-liked amongst the lumber bosses and at the docks. Yes, I checked up on you after you approached me at Mrs. Smith's. I do not grant favors lightly. But you are known to be an honest hard worker, and people trust you. Mrs. Grey certainly does, and so do I."

His expression went from surprise to embarrassment, and then to completely shuttered. That last occurred at the mention of Mrs. Grey. *Very* interesting.

He said, "You believe criminal charges will be brought? Against the mayor, the chief, and their accomplices?"

"It is only a matter of time. I will be paying a visit to the district attorney, but I am certain he is already aware of the situation and is working toward that same end."

Mr. Jacobs glanced around. "Mrs. Baldwin, I swore I'd help you, and I mean to abide by that. But I am very late. May I consider it? I will need to—to form a plan, to determine how to uncover the information you require."

"Of course." She smiled in satisfaction. He was

exactly who she'd thought him to be: a good man, conscientious to a fault. "Thank you for your time. I will keep you no further."

He started to leave, then paused. "There is something that might aid in my search. Can I assure the, ah, lackey in question that if he testifies, he may be granted immunity?"

"That is for the district attorney to decide. But if this man was foolish enough to be tricked into such abhorrent behavior, shouldn't he suffer the consequences?"

"Yes. I suppose someone that dumb deserves what he gets. Good day, Mrs. Baldwin."

He tipped his hat, and she bent her head in acknowledgment. "Good day, Mr. Jacobs."

She watched as he strode up the block. *Just the man for the job. I was correct in my assessment. A truly upstanding citizen, and one who will no doubt become an asset to our cause.*

Satisfied that the wheels of justice would soon be set in motion, with the aid of Lucky Jacobs and others like him, she continued up Fourth Avenue toward Charlton's. The morning's errand had taken longer than expected, and LeGrand would be awaiting her arrival at the store. He was also a good man, who wouldn't be cowed by the mayor or anyone else, and would support her unequivocally in her quest to clean up the city.

Beginning with the "dirty" mayor and chief of police, and whoever was with them. They had better watch out because Lola Baldwin was on a mission, and when she set her mind on something, she got it.

Always.

Chapter Twenty

After Lucky left, Solace rose from the sofa, made a cold lunch for Allen—she couldn't imagine eating anything herself—and puttered around the house with no real idea of what she did, until Allen grew tired and went to take a nap. She heard the bed creak under his weight—they really must tighten the springs—and waited until he stilled and the house was quiet. Then she walked to her chair in the living room and sat carefully down.

She neither cried nor shook. She did nothing. She only stared at the familiar-yet-suddenly-alien comforts of home. The place where she should feel safest, but which now felt *wrong*.

When had her life become so foreign? Growing up, moving around as her father pursued his photographic endeavors, she had made friends easily enough wherever they went. But they never stayed more than a year or two in any one place, and after exchanging a few letters, her "bosom bows" drifted away like seeds on the wind to plant new friendships elsewhere.

By the time her father had died and she'd met Allen, she was ready to settle down and start a family. But then Allen's career had become as unstable as her father's, largely due to his changing health. True, their tenures in each location were longer than those of her childhood, but that only made it more difficult to leave.

Eventually, she had stopped trying to make friends, and her world had shrunk to Allen, herself, and their little home. Now, the truth could no longer be ignored: She was alone.

Of course, the sisters at the school and Father Henderson would be compassionate, and even provide real, practical aid, should she ask for it. But she could never, ever discuss her situation with them, for they would either think Allen a ruthless, calculating killer, or that he belonged in an insane asylum, not in charge of young children. There was no middle path, unless Solace could prove his behavior stemmed from physical illness rather than mental frailty.

Besides, she hardly knew the sisters or the priest. Allen had worked with them in preparation for the school year, but Solace had not. And though she had spoken with Father Henderson about her linguistic interests, that hardly constituted a lasting camaraderie.

Then there was Adina, who seemed genuinely interested in pursuing a friendship. But a half hour's pleasant chatting did not invite return confidences about Allen's potential as a brutal killer, or Solace's sinking despair at his description of that poor woman's corpse.

And… That was it, the sum total of their social circle. They had befriended no other St. Mary's parishioners, and beyond a few tradesmen—and Lola Baldwin—had met no one else.

Except Lucky Jacobs.

Lucky was… Well, she couldn't put into words *what* he was. To her alone, or to her and Allen together. But the house felt…empty…now he'd gone. Small and colorless, like her father's photographs. Life made thin, flat, and gray.

Why had he helped them? Out of charity? Or…something more? Did she want to know?

At the back of the house, Allen stirred. The bed creaked and then the floorboards.

She stood. No, she did not want to know. She was grateful for Lucky's aid, nothing more. She called toward the bedroom, "That was a short rest. Are you feeling better?"

The only response was the squeak of Allen's sock drawer as he pulled it open. She really must remember to fix it for him. "I'll put the kettle on for tea, then."

The house was silent, as though her voice had frozen Allen's movements.

Suppressing a shiver of unease, she moved through the arch into the hall, and from there toward the kitchen. It was such a tiny hallway; a few steps to the kitchen before her, another few to the bedrooms on the right, with a thick, muffling runner covering the whole of it. One moment she was moving, lost in thought, the next—

Allen slammed into her, knocking her head into the kitchen door molding. Pain split her skull and she bit her tongue, tasting blood, then he punched her in the back and she fell against the flower table in the hall, the glass vase shattering, splintering across the floorboards onto the runner.

"Allen…" she managed, but he yanked her head back and covered her mouth and nose with his palm.

"Who *are* you? What have you done with my wife? Where is Laura?"

She shook her head, hot tears streaking her cheeks. *Why, God? Why is he doing this?*

He dropped his hand, and she gasped in a quick, deep breath before he shoved her hard against the wall. For such a slight man, he was strong, and she had the sudden terrible realization that he *could* have stabbed or drowned all three of those poor women.

No! His illness makes him confused, and he's frightened. He is not *a killer*.

Then as her vision cleared, she saw the black rage twisting his face into a grotesque mask, nothing like the dear, sweet, scholarly man she had married.

"Allen! It's me—Solace. *I* am your wife. Remember? Please, we were married in Minnesota. Your mother came. It was right before she died."

It was the wrong thing to say. He'd started to look doubtful, but at mention of his mother's death, he snarled and grabbed her throat, lifting her up until her toes skimmed the floor. His breath was hot on her mouth, like an evil version of a lover's caress. *"Never speak of that good woman.* She is alive and well, and you are a demon's whore, come to deceive me!"

He was crushing her windpipe. She tried to kick him, but she had no leverage, and her skirts got in the way.

Just when she must pass out, never to wake again, something caught his attention and he let her go. She dropped like a ragdoll onto her side, cheek pressed into the carpet, sucking air through her nose and mouth, too stunned to attempt anything else. Allen stepped into the living room, and she knew she should force herself to rise and run for the door—go to the neighbors, or the church, as Allen himself had begged her to do.

Or to Lucky. He would know what to do.

But she couldn't, she could only breathe, the blessed oxygen filling her body, her lungs working overtime to restore functions her brain had been about to shut down.

Allen shuffled across the living room to the hall, and renewed panic got her up on hands and knees, crawling toward the door.

"Where do you think you're going?" He kicked her in the side, and she fell half onto the kitchen floor, the pain excruciating. She *couldn't* faint—she must stay alert and try to escape.

And then—he was gone. Just like that, out the front door, leaving it open behind him.

Solace lay still, breathing hard, unable to move or think. Her only certainty was that Allen had attacked her, viciously and without provocation. In the past, there was a clear build up to his rage, and she knew fear of his condition drove him more than anything else. There was also immediate regret, accompanied by an apology and obvious shame at his actions.

But this…

This was different in every way. He had not recognized her, had suspected her of harming his first wife, and had beaten her for it. *Beaten*, not simply hit.

She touched her side and winced. It was tender but likely not permanently damaged. Her throat was swollen and raw, and she couldn't speak yet—she could barely swallow and would have ugly bruises. But she was alive, which was all that mattered.

Suddenly there was the sound of feet on the steps outside. *He'd come back*—he'd gotten a shovel or an axe—*he would kill her*.

She twisted, desperation driving out the pain as she scrabbled across the slippery linoleum toward the pantry door leading to the side yard. She wouldn't make it—her palms were sweaty, they slid over the shiny, waxed floor, and she was still too weak to get any purchase with her full skirts tangled between her legs.

He paused at the open front door, the dry hinges creaking as he pushed it wide.

I will not die today! I will not *die!*

He stepped into the hall, shoes crunching on the broken glass from the vase. Then he paused again, as though listening to ascertain her location.

She'd reached the table and pulled herself up, then pushed off it, hurling herself toward the counter. Maybe she could push off from there to the door—*she was too late—he was coming—almost in the kitchen.* The utensil drawer—she yanked it open and grabbed the butcher knife, willing her grip to be firm, and then he was at the door, and she whirled to face him.

But it wasn't Allen. Lucky stood in the doorway, his face white with shock when he saw her. "*Solace!* What has happened? *What has Allen done to you?*"

And then he was crossing the room and she dropped the knife and stumbled forward to the protection of his arms as she sobbed out her fear and pain.

"Shh," he murmured and then lifted her up, hooking a chair with his foot and sitting on it, cradling her on his lap. "I'm here now—listen to me—*I won't let him hurt you again.*"

As he had earlier, he stroked her back and her hair, and she let him, feeling protected and…loved. No, it was mere kindness. But he rocked her gently, and he was so strong and felt so safe, that after she'd cried herself out, she rested her head on his chest and just breathed him in, his beard stubble tickling her forehead.

Noticing she had calmed, he shifted her to look into her face. He was so close that if he wasn't "just being kind," he might attempt to kiss her. She didn't know how she felt about that. She was too numb. She *shouldn't* want him to; Allen was her husband, for better or for worse. And she loved him—truly, she did. But today, he had betrayed his vows to "honor and cherish," and here in Lucky's arms, everything was different and not part of her ordinary life.

Extra-ordinary.

"Solace…," he breathed. And then he saw her neck, and his expression went black with fury. "*Good God*—did he do this to you? Did Allen do this?"

She shook her head, but it was no use. Who else could it be?

Lucky lifted her off his lap and pain shot through her side. She gasped and he immediately let go, making her stumble and grab the table for support.

"What is it? Where else did he hurt you?"

She couldn't think. Her head spun, and she leaned over, willing herself to stay conscious. Instantly he was at her side, taking her elbow and helping her to the chair.

"Sit," he ordered tersely. "Tell me everything."

"I…" She swallowed, gagging over the swelling in her throat, the motion making her lightheaded again. She shook her head to clear it, but he misunderstood.

"*Tell me*. Now."

He towered over her, fists clenched as though this kept him rooted to the spot. If he unclenched them, she didn't know *what* he would do, but it would be explosive.

"I'll tell you," she whispered hoarsely.

His face went white again, and he fell to his knees, cradling her neck in his big hands. "Your voice—"

She placed her hands on his. "I'm fine. No—listen—I *will be* fine."

It was so difficult to speak. Before she could ask, he was up and banging cupboards open until he found a glass, then filled it at the sink. He brought it to her, holding it to her lips until she forced down several swallows. It burned at first, then gradually eased her throat.

"Thank you."

He put the glass on the table and pulled a second chair out, straddling it, hands gripping the back like a barrier between them. His jaw was set, expression grim, his body taut as a bowstring. "I know Allen did this. That he…choked you, and—what—kicked you?"

"Yes. But he didn't mean it! He—he was confused. You've seen him—you know."

"If an automobile runs a man over, he is dead whether the driver meant it or not. Do you understand? Allen could have *killed* you. However much he may not intend to harm you, he *did*." His expression was like granite. "I told you of my father's job at the meat factory. But I left out how he drank away his paychecks and beat my mother. One day he came to work drunk, slipped in the blood on the floor in the grinding room, and…"

His voice trailed off, as though he saw that far away time, instead of Solace and the bright kitchen in which they sat. Then he refocused on her. "They didn't find enough pieces of him to bury. The point is, he was not a good man. If he hadn't been killed, he would have killed my mother. Or my sister. Or me."

"Allen's not like that!"

"They never are. My mother defended him until the day he died. Until the day *she* died. It's partly why I left and came out here. I couldn't stand the memories."

He rose and replaced his chair under the table, then watched her for a moment. "I won't let that happen to you. You have stood by him for how long? Ten years? No one can doubt your loyalty. But no one expects you to *die* for him. Not even the Church."

She shook her head, the tears rising. "No—please! He didn't mean it! He—he'll get better when school starts. He always does!"

Lucky turned away, and she leapt up, wincing with the pain.

"No! Don't hurt him! You must promise me you won't hurt him!"

He ignored her, moving toward the doorway, and she limped after him, clinging to his arm so that he had to stop and face her.

"Please! If you have any friendship for me, don't hurt my husband."

He stared her down, blue eyes inscrutable, and his voice held an edge she had never heard in it before. "It is precisely because I am your *friend* that I can't let him get away with this."

He started to pull away, and in desperation she grabbed his shirt.

"*No!* Don't you see? It's not just Allen."

Her voice broke. The tears ran, hot and fierce, down her cheeks—tears of fear—and of shame. She shook her head, holding his gaze, willing him to understand.

"I couldn't bear it if you hurt him, but not *only* because of him. God forgive me—I couldn't bear it if you hurt him and were sent to jail for it. I can't bear to lose...*you*."

Chapter Twenty-One

For a moment, Lucky couldn't understand what his brain told him his ears had heard. Solace stood before him, gripping his shirt so tightly, one of the buttons had popped off. Tears streamed down her cheeks, her hazel eyes locked with his as she begged for her husband's life.

Her son-of-a-*bitch*, prostitute-murdering, wife-beating husband, who Lucky would kill with his own hands and enjoy doing it, before he let the man *ever* lay a hand on Solace again. But just like his mother, Solace pleaded for the life of her rotten husband. The rage burned up from Lucky's gut, the need to kill roaring in his ears until Solace swam before his eyes.

And then she said something, a thing so unexpected, so wrenching in its intensity, that it was like cold water on an oil fire. It should have dampened the flames, but instead, it set off sparks of a different sort, unmatched in their heat and crackling power.

He grabbed her shoulders and shook her. Not to hurt her, but to make sure she was real and knew what she said. "Say it," he commanded. "Say it again!"

She gasped but nodded, shifting her grip so that their forearms were locked, as though they performed a bizarre dance, pulled close, yet held at arm's length.

"Please, I'm not free. But you—your…friendship— means everything to me. I—I need your help." She dropped her gaze, white cheeks turning pink. "I've already lost my husband, my parents. Please don't leave me. *I couldn't bear it…*"

This last was barely a whisper, and all the rage, the passion, the sparks crackling inside him warred with each other while he stood perfectly still, not releasing her, but not drawing her any closer. She, too, did not move, trusting him to do the right thing.

Good God, she *trusted* him, when half of him wanted to throw up her skirts and have at her like a rutting bull, and the other half still thought killing her husband would solve all their problems. And yet neither half was thinking objectively or in possession of all the facts.

Despite it all—despite *every* indication—he still couldn't put Allen Grey into the role of coldblooded killer. These were not crimes of passion. Ellie's death especially had required calculation and a precision of which Allen was incapable. The man couldn't tie his shoes. How could he kill Ellie, *freeze* her, then days later wrangle her corpse to the yard?

Forget how. The real question was *why*? It made no sense. But flaring up in anger and beating Solace *did* fit with Allen's confused and unpredictable condition.

With more self-control than he'd ever known, Lucky set her aside and moved to the sink. He twisted the faucet on and splashed cool water on his face, then drank great gulping handfuls of it until his head cleared. He shut off the tap and found Solace beside him, calmly offering a towel. He used it to dry his hands, then blew out a breath.

"I won't leave you," he said flatly, and she flinched. He hadn't meant to sound angry, but it was the best he could do under the circumstances. "However, I won't allow your husband to hurt you again either. Where is the nearest telephone?"

"There's one at the corner store, four blocks away."

He left the kitchen and headed for the back of the house, Solace following as he entered the bedroom, threw open the closet, and rummaged through it.

"What are you doing?"

"Where is your overnight case?"

"My… You can't be suggesting that—that we—"

"Of course not," he said impatiently, although he'd considered it. Fortunately for her, he had a roommate and a conscience, both of which seemed damned inconvenient at the moment. Besides, Sadie had strict rules about female visitors. He abandoned the closet and gazed around the room. "Or at any rate, not with me. But you can't stay here, and since you know no one in Portland, I've an idea where you can go."

"Where?" she asked cautiously, as though suspecting she wouldn't like his answer. Which she wouldn't.

"To Mrs. Baldwin."

"*What?* I couldn't! Why, she—and we—I can't have her knowing my business like this! It would be too awful!"

He bent to look under the bed. "Ah-ha!" He wrenched the overnight case out and threw it onto the coverlet, then went to the dresser and opened the top drawer. It held men's socks, and he shoved it closed—it had a terrible squeak—and tried the next one down.

Solace grabbed his arm and pulled him around to face her. "Stop that! I'm not going anywhere! What about Allen? He can't be left alone. He'll hurt himself!"

Lucky slammed a fist on the heavy dresser so hard it bounced. "*I don't give a damn what happens to Allen!*"

She jerked away, and he inhaled, then exhaled. "I'm sorry, but you must see that you aren't safe here. What's to prevent his returning to beat you again? Or…worse?"

Solace shook her head, but the flash of terror in her eyes said she feared this very thing. She sank onto the bed, hugging herself as though cold, despite the heat.

"If you tell Mrs. Baldwin, she will report it to the police. Allen will be arrested for insanity and sent to the asylum. He will *die* there—I will *not* kill my husband."

Past caring for her sensibilities, Lucky shouted, "*What if he comes home and kills you? Will your* death be better for your precious marriage than *his?*"

She rose from the bed, hazel eyes flashing. "Of course not! But I can't let Allen die, either! Are you listening to me? He's not out of his mind! He's unwell—there is something wrong with him. I don't know what it is, but it's not always there, and when he is himself again, he is the sweetest, gentlest man you could ever know."

She was no longer shouting, and there were tears on her cheeks, and something inside Lucky cracked. He wanted to reach for her, to comfort her, but the love she felt for her husband shone in her face, bathed in the light from the lowering sun that slanted through the window.

He scrubbed a hand over his eyes, breathing deeply until the fear and rage dissipated. "We'll tell Mrs. Baldwin…there is a problem with the house. The foundation. It isn't safe for you here, but Allen and I will fix it. That should buy us a few days."

"You—you'll be here? You'll…take care of him?" The hope in her eyes was unbearable.

"Yes," he managed. "He will come to no harm on my watch. Now, will you pack your case, or shall I rifle through your belongings and choose what I think best?"

She was silent a moment before saying hesitantly, "Must it be Mrs. Baldwin?"

"She is well-known and respected. She has

connections, not to mention a large home with rooms to spare. You won't be the first woman she has taken in."

He stared unseeing at the open drawer before him—it could have contained her unmentionables, for all he knew—while their conversation replayed in his mind.

She had admitted she cared for him. But only as a friend—she loved her husband. Yet even if she did not, Lucky would regret anything resembling adultery. She was not free; she would be Allen's wife until the day he died. Even were he arrested, they would still be married, and she'd be as far from Lucky's reach as she was today, though she stood a mere arm's length behind him.

Bitterly, he squeezed his eyes shut and clutched the hapless drawer to stop himself from hurling it through the window. He would get through this. If a friend was what she needed, that's what he would be. And the best way—the *only* way—to serve her, protect her, ensure her happiness, was to prove Allen's innocence, and help her to halt, cure, or hide his condition.

He heard the rustle of her skirts before she lightly touched his arm. He pulled away and moved to the door, the feel of her fingers burning through his coat. "I'll wait in the kitchen. If Allen comes home, stay here and let me handle him." He risked a glance at her.

She hesitated, eyes dark with emotion. Then she nodded. "I'll only be a moment."

He nodded also, then ducked out the door.

~:~:~

By the time Lucky saw Solace safely ensconced at the home of Mr. and Mrs. LeGrand Baldwin on East Ankeny, it was supper time. Solace had assembled her necessities quickly, and they had walked to the store to use the phone, so Lucky could apprise Mrs. Baldwin of his intent to drop one of his "strays" at her doorstep.

She'd seemed unsurprised, merely asking pointedly if he had decided to help with her "little problem." She wouldn't be more specific, as anyone could be listening on the party line. But he understood. And so he'd drawn a deep breath and consigned himself to Hell.

"Of course. I am at your disposal."

At this, she had said she would expect his "friend" shortly. He sensed her curiosity across the line, but here, too, she had not pressed for details, and they rang off.

Lucky hefted Solace's bag—heavier than it appeared, as it was filled with books—and they backtracked the two blocks to the streetcar stop on Morrison. Once they'd paid the fare and found seats, it was a slow ride downhill and across the bridge to East Portland. After the fourth stop in as many blocks, Lucky reflected it would have been faster to walk. But though she wouldn't admit it, Solace was in a lot of pain. And now he was, as well, though of a different sort.

At least if they'd walked, he would have been spared sitting, pressed against her, for the whole trip. The streetcar wasn't as bad as the wagon had been, but each time it ground to a halt, they bumped together, no matter how rigid he kept himself. Worse, the trouble wasn't even lust, although that was *some* of it. But more than that, he wanted to take her hand, rest her head against his shoulder, and assure her no harm would come to her. Yet due to the nature of their *friendship*, a single man and a married woman, he was denied even that.

And so her nearness, coupled with the forced inactivity when he would rather have been combing the streets for Allen, did nothing to improve his temper. Plus, he'd again forgotten the murders and the missing envelope, about which he still recalled nothing useful.

All things considered, he was glad to leave Solace in Mrs. Baldwin's hands. She'd answered his knock herself and, after a flash of surprise at the identity of his "friend," had ushered Solace inside, commiserating about the "poor quality of new homes these days." Through the doorway, Lucky saw warmth, and light, and two teenage boys running down the staircase, one close to twenty, the other a little younger: Mrs. Baldwin's sons.

She murmured something to Solace before handing her off to the two young men. Then she faced Lucky.

"Mr. Jacobs, a word. When you called, I wondered if this was the friend you had mentioned previously. But as it is clearly not, and another victim was found…?"

She was an intelligent woman who would not leap to conclusions, but her curiosity was natural. Lucky gave her a grim nod, and she gave him a sympathetic one back.

"I am sorry. It is worse when there is hope first." She straightened. "Mrs. Grey will be well cared for while you are fixing her…house."

He looked past her to Solace, who smiled tentatively at something the younger son had said, while the older one lifted her bag and exclaimed over its weight. The whole domestic scene only reminded Lucky of how far removed he was from anything like it. His home had never been one that welcomed a new friend and made that person one of its own. Hell, his family was barely familial to each other, let alone to anyone else.

He returned his gaze to Mrs. Baldwin and managed a terse, "Thanks."

She nodded as though understanding more than he wanted to reveal. Then she shut the door, closing him off from something he'd just discovered he wanted—nay, *needed*—for himself. But it was hopeless, because without a certain woman at his side, no life would be complete, no matter how covered in domestic trappings.

He turned his back on the Baldwins and ran down the steps toward Sixth Street. At least he could walk off his mood while searching for Allen. God knew where the man was. In truth, he had better stay hidden a while longer, because despite Lucky's promise to Solace, beating Allen to a pulp was still the best plan he could think of.

Since he had to go through downtown, he might as well start with the yard at Erickson's. If nothing else, he could inspect the site where Ellie's body was found.

It was still light out, and the walk west across the bridge restored his equanimity. At Second, he turned north toward Burnside. It was the most direct route, which he took unconsciously. But two blocks later, as he neared police headquarters, he regretted the choice.

You're a damn fool, and a terrible double-crosser. You can't feel simultaneously guilty about losing a bribe and *not telling Mrs. Baldwin the truth.*

Speaking of which, he should stop by the Gem. He could decide later what to do about the job itself. Quickly, he turned right on Oak, walked east toward the river one block, made another right onto First and, a few doors down, ducked into the Gem's dim interior.

It was early, but workmen already occupied half the tables and the bar, dining on bread and bowls of stew. The savory smells hit Lucky like a wall of comfort, and he realized he hadn't eaten all day. The bartender, an older, rotund man with a shiny pate, glanced up from the glass he was toweling and nodded pleasantly as Lucky pulled out a stool and sat, removing his hat. Whatever had happened, at least he hadn't alienated the staff.

The man set a tumbler before him. "What'll it be?"

"Just water tonight. And a bowl of beef stew if you've got any."

The bartender's eyebrows rose. "Water? Thought your tastes ran to harder stuff."

Lucky shrugged sheepishly. "I had a rough day yesterday and overdid it a little."

"If that was 'a little,' I'd hate to see you on a bender. Well, you're in luck. A man came in on Monday with a side of beef to sell in a hurry. Guess his ice box broke. Shame for him, but we've had meat all week, despite the shortage. But maybe the strike's over anyway, or so the papers say. Sure I can't interest you in another brandy sling to celebrate?"

"No, thanks."

"Suit yourself." He poured the water, then caught another patron's eye and moved away.

The man was only joking, but Lucky's stomach sank. What the hell had he done? He wasn't a prohibitionist, and even shared a beer now and then with the sawyers on his crew. But he disliked getting drunk and its aftereffects, and so he usually kept it to one drink.

Except yesterday, when he'd imbibed so much, he couldn't remember an entire night of his life. An occurrence eerily similar to what Allen experienced on a regular basis. Was it possible Allen *had* killed Ellie? Could Lucky commit murder with no memory of it?

No, he couldn't. But a bar brawl? His father's specter hovered nearby, leering maliciously: *Vaisiai nepatenka toli nuo medžio.* Fruit doesn't fall far from the tree.

Last night, Lucky had craved oblivion and a release for his pent-up energy. Most days, he could shove a tree into a giant saw to relieve his feelings. With Jones shut down, had his physical frustration exploded here instead?

He was nothing like his father—*nothing*. But…there was that blinding rage he'd felt at finding Solace, broken and hurt in her own home, after her husband tried to *kill* her.

The murder-lust surged, and he gripped the bar, shaking his head to clear the red from his vision. The waitress, arriving with his stew, set it down barely within reach before scurrying away like a frightened mouse.

Was he like his father? Allen had the excuse of being wrong in the head, or perhaps physically ill as Solace insisted. But if Lucky was violent, the blame lay solely on himself.

The bartender reappeared with a fat white envelope. "Figured you'd come back for this."

Some of the tension left Lucky's shoulders as he took it from the man. It was heavy for a place as small as the Gem, which possessed only a dozen slot machines.

The bartender caught his frown and said, "Owner also runs Fritz's. Payment in there's for both clubs—ten dollars each for fifty machines."

Lucky barely managed not to gape. *Five hundred dollars?* He'd had no idea the fines were so high. He shoved the envelope into his pocket. "Thanks."

The bartender started to leave, and Lucky motioned him back. "Wait. This may sound dumb, but…did I do anything last night that I should apologize for?"

The man didn't blink. "Nah. You drank a lot and gamed. But you asked me to hold that envelope for you, then forgot about it. You seem a good sort—hate to see you in trouble. Or me—don't want to get in the middle of anything. So, we square?"

Lucky nodded slowly. "Yes. Thank you."

The man resumed his duties, and Lucky wolfed down the stew. Then he paid, leaving a generous tip for both the bartender and the waitress to prove he *was* unlike his father. The belief that tipping created a "dependent servile class" fit neatly with Mykalos Jacobonis's own inclinations, which were to be a cheapskate.

I don't have to be like him. In this or anything else.

Fury at Solace's condition did not make him a bully. He put his hat back on and aimed for Erickson's.

The evening was warm, but the Willamette River, a block to the right, moderated the temperature. By the time he walked down First and turned left onto Burnside, then reached Erickson's, it was half-past seven, and a crowd spilled through the open doors.

The eight-story brick building was massive, taking up most of the block. The restaurant had good food and service, but it was out of Lucky's price range, which tended toward smaller places like the Gem. The saloon yard was also two blocks from Police Headquarters, so whoever had dumped Ellie's body here was either gutsy or stupid.

Or out of their mind.

Lucky shook his head. It might suit his own purposes if Allen were sent away, but it wouldn't serve Solace.

He walked the length of the building and turned right, following the saloon's wooden fence around onto Couch Street. A few yards down, he discovered the gate Allen had described, now padlocked in an attempt to secure the area and preserve any evidence.

He glanced up the street. Most of the traffic was a block south on Burnside, and none of the pedestrians walking by paid him any heed, so he pulled a pin from his hat band and reached for the lock. Some skills he'd acquired during his misspent youth still came in handy. He jimmied the pin until the tumblers released, then removed the lock and entered the yard. Another old trick—act like you're on the level and folks will think you are.

He shut the gate and looked around. It was as Allen had described: weedy, with an old trough and pump near a door in the saloon's wall. A depression in the tall, dead grass might be where Ellie had lain, but Lucky saw no bloodstains, supporting the theory that she had died elsewhere, and confirming Allen's memory of the blood on her body being dried, not fresh. The trough's grayed interior was littered with leaves, but the pump was functional and gushed rust-tainted water when he tried it. So Allen's cuffs could have been stained from that. He tried the saloon door, but it was locked, the hinges rusty.

Nothing he saw proved or disproved Allen's guilt or innocence. Lucky took one final look around, then returned to the gate and grabbed the handle, only to have it yanked open from the other side. He pitched forward, his knees slamming into the wooden sidewalk, his palms skidding across the rough planks. "What the—"

He twisted and squinted up—to find Detective Jenkins looming over him, grinning wolfishly.

"Jacobs—what the hell are you doing here?"

Chapter Twenty-Two

Jenkins bent and offered Lucky a gloved hand. Though not in uniform today, his plain clothes were, as usual, so crisply starched, he looked like he'd just stepped off an ironing board. For a man who had previously accepted the bribes for the chief, Jenkins was awfully buttoned up. Though not tall, he had a beefy physique, and he pulled Lucky up with ease, then waited as he dusted himself off.

"What are *you* doing here?" Lucky growled, then realized what a stupid question that was. "Sorry. I don't like falling on my face."

"And I don't like my evidence disturbed." Jenkins retrieved the steel padlock and inspected it for damage, then snapped it back onto the gate. "If your skills include lock-picking, I can see why Miller tapped you to collect the envelopes. You could just take the money from the cashbox, if necessary."

Lucky ignored the barb. "While we're on the subject—"

He reached into his pocket for the envelope from the Gem, but Jenkins made a negative motion with his hand.

"Not here. Hunt doesn't want officers seen accepting envelopes of any kind in public."

Lucky withdrew his hand. "What am I supposed to do with all this cash if I only deliver it once a week? It's not like I have a safe." Especially one that could hold contributions *this* big. Did Jenkins know the value of the bribes? Probably. Only Lucky was that naïve.

Jenkins shrugged as they moved up Couch toward Third. "Not my problem. Why are you poking around here, anyway? Think you can solve the murders—maybe impress a *lady* friend?"

Lucky glanced at him sharply. Had he connected Lucky to Solace? It wouldn't be difficult, after Lucky had quizzed Molly in front of Officer Peters, before driving the Greys home from the library. Even Mrs. Baldwin had "checked up on him," as she put it. Of course Jenkins would do as much for the new collections man.

"I don't know why I came. As I said, Ellie was a friend, and I'd like to help." It was the truth. He'd just omitted a few details, such as *why* he wanted to help.

Jenkins chewed his lip, staring ahead and giving the impression that he noticed nothing. Which was certainly an illusion. They reached Burnside, and Lucky paused. He needed a few things from Sadie's before heading to the Greys' home. Hopefully, Allen had found his way home already, because Lucky was out of ideas. The library had closed hours ago, as had the church offices, and where else would Allen go?

Regardless, it was better if Jenkins didn't tag along. The detective must know Lucky's address, as Peters had jotted it down in his notebook. It would be on record somewhere, as would that of the Greys. But something about Jenkins's attitude was disturbing, like a terrier seeking the best place to dig up a new bone.

"Where are you off to now?" the detective asked casually.

"Home," Lucky said truthfully.

"Oh? Early to bed, are you?"

"Lumber's an early business."

"Right. But it's still light out. Sure you don't want to stop somewhere for a...*drink?*"

Lucky gritted his teeth and wished once again that Portland wasn't such a small town. In fact, it was growing by leaps and bounds, but it still seemed everyone knew everyone else's business.

"Not tonight." He tipped his hat pointedly and walked away, pretty sure he heard Jenkins's malicious chuckles behind him. Whatever the detective was after, Lucky devoutly hoped he himself hadn't given it to him.

At Sadie's, he packed his toothbrush, shaving kit, and a change of clothes into a sack. He also grabbed his hunting knife, since he didn't own a gun, and a small supply of cash from the Bible. Hopefully, he would need neither, but it was best to be prepared. For what, he had no idea. But it seemed prudent to be armed in case Allen was still inclined to violence when he returned.

While he had the Bible out, he tried inserting the envelope from the Gem, but it was too big, so he reluctantly put it back in his coat. Five hundred dollars was too much to carry around, but he couldn't leave it here either. He'd deliver it to the station in the morning, Jenkins be damned.

As for tonight's planned pickups, well, they hinged on when or if he found Allen, and what happened after. He flexed his fists. No, he wasn't a bully. But he could throw a mean punch when necessary, and smashing a wife-beater's face seemed to qualify.

When he had everything tossed into his satchel, he went down to the kitchen to round out his supper. He told Sadie about the Greys' "foundation" issues, and that he had left Solace with the Baldwins, so he and Allen could get an early start on the morrow. To this pack of nonsense, Sadie raised her eyebrows, which he took to mean she understood full well why he'd taken responsibility for Allen Grey, and that it had nothing to do with *Allen* at all. He responded with a self-aware half-smile, then winked at Mary, hiding behind Sadie's skirts.

Next, he headed for the parlor to give Sam the same information. A Jones man was there and told him the creeks were finally clear, and the saw would be fixed soon, so business would resume on Monday. The news gave him a pang. Somehow, the time he'd spent helping Solace felt more real than his normal routine. When he resumed working ten- or twelve-hour days, six days a week, everything would change.

As it should. She has a husband who she'll stand by, no matter what. You may as well let her go now, instead of hanging onto nothing, for no good reason.

But only when she was safe.

On his way out, he made a final stop at the telephone in the hall and asked the switchboard operator to ring the Baldwins. One of the sons answered and assured him that Mrs. Grey had eaten supper and then gone upstairs to rest, and should he go get her? Lucky thanked him and said no, but if she asked, he was still searching for the source of the problem with the foundation.

"Yes, sir," the son—possibly the younger one—said and rang off.

Lucky shouldered his satchel and left the rooming house, heading down Fifth and turning onto Washington. He considered taking a serpentine route, going down Fifth to Salmon, and then doubling back up Sixth to Washington, then up a block to Seventh and down again, and so on, in hopes of spying Allen. But on balance, it made sense to determine if the man had made it home already, and if not, search outward from there. Surely Allen would have come to his senses and returned by now, assuming he remembered where he lived.

Lucky grunted in frustration. How could the man be so lucid one moment, and so…*not lucid* the next? Was Solace right, and this was a physical illness that might be treated, over which Allen had no control? Or was Allen mentally insane? If so, that alone made him a criminal according to the law, and he must be incarcerated even if he'd never committed a crime.

Either way, Lucky had sworn to Solace he would find Allen, so he examined any and all passersby, but saw no sign of his quarry. Fifteen minutes later, he arrived at Myrtlewood Lane and let himself in with the key Solace had given him, calling out, "Hello…?"

He had expected no answer and got none. The house felt empty, but he checked all four rooms to be sure, then stood in the hallway, wondering what to do next.

It was then he realized his mistake. Being here, in the center of the Grey home—*her* home—was to be enveloped by her. The house was peaceful and dark. He hadn't lit the lamps, but moonlight shone through the lace curtains and lent a soft glow to all it touched. Lucky breathed in the smells of flowers and lingering sunshine and *Solace*, then closed his eyes and gripped the nearest wall to stop the overwhelming *need* to be near her.

Knock it off, you bastard. Find Allen, prove he's innocent, and then—

He opened his eyes, seeing nothing around him.

Then…what?

Live out his days in the same town with her, knowing he could never have her? Find a nice substitute and settle down to live a lie? He shook his head. Was it really only a week since he'd delivered her mulch from Fisher's? A single fateful moment that changed his life forever.

Fisher's.

It was Friday. Earlier in the week he'd told them that, thanks to Jones's continued shutdown, he was available again this Saturday. Which was now tomorrow. But he'd also promised Solace he would look after Allen.

"Mush for brains," he muttered, then stilled, listening intently.

There it was again—the snap of a twig in the bushes beside the front steps, to accompany the rustling noise his subconscious had registered moments ago. Perhaps an animal—except Lucky's instincts said it wasn't.

Willing the floorboards not to creak, he tiptoed to the kitchen and leaned across the counter to peer through the sheer curtains, keeping hidden as much as possible.

At first, nothing appeared out of the ordinary. The moon was waxing, nearing its first quarter, but it was inordinately bright and almost at its zenith. The yard was bathed in silver-white light that altered depth and threw shapes and shadows into sharp contrast. A movement caught his eye, and he held his breath, watching as the figure of a man separated from the bushes directly in front of the window and moved to the walk, bending near the steps. If he turned a few degrees left and glanced up, he might see Lucky behind the curtains.

Lucky stayed absolutely still, heart thudding. Was it Allen? Probably not—the shape was too bulky. And why would Allen sneak around his own front yard?

Then again, logic played little role in Allen's "spells."

The man picked something up off the ground, but

Lucky couldn't see what it was. Then the man straightened as though startled, his head swiveling left and right, before he pivoted and ducked back into the shadowy bushes by the window.

But not before the moon bathed him in a sudden eerie light, giving Lucky one perfect view of his face, like a photograph taken with a bright, well-timed flash.

Then Detective Jenkins was gone from sight, snug against the wall of the house, and Lucky staggered back from the window, only to have a new movement catch his eye: Allen had returned at last. He opened the gate and strolled into the yard, just as though he hadn't viciously beaten his wife hours earlier.

Lucky curled his fingers into a fist, tense and poised. What should he do? Run out and smash Allen's face in? Besides having sworn to protect him, he was loath to alert Jenkins to his own presence. So far, it was doubtful Jenkins knew *how* involved he was with the Greys. The comment about a "lady" could have meant anything. But what was Jenkins up to, hiding in their yard? And had he been lurking there *before* Lucky arrived?

Allen came up the walk and began poking around the bushes on the far side of the steps, much as Jenkins had done on this side. Whatever they both searched for, Jenkins appeared to have already found it.

So what do I do now?

At any moment, Allen would give up on that side of the yard and move to this one. Surely even *he* couldn't miss the large police detective hiding in the bushes. In his unpredictable state, what would he do? And Jenkins. Was he aware of the incident with Molly? Was that why he'd come—to find proof that Allen's violence toward prostitutes was habitual?

Allen straightened and headed across the walk, and Lucky's decision was made for him. He raced to the hall and flung the door wide, bursting onto the porch and startling Allen just as he neared the second set of bushes.

"Allen! There you are! I've been waiting for you. We won't get much work done tonight, but if we rise early, we'll have it put to rights in no time."

"We will…?" Allen asked, clearly confused. Lucky only hoped Jenkins would be too worried about his own discovery to catch such nuances in Allen's tone.

"Yes. But don't bother poking around the foundation now. It's far too late. And I'm so glad you stopped by the boarding house. This is too big a job for one man."

"It…is?" Allen stood, rooted to the spot, so Lucky bounded down the steps and took his arm, pulling him onto the porch and into the house.

"Yes. I haven't been here long. Thank you for giving me your key while you phoned Mrs. Grey. I trust she is settled in for the night. When we get it all fixed up, you can call her tomorrow and tell her it's safe to return."

"Ah." Obviously, Allen was accustomed to covering up his forgetfulness. He removed his arm from Lucky's grasp, clearing his throat. "Yes, I see. Well, then. Perhaps we should call it a day?"

He lit one of the gaslights on the wall as Lucky shut the front door and glanced through the kitchen at the window. Nothing but black showed beyond the thin curtains, and he suppressed a ripple of unease. What had Jenkins found? And how had he known it would be here, of all places?

Lucky steered Allen down the hall, away from the kitchen. "Yes. A good night's sleep will be just the thing." He hesitated. "Do you know who I am?"

Allen met his gaze guilelessly. "Are you a friend of my wife's?"

"Something like that. Lucky Jacobs, from St. Mary's. About your wife—do you recall when you saw her last?"

He searched Allen's face for any sign of remembrance or knowledge of his actions, but the man only smiled.

"This morning, of course. I made coffee. She was so pleased. Shall I make some for you now? I know how—it's no trouble."

Lucky's heart sank. Despite his promise to Solace, he'd wanted to thrash Allen, to make him pay for each and every bruise he'd given his wife. But if she was right, and Allen had no understanding of or control over his actions, then Lucky couldn't punish him. It would be like punching a baby for spilling its milk.

"No, thank you. Perhaps in the morning."

Allen nodded and stepped toward the bedroom, then hesitated. "Did…Solace—my wife—did she tell you where to sleep?"

An unwanted wave of pity washed over Lucky. What would it be like to not recall your own wife's name? To wake up and not know where you were? It must be terrifying in the extreme. And when a man was terrified, he often reacted not with flight, but with fight.

"Yes," Lucky said quietly. "I'll be on the sofa."

Allen beamed. "Wonderful! I hope you will be most comfortable."

"I'm sure I will." Then as Allen moved to leave, Lucky added, "Wait—if you don't mind my asking, what were you looking for outside?"

"My shoe."

"Your…shoe?"

"Yes. The left one. I threw it in the bushes this morning. At least, I think I did. I don't always remember things now." Allen's expression fell, then brightened again, like a child speeding from sorrow at a broken toy to excitement over a new treat. "But you can help me find it in the morning, can't you? I'll make the coffee, and you'll find my shoe!"

Lucky swallowed the lump in his throat. Allen *was* a child, albeit a very large one. What must Solace deal with every day in order to care for him? A pre-schooler's mind and needs inside the body of a full-grown man— her husband, who *should* care for *her*.

"Yes," Lucky said. "Everything will be fine in the morning."

Allen smiled again before disappearing into the bedroom, and Lucky turned down the lamp and went into the living room, hoping Jenkins had departed. Even so, he was in for a sleepless night. For if Jenkins and Allen *had* been searching for the same thing, then…

What in God's name did the detective want with Allen's shoe?

Chapter Twenty-Three

Saturday July 30

"INSANE PRISONER CREATES A PANIC –
Armed with a stick of stovewood and a flat
iron, McIntyre attempted to brain one
man, and it took seven prisoners and Deputy
Sheriff Davis to disarm him. He will be taken
to the Oregon Insane Asylum tonight." —*The
Oregon Daily Journal*

Lucky woke early the next morning to the smell of coffee brewing and bacon burning. Not *only* bacon—his eyes flew open and he sat up on the sofa. The room was gray in the pre-dawn light. Except the mantel clock said it was an hour *past* dawn, and the air drifted around him in a thick, lazy haze. In an instant, he was on his feet, running for the kitchen.

Oily black smoke billowed from it, while Allen stood at the stove, beating a grease fire with a linen towel. A coughing fit overtook him, and he staggered, dropping the towel onto the stove where it burst into flame, a vicious white heat amid the crackling grease.

Lucky grabbed Allen under the shoulders and pulled him through the hall and out to the front porch, still coughing. He released Allen, then sucked in a deep breath of air before running back into the house. Grabbing a heavy quilt off the sofa in the living room, he raced to the kitchen. The fire was still contained on the stove, thank God, the grease-soaked towel wicking the flames up and away from the wood counters or the floor.

Lucky half-unfolded the quilt and threw it over the entire stove, including the cast-iron skillet Allen had used to cook the bacon. Smoke and flames pushed out on either side as he slammed down on the heavy layers of batting. The heat seared his forearms, but he pounded mercilessly, smothering the oxygen underneath until the flames sucked in a last breath and died. Then he pulled the quilt and skillet off the stove, threw them on the floor, and doused them with bowls of water from the sink.

When the last lingering sparks sizzled out, he threw up the sashes on both the side and front windows, stretching across the counter to reach the cool, clear air outside. He gasped in great gulps of it while the smoke behind him wafted lazily toward these new exits, taking its time, but finally thinning and drifting away. Lucky's heart thundered, and his limbs shook with the effects of near disaster, but he pushed off the counter and went to check on Allen. The man sat where he'd been dumped, arms wrapped around his knees, rocking to and fro.

"I did a bad thing. I wanted to surprise Laura. She loves coffee and bacon, and I wanted to make it for her. But I forgot to put the lid on the pan. And now"—his eyes filled with tears and his body shook—"now I've ruined everything. Is…is she hurt?"

Lucky sat on the steps below him and drew in another blessed breath of fresh air, then blew it back out again. "Your wife is fine, Allen. She isn't home. Remember?"

The relief on Allen's face was pitiable; he'd genuinely been afraid he might have killed his wife. Whichever one he currently remembered.

Good God—what if Solace *had* been home and hadn't woken in time? What if that lazy, deadly smoke had found its way to her bedroom, soothing her into a deeper sleep, before stealing the breath from her forever?

The image of Solace, dead in her bed, thanks to the well-meant but incompetent efforts of her own husband, turned Lucky's blood to ice, and suddenly he was on his feet and retching into the bushes by the steps, his fear and the contents of his stomach coming out in equal measure. He was not a crying man, and it was a surprise when he scrubbed a hand over his face a moment later to find it wet with tears.

So close. It could have been her. So close…

He gave himself a shake, then looked up to find that Allen had come down the steps and was peering intently at the bushes.

"Did you find my shoe?"

"No," Lucky said shortly, and went inside to assess the damage.

~:~:~

Peters watched as Detective Jenkins hurried upstairs to the chief's office, looking around as though worried about prying eyes. That could only mean he had information about the murders. Peters glanced around also, then followed him up to the chief's slightly ajar door, pausing as Jenkins's muffled voice said, "…not Creffield," then something about "Jacobs."

All week, Peters had tried to fathom why the detective was so dismissive of his ideas about Jacobs being the killer, since the man admitted to a past relationship with the latest victim. Moreover, Peters had seen Jacobs in this very building at least twice after noticing him at the docks on Tuesday, *while* Jenkins was also there. An odd coincidence, to say the least.

Peters leaned in to push the door wide and enter, but Jenkins's next words stayed him.

"Jacobs most certainly may have killed the whore, Ellie. But I am not convinced he killed the other two victims, so I am still investigating Allen Grey. They're both likely suspects. I telegraphed the police in Chicago, where Jacobs hails from, and learned he was arrested a few times on minor charges, but never jailed."

Hunt grunted. "Didn't you check up on him before tapping him for the collections job?"

Peters jerked back. Collections? Surely the rumors weren't true that the chief was on the take? But if Peters understood correctly, then Jenkins was in on it too. His blood boiled, and he clenched his fists to stop from bursting into the office.

Jenkins responded, "I felt his criminal behavior could be an advantage, though I didn't initially think it extended to murder. But he's adept at picking locks, so if that Martin fellow gives us any trouble, Jacobs can break in and take the fines from the register."

"Lock-picking?" Hunt demanded. "How do you know that?"

"Caught him doing it at Erickson's yard yesterday."

"Erickson's? Why the hell haven't you arrested him then? He knew the whore, killed her, dumped her body, and returned to the scene. What more do you need?"

"It's only my theory, sir. We have no hard evidence."

"Well, go and get some, goddammit!"

"Yes, sir. I plan to look into Jacobs further. But I still feel Allen Grey is involved somehow. For one thing, they know each other. Maybe they're cohorts—maybe Grey committed the first two killings, Jacobs the third.

May I have permission to investigate them both?”

“Yes. Just get me one or both of them. I don’t care which, so long as someone’s in jail!”

“Yes, sir. I have a lead to pursue on Grey that can’t wait, and then I’ll look into Jacobs.”

“Good. Keep this up, and you’ll get that promotion within the month.”

Peters felt the words like a physical blow. Hunt planned to promote *Jenkins*, when the chief *knew* Peters had been first to propose Jacobs as a suspect?

Footsteps approached the door, and Peters quickly went around the corner, waiting out of sight until he heard Jenkins move down the stairs, whistling tunelessly. If the detective wanted to waste time on Allen Grey, let him. Peters went downstairs to retrieve his helmet, then headed out into the heat. First, he’d see what Jenkins might have missed at Erickson’s, and then he’d visit Jacobs’s boarding house.

If evidence was what Hunt wanted, Peters would find some, if he had to overturn every stone or look under every blade of grass in Portland.

Then they’d all see who earned a promotion first.

“Allen,” Lucky said for what seemed like the hundredth time as he guided the wagon off of Sixth Avenue onto Flanders. “I can’t leave you at the library. You’re helping me with my deliveries—it’s your job for the day. It has been, *all* day.”

“It has?”

“Yes.” Lucky pulled up under a shady maple in front of the address he’d been given for the next delivery, an ice box fresh off the train from Wisconsin. It was a special order, and Mr. Fisher-the-Elder had said it was anxiously awaited.

"When did I start?"

"Today. A few hours ago. Don't you remember?" Too late, he realized the asininity of the question, but Allen didn't notice. Lucky set the brake and jumped off the bench, aiming for the back of the wagon.

Allen followed more slowly. "Am I not a teacher?"

Lucky pressed his lips together, knowing he would still sound curt, and wondered how the hell Solace maintained her patience and serenity while caring for a nearly six-foot-tall child.

"When school starts, you'll be a teacher again. But today you're helping me. Because…" He fumbled for an excuse, then realized the answer lay right in front of him. "Because I can't lift the heavier deliveries by myself."

The ice box was four feet tall by two and a half wide, and at least eighteen inches deep. Made of oak with brass hinges and lined with zinc, it had a removable drip tray below the double front compartments. Considering the modest dwelling before them, it was a wonder the customer could afford it. Sadie had need of a modern ice box if anyone did, but even with a full house of boarders, she could only afford a much smaller one made of cheap pine and lined with tin.

Allen's face cleared. "Of course. How silly of me. I'll be glad to help you today."

"Thanks," Lucky said drily, since Allen had already been "helping" for the better part of four hours. But his tone was lost on the man, who now threw himself into the role of delivery assistant with enthusiasm, as if it was a new and exciting adventure he had chosen for himself.

You're a fool, Lucky told himself. *Solace does this week in and week out. You can make it through one damn day*.

"Wait here," he told Allen, then mounted the porch and knocked on the door.

Mr. Fisher had said the customer had requested Saturday delivery, presumably to be present for the ice box's arrival. However, the door opened on a young, bird-like woman wearing a ruffled white shirtwaist and light blue skirts, who squinted nearsightedly up at Lucky.

"Yes?"

"Good afternoon, ma'am. I'm from Fisher's. I believe you are expecting an ice box?"

"Oh, thank goodness." She had a high, breathless voice and a nervous manner that made her appear constantly on the verge of giggling. "We have been without an ice box for *days*—all week, in fact! Walter had to take everything out and put it in the Howards' new meat freezer."

"Oh?" Lucky asked politely, listening with one ear as he checked on Allen by the wagon. Surely the man could stay put for a minute. But after the fire, caution was the better part of valor.

The woman prattled on. "Mr. Howard—he's the butcher—told us of the packing strike last week, so Walter bought all this meat, and then the ice box broke on Monday. But the Howards' brand-new electric freezer was empty, also because of the strike, and it's so close by, in the new space they are expanding into, and right on the way to the police station, so what could be more convenient?"

Lucky brought his attention back to her. She was pretty in a childish sort of way, with light brown hair in ringlets and bright blue eyes in a cherubic face.

"The police station?"

"Yes. Walter is a police officer. Or a detective, I should say. Detective Jenkins. I am Mrs. Jenkins." She blushed and tittered nervously.

Lucky stared. So this was the woman brave enough to marry the stoic Jenkins. Hardly a woman—no more than twenty, and in every way the opposite of her husband. Where he was stocky and dour, she was small-boned with the guilelessness of a schoolgirl.

"The name's Jacobs," Lucky said, tipping his hat, then moved back down the walk toward the wagon.

She followed, still chattering. "Anyway, Walter took all our meat to the Howards' freezer Monday morning, but now he will be so pleased that the ice box is here, and the strike is over—or never begun—or something. But we haven't had meat for dinner all week, though I offered to go to Howard's and retrieve some of ours."

"Oh?" Lucky climbed into the wagon bed to wrangle the ice box closer to the edge.

"Yes, but Walter wouldn't hear of it. He won't let me put out the slightest effort. I have a delicate constitution, you see, and my father made sure he—Walter—knew it."

"Oh?" Lucky said again.

Her eyes were bright enough, her cheeks pink, but she was tiny and had yet to mature into womanhood. Not like… Well, not like some women he knew, who exhibited a quiet strength he found far more appealing than this little thing with her incessant chirping.

He motioned Allen closer to the wagon and explained how he should support the ice box on that side as they lowered it to the ground. It took some doing, and a lot of patient instruction in proper lifting techniques, but eventually they got it into the street, up the walk, and through the house to the kitchen at the back.

"Please put it there," Mrs. Jenkins said, indicating a spot near the back door with a hole in the wall, where the ice could be replaced from the back porch. "Of course, the ice compartment doors won't line up, but Walter can fix that. It's so nice to have a husband who can fix things. My father wanted me to marry an intellectual, but I fell in love with Walter instead."

Lucky hid a smile, wondering if Jenkins would view this as a compliment. Probably not; he seemed to enjoy feeling smart and superior as much as the next man. Possibly more.

When the new appliance was in place and Lucky had added a block of ice to it, Mrs. Jenkins said, "Walter takes care of all our bills. Did he—have you—are you expecting payment today?"

Lucky smiled reassuringly. "Fisher's will send a bill, and your husband can pay it."

"Thank goodness! I wouldn't know where to find our checkbook. Or perhaps you would need cash. Which is not a problem—we have plenty of money. My father gave me quite the dowry, insisting I continue in the style in which I was raised, despite Walter being so poor."

Lucky began to feel sorry for the—apparently literally—poor detective. Perhaps he was close-mouthed as a defense against his wife's verbosity, and his correct appearance and ambition stemmed from the fact that he was not as wealthy, nor as smart, as her father wished.

"But here I go again!" she said now. "I really must learn to hold my tongue. I am so sorry for keeping you. Have you many more deliveries to make today?"

"None. You are the last."

"Oh! But that is wonderful!"

He stared at her in confusion, and she blushed and

giggled again.

"Oh dear, that did sound funny. But I was only thinking that perhaps you could drive me to Howard's and back? I am sure Walter would pay extra for it, and then I can surprise him by bringing our meat home and having it all stored away before he gets here."

In truth, Lucky had hoped to finish early so he could check on…whatever needed checking on. The morning spent caring for Allen and making deliveries had driven all else from his mind, and he had no plan. On Monday, he would resume work for Jones, no closer to solving Ellie's murder or uncovering Allen's role in it, nor to discovering how to appease Mrs. Baldwin while fulfilling his obligation to Miller. Or to Chief Hunt—or whoever *his* boss was.

But gazing down at the expectant Mrs. Jenkins, he found he couldn't refuse. "Happy to oblige."

"Oh, thank you! Let me get the key to the freezer. I'll only be a moment."

In the end, it took several "moments" to locate the key, for it was missing from its hook by the door. Mrs. Jenkins talked nonstop as she hunted for it, before finally locating it in a pair of her husband's pants, lying forgotten on her mending pile. "Of course, Walter should not have been gardening in *these* pants, even if they are dirt-brown already, and now they're torn. But gardening is his passion, and I couldn't scold him for it, nor for wearing his police gloves while weeding, though he did get something awful on them. Or perhaps he was emptying the mousetraps. Whatever it was, the smell was just *terrible*."

Lucky forbore to respond, and sometime later, he pulled the wagon up in front of Howard's Meat Market.

He helped Mrs. Jenkins off the bench, while Allen scrambled from the now-empty wagon bed, and then she led them through a side door into the new, second shop space, which was still under construction.

The room was bare except for an enormous structure that must be the famed electrical freezer. It took up most of one corner, with a pile of lumber in another. In the wall opposite the entrance, a partially finished door had been framed, providing access to the main shop. The sounds of commerce drifted through it, an odd counterpoint to the dusty quiet of the annex.

Mrs. Jenkins said, "You both have been so helpful! Mrs. Howard will be glad to have her freezer back. I can only imagine how much meat will be coming in soon!"

She went to the freezer, which was nine feet tall by ten feet wide, and made of polished wood. The front had three main sections, including two glass-paned half-doors on top, with three carved wood doors below. These were chained together, but the unit's side wall held a full-height door with a tumbler lock, into which Mrs. Jenkins inserted the key and twisted it.

"There is not much to remove. Just a side of beef and some chicken, and—oh!—a leg of lamb. Or was it pork? No, definitely lamb, for the only pork we had was a side of bacon. Now, it should all be just…" Her voice trailed off, and she stared blankly at the freezer's interior.

Coming up behind her, Lucky saw that, due to its insulated walls and the cooling unit at the back, this cavity was four feet square by six feet tall. Cold air wafted from it, despite the day's heat, and he shivered. Wood shelves lined one side, while rods suspended from the ceiling sported huge meat hooks, large enough to store several sides of beef, or whole pigs or lambs.

However, at the moment, it was entirely empty.

He frowned. Had someone stolen the Jenkins's meat? But…why?

"I don't understand," Mrs. Jenkins said. "Did Walter…? But no, he couldn't have, for where would he put it? You only delivered the ice box today!"

She hurried to the main shop, and Lucky had no choice but to follow, Allen trailing behind like an obedient dog. Both Howards were with customers, their plump, genial faces focused on the job at hand, not the small angry personage who had just invaded their shop.

Mrs. Jenkins paused dramatically, then cried out, *"What have you done with our meat?"*

The Howards and their customers gaped at her.

Mrs. Howard recovered first, murmuring apologetically to the woman across from her at the counter, before stepping around it to usher their odd trio back to the annex. "Now, now, dear," she said to Mrs. Jenkins, "what nonsense! Of course we haven't moved your meat. Why, you have had the only key this whole time, for Hiram misplaced the spare."

Mrs. Jenkins glared at her. "We had a whole side of beef. Where has it gone?"

"I am sure you have only got the wrong compartment. Mr. Jenkins always says you are too flighty by half. Perhaps he is right after all!" She wiped her hands on her full-length white apron, then bustled to the freezer's side door, flinging it wide. "There, you see—or—oh my…"

In a perfect imitation of Mrs. Jenkins's own response to the vacant freezer, she stared blankly, then peered through the glass front doors at those shallow, also meatless compartments.

"I don't understand." She called loudly into the store, "Mr. Howard! Hiram! Do come in here!"

Her husband came to the door, alarmed. "Whatever is the matter? I am with customers!"

Just then Lucky became aware of a commotion outside. Or in the next room? Loud voices, the sound of many feet—it *was* in the shop, but it was *also* outside. The hairs on the back of his neck prickled as he stared at the large, empty contraption before him. A *brand-new* freezer whose shiny tin floor, he now saw, had a rust-colored liquid dried on it in places.

Everything receded, and he moved in slow-motion, as if in a dream. Allen looked confused as hands shoved him aside. Mrs. Jenkins's face lit with a smile of recognition, which became uncertain as Officer Peters rushed in, followed by several uniformed cops. The Howards glanced from these to a second group of officers entering from the shop, and then at each other.

Peters shouted, "Stand back and make no sudden moves! I have an arrest warrant!"

"Allen Grey is innocent!" Lucky heard himself say, which was the right response, but to the wrong question. He knew it, and yet his brain could not correct his speech in time. For of course it was not *Allen* who'd admitted to a relationship with Ellie, nor he who had been nosing around, asking troublesome questions.

Lucky said, "This isn't right. I didn't kill her."

Peters shrugged. "The evidence tells a different story. Take him in."

Chapter Twenty-Four

When Solace woke on Saturday morning in one of the Baldwins' guest bedrooms, her side ached and every muscle in her body was sore, as if she'd been put through a wringer. Her throat was the worst—raw, like she'd swallowed knives, and tender on the outside.

She rolled carefully onto her undamaged side and sat up. A hand mirror lay on the bedside table, and in the light leaking through the curtained windows, she could just make out her reflection. Aside from the circles under her eyes and a puffiness to her lower lip, her face looked relatively normal. There was a cut on her brow from Allen knocking her head into the doorframe, but it was not very noticeable, and could be covered by her hair.

Her neck was another matter. The bruises which had begun forming yesterday were now purple, and looked exactly like what they were: handprints left behind when her husband of ten years had choked her. She angled the mirror, but there was no denying it. Anyone seeing them would know exactly what had happened to her.

A suspicious hot dampness threatened her eyes, and she fought it down. *Don't be ridiculous. Crying will change nothing, and you have no time for it.*

She planted her feet on the thick rug and stood, reaching for her overnight bag, which sat on a silk-upholstered chair nearby. She chose a blouse with the highest possible neck, but the boning poked her bruises and made her gag. She clawed it off and flung it on the bed, then flung herself down after it, heart hammering, her whole body shaking.

Stop it! This is not you. You are strong, and you will *get through this.*

But not by cringing on the bed. She forced herself up, scowling at the blouse. Then she retrieved her nail scissors from her bag and carefully cut out the boning. When she buttoned the neck again, it was not as fashionable, but it was also less stiff, covering the bruises while allowing her to breathe.

Satisfied that this was the best she could do, she finished dressing and fixed her hair, then went downstairs. The hall clock said it was nearly nine, but she heard voices through the closed dining room door. No point delaying.

She twisted the handle, opened the door, and—

The maelstrom crashed to a halt. Three heads swiveled and three pairs of eyes peered at her curiously, while the fourth, belonging to Mrs. Baldwin, regarded her *in*curiously, then indicated the empty place next to her. The older son—Pierre?—leapt up to pull out the chair and push it in as she sat, before reclaiming his own seat. Mr. Baldwin nodded at her over the *Oregonian*'s top edge, then resumed reading it, and the younger son— Myron?—stared open-mouthed, until Pierre kicked him under the table and he went back to wolfing down his breakfast.

"Good morning," Mrs. Baldwin said. "I trust you slept well?"

"Yes, thank you."

Solace fought the urge to tug her collar or touch the scab on her forehead, while the heat rose in her cheeks. *Mrs. Baldwin knows—they all do. Lucky said I am not their first woman guest needing temporary housing, so they must all know* why *I am here.*

It was too humiliating, having her private business known by total strangers, and by Mrs. Baldwin in particular. And yet…

LeGrand Baldwin, a pleasant-faced man nearing fifty, with neatly trimmed dark hair and graying sideburns, kept reading, fully absorbed in the paper's contents. Much like the night before when he had greeted her politely, then made no comment when she excused herself early for bed. His two sons continued eating as though this were both their first meal in days and the last one they would ever get, pausing between bites to argue vigorously before shoveling more food in. And while Mrs. Baldwin *had* looked at Solace, her gaze held neither pity nor censure.

So perhaps they all knew and…didn't care. Or rather, they *cared*, but did not *judge*.

Solace felt her shoulders relax, and suddenly, she was starving. The double doors on the far side of the room swung open, and a plump blonde woman entered, wearing a maid's gray dress and white apron. She bore a silver coffeepot and a basket of rolls, both of which she set gingerly on the table as though afraid of spilling, before glancing uncertainly at Mrs. Baldwin.

"Thank you, Molly. You may serve our guest some eggs and bacon if you please."

"Oh—yes, ma'am!" Molly removed the lid from a silver platter on the table and enthusiastically piled food on a plate, then plunked it in front of Solace so hard it bounced.

Myron started to laugh, then winced. "Ow! Knock it off, Peri, or I'll kick *you* next time!"

"*Idiot!*" Pierre stage-whispered. "Ma says we can't laugh when they're training!"

Molly's face went beet-red, but Mr. Baldwin set down his paper and said kindly, "Thank you, Molly. Would you be so good as to pour me some more coffee?"

"Yes, sir. Of course, sir." She reached quickly for the pot, then stopped herself, taking a steadying breath before carefully lifting it and filling her employer's cup to just below the rim. Then she faced Solace, took another breath, and said, "Ma'am? Would you like some coffee?"

All at once recognition dawned, and Solace exclaimed, "I know you! From the library. You were the—" She stopped herself just in time as alarm leapt into the young woman's eyes.

"Molly is new to us," Mrs. Baldwin said smoothly. "She is training to be a maid. And doing very well, I might add, as this is only her third day."

Poor Molly set the coffeepot down, whispering something about "burning toast," and fled to the kitchen.

"I'm terribly sorry—" Solace began, but Mrs. Baldwin raised a dismissive hand.

"No matter. You meant nothing by it, you were merely surprised. And if she is to improve her situation, she must know that some folks will understand her past and comment on it. It is human nature to be curious. But also to be compassionate."

Solace nodded slowly. "I understand. Thank you, Mrs. Baldwin, for your kindness and compassion in letting me stay here."

"Think nothing of it. And please, you must call me Lola. It seems silly to keep to the formalities when you may be here a while if your, ah, foundation can't be fixed right away."

"That reminds me," Pierre broke in. "Mr. Jacobs called last night. He said you're not to worry, he's got it all under control, and he'll call again when he knows what's what."

If any of them found it odd that Lucky had phoned instead of Allen, they gave no sign.

Mrs. Baldwin—Lola—nodded decisively. "A good man. He is doing some work for me as well."

Solace was not even surprised by this. "Yes, he's very…capable."

Myron glared ferociously around the table. "I'll bet *his* mother lets *him* canoe the Willamette!"

Myron's mother didn't even blink. "You're fifteen, while Mr. Jacobs is nearing thirty. When you are his age, you may do as you please, but not before."

"Gilbert's mother says—"

"What Mrs. Herren says has no bearing on this discussion. Now, Peri, I believe your father has store business to discuss with you. Myron, you may join them after your chores."

Pierre rose with a superior air—one that told Myron, *I am older than you, and far more important!*—and carried his dishes to the kitchen. Myron looked mutinous, but confronted with his mother's unmoving expression, he grudgingly gathered his own dishes and left. Mr. Baldwin snapped the paper shut and rose, tucking it under his arm and coming around the table to kiss his wife's cheek. He smiled at Solace and betook himself through the doors to the front of the house, leaving his dishes behind.

Mrs. Baldwin—*Lola*—frowned, then sighed. "I suppose he's earned the right to expect someone will clean up after him. Those two boys, however, need to remember where we came from."

Solace made a polite noise and was about to take her third—or was it fourth?—slice of bacon, when a deafening clatter came from the kitchen, followed by feminine screeching, and then something *clunked* against the dining room doors and slid to the floor with a squishy *splat!*

"What in the world…?" Lola was out of her seat and across the room by the time Solace rose to follow her into the kitchen, still clutching the bacon.

A scene of comical proportions greeted them. Red-flushed Molly wielded a butter knife at a tiny figure with the black hair and silk robes of a Chinese sing-song girl, who crouched on the floor like a cat, holding a wooden platform shoe ready to hurl at Molly's head. Pierre was nowhere to be seen, but Myron sprawled near the sink amid the broken crockery and crumbled remains of a platter of toast. His awed gaze alternated between the buxom maid and the petite visitor, whose silk robe was not as tightly secured as it could have been.

Molly raised the knife higher and shrieked, "Poison me, will you? You lying little—"

"*Poison?*" the girl shrieked back. "I no poison you! I help—do what you ask!"

She dropped the shoe and fished around in her copious sleeves, coming out with a small packet wrapped in brown paper that had a green twig tied into its securing string. She rose and gesticulated with this as she spoke, the wide arcs of her sleeves flapping like silky pink butterfly wings.

"You say need *yànwō*, so I get for you!"

"I don't know what *yànwō* is!" Molly spat. "I said I

needed—" Abruptly she became aware of her audience. Her face blanched, and she lowered the knife. "Ma'am— I can explain—"

Lola's swift glance took in the situation. "Myron, leave us."

He scrambled up. "But I can help. You might need a man, in case they get violent!"

Solace suspected his noble offer had less to do with protecting his mother, and more with the fact that the Chinese girl's bosom was already half-exposed and might soon be fully visible if she continued gesticulating. Clearly Lola had similar suspicions and flattened her lips at him.

Myron gave it one more try. "But Ma—"

"Leave."

He cast a last regretful look at the two women before slouching out the open side door.

Lola closed it after him and faced Molly. "Now then, what is this about?"

The Chinese girl shot up to her full, tiny height, which couldn't have been more than four and a half feet, and scowled at the two other women. "I do Miss Molly favor! Say need *yànwō*, so I get for her. All the way from Gardens. But she no like, say I try kill her." She waved the packet defiantly under Lola's nose. "How this kill her? Is *yànwō*!"

Lola ignored the packet. "And what, exactly, is *yànwō*?"

"*Bird's nest,*" the girl said with exaggerated patience. "For—"

Molly snatched a ripe plum from a bowl on the counter and hurled it. Her aim was perfect—the fruit smacked into the girl's temple, exploding into pulpy chunks and sticky juice.

"Molly!" Lola gasped.

"*Jīnǚ!*" the girl screeched, launching herself at Molly. "I kill you for that!"

Solace dropped the bacon slice into the refuse bin and coughed loudly, startling the others into silence. "I wouldn't want to impose, but I wonder if I might speak with Molly and—"

She paused inquisitively, and the girl abruptly straightened, then bowed low, saying with extreme dignity, "Hua Shui. I am *very* pleased to make your acquaintance."

"Er, yes. I'm Mrs. Grey." To Lola, Solace said, "I think this is something Molly would rather not discuss in front of her employer. But if you'll allow me, I may be able to help."

Lola pursed her lips. "Very well. But Molly, you must know that you can trust me."

"Of course, ma'am! But—you see—" She faltered, wringing her apron in abject misery.

"Never mind." Lola turned to Solace. "Come upstairs when you are done. I have something to show you."

When she had gone, Solace said to Molly, "Are you sure?"

Molly gave an embarrassed nod. "I'm reg'lar as a clock, an' it's more'n a week late."

Hua Shui made a "Pfft!" noise and folded her hands into her sleeves. Solace ignored her and asked Molly, "Do you know who the father is?"

"No point in guessing. You know what I do—*did*. Please, you can't tell Mrs. Baldwin. I'd be so ashamed. An' she won't approve of how I'm dealing with it."

That was likely true. But approving or not, Solace

felt Lola would understand. "I won't tell. But if this is your chosen path, you must do it soon or the *yànwō* won't be as effective."

Hua Shui slapped a hand on the counter. "That what I say! But she no listen—say I poison her. Why I do that? We sisters—same *lā pítiáo*—I help her!"

While Solace's knowledge of Chinese didn't extend to the vocabulary of prostitutes, Hua Shui's meaning was clear. Even Molly understood and glared at her.

"You be quiet! He ain't my pimp anymores 'cause I don't *have* a pimp!" She faced Solace again. "So this— this *yànwō* really is what I should take? To—to do it?"

"Yes. It's only wild carrot seeds, or bird's nest, which is what *yànwō* means in Chinese."

She took the packet from Hua Shui and gave it to Molly, who still hesitated. "But this twig—it looks like hemlock."

"Yes. It does. You should never pick wild carrot yourself because hemlock is so similar. But I grow this myself, and trust me, it is *not* poisonous."

A sudden vision of Lucky rose before Solace, leaping up to knock what he believed was a deadly plant from her hands, followed immediately by another memory, of when he'd approached her for a very different reason. With difficulty she pushed both images away.

He was only being kind, both times. That is what friends do for each other.

Molly said stiffly to Hua Shui, "Thank you. I'm sorry I didn't believe you."

Hua Shui lifted her chin airily. "It is not a problem. I forgive you. One teaspoon, crushed. In drink. Every day, until is done." She bowed low to Solace. "It is very nice meeting you, Mrs. Grey. Perhaps we meet again soon."

Then she retrieved her shoes and slipped out the door.

In answer to Molly's unspoken query, Solace nodded. "That is the dose I've been told."

Molly lowered her gaze, but not before Solace saw the tears in her eyes. "I was allus so careful. What kinda odds is that? Right when I get out, this happens."

"Molly, are you certain you want this? Perhaps you should wait a day. That long won't make a difference. But you need time to think before doing anything you may regret."

Molly shrugged. "Can't make a new life if I got to take care of someone else."

Solace had no response to this, so she offered to help clean up the mess. But Molly, still embarrassed, shooed her out of the kitchen, and she went to find her hostess instead.

Lola's upstairs office was on the eastern side of the house, with a large maple shading the windows. It was plainly furnished with a serviceable oak desk and a large bookcase. Every surface was crowded with papers and books, and Lola sat in a swivel chair, spectacles perched on her nose, working at a typewriter.

She looked up when Solace entered. "Was everything resolved satisfactorily?"

"I…think so." Molly had seemed so sad. But this was what she wanted, wasn't it?

"Hmph. Well, just because I left does not mean I don't know what happens in my own house. Molly has more options than she thinks."

"You mean adoption?"

"That. And raising her own child."

Solace stared at her. "But…how would she work? With a newborn, and later, a child?"

"The organizations I work with understand that dilemma well. We have plans to provide childcare to help unwed mothers get back on their feet. And we will also encourage the father to do his duty."

"How? By forcing the men into marriage?"

"I prefer to call it promoting a strong family life," Lola said wryly. "Perhaps that sounds high-handed, and often a divorce is granted shortly after the wedding. But then the man is liable for child support, whereas if they are never married, he goes scot-free. As a Catholic, the idea of divorce must be shocking to you. But I am surprised you are not more shocked by Molly's intentions."

"I suppose that would seem odd," Solace admitted. "I had an unusual upbringing, and I have strong feelings about the plights of females in these cases."

"But you do not believe in divorce? Even when the woman's safety is at stake?"

This dove into more personal waters, so Solace said, "You had something to show me?"

"Very well. We will discuss this later." Lola rifled through the desk and came up with several typewritten papers secured with a metal clip. "This is a petition demanding that Mayor Williams do his job and close the gaming halls. He should have done so already, but instead, he and Chief Hunt are lining their own pockets with bribes from the owners."

Solace took the papers and skimmed them. "What has this to do with me?"

"With your language skills, I wondered if you might translate them for me. We have many immigrants in Portland who cannot read English, although they have been naturalized and can vote: Germans, Italians,

Russians, and of course Chinese and Japanese, among others. We must get the word out so they understand what to vote for."

"Are they literate? In their own languages?"

"I am hopeful that enough are, so that word can be spread throughout their communities."

Solace suspected Lola of inventing busy-work for her, but she was still grateful. "I'll be happy to help."

"Thank you. If we finish these today, I can deliver them to the woman who has volunteered to help pass them out. I believe you may know her—Mrs. Adina Donner."

"Why, yes! She called on me yesterday."

Was it only a day since they had sat on the porch and laughed? A sharp pang of loss stabbed Solace. Once Allen's condition was known—for she was ever more certain it *must* come out—surely Adina would realize the unsuitableness of the connection and terminate it.

Lola said, "She mentioned that she had made your acquaintance. She and her husband support the organizations I work with. They donate money and time, a rare combination."

Mr. Baldwin poked his head in, giving Solace another polite nod before addressing his wife. "My dear, I believe we must subscribe to the *Daily Journal* after all. Three papers seems excessive, but there is not a thing about Creffield in today's *Oregonian* or the *Gazette*."

"Very well. Whatever you think best."

A shiver ran up Solace's spine. "Creffield? Has there been another murder?"

Mr. Baldwin smiled reassuringly. "On the contrary, they found him yesterday outside of Corvallis, at the home of one of his disciples, Mrs. O.V. Hurt. I heard of it from someone in the know, but I'm not sure it is common knowledge, since the papers don't seem to have the story yet."

"But that is wonderful! The murders are solved!"

"I'm afraid not. He has been hiding under the house for a month, maybe two, with no food since Mrs. Hurt was sent to the asylum two weeks ago. He can barely stand, let alone walk, and there is no possibility of his guilt, in these murders at least."

"Creffield is *not* guilty? There is no doubt?"

"None. At least, not of murder. They've got him on the adultery charges, though."

Solace's brain whirled, and then her blood froze as the implications crashed into her.

If Creffield is not the killer—cannot be the killer—then... Is it Allen after all? No—impossible!

And yet…the bloodstains…the rash…he had *touched* the body. And…

His murderous strength as he grasped my throat…

She couldn't feel her extremities. She closed her eyes, forcing the memories away, shutting them off until she could breathe again. When she opened her eyes, she found Lola peering at her over her spectacles, though when she spoke, she addressed her husband.

"LeGrand, you know this is my work time. Go find something to occupy yourself and those two boys, and leave us in peace."

"Of course, my dear." He smiled at Solace again and retreated.

Before Lola could ask what had upset her, Solace lifted the top sheet off the stack of papers, feigning interest in it, although in truth, she had no idea what it contained. Fortunately, Lola took the hint, and they settled down to work quietly together.

Sometime later, there was a faint knocking on the front door, and Solace turned from her seat by the window to find the room in shadows. Lola had switched on her desk lamp and was reviewing the documents she had typed, and Solace squinted at the clock on the bookcase. Molly had brought them sandwiches at noon, but they had otherwise worked uninterrupted for hours.

Solace said, "I had no idea it was so late. I wonder why Lucky—Mr. Jacobs—hasn't called?"

Lola frowned. "That is odd. I would have expected a report by now. Where has the day gone? I will have to take the car if I want to get these flyers to Adina tonight."

Someone answered the door. The distant sound of voices drifted from below, and Solace stretched and stood, adding her latest translation to the pile on the desk.

Suddenly, someone shouted, and feet thumped up the stairs. A bony, barefoot little girl in a too-large dress ran into the study, followed by a breathless Myron. The girl had the gray pallor of malnutrition, her braided blonde hair dull, but her eyes sparked fierce with determination.

"Are you Mrs. Grey?" she demanded of Solace.

A stone settled deep in the pit of her stomach. "I am. Why—is it my husband?"

Lola stepped forward. "I am Mrs. Baldwin. May I help you?"

The girl glanced between them, and her mouth firmed. "Right. Mrs. Sadie said I could tell you too. She didn't want to phone 'cause that ol' busybody Missus J.B. Smith is allus listening on the line. Anyway, she says come quick—Mr. Lucky's been arrested! They say he kilt all those women, an' Mrs. Sadie says if we don't git him out fast, they's gonna lynch him!"

Chapter Twenty-Five

Monday August 1

> "REBUKED AT JAIL BY VISITORS – 'I am not crazy; I am Elijah!' Thus spoke Joshua Creffield. He raised himself from the cot, propped his head on one hand, batted his eyes at the men on the other side of the bars, and lay down again." —*The Morning Oregonian*

Lucky stared through the iron grillwork at the dark corridor beyond. Strange. For all his misspent youth, he had never been in a jail cell before.

After two days, he didn't like it.

Three stone walls, dank with mold and rot, or worse, and the fourth a grid of flat metal bars, too closely riveted for a man's hand to pass through. In the center of this was a barred metal door with a solid panel in its center to discourage attempts at kicking one's way out.

This couldn't be happening. He was trying to *solve* Ellie's murder. But when he told Officer Peters that he'd been working with Detective Jenkins, the man frowned, saying cryptically, "I wouldn't call Jenkins friend if I were you, for he will not get you out of this."

For the thousandth time, Lucky circled his cage. Light filtering through the high, also barred window showed it must be Monday mid-morning, and he was no closer to understanding what had happened. Well, he knew the *what*: He was being accused of Ellie's murder, maybe the others as well. It was the *how* and *why* he couldn't fathom. And the *who*, for someone had done this to him.

Peters refused to elaborate, and the only conclusion Lucky could reach was that someone had led Jenkins to regard him as a suspect, for surely he wouldn't do so on his own. Lucky forced himself to sit on the metal cot that, with the piss pot and water jug, constituted the cell's only adornments. He had to think, focus on the facts, or he'd never uncoil it.

Fact one: Ellie was murdered by someone who knew of the Howards' freezer, as she could not have been frozen by any other means. Before the strike, Union Meat and other distribution companies had filled their own freezers, and no other local business possessed such technology. But the Howards' freezer had arrived after meat deliveries ceased, and so was empty.

Supposedly, Lucky had heard of it at St. Mary's, along with all the other parishioners. However, Jenkins had already rented the freezer before Lucky—supposedly—killed Ellie. So, he was forced to infiltrate the shop on Sunday night and pick the lock, a skill Jenkins knew he possessed. Lucky then allegedly replaced Jenkins's meat—already frozen, and therefore effectively bloodless—with Ellie's corpse, staining the floor with *her* blood in the process.

Fact two was more disturbing: Murder was a hanging offense, so someone wanted Lucky dead. But who? A gaming boss? No one at Jones or Fisher's could hate him that much. But he *had* nosed around the clubs, asking after Ellie, and not being subtle. Anyone—owners, staff, patrons—could have overheard and decided he was a threat, about Ellie, or whatever else they were up to.

He splashed water on his face from the jug on the floor. It was not much cooler than the heavy air, but the rivulets ran down his jaw and neck, clearing his head. He took a deep breath and leaned against the stone wall.

As for fact three, it was even more incredible: At the jail, they'd photographed Lucky holding a slate bearing his name and the charge of "Murder." But they'd also pressed his fingers onto an ink pad, then rolled them on paper. They called it "fingerprinting," a process Jenkins had brought west from New York. It was too fantastical, right out of Mark Twain's *Pudd'nhead Wilson*, that fingertips had unique patterns, which the skin's oil and sweat residue imprinted on objects, and which could be "lifted" off later with powder and tape, then used to identify a suspect.

Not only were Lucky's fingerprints on the padlock and gate of the lot where Ellie's body had lain, but—fact four—they were on the coins he had given her, found in her pocket, still wrapped in Sadie's dishcloth. No other fingerprints were detected at the lot or on the Howards' freezer, and—fact five—he'd blatantly admitted to a prior relationship with Ellie.

So the theory now was that he had paid Ellie for sex—the lowest streetwalkers charged fifty cents, so his sixty seemed generous—then murdered her, broke into the freezer, left her there for five days, and when he feared the strike was ending, moved her to Erickson's.

Taken altogether, it almost made sense. Almost, for if he killed her, why not take the coins back? Why leave them in her pocket, covered in an easily identifiable cloth belonging to his well-known landlady?

Behind him, keys clanked and metal scraped, and

Lucky turned to find Detective Jenkins unlocking the cell door, his canny grin in place. "There you are. Been looking all over for you."

"Funny. When the hell am I getting out of here? You know I didn't kill anyone."

Jenkins leaned against the metal doorframe. "Well, that's the thing. You've heard Creffield's in the county jail? Found starving after weeks under a house down south. Couldn't have killed the women up here. Unlike you, who had the opportunity and the history, with at least one of them."

"I told you, Ellie was a friend. I wanted—still want—justice for her."

"Maybe. Or maybe you tried to cover your tracks by hunting for her so-called 'real' killer. Working with the police, who would suspect you?"

"But *why* would I kill her? I hadn't seen her in a year. What motive would I have?"

Jenkins shrugged. "Maybe you hadn't seen her, and maybe you had. We have witnesses who will testify that you were a regular at the massage parlors in the North End. Your boarding house is close by, so it's certainly believable."

Lucky sucked in a breath. The witnesses had to be lying, probably paid to testify against him. It wouldn't be the first time the wheels of justice were hand-cranked. But by whom? It was all so ludicrous. He was no saint, but he was also no "regular" at any house of ill-repute.

Jenkins's beady eyes bored into him. "As for why, perhaps your circumstances changed, and you feared losing your…freedom."

"What does that mean? Before this mess, I had no reason to fear my liberty was at stake."

The detective stepped into the cell, hands clasped casually behind his back. "There are many ways a man's liberty can be threatened, such as from a past indiscretion which he hopes to conceal from a lady, so it won't interfere with his *future* plans."

Lucky stared. Did "lady" mean Solace? And did Jenkins imply Lucky had killed Ellie to hide their brief fling? He shoved a hand through his hair.

"What plans? There is no 'lady' in my life—none with whom I have any possible future."

Jenkins removed a toothpick from his breast pocket and methodically applied it to his teeth. "So you say. But at Howard's, you accused Peters of being after Allen Grey. That confused me, until I realized how much the evidence points to him as well. For instance, he learned of the freezer at St. Mary's at the same time you did. And his shoe was in the yard with Ellie's body. We know it's his; I followed him home from there, and he most certainly wore only one shoe. He tossed that one into the bushes by his house, and I retrieved it later."

Black spots danced before Lucky's eyes. Calm—he must remain calm. "But you now believe *I* am guilty. Either the shoe implicates Grey or the fingerprints implicate me. Not both."

"True. Unless you are working together. Or…you are framing him."

The blood in Lucky's veins turned to ice and his pulse slowed. *This can't be happening.*

The detective examined the toothpick with great interest, then tucked it in one corner of his mouth. "Grey is the perfect scapegoat, with his history of violence against prostitutes. Yes, I read Peters's report. But you saw an added benefit. If Grey hangs for your crimes, his widow is ripe for the taking. So, you plant something of Grey's at the scene, and presto—she's yours."

And there it was—his worst nightmare realized. *Solace*.

All he'd wanted was to protect her, but Peters knew of their connection and had leapt to his own conclusions. And damn it to hell, it *was* logical when viewed from the outside. Killing Allen *had* occurred to Lucky, but not so Solace could remarry, only to keep her from harm.

He sat on the cot and rubbed a hand over his eyes. He must tread carefully to prove his own innocence, without further implicating Allen. "I can understand Grey coming home from Erickson's without his shoe if he's the one who lost it there. But if *I* planted it, why would Grey travel *to* Erickson's wearing one shoe, instead of simply putting on another pair?"

Jenkins flicked the toothpick into a corner of the dirty cell. "Perhaps he was confused, another behavior he frequently demonstrates. Or he thought the shoe was lost on a previous excursion and retraced his route to find it."

"That makes no sense. And how could I have planted it at the saloon in the first place?"

"You've been seen at the Greys' several times, 'helping' around the house. Easy as pie to steal the shoe and use it for your own nefarious purposes."

"But…" The whole thing was absurd—worse than any farce Lucky had ever seen.

He clenched his fists, slippery with sweat. Now that Creffield was exonerated, it seemed the police were desperate for new suspects. So either he or Allen must be proven guilty, which meant Solace would either lose her husband or Lucky. Or, God forbid, both.

He stood and paced the cell. "Yes, I know the Greys,

from St. Mary's. And I helped build their shelves for them. It's the least I could do, as they are new to town."

Jenkins didn't move, and Lucky stopped abruptly. His nervous pacing and verbose denials played right into the detective's hand. A slow smile curved Jenkins's mouth, like a cat with a plan for its mouse. He moved to the cell door, then stopped.

"One more thing—small, but significant, and I believe it's the real reason you killed Ellie. Her death always seemed different from the others. More…personal. And then I had a revelation. You not only covet Solace Grey, you wish to marry her. But it wouldn't matter if she were freed by her husband's death, because *you* would not be free."

Lucky's jaw worked, but no sound came out.

The cat's grin became malicious. "We know Ellie was with child—*your* child. If Mrs. Baldwin found out, she would force you to marry the whore, and then Mrs. Grey would be lost to you forever. Catholics frown on divorce, I believe. But if Ellie—and her baby—were dead…"

Jenkins trailed off, and the black vortex swirled around Lucky, swallowing him whole.

Ellie was expecting. She and *her baby were murdered.* That was why she'd wanted to turn her life around—was willing to meet with Mrs. Baldwin. A new beginning, for a new life.

Wave after wave of nausea soured his gut, his face was icy hot—*cold dead corpse, thawing on a hard metal table—with a dead, frozen baby inside, just beneath his fingers…*

The last thing Lucky heard was Jenkins bolting the cell door and whistling down the corridor, before the blackness overcame him, and he fell back on the cot in despair.

~:~:~

Lola paused outside Chief of Police Charles Hunt's slightly-ajar door, not to eavesdrop—that would be crass—but to adjust her hat, which had loosened on the walk here. If Hunt was so careless as to leave his door open while conversing with persons unknown, and if Lola happened to overhear what they said, that was not eavesdropping, it was serendipity.

"You're sure?" The speaker was Hunt, followed by a man's voice she didn't recognize.

"Positive."

"Why wasn't I informed sooner?" Hunt sounded angry, but then, he usually did.

"I only just completed the autopsy. I had two embalmings on Saturday and one that couldn't wait on Sunday. I had to work the Lord's Day, for Chrissake."

Ah. John Finley, then. Coroner-cum-undertaker.

Hunt grunted something, and Finley said, "You don't want to know why it couldn't wait. The point is, I finished her up just now, and she was with child. Some weeks along, in fact."

Finley must be referring to Ellie, the girl found at the saloon, for whose death Mr. Jacobs had been arrested. Falsely so, for he was no more capable of murder than a pig was of flight. But…this was an interesting development. Had Mr. Jacobs known of her condition? Was it his child, and was that why he had originally sought aid on her behalf?

Lola glanced around the upper floor of the station, but it was largely empty, and no one paid her any heed. Most of the patrolmen had gone to the county jail, where a mob had gathered outside Creffield's cell. Her hat was as fixed as it could be, but her skirts appeared to need attention, so she stepped closer to Hunt's door, where, if anyone asked, the light was better.

Hunt was saying, "…told anyone else?"

"No. I performed the autopsy without assistance. As soon as I discovered her condition, I came here. If you wish to release the information, it's up to you."

Hunt swore. "The papers would have a field day. Prostitute murdered, *with* her baby."

"At least you have a suspect in custody."

"Hmph. I suppose so."

"Surely with Creffield *and* this man in jail, your department looks very good right now."

"Perhaps. But Creffield has only been charged with adultery, and—"

"Mrs. Baldwin, may I help you with something?"

Lola looked up to find the uniformed officer from the library—Peters?—regarding her solicitously. Inside Hunt's office, conversation ceased and chair legs scraped across the floor. Calmly, she gave her skirts a final twitch and smoothed an invisible wrinkle from her jacket.

"I need to see Chief Hunt on a most urgent matter."

Peters's glance at the open door was speaking, but she refused to dignify it with excuses or a denial. The young boy had no business criticizing *her*.

Hunt's door widened, revealing the Chief himself with Finley standing behind, holding a sheaf of papers. Hunt's white hair stuck out all over, ringing his bald pate, and his neatly trimmed gray-and-white mustache drooped over his downturned mouth. Finley, by contrast, was pleasantly handsome, his hair still thick and dark, though he was near sixty—not much younger than Hunt.

Perhaps their respective jobs accounted for the differences in their aging and temperament.

"What do you want?" Hunt barked.

Finley laid the papers on the Chief's desk. "I'll leave you to your work. If you have questions, I'll be in my office."

He slipped around Hunt, bowed politely to Lola, and betook himself away. Peters also seemed to suddenly have business elsewhere and fled, leaving Lola alone with Hunt.

"Well?" he growled. "Here to discuss more of your womanly concerns? Want to dress my officers in petticoats and hold a garden party to benefit the poor?"

She met his glare with a level gaze. "I wish to discuss the arrest of Lucky Jacobs."

That startled him. "What of it?"

"Must we converse out here?"

He grunted and moved aside, allowing her to step into his office while he closed the door behind her. Perhaps he'd learned his lesson on *that*, at least. He indicated a high-backed chair in front of his desk, waiting while she settled herself, then returned to his own leather swivel seat.

"Well? I'm busy. Say your piece, and let's get on with it."

"Thank you for taking the time to speak with me." She would *not* stoop to his level. "I wish to know when you will be releasing Mr. Jacobs and dropping all charges against him."

"Oh? And why would I do that?"

"Any evidence against him is circumstantial. In fact, it seems he was helping Detective Jenkins with the case. If his—what do you call them?—fingerprints were found near that woman's body, they were left after the fact. There is no evidence he knew the first two women, and his connection to the third was in the past. Additionally, I understand Jenkins is ambitious. Perhaps he believes solving these murders quickly will curry your favor and garner him a promotion."

Hunt leaned back, scowling. "And how do you know any of this?"

"I have my sources." No need for him to discover how much his officers told their wives, and how much they had told her. "Furthermore, Mr. Jacobs has an impeccable reputation in the lumber industry, as well as at the docks, where I understand he occasionally works."

An odd expression crossed Hunt's face. "A man can be a hard worker and also a killer."

"Not this man. If he is not released at once, you can expect to hear from our lawyer."

"*Our* lawyer...? Speak plainly. What has LeGrand Baldwin to do with Lucky Jacobs?"

"Nothing on a personal level. But professionally, Charlton's will sue you and the Police Force—perhaps the city, as well—for falsely imprisoning one of its employees."

That got his attention. "*What* in the name of Providence are you talking about?"

"Mr. Jacobs has also been working for me, helping Charlton's determine the lay of the land as we prepare to open our store on Washington."

It was essentially the truth, although if questioned, Mr. Jacobs might not *know* he worked for Charlton's. She had only hit on the inspiration this morning and informed LeGrand of it at breakfast. If pressed, she would have to admit that Mr. Jacobs had only been "hired" the day before his arrest. But hired he was, and that's what counted.

Hunt said sourly, "He does get around. But even Charlton's can't help if he has no alibi."

Lola kept her voice serene. "That *is* the crux of the matter. He cannot have killed Ellie, for I believe Finley estimates her time of death as sometime Sunday afternoon. Is that correct?"

"Obviously, you know it is."

"Then I will tell you that Mr. Jacobs was with me on Sunday during the dinner hour, and prior to that, a dozen witnesses saw him at church. After we spoke, he met with his foreman, performed repairs around his boarding house until supper, and then went to bed, all also witnessed by his many housemates. Finally, should Finley decide Ellie died on Monday, I understand Mr. Jacobs was at the lumber office in the morning, then with a friend all afternoon. And you know where he was that evening, assuming your officer filed an accurate report."

Hunt's expression didn't change, but after a moment, he stood and turned to the window. She wouldn't back down, but she could wait. Hunt liked to be in charge of every detail, down to reprimanding officers for forgetting their gloves. He did *not* like others taking command or knowing more than he did. But if given time to preserve his dignity, he'd likely come around.

A minute later he faced her. "Very well. Jacobs is still a suspect, but he may go for now, on one thousand dollars' bail. I'm sure *Charlton's* can afford that much for such a valuable employee. If the charges are dropped, bail will be refunded. Good day to you, Mrs. Baldwin."

Ignoring his rudeness, she accepted the win. "Thank you. I will see myself out."

Leaving his office, she hurried to the clerk's window on the ground floor. A young man greeted her—was *everyone* employing children these days?—asking, "May I help you, ma'am?"

Taking out her pocketbook, she withdrew the check she had torn from the Charlton's ledger LeGrand kept on his desk in the study.

"I wish to post bail for Mr. Lucky Jacobs."

The clerk looked at her blankly. "Jacobs, you say? But you can't—it's too late."

He wasn't much older than her sons. She put on an expression that *they* knew well. "Chief Hunt assures me I may. Shall I ask him to come and discuss it with you?"

The poor boy rose hastily and cast a wary glance through the window at the stairs. "Please, ma'am—I didn't mean to say that Mr. Jacobs *can't* be released, only that he already *was*."

The clerk inclined his head toward a door across the room, just as Mr. Jacobs himself emerged from it. A sunburned man in rough worker's garb stepped forward, and Lucky shook his hand, clearly thanking him.

Abandoning the relieved clerk, Lola crossed to them in a few strides. "Mr. Jacobs, I am glad to see you freed. But how were you released so quickly? I only just spoke with Chief Hunt."

He paled when he saw her—an odd reaction—his gaze flicking worriedly to the other man. He had no hat to tip, but he bowed politely. "Mrs. Baldwin. What are you doing here?"

She looked from him to the older man. "I came to bail you out, but I see my services were unnecessary."

How the Chief must have laughed at her, when he knew all along Jacobs would be released! She disliked being made the fool, but now was not the time. Or perhaps Hunt really had not known what was happening in his own station. Either way, he would get his due.

The older man doffed his wool cap, which, with his high rubber boots, identified him as in the shipping industry. His hair was mostly white, with a few blond streaks remaining.

"Mrs. Baldwin? Pleased to make your acquaintance. Miller's the name. Mr. Jacobs is sort of an employee of mine. I heard of his troubles and came to post his bond."

Why would a man who only "sort of" employed Mr. Jacobs post a thousand-dollar bond for him? Never mind that she had just tried a similar scheme herself.

"That was most kind of you."

The young clerk, who had disappeared from his desk behind the service window, now came through the door Mr. Jacobs had just exited, carrying what must be Jacobs's confiscated belongings.

Mr. Jacobs paled and said hurriedly, "Mrs. Baldwin, perhaps you could wait outs—"

The clerk reached them and said loudly, "Here you are. One men's coat—check. One pair men's boots— check. One hat—hunting knife—check, check. And one envelope containing five hundred dollars cash. It's all there, so *whoever* you're to give it to won't be disappointed."

Mr. Jacobs went from white to red, as the clerk winked and passed the fat envelope to him. He tucked it hastily into his coat, refusing to meet Lola's gaze.

And the penny—or rather, the wad of cash—finally dropped.

"Mr. Jacobs. Might I have a word with you, please? *In private.*"

Chapter Twenty-Six

Lucky could think of no distraction—her grim expression said she *would* have the truth. He'd barely had time to assimilate his release or that Miller had put up his bail. He would have to face Mrs. Baldwin eventually, but now that his own freedom was achieved, every fiber of his being thrummed to prove Allen Grey innocent and ensure Solace's safety.

For if the police had decided against Lucky's guilt enough to allow him out on bail, they must be focused instead on Allen's. He was the only remaining suspect, since Creffield had been exonerated. The whole thing was maddening, not least because Lucky was so close to understanding, but still the solution eluded him.

Just then, the door to the station opened with a *bang!* and two people entered. The first was a uniformed patrolman. The second, dragged behind him by sheer force, was a little over four feet tall and shrieking in Chinese. When she saw Lola Baldwin, Hua Shui abruptly ceased both her cacophony and her ragdoll act, and instead attempted to stand and execute a low bow, in which she was hampered both by her high platform shoes and the officer, who refused to loosen his grip.

"Mistress Baldwin," she said. "How do you do? I am most pleased to see you again."

Mrs. Baldwin seemed unsurprised by either Hua Shui or her state of disarray, which today included a red silk robe knotted at her waist and a gold ribbon tied under her black hair. It was clear the women had met before, both by Hua Shui's greeting and Mrs. Baldwin's response of, "Yes, quite. And how are you today?"

"Oh," Hua Shui answered airily, as if the officer wasn't still clutching her, and they weren't all standing in the middle of a police station. "I am quite well, thank you." Her haughty gaze passed over Miller and Lucky without acknowledgment, but she aimed a look of vicious scorn at her captor. "But see, I have little bit trouble. This man, he say I go jail because walk down street in robe. Why that a crime, I ask you?"

The officer's nostrils flared. "Everyone knows you were not going for a walk in your night robe in broad daylight. But even if you were, public indecency's a crime." He did loosen his hold, however, evidently deciding she was unlikely to bolt, as he stood between her and the exit, and he outweighed her by a hundred pounds.

She made a show of yanking her arms free and straightening the dirty robe. It kept falling open in new places with every twitch, and Miller stared, transfixed. Then he shook his head as though to clear it.

"Jacobs, I'd best be on my way. Stop by the dock tomorrow so we can discuss, er, these matters. Good day, Mrs. Baldwin." He sent one last bemused look at Hua Shui, tugged his cap politely at everyone else, and escaped out the door.

Lucky bastard.

Mrs. Baldwin watched his departure, lips set in a thin line. Then she faced Lucky. But for the second time in as many minutes, Hua Shui saved him. Still acting as though this were a social gathering, she said, "Mrs. Baldwin, may I inquire, how Miss Molly? She take *yànwō*, yes?"

Lucky stilled. It couldn't be a coincidence. "Another bird's nest? Who took it and why?"

Mrs. Baldwin regarded him quizzically, but Lucky focused on Hua Shui. Something tickled his subconscious…a certainty that he was on the brink of finally uncoiling Ellie's murder.

"For *baby*," Hua Shui said with the exasperation of one speaking to dolts and idiots. "Miss Molly no want. No good have baby in our business, and now she maid, can't keep. Take *yànwō* seed, no baby."

"A seed…for no baby? *Yànwō* is a plant? And it…" The knowledge electrified him, set his every nerve on fire. Ellie—*yànwō*—but she wouldn't. Would she?

He understood why prostitutes ended unwanted pregnancies. But he felt sure Ellie would want to keep her child. No—she *hadn't* taken the *yànwō*. That was Hua Shui's point: Ellie *should* have taken it, but didn't. Lucky saw the wheels spinning in Mrs. Baldwin's sharp mind as well. No hope for it—he might never meet Hua Shui again. He moved directly in front of her.

"Do you remember me?" Her only response was a contemptuous sniff, which he took as an affirmative. "When we talked, you said my friend Ellie did *not* take the *yànwō*, is that right?"

She nodded vigorously. "That right. She no take. *Want* baby. But father, he—" She stopped, looking around as though suddenly remembering the semi-empty police station in which they stood. Fewer people meant less background noise, and their voices had not been quiet. "Never mind about that. I forget, not know father. Never see him, not know name. I go jail now, yes?"

This last was directed at the officer, waiting patiently

nearby. He started to speak, but Mrs. Baldwin cut in, "Is that necessary? Perhaps I could—"

"No, no, is fine!" Hua Shui grabbed the officer's hand, attempting to wrap his fingers around her bony wrist while shaking her head at Mrs. Baldwin. "No want go with you—not be maid. Want go to jail!"

Mrs. Baldwin pursed her lips. "A moment ago, you indicated the opposite. I can offer an alternative. You do not have to be a maid, per se."

"I change mind—jail good. Free dinner, yum-yum, and bed all for me. Very nice!"

It was clear she would remain obdurate. The officer shrugged and led her away for booking, leaving Lucky alone with Mrs. Baldwin.

She eyed his sock-covered feet and the boots still in his hands. "I will await you outside."

She marched from the station, and with a resigned sigh, he found a bench and sat to put the boots on. He donned his coat, the envelope of cash burning like a brand through the lightweight wool, then rose and pushed out the door into the hot summer sun.

~:~:~

Solace knew the moment Lucky stepped outside, and the relief shuddered through her like a tidal wave, so that she almost gasped aloud. *He is free—thank God!* Free, and whole, and apparently unharmed, although he was too far away for her to be certain of that last.

In theory, she stood catty-corner from Central Police Station at the intersection of Second and Oak, listening to Adina chatter about inconsequential things, while keeping an eye on Allen, who paced nearby, absorbed in a book. In reality, her mind and spirit had been elsewhere since that moment two days ago when little Mary announced Lucky's arrest.

She hardly knew what had passed in the intervening time; it was all so chaotic. Lola—it still felt unnatural to call her that—had insisted Solace sit, and then with her usual force of will had begun to handle everything before Solace could comprehend what needed handling.

First, Lola made Mary repeat what she knew, twice. Which wasn't much, only that Lucky was making deliveries with Allen—even this small bit was incomprehensible to Solace—when the arrest occurred, and that Mary's original errand was to find Solace and reunite her with Allen.

"But how did you know where to find me?" Solace had managed to ask.

"After the police taked Mr. Lucky, Mr. Howard— they was at the butcher shop—taked Mr. Grey to Fisher's. But Mr. Fisher don't know him, and said to try Sadie's, in case he lived wi' Mr. Lucky. Course he don't, but Missus Sadie knew you was here, so's she sent me over. She says she'll keep an eye on 'im untils you get there."

Solace involuntarily lifted a hand to her throat, still covered by the high collar. "And…how is Mr. Grey? Is he well?"

Lola glanced at her sharply, but in the event, Mary didn't understand the question—wasn't anyone not on their deathbed "well"?—and only said, "Missus Sadie gived him tea and tol' him to lie down in the parlor. She says he's worn right down from all the 'citement, but he'll be fine when's you come back."

Lola turned to Solace. "Perhaps you had better go with Mary now." She paused, stern gaze dropping to Solace's neckline before meeting her eyes again. "Unless you feel unsafe?"

For one brief, insane moment, Solace had considered staying with Lola, who would be thinking of ways to help Lucky. But what could Solace do? She had no useful connections and no ties to Lucky that gave her the right to stay. None she could acknowledge, at any rate.

So instead she had said, "No. I will be fine. His…episode…was an aberration."

With her too-perceptive intuition, Lola had said softly, "Never fear. Mr. Jacobs is a good man, with friends who support him. But justice can be a slow, daunting process. Go, take your husband home, and LeGrand and I will see what can be done."

Mary was impatient to be off, and so Solace had gathered her belongings—except the books, which were too heavy to carry—and was soon outside and hurrying to keep up with the child, who was quick for such a thin, starved little thing. Meanwhile, Lola had shut the door on their departure, but had not forsaken Solace. By the time she arrived at Sadie's, the Donners were waiting in the parlor with Allen.

Adina said, "Lola called. We have both a car and rooms to spare. Do *not* argue. I won't hear of it. You *would* be fine on your own, but you will be *better* with us. There, it is settled."

And with a wry smile from her husband, it was. Allen and Solace were whisked away in the Donner's automobile, a bright red contraption with mahogany leather seats, a windscreen, and a black cape top, to their "home," which turned out to be a mansion in every sense of the word. It was full night when they arrived, and Solace had no idea of their route, only that they were in the hills above Portland, facing east, with a view of the river far below. Disembarking from the car, she looked up—and kept looking up. The structure towered above her, comprising three stories of living space, with, as she later learned, servants' quarters below the attic.

It was too much. *They* were too much. But it was also too late; she'd accepted their hospitality. However, their own frank acceptance of herself, Allen, and their situation soon put her at ease. As much as she could be, at any rate, given the circumstances.

Sunday had passed in a mix of exhaustion and restlessness, due to Solace's inability to do or learn anything useful. She had no right to ask after Lucky, and could not discuss him with Adina, even had they been alone. Which, for most of the day, they were not. If the Donners found it strange that Allen refused to leave her side, they forbore to comment. But she caught them once in the drawing room, heads bent and whispering, when she returned from sending Allen upstairs for a nap.

They started guiltily when she entered, and Solace had swallowed her pride and accepted that her secret was out. Allen *was* acting like a child—once again sweet rather than violent, but still a child. Surely the Donners would mention it at church, and all would be lost. With sudden fierceness, she had determined not to dwell on it, but to accept their charity while it lasted, for the memory of their kindness must sustain her when, inevitably, she and Allen were forced to move again.

Somehow, she had survived until this morning, and then—*glorious moment*—Lola had telephoned Adina to say she was going to the police station, and Lucky would be freed by noon.

Adina had replaced the receiver, turning to see the terrified hope Solace couldn't hide. "So that's how it is.

No, don't deny it. I am not judging you. But I believe Lola may want company at the station. I am determined to go, and as my guest, you must accompany me."

"I—whatever can you mean? I have no desire to—to go to the police station."

"Don't be absurd. Lola is my friend, and yours too, now. And—for I see the objection forming on your lips—there is no reason your husband can't come. The drive will do us all good. We'll leave in half an hour."

And so here they were, Adina chattering, Allen reading, and Solace unable to sit or stand or pace, her mind too focused on the building across from them.

And then its doors opened and Lola exited, but Lucky wasn't with her—*why not?* She waited, so Solace must also wait…and wait…and when she could wait no longer, she took a desperate step toward the sidewalk's edge—and then he was there, and she breathed in the sight of him. Adina appeared at her side, and Solace was grateful, even knowing it meant her feelings must be writ clear on her face. Those inappropriate, unwanted, shameful feelings she could not control.

Lucky stepped toward Lola. Then his gaze landed on Solace.

And he jumped into the street and strode toward her, ignoring automobiles, carts, and pedestrians alike. Adina clutched Solace's arm, but she needn't have bothered, for Solace was rooted to the spot. She must memorize his face, for who knew when or if she would see him again? Her heart thundered as he leapt onto the sidewalk and stood before her, blue eyes boring into hers as they had at their first meeting. Was it only nine days ago?

He swallowed, Adam's apple bobbing. He lifted a hand, checked himself, and let it drop. "Solace—Mrs.

Grey." His gaze shifted to Adina. "Mrs. Donner, is it? I believe we attend the same parish. I—"

He got no further, for Lola, who had immediately followed him from the station, arrived and also mounted the sidewalk. "Mr. Jacobs, do not think to avoid your day of reckoning so easily." She addressed Solace and Adina. "Forgive me, but I *must* speak with Mr. Jacobs alone for a moment, on a matter of urgent business."

Lucky ignored her, focusing on Solace. "Mrs. Grey, I have a question for you. Do you know what *yànwō* is?"

Lola frowned. "Mr. Jacobs, this is hardly an appropriate topic when ladies are present."

"On the contrary, a skilled botanist is *just* the person with whom I should discuss this."

Adina sent Solace an assessing look, then said, "I, however, know nothing of plants. But I do know Mr. Grey, and will sit with him on that bench"—she indicated an iron seat down the block, toward which Allen already wandered, still absorbed in his book – "until you are ready to leave."

"Thank you," Solace said with sincere gratitude, then faced…Mr. Jacobs. She *must* retrain herself to think of him thus. And yet it was unlikely she would see him again after today, so what was the point? With a mental sigh, she said to him, "I am very familiar with *yànwō*."

"You are?"

"Yes. I grow it myself—you have seen it in our yard. It is an anti-spasmodic. Topically, it reduces wrinkles, and if taken internally, aids in elimination and treats gout and other ailments."

"I see. And…ah…" His cheeks reddened, and Lola made an impatient gesture.

"In the interest of hurrying this along, I believe Mr.

Jacobs wishes to know about its use as an abortifacient."

The blush deepened in Lucky's cheeks, but Solace felt her own expression clear. "Of course, I remember now. Hua Shui gave it to Molly."

He said, "How the h—er, in God's name, do you know Hua Shui? Or Molly?"

"Molly works for the Baldwins, and Hua Shui was a visitor there. How do *you* know them?"

"They are…were…ah, friends, of Ellie's. The most recently murdered woman."

"Oh. I am sorry. I didn't mean to pry. Mrs. Baldwin mentioned you knew her."

He cleared his throat. "Never mind. But tell me, is this *yànwō* safe?"

"It is when purchased from a reputable source, such as the Chinese Gardens, and if taken correctly. Molly should be perfectly fine if she chooses to use it."

Lucky frowned. "I was not asking for Molly, but for…" The color rose in his cheeks again. "In point of fact, I understand Ellie may have needed it."

"Ellie? Then she was…"

Tightness gripped Solace's chest. She should have realized. Even after Lola explained that Lucky was connected to Ellie, it had not occurred to Solace *how* personal his interest might be.

"I am sorry," she said stiffly. "It is none of my business."

He said hurriedly, "No, you misunderstand me. I was not—it's not—she *may* have needed it. I am only repeating what Hua Shui said and trying to piece it all together. Before last week, I had not seen her in over a year—I swear to you."

Lola's mouth turned down disapprovingly. "Then

how did you know of the pregnancy?"

His face fell. "It's true, then? I wasn't certain. It was a guess, based on Hua Shui's words and—well, it's no matter."

Lola's frown deepened. "Isn't it? Are you certain you had *no* contact with her until last week?"

"Yes, I am certain. How did *you* learn of it?"

Her cheeks pinkened. "I overheard the coroner telling Chief Hunt about it. Finley completed his autopsy this morning and claimed no one else knew the results."

Lucky said grimly, "And because I admitted to knowing her, you thought I had more reason than Finley to understand her condition? Let me assure you—*both* of you—I did *not*. Hua Shui told me Ellie refused to take 'bird's nest,' but I only just discovered what that meant."

Lola sniffed. "In any case, we can discuss this further when we discuss that *other matter*." She looked pointedly at his coat pocket, and he reddened again.

Just then, Adina approached them. "Solace, forgive me. I had hoped to give you more time, but Mr. Grey is growing restless. Perhaps we should leave?"

Solace glanced at Allen. He had risen and closed his book, and now regarded his surroundings in confusion. Probably he did not recall how he'd gotten here.

"Of course." She forced the lump in her throat back down and faced Lucky. "I am sorry I wasn't more help about the wild carrot. It really is completely safe."

"Wild carrot?" He seemed confused.

"*Yànwō* is what the Chinese call it. Because the dying flowers resemble a bird's nest."

Something lit his eyes, as though this one thing had sparked an idea. How she wished she had the right to discuss it with him—hear his opinions, and have her own questioned and critiqued and *heard*. From the sudden regret in his eyes, she guessed his thoughts ran in a similar vein.

All he said was, "Thank you for the information." He faced Lola. "Ma'am, I'm not avoiding you. But I've been in a jail cell for two days. I need a bath and fresh clothes. In short, I need to go home before I do anything else."

"Very well. Please join us for supper tonight. Come over as soon as you may."

Lucky tipped his hat to her, including Solace and Adina in the gesture with heartbreaking casualness, though it was the right and proper thing to do. But she allowed herself to watch him walk away, knowing it should—*would*—be the last time she saw him.

Then she said to Adina, "I'm ready," and went to retrieve Allen, feeling Lola's sharp gaze piercing her back all the while.

Chapter Twenty-Seven

Chief Hunt tossed the signed testimonial he'd been reading onto the growing pile on his desk and glared at the man standing opposite him. "*Another* one!"

Detective Jenkins stood, ruler-straight as ever, with not a thread nor a hair out of place. Too bad. A good dressing down would have relieved Hunt's feelings. He came around the desk and stood next to the detective, who kept his gaze forward. He was stocky, but Hunt towered over him and had control of his career besides. A quiver of Jenkins's mustache was the only sign he might be nervous, and Hunt smiled grimly.

"You'd better have an explanation for this—this *fiasco*." He grabbed the stack of letters, shoving them under Jenkins's nose. "Jacobs is quite popular—lumber bosses, shipping companies, the *priest* at his goddamn church!" He pulled a letter out at random. "'Mr. Jacobs is an upstanding member of the community who has never once stepped out of line.'" Another. "'Mr. Jacobs was at Sadie's boarding house all of Sunday afternoon...'" A third. "'I represent Mr. Jacobs in a civil suit against your department for wrongful arrest...'"

Hunt threw the papers on the desk. "A civil suit! You know what an investigation could lead to. I will not have the papers call me 'the only blot on the city'—*again*. Do you hear me? If you can't find the person who *actually* committed these murders, I will make certain you never work as a detective again, *anywhere*. Is that clear?"

Jenkins had grown gradually paler, his hands clenched so tight, he'd pulled one of his gloves partway off, exposing red, sun-burned skin, attesting to the man's odd love of working outdoors in his garden. Before Hunt could give him a dressing down after all, Jenkins quickly tugged the glove back into place. Meticulous, even now.

"Sir, Peters arrested him while I investigated—"

"You are Peters's superior! Don't foist your incompetence on him!"

"But Jacobs knew the victim—intimately. He may be the father of her baby. If it came out that he impregnated a whore, his reputation would be sullied. I—"

"Silence! Your bungling makes us all look incompetent! The Creffield business, too. All that manpower, wasted, when he was under a house in Corvallis the *whole time*. We'll be the laughing stock of the entire country! No one will attend the fair, and all that money will be *gone*, with no revenue to replace it!"

"But sir, Jacobs's fingerprints were found in the yard, and on the lock and the coins…"

Hunt twitched his mustache. "Fingerprints! Bah! I don't even believe it's true that every man's is unique. That's your claim, yet—"

"But Scotland Yard—"

"—*even so*, they prove nothing. *Nothing!* Only that he was there, not *when*, or *why*. He admits giving her money—*charity*—from the goodness of his sainted heart! And you know as well as I he had good reason to visit Portland's saloons. Including Erickson's!"

Jenkins's face flooded with color, his only reaction. The man was stoic, Hunt would give him that, though his career—his whole life, even—could be ruined by this.

"Sir. Those very reasons led Peters to arrest Jacobs.

He acted rashly, and should have waited for me to guide him. But the letters you received—the writers don't know of—that is—"

"His other *other* job? Of course they don't know! He's *good* at it—discreet, reliable, a trustworthy, honorable man—*not a goddamn killer of women and babies!*"

He turned his back on the now trembling detective and stared out the window. Good. Maybe a little terror would make the man do his job better.

Except Jenkins didn't appear to be "trembling with terror" so much as shaking with fury. Ambitious son-of-a-bitch; likely saw his promotion vanishing for good this time. But…there was something else. How had Jenkins learned the dead girl was pregnant? Could *no one* in the department keep their damned mouth shut?

Hunt said through his teeth, "Between this, and the teetotalers, and the gaming—what a goddamned nightmare. We'll *all* be lucky to keep our jobs." He faced Jenkins. "Find me the real killer—*yesterday*—and I'll fire Peters instead of you. Fail, and you're both gone. Understood?"

"Yes, sir. I'm still investigating Allen Grey. I will pursue that lead immediately."

There it was. Hunt had been waiting for Jenkins to display the detection skills he was known for. Grey was as good a suspect as any. "I'd forgotten about him. Well, you'd better be *damned* sure he has no alibi before you arrest him."

"Yes, sir. I've compared his movements to those of the three dead women, and I don't believe anyone can vouch for him. But I'd like to interview his wife to learn if he's been violent toward her as well. Tonight, if I have your permission."

"Hmph. Glad you're showing sense this time. I expect a full report tomorrow!"

Jenkins gave a curt nod, staring at a point on the wall, awaiting dismissal. Hunt studied him. Rumor had it his wealthy father-in-law was displeased by his lack of advancement. Jenkins pursued his job with zeal, but he was not above twisting the facts to satisfy the greater good—or Hunt's directives. Especially if it brought him closer to his own goals.

Yes, Jenkins was a good soldier, with ambitions to be a general. But would this current failure make him a better officer? Or a bigger thorn in Hunt's side?

Only one way to find out. "Go."

Hunt faced the window again as Jenkins hurried off on his mission. What a mess. Lola Baldwin would have a field day if she found out. A thought struck him. She'd been outside his door when he learned of the dead woman's pregnancy. Could *she* be the tattletale? He frowned, turning the idea over. Undoubtedly she *could*. But by all accounts, she had gone directly from his office to the clerk's window, spoke with Jacobs after he was released, and then left shortly after that. She had not interacted with Detective Jenkins or anyone else relevant.

Not her, then. Peters? But he'd come to Hunt's door after Finley commented on Jacobs's arrest—too late to hear their conversation about the pregnancy. So…was it the coroner himself?

Hunt strode to the door and barked at the nearest officer, "Get Finley on the phone!"

When the operator connected the call, Hunt took it at his desk. "Goddamn you, Finley, what's this about you blabbing details of the victim's condition to my detectives?"

There was a moment of silence on the line before Finley said, "I don't know what you mean. I said I'd told no one, and I didn't. I came straight to your office after the autopsy, and I spoke to no one here or in your building about it, except you."

Finley seemed genuinely puzzled by the accusation, and Hunt's bluster dissipated. "But *someone* told him. If not you, then who?"

"I have no idea. But if I were you, I'd find that person. You have a loose cannon—someone who may 'blab,' as you say, to the papers, besmirching the department and making your job even harder. And with the liquor vote coming up, not to mention the fair…"

He trailed off, but the implication was clear, and Hunt grunted and hung up. Incompetence and loose tongues on the Police Force wouldn't secure his position as chief or bring business to the exposition, and therefore, industry to Portland. What a *goddamn* mess.

It was late evening when Solace and Allen arrived home. It had been a struggle to convince the Donners to let her leave with Allen, but as he had been nothing but sweet in their presence, she at last won them over on the condition that Adina would come by early the next morning to check on her.

"And," Adina had promised, "it will be *far* earlier than any respectable visit should be made, so you had best be ready for me."

Solace had smiled her thanks, collected their belongings, and accepted yet another ride in the Donners' automobile to get them home.

Home.

Relief washed through her as she and Allen moved up the walk, the Donners' chauffeur driving away up the lane behind them. She would be safe here, from unwanted feelings and emotions, able to hide away for a time and heal, before facing the world again.

Allen, too, seemed glad to be back, looking around excitedly, taking in the garden, the house, everything, as though he'd been gone weeks or months instead of days.

"Solace!" he cried. "How your flowers have grown!"

He reached for a bunch of wild carrot, and Solace grabbed his arm. "No, don't touch those!"

"Why not?" He shrank back, peering at the white umbels, and gasped. "It's not hemlock…? You haven't planted hemlock in the yard, have you?"

A pang shot through her at his confusion. "No, of course not. But it is very similar, isn't it?" Similar enough to have fooled Mr. Jacobs, albeit temporarily.

"Then why couldn't I touch it?"

She smiled, because if she didn't, she would cry. Of course he'd forgotten. "Your skin is sensitive to this plant, and you will get a sunburn-like rash if you touch it. But it's only wild carrot."

"Wild carrot?" He seemed intrigued by the name, and this time, her smile was genuine.

She picked a stalk and held it out to him. "Also called Queen Anne's lace. See the red dot? Or *yànwō*—bird's nest—if you prefer. They're one and the same."

Something about that struck her as important, a memory from a recent conversation. At the Donners' home? Or with the Baldwins…? No, at the police station, with Lucky and Lola. They had discussed the use of wild carrot to end unwanted pregnancies. But why should her brain raise the memory now? She stared at the flower in her hand, trying to let the thought rise and clarify on its own. But nothing came to her, beyond the fact that Ellie was pregnant and planned to take *yànwō* to end it.

Or had she? Hadn't Lucky said Ellie *refused* to take it? That seemed important. And if Lucky were not the father—in this she believed him implicitly—then who was? Would that man have wanted the baby aborted enough to kill Ellie if she refused?

If only Solace could discuss it with Lucky. But…she couldn't. Nor could she discuss it with her husband, who now turned and mounted the steps to the porch, saying, "I'm tired. I'll go to bed early. You'll come in soon?"

"Of course, dear." With a sigh, Solace tossed the blossom into the yard and followed him into the house.

~:~:~

Across the river, Lucky sat at the cleared dining table in the house on East Ankeny, awaiting Mrs. Baldwin, who was overseeing Molly's cleaning efforts in the kitchen. During dinner, she had been polite, but Lucky wasn't fooled. The set of her lips, the glint in her eye, told him she would wait only until her family dispersed before demanding an account of his behavior.

If his hat were not hung on the coat rack in the entry, he would have twisted it in his hands. The sympathetic looks her sons sent him as they beat a hasty retreat didn't help. Even Mr. Baldwin made himself scarce, leaving Lucky to stew.

At last the doors to the kitchen swung open, and Mrs. Baldwin returned. She resumed her place at the foot of the table, sitting erect, hands in her lap, studying him.

"Mr. Jacobs, I am not one to dilly-dally. When I asked you to discover who collected the gaming bribes for Williams and Hunt, I believe you already knew the man's identity. Am I correct?"

At least it would be over quickly.

"Yes. I have been collecting them, but only for the last week." As if that made a difference. "In any case, I did it, and it was not my finest moment. At the time, I still hoped to find Ellie alive. I believed having a reason to visit the clubs so often, since I am not a regular at any of them, would facilitate asking after her."

She made no response except to compress her lips further and regard him more critically. He waited. She was not his employer, despite what she'd hinted to Hunt, nor did she hold any power over him. But he respected her and disliked losing her approbation, especially over anything so transitory as this ill-fated venture.

Finally, she said, "Perhaps your motives were noble, but the fact remains that you aided in the collection of bribes meant to enable this city's gambling culture. Therefore, I have to wonder, if you would do this, why would you not visit any number of houses of ill-repute? And impregnate the occupants, willy-nilly?"

Lucky choked a laugh into a cough. Her expression was so severe, but the way she had framed the question... However, this was her passion, so why shouldn't she speak frankly? Or perhaps it was merely hysteria on his part. It had been a very strange seven or eight days, and was unlikely to soon settle down.

Her brows lowered, and he said quickly, "I apologize. I am not myself. Let me assure you, I knew Ellie before she, er, changed professions. Neither have I impregnated any other prostitutes, nor even had relations with any, that I know of. I am not a regular at any house of ill-repute, but *especially* not hers."

The kitchen doors banged open as Molly entered, bearing a stack of clean china destined for the mahogany hutch by the wall. She did not seem to have overheard Lucky's comment, but his cheeks burned nonetheless at the implied insult to her former crib.

Mrs. Baldwin nodded. "It is bad to sin. But it is worse to feel no shame. I believe you regret taking the bribes and that you did not dishonor Ellie. But at the police station, you said your guess about her condition stemmed from a conversation with Hua Shui and *something else*. If not your personal knowledge, then whose? I overheard Finley state that no one else knew before he told Hunt, which occurred mere moments before your release."

Lucky considered the matter but saw no reason to demur. "Detective Jenkins told me."

Abruptly, Molly dropped a gravy boat and it clattered off the side of the hutch. Thankfully, it did not break, but her face was white and splotchy, and her hands shook as she lifted it and placed it with extreme care on the shelf.

"Sorry, ma'am. I'll be more careful."

Mrs. Baldwin frowned. "Are you well, Molly?"

"Yes, ma'am. I was only startled by you all mentionin' Mr. Jenkins."

"You know him?"

Molly shuddered, but she managed a nod, eyes downcast before she raised them quickly. "But not—I never—he warn't a customer or anything. I mean of mine. He come to our house a lot."

"You mean to make arrests and such?"

"Oh, no, ma'am! He come to fu—I mean, he *was* a customer, just not mine." She reddened but did not look away. "He was real creepy-like, and not in a sneaking around kind of way, althoughs he did that, too. But I warn't his type, which is good, 'cuz he give me the willies, and most o' the other girls, too."

Mrs. Baldwin's frown deepened. "In what way? If you don't mind my asking."

"Oh, no, ma'am, I don't mind you asking, if'n you don't mind my answers." She paused, marshalling her thoughts. "Well, he's jus' known for havin' unnatural tastes. You know—handcuffs and ropes and such. Or, sorry, mebbe you don't. But anyways, he likes to hurt and be hurt, if you git my meaning."

From her grim expression, Mrs. Baldwin did.

For Lucky, the revelation of Jenkins's character was not as surprising as it could have been. The men who publicly seemed the most strait-laced were often the ones with the most reprehensible—or at minimum, the least socially acceptable—private interests. But with Jenkins, it went farther. Recalling their conversations, Lucky realized the detective's words often held an underlying cruelty, as though he enjoyed inflicting discomfort. At the time, Lucky had excused it as a necessary part of Jenkins's job. But seen in this new light…

Molly closed the hutch, using her apron to dust its glass front. "Anyways, he has a type. *All* men do. Whores know it, but respec'able ladies don' believe it. For him, he likes 'em young an' brown-haired. Like his wife, which is lucky for me, 'cuz I ain't neither."

An electric tingle rippled through Lucky as something, a missing piece of the puzzle, clicked gently into place. "Molly, who did Jenkins visit when he came to your house?"

Her gaze shot to his. "Why, Ellie o' course. I thought you all knew."

Chapter Twenty-Eight

After Allen went to bed, Solace cleaned the fire-damaged kitchen. From Allen's confused memories, she gathered he had tried to cook bacon, but the popping grease ignited a stove fire. If Lucky—*Mr. Jacobs*—had not been there, the house would have burned down and Allen with it. Instead, there were only ash stains on the stove, counter, and walls, and one of Solace's quilts was ruined. Her cast-iron skillet, rusty from being doused with water, needed to be soaked in vinegar and re-seasoned, but she set it on the counter by the door to deal with in the morning. The whole house still smelled of smoke, but thankfully, there was no lasting damage.

If only her heart were so fortunate.

Though exhausted, she was too keyed up to sleep, so she retreated to her chair in the living room and attempted to read. But even that was difficult as her brain whirled with all the events and emotions of the past week. Trying not to think about it was more work than letting the thoughts come. But as those thoughts were unbearable, she pushed them away in a never-ending cycle of anguish and despair.

She had just determined to lie down after all, when a knock came at the door. The mantel clock said it was nearly nine. Who would call so late? Adina? She had been anxious about Solace being alone with Allen. Perhaps she had decided to come now rather than waiting until morning.

Solace set her book on a side table and went to open the door. But instead of Adina, she found Detective Jenkins on the porch, dressed in what must be his street clothes: black greatcoat and trousers, with a gray derby pulled low over his brow.

"Detective, may I help you with something?"

"Sorry to bother you so late, ma'am. As you may know, we have arrested that man I told you of before—Creffield."

"Yes, I heard. It is a relief that he is safely in jail."

"Agreed." He seemed distracted, peering past her into the house. When he met her gaze again, his was…intense. "You are also aware, I believe, that another man was suspected of committing these heinous murders—a Mr. Jacobs. Do you know him?"

Her heart thudded, and she prayed for outward calm. "We attend the same parish."

"Yes. But your…friendship…goes deeper than that. Does it not?"

Solace's palms were slick and her brain spun. What was he after? Surely Lola's testimony, with that of Lucky's other employers and friends, had exonerated him. Or did Jenkins attempt to put him away on a charge of adultery, like the one on which they held Creffield? At least Allen was safely in bed, fast asleep, so she needn't fear him doing or saying anything damning in the detective's presence.

She kept her voice steady. "Mr. Jacobs helped my husband with improvements and repairs to our home. Allen and I both are grateful to him."

A glint came into the detective's eye. "Speaking of your husband—but perhaps I could come inside? It is awkward conversing across the doorstep, is it not?"

He moved forward, and even if good manners hadn't precluded it, she couldn't have shut him out, for his bulk was too great. She had no choice but to let him in.

He removed his coat and hat, hanging them on the pegs by the door, then went into the living room. She followed and found him pacing the perimeter, examining the books, photos, and other décor, but saying nothing.

Foolish of her to mention Allen, but it couldn't be undone. "What may I help you with, Detective?"

He faced her, his genial expression unwavering, though it didn't reach his eyes. "I have a few questions for your husband. Is he at home?"

Sudden irrational fear gripped her—should she lie and say she was alone?

Before she could decide, Jenkins spoke again. "Never mind. I should probably get better results from asking *you*, shouldn't I? You are so much more…aware…than he."

Breathe. She must breathe. Could Jenkins arrest Allen and commit him to the asylum without a warrant? What was the detective after? She *must* remain calm and reveal nothing. But despite her efforts, he saw something in her face and smiled grimly.

"I thought as much. So I will ask you, how did your husband acquire the rash on his hands and forearms last Friday?"

His words were like a physical blow, and she staggered. "How…?"

"An interesting thing, that. The dead whore had a similar rash when we found her at Erickson's. Which, incidentally, is also where we found one of your husband's shoes."

Oh God—what was happening? Surely Allen was

not a serious suspect?

"What shoe? How can you be certain it's his?"

He grinned, a baring of teeth, like a cat sighting a mouse. "I followed him home. He wore only one shoe, and its match was found at the saloon yard."

Something about that seemed wrong, and she straightened. "How did that come about?"

His confident expression faltered, then re-firmed. "I saw him throw the shoe into the bushes by your porch, and I later retrieved it. We have both shoes in evidence, and I can swear to their belonging to your husband. So if you think to bear false testimony, it will do no good."

"You were *patrolling* at Erickson's, very early on the self-same morning my husband was there. But detectives don't normally patrol, do they? You said so yourself."

Anger flashed in his eyes; he had not expected a mere woman to pick his theory apart. "There is also your husband's violence against prostitutes, religious attacks perpetrated to save their souls. But when he killed Ellie, he also killed her unborn child. Murdering a whore—" He shrugged. "But her baby… That is another matter."

"Her…baby." The hairs on the back of Solace's neck rose. "Where did you hear this—this rumor?"

"It's not a rumor," Jenkins said, watching her carefully. "The coroner told me."

The blood left her extremities. "When, exactly, did Finley give you this intelligence?"

He frowned. Most likely, he'd expected her to be too shocked by the revelation to do more than accept it. And she *was* shocked—dizzy and cold with it, but not from the "news" she had already known. Rather, from the clicking of cogs and wheels in her brain, as thoughts which had hitherto drifted, not fully formed, suddenly settled into sharp, cohesive focus.

"Saturday, right after he finished the autopsy."

She gasped, then clapped a hand over her mouth, but it was too late. She shouldn't have asked him—should have gotten him to leave, then gone to the police.

But with that one gasp, he saw his mistake. His face hardened, and he moved so fast, she had no time to turn and run in her heavy skirts. He grabbed her by the forearms and dragged her into the kitchen, forcing her into a wooden chair. She fought him, but his bulk was too great, his fury too strong. He removed his belt and looped it around her wrists behind the back of the chair, cinching the leather so tight, she cried out.

"Shut up!" he snarled.

He reached for a nearby dish towel, and she wondered, *Should I scream? Try to wake Allen? Or if I stay silent, will Allen live, and only I will die?*

She opened her mouth and he punched her—her nose crunched and she saw black as blood poured down her face. He knotted the towel around her throat, then began yanking drawers open until he found her butcher knife—the same one she had hoped to use when defending herself against Allen. He brought it to her cheek, and she had never seen such cruel purpose in a face before. Allen's madness was disturbing; this was *horrifying*.

The tears rose, unwanted, and he smiled at her fear. He reached behind her head and began pulling the pins from her hair until its brown length cascaded around her shoulders. He slid a finger into one smooth curl and licked his lips.

"You leave me no choice. Fortunately, I had already planned to frame your husband for the first three—or rather, *four*—murders, so killing you only makes him *more* believable as a suspect. It's such a shame he's so fond of violence. But first, shall we have a little fun?"

He inserted the knife into her skirt and tore it clean down the front, then did the same with her petticoats. "Yes, I think we shall," he murmured, surveying her lace drawers. And the look in his eyes now was worse than any she had yet seen.

~:~:~

"Are you sure?" Lucky demanded of Molly over the blood roaring in his ears. "Are you *sure* about Jenkins and Ellie?"

"O' course. He chose her special, paid extry even, t' make sure she was 'at home' when he wanted her. He was hoppin' mad about the baby. Told her t' get rid of it, but she wanted t' keep it. That made 'im madder—didn't want her *unavailable*. An' he were afeared she'd talk. He wants to be chief someday, mebbe run for government. With a whore's bastard in the wings, he'd never win. An' if his wife's hoity-toity family found out, they'd sue for divorce, which he can't have, neither."

Lucky fell back in his chair, the revelations slamming into him until he came to one climactic conclusion. Surely it was impossible…?

And then Mrs. Baldwin spoke the truth he couldn't quite comprehend. "Mr. Jacobs, I believe Detective Jenkins had reason to harm Ellie. And when Peters arrested you, it played into Jenkins's hand, for you could be framed without any of it blowing back onto him."

Lucky scrubbed a hand over his face. It was so farfetched, and yet… He straightened. *He* had been exonerated, but there was still another "suspect."

"Allen Grey!"

Startled, Mrs. Baldwin and Molly looked at him.

"Framing me didn't work, but Allen is next on Jenkins's list. If he tries to set Allen up—"

Lucky stopped. It wasn't his secret to share, and he understood how Solace feared this exact scenario. If Allen's illness came out, the murder charges would hardly matter. Either he'd hang for crimes he didn't commit, or he'd go to the asylum to die a much slower, more horrible death, with both results killing Solace, emotionally, spiritually, and possibly physically.

"It would be bad," he finished lamely.

Mrs. Baldwin pursed her lips. "Mr. Jacobs, I understand the Greys' situation more than you realize. I will do everything I can to ensure nothing damaging is said of either of them."

"Thank you. I—that is, I am sure Sol—Mrs. Grey—would appreciate that."

From her expression, she understood *his* situation too. "Do the Greys have a telephone? We should warn them to steer clear of Jenkins until Hunt has been alerted."

"No. The nearest is in a shop down the block. Closed at this hour."

Molly made a slight motion with her hand, and Mrs. Baldwin turned to her. "Yes, Molly? Do you have something to add?"

"Begging your pardon an' all—I don' want t' butt in. But Mr. Jenkins, well, he's dangerous. He broke Hua Shui's arm once, afore he went on t' Ellie. But 'specially now when his plans are fallin' apart like. It's allus them controlled types. Sumpin' goes wrong, and they snap. Most times, they just hit a girl or break a vase or sumpin'. But we knows he kilt Ellie…"

Cold fear gripped Lucky, and he shot to his feet, but

Mrs. Baldwin said, "Stay. I'll telephone the station. A patrol car can get to the Greys' house faster than we can."

Every nerve in his body strained for action, to find Solace and keep her safe, but he saw the sense of Mrs. Baldwin's plan. Instead, he paced restlessly while she went to make the call. He would have followed her, but it would only impede her progress. Molly gave him a sympathetic look and returned to the kitchen, leaving him alone for agonizing minutes. What was taking so long? Surely it should be a short conversation?

When Mrs. Baldwin returned, her face was white. "No one answered at the station, so I called Hunt's home. Jenkins came to him this evening with the evidence laid out against Allen Grey, and Hunt—" She swallowed. "Hunt gave him permission to question the Greys. He's probably there now. I convinced Hunt to send someone to their house, but we may be too late."

"No."

She blinked. "What? The police are on their way—"

"No, I won't sit here and wait," Lucky said flatly. "If I may, I would like to borrow your car. If not, I'll run. Either way, I'll not do *nothing* while that *monster* is with Solace."

"Of course. I will get the keys for you. You know how to operate it?"

"Yes," he lied, and followed her in search of her husband, who held the literal key to Lucky's sanity and freedom. For if anything happened to Solace, he'd kill Jenkins himself, and then Hunt for hiring him. And then anyone else who'd endangered her for good measure.

Solace, hold on—I'm coming...

Chapter Twenty-Nine

Jenkins shoved Solace's torn skirts roughly aside, then slowly and precisely, he placed the knife point against her calf. He used just enough pressure to prick her skin, so that blood trickled down her leg, and she bit her tongue to keep from moaning. What was it the papers said? Ellie had been stabbed, multiple times. The look in his eyes was of pure pleasure at the pain he caused her, and she fought down the nausea and revulsion.

She must *think*—she could *not* give in to the terror. Perhaps if she got him to talk, it would delay whatever he had planned, long enough for…what? No one knew he was here, and no help would come, no matter how much she delayed the inevitable.

But she had no other ideas, so she said, in a voice that must have been steadied by God, for *she* couldn't have done it, "I still don't understand. You're a police officer, sworn to uphold the law. Why kill all those women?"

He gave her a look of utter scorn. "I'm no killer! Killing's a chore, and when it's done, there's no more fun to be had. I didn't kill 'all those women,' as you say. *I* didn't kill anyone at all. Ellie's death was…unfortunate. But entirely her own fault."

He moved the knife to her other calf and nicked it also. She bit back a gasp, refusing to give him the satisfaction. "But…the women found in the rivers…"

He laughed then, a horrid sound, like a crow's rough caw. "Stupid woman. I didn't kill them. We all thought

Creffield did, but he was incapacitated at the time."

Her brain whirled. He had no reason to lie to her, and yet, if not him, then…who?

Jenkins said, "The Police Force looks damn foolish. But I can fix all that. Once your husband is arrested for *all* the murders, Hunt will see what an asset I am."

"You plan to blame Allen for killing the first two women, and Ellie, and…me?"

"It is the perfect solution. He displayed his violent tendencies in public, and once it's known he suspected your adultery with Jacobs—well, who will *not* believe he's a killer? Such a tragedy that I arrived too late to save you. I heard you scream—" He jabbed her calf again, grinning evilly at the sharp gasp she couldn't suppress. "—but when I broke in, you were already dead. Mr. Grey attacked me, and I had to kill him in self-defense."

Solace swallowed. There *must* be a way through this.

He watched her dispassionately, then set the knife on the table. "I believe we'll skip the fun and go straight to the killing. I have no taste for it, but it must be done. Lucky for you, the first two women were strangled. The less you struggle, the less it will hurt, and the more quickly you will lose consciousness."

She said in desperation, "If that's true about the first women, then how can you frame one man for all three crimes? Since Ellie was—"

"Don't speak of her!"

He rose and went to lean over the sink, and suddenly she understood what had happened.

"You didn't mean to kill her. You wanted her to abort her baby, but she only pretended to take the medicine. It must have made you angry when she fooled you."

That got his attention. He turned, face dark with rage.

"Ellie was a dumb bitch. She couldn't outsmart a flea."

Solace kept her voice low, soothing. "Of course not. You found out—you really *are* smarter than she."

"Obviously I'm smarter than a whore! I purchased wild carrot seeds from the Chinese Gardens, but she gave them to another whore, so I had to get more."

He paused, and in the silence, Solace heard the faint squeak of rusty bedsprings from the back of the house.

Allen—no!

Jenkins didn't seem to have noticed, so she said quickly, "You returned to the Gardens…?"

"I did not! That Chinaman gouged me, but I got him back. I raided his opium den a week later and threw him in jail. No, I picked the seeds myself this time."

Solace stilled. "*You* picked them. But…how did you know what the plant looked like, when you only had the seeds before?"

"Think I'm that stupid, do you? I went to the jail and made that cheat describe it to me. Tall stalks, white flowers, umbrella shape. It grows all over around here!"

The bedroom floorboards creaked…she *must* hold Jenkins's attention. "What of the rash you mentioned? If you knew of it, were you not concerned about it?"

"Of course not! The Chinaman warned me. I wore gloves when I picked the stalks and removed the seeds."

An image of Lucky rose before her, rushing to save her from accidental poisoning—or so he'd thought. Two very different plants. Yet, to the untrained eye, very similar. Nausea roiled through her. Jenkins had picked hemlock by mistake. Even a couple of seeds would have been fatal—Ellie never stood a chance.

Neither did Solace. Jenkins was restless, pacing the kitchen, and she knew she could only keep him talking a little longer. Hot tears threatened; she would never see Allen, or Lucky, or any of her new friends again. Just when she might have found a permanent home, she would die, and never know the joy of truly belonging.

She swallowed. What would be, would be, and she would find a different sort of belonging when this was over.

No further sound came from the bedroom, but just in case, she said, "So you gave Ellie the seeds you picked, and she…"

"Died. Who cares? *I* didn't kill her. She brought it on herself."

Oh no—was that a noise in the hall? With every bit of strength she possessed, she refrained from glancing that way. *Dear God, let him return to bed. Let him not be killed as well!* Jenkins was about to pace past the doorway—she jerked the chair sideways as though trying to break free, the legs loudly scraping the floor.

Jenkins leapt toward her. "Stop that!" He blocked her view as he yanked the chair to the room's center. "I'm tired of this. It is time for you to join the other whores!"

He reached for the towel around her throat, pulling it tighter—cutting off her airway—silver spots before her eyes—limbs tingling—in moments, it would end—*she* would end. *Dear God, let it be quick—Allen—run! Get out of the house—save yourself!*

And then…she couldn't help it…her heart cried out, and in her last moments, she didn't suppress it: *Lucky*…

It was almost over. She would lose consciousness at any second. All sound was gone, and sight would soon follow. But then…

The oddest expression crossed Jenkins's face. He froze. His eyes bugged out, then rolled up. His fingers went slack and the towel loosened. And then he toppled over like a felled tree.

Allen stood behind him, wielding her cast-iron skillet, his voice faint over the rushing in her ears. "What an awful man. Are you quite well, my dear?"

~:~:~

Solace hardly knew what happened next or in what order. Even two days later, it was an indecipherable jumble of events and emotions. Allen had untied her, of that much she was certain. And then the police had arrived, Lucky with them.

Lucky.

The sight of him, when she had expected never to see him—or anyone—again undid her. But Allen was there, and a crowd of officers, and she couldn't go to Lucky, nor he to her.

Which was right and proper, and now she was glad of it. But as Allen patted her awkwardly while she wept out her terror, she would have given her soul for just one minute in Lucky's arms. She couldn't tell from his granite-like expression if he felt the same. He probably did not; it was *better* he did not. In fact, he'd hardly said a word to her after determining she was unharmed, which made her weep all the more, *because* it was so proper.

At some point, the police took Jenkins to the jail. Allen always had been stronger than he looked and had struck a resounding blow to Jenkins's skull, but no permanent damage was done. Mercifully, when questioned, he'd only recited the facts he knew, and any confusion was put down to over-excitement. And thanks to Lola's call to Hunt, plus Molly's testimony and Lucky's corroboration—not to mention the knife, Solace's torn skirts, bloody nose and calves, and the marks left by Jenkins's belt on her wrists—it was obvious Allen had only acted to save her.

When the officers were done questioning them, Lucky had reappeared with her recently-emptied overnight bag in his hand, its sides bulging once more.

"I couldn't find Allen's bag," he'd said brusquely, "so I put a few things for him in yours. I'll take you to the Donners' now. No, don't object. You're not staying here, and that's final."

Allen had beamed, trailing Lucky into the hall, and mutely, Solace had copied him, taking her bonnet off the peg and following the men outside and down the walk. A car was on the street, but it was too dark to discern any detail, and she was too much in shock to ask whose it was or how Lucky came to be in possession of it. They boarded it, and Lucky drove to the Donners' home. He'd carried her bag to the door and knocked, waiting for it to open, then tipped his hat to Allen, gave Solace a curt nod, and was gone. And she hadn't seen him since.

But Lola called at Adina's on Wednesday to relay the facts of the case, which she had gleaned from one of her many connections in city government. Faced with the overwhelming evidence, Jenkins had confessed to killing Ellie and supplied the remaining details.

"You were correct," Lola said to Solace, while accepting tea from Adina. "He feared being seen picking a known abortifacient, so he took the train to Oregon City. Unfortunately, the field he chose held *both* wild carrot and hemlock, and as a city dweller, he failed to realize he had gathered two similar plants until Ellie died. He rubbed the remaining wild carrot on her calves as if she had picked it herself, and he placed a few stalks in her pocket as 'evidence.'"

"So that's how she got the rash," Solace said. "He must have done it soon after death or the skin would not have reacted."

"Yes. And of course, he wore gloves throughout. Hunt forbids his officers from dressing sloppily in public even when off-duty, which in this case had the unintended consequence of Jenkins's not being affected by the toxins in either plant."

Solace set her cup down. "Allen must have touched the wild carrot at Erickson's. I did wonder how sweeping up a few leaves from our kitchen could so affect him, even with his sensitive skin. But what made Jenkins change his plans for Ellie's supposed cause of death?"

"He quickly remembered she was from the country and would never mistake hemlock for another plant, no matter how similar. He decided to connect her death to the murders, but he knew what the papers did not: The first two women died of strangulation, not drowning."

"Oh," Adina gasped. "How terrible."

Lola nodded matter-of-factly. "Yes. But also inconvenient for Jenkins, as he couldn't simulate strangulation on Ellie post-mortem. However, he knew from his prior cases with Finley that the blood in her body would still be present, albeit pooled due to gravity. So he stabbed her in her sides and back, to make her bleed as though this was what killed her."

"How did the Howards' freezer come into play?" Adina asked, and Lola grimaced.

"Mrs. Jenkins never visited the shed where Ellie died, but in this heat, the smell would soon be noticeable. Hearing of the freezer was a boon, and Jenkins rented it straightaway on Sunday afternoon, moving Ellie into it that evening before rigor mortis set in. He really did have meat that might spoil, but he sold it to a saloon on Monday morning, telling his wife it was at Howard's."

Adina said slowly, "Then on Thursday evening, the papers reported that the meat strike was ending, and he knew the Howards would want their freezer back."

Lola nodded. "As well, he needed Ellie to be found, to connect her death to the others, and to stop Mr. Jacobs from nosing around. Jenkins determined to throw her into the river and then 'discover' the body, in a manner similar to how the other two were found. He carried her from Howard's in a burlap bag, but she was heavier than expected, and he paused to rest in Erickson's yard, just before Mr. Grey entered it. Luckily, Mr. Grey did not see him, or he might have been Jenkins's next victim."

Solace said, "But once he saw that Allen was…"

The heat rose in her cheeks, but Lola said calmly, "Unwell. Yes, Jenkins had been hiding across from the alley on Monday evening when your husband accosted Molly. He intended to intimidate her himself, but Mr. Grey got in the way. So, when Jenkins saw your husband again on Friday, he left Ellie's body in the grass and hid outside the yard. He hoped your husband's confused state would play into his own hand, which it did."

"And accusing Mr. Jacobs of the murders?" Solace asked. There. She had spoken his name without faltering.

"Peters thought he was the killer all along," Lola responded, "but Jenkins did not. However, when the police found the coins in Ellie's pocket, which Mr. Jacobs admitted giving to her, he became an ideal suspect. Jenkins was a proponent of fingerprinting techniques, so he made sure Peters heard him tell Hunt about the lock and coins, while taking credit for Peters's theory about Mr. Jacobs. Peters became incensed and rushed to arrest Mr. Jacobs, letting Jenkins achieve his goal without dirtying his own hands."

"What of Solace?" Adina asked. "How did she fit into Jenkins's plans?"

"At first, not at all. After Mr. Jacobs was freed, Jenkins deflected blame for the bungled arrest onto Peters and told Hunt he wished to question Solace to reinforce his case against Mr. Grey. But in reality, Jenkins wanted to frame him. However, he thought Ellie's pregnancy was common knowledge, and so gave himself away to Solace, making her a liability."

Solace shuddered. "Since both 'suspects' were connected to me, it was the perfect fit. Kill me, frame my husband for all, and Jenkins would get away scot-free." She shivered. How close both Lucky and Allen had come to hanging for murder. How close *she* had come to death.

"Speaking of your husband," Lola said, "how is he?"

The question was blunt but not critical, and Solace drew in a breath before answering. "He is resting, still recovering from the ordeal. But otherwise, he is fine."

Adina looked from one to the other of them. "Forgive me, Solace. As he is now living in my house, I can say with certainty that he is *not* fine. But I believe Lola may be able to help him. Help you *both*."

Solace's hands shook, and she set her teacup on the coffee table with a *clink!* She rose, trying to steady her voice. "I appreciate your concern. But he is only over-excited. He—"

"Sit down," Lola interrupted.

It was a command, though delivered kindly, and Solace fought to swallow her shame and terror. Perhaps it would not be so bad if they knew. And what a relief to discuss it openly, to not force it all down, locking everything tightly inside. But…

What if she were wrong? What if the help Lola offered was to have him committed? What would she do then? How would she survive? Not divorced or widowed, but not truly married either, caught in a limbo from which there would be no escape.

Adina said, "Solace, do please sit. No scheme of Lola's will harm Allen. Isn't that right?"

Lola inclined her head. "If you will speak frankly with me and listen to what I propose, I think we may help your husband, while avoiding any stain on his character—or on yours."

Solace's limbs felt so rigid, she wondered if she *could* sit, but somehow she managed. She knew she must appear uncomfortable, angry even. But she couldn't help it. "I'm listening."

Lola said, "First, a few questions…"

What followed was one of the most agonizing quarter hours Solace had ever endured. Lola quizzed her on Allen's behavior, his habits, his words, and every "odd" thing he had ever done. She asked when his actions had crossed from merely eccentric to concerning. And she paid particular attention to any episodes of violence. She made no comment and took no notes, only asked clarifying questions as needed.

When she was satisfied that Solace had told all, she sat back, silent for such a long time, it seemed certain she had changed her mind and commitment would be the end result after all. Finally, she spoke, and after another quarter hour, she rose and departed.

Adina saw her out, then returned to the parlor and sat on the sofa next to Solace, smiling. "You appear almost as much in shock as you were the other night."

Solace turned to her in wonder. "I hardly know what to say or think, or even feel. Can any of this be real?"

"You are not accustomed to having friends. You have been handling things on your own for far too long. It must have begun with your father, and that is why Allen felt familiar to you, and why you chose him as your husband." Solace started, and Adina's smile widened. "While Lola was studying German research into brain diseases, I was reading the Austrian psychologist Freud and his theory that we all wish on some level to 'marry our mothers.' Or in your case, your father."

Solace's mouth worked, but Adina continued breezily. "Never mind. It is not my intent to psychoanalyze you, only to point out that you have had to be in charge, all on your own, since you were a young child. You are not accustomed to letting people in, or to receiving love and aid. But you have friends now, and Lola is a powerful ally."

"Amen to that," Solace said with feeling, and Adina laughed. Solace shook her head slowly. "Tell me, am I awake? Did Lola say there is a sanitarium in East Portland, at which she can secure a bed for Allen? And the doctors there will treat him as if he has any other disease, and not send him to the asylum? Or arrest him?"

"Yes, darling Solace, you are fully awake, and that is precisely what Lola outlined. No one who knows your husband believes he murdered the first two women, for it is clear he is only violent when lashing out; that is, when he is afraid. He is no cold-blooded killer, merely a man whose mind sometimes does not work the way it used to." Adina paused and gave a delicate shudder. "Yet now we know the original killer is *not* Allen, nor even Jenkins or Creffield, it does make one wonder who *is*."

Solace also shuddered, but for once, Portland's wildness and the anonymity of a larger city felt protective, not oppressive. Besides, her mind was still too absorbed by her conversation with Lola to share Adina's thrills over a killer on the loose.

She could hardly credit it. Not only had Lola solved the seemingly insurmountable difficulty of Allen's care, but she had also solved another one: the not-small matter of Solace having no income, nor any means of paying for said care.

"And do you truly think I can run a boarding house?"

"Not quite a boarding house. Only one or two women at a time, renting your spare bedroom. Women who might not do well in a large house, or who can't afford a higher rent. The foundations with which Lola and I work will help with your expenses, should the income from your boarders be insufficient. And she will speak with your landlord, in case he objects."

Solace opened her mouth, closed it, then opened it again, at last managing, "Thank you."

"Don't be silly. You are helping us with our cause. Besides, it will mean you and I will *have* to be in each other's company. You will not be allowed to put me off." Adina paused, then frowned. "Why Solace, whatever is the matter? Solace—are you…crying?"

It was so absurd—she should be *happy*. And yet the tears *would* come, and she couldn't stop them. "Y-y-yes! B-b-but I don't know *why*…!"

"I do. It's hope. You haven't had any for a very long time, and it's overwhelming you. Come here, darling. I'm here, and Robert and Lola, too. You are no longer friendless, and you don't have to face anything alone, ever again."

Chapter Thirty

Late August 1904

"MANY MYSTERIES BAFFLE POLICE – In
Two Months Eleven Persons Have Vanished
in Portland – The police were kept busy during
the months of June and July endeavoring to
locate them. Their whereabouts is still
shrouded in mystery, and may never be
discovered." —*The Oregon Daily Journal*

Jones's foreman, a man named Neuland, squinted at Lucky across the counter of the business office on Sixth. "You sure about this?"

No, goddamn you! But it was the only honorable thing he *could* do under the circumstances, so he gritted his teeth.

"Yes. Send me back to the logging camps. You don't have to make me a boss or even a sub-foreman. I'll do anything. High-climb, notch, run the skid. I just—I can't stay in Portland."

Neuland set his board clip on the counter and examined Lucky. "It will be a big pay cut. And it's nearly September. Only a few weeks, maybe a month or two, and you'll be out of a job and have to go somewhere else. Weren't you going to Alaska? Why not go now? Seems like a better, more permanent solution."

Lucky scrubbed a hand over his face. Couldn't the

man just do what he asked without all these questions?

Lucky *had* to leave. He would not—*could* not—live in the same city as Solace, knowing she would never be his. And yet, until he was absolutely certain of her health and safety, he couldn't move so far away that he would be unable to help if she needed it. The logging camps west of Portland seemed the best compromise. And a few weeks might be all he needed to assure himself she was settled. Besides, he could burn off his frustration, perhaps even forget her, with the twelve- or fourteen-hour workdays filled with brutal physical labor.

And he must forget her.

From Sadie, he'd heard that Allen would go to Dr. Coe's Nervous Sanitarium in East Portland. The fledgling hospital would be expanded next year, as Dr. Coe had received a contract to care for patients from the District of Alaska, where no such facility existed. It was close enough that Solace could visit regularly, and it carried much less stigma than the Insane Asylum.

Even better, Solace could stay in her home, as she would soon begin letting her spare room out to women in need of temporary housing. These women would be vetted first, and only those truly wishing to change their lives would go to Solace.

"An' what's more," Sadie had continued, beaming, "Mary will go to live wi' her!"

"Is that right?" Lucky smiled at the girl standing at Sadie's side, and she grinned back.

"Yessir, Mr. Lucky. Missus Sadie's done taught me a lot about keepin' house already, an' I can larn more, an' help Missus Grey clean and cook and all sorts o' stuff. An' I kin sleep in her pantry, same as here, so that's all right."

What a change had been wrought in her, though it was barely a month since Mrs. Baldwin had delivered her, too thin and shrinking from everyone and everything. It warmed Lucky's heart, both to think of Mary in a nice, quiet home, and also of Solace having the company. She would make an excellent mother…

Christ, how even that small thought had sent longing through him. He'd shoved it down. Mary would be good for her, as she would be good for Mary. End of story.

"I'm not ready to go to Alaska yet," he growled at Neuland now. "It's already autumn up there. No one with any sense would go before breakup, when the ground thaws in the spring. After the logging camp, I'll find something else."

Neuland gave him a sly look. "Like dock work?"

Lucky fought back another growl. He'd given the five hundred from the Gem to Miller to deal with, then "resigned" from the collections position. And good riddance. But whether one of Hunt's officers had blabbed, or someone saw Lucky at the clubs and put it together, news of his ill-advised "job" had spread. Mrs. Baldwin alone had been strangely silent on the subject, though he expected any day to hear from her. But everyone else was hell-bent on ribbing him about it, including Neuland, apparently.

Lucky glared at him. "Can you just make it happen?"

"Fine, fine, hold your horses. Let me see what I can do. But just so you know, you can come back and work for Jones any time. You're a good man, and this job will always be yours if you want it."

Lucky swallowed, then cleared his throat. "Thanks," he said gruffly and left.

Out on the street, he paused. What now? It was

Sunday, and despite his impatience, nothing would happen before tomorrow. He could go back to Sadie's, but being stuck inside with a bunch of rowdy men, or worse, the bible-thumpers, was intolerable.

He picked a direction at random and began walking. Every instinct tried to turn him uphill toward Myrtlewood Lane, but he forced himself to resist.

Solace…

He would never see her again. She would never betray her husband, and divorce was out of the question. In time, she would forget him, and perhaps he—

It was useless. While he was in Oregon, he would come to town to check on her whenever he could, without her knowing. He *had* to be sure she thrived. That knowledge alone would sustain him when it came time to leave her permanently.

Meanwhile…

He looked up to find he stood in front of the Gem.

Well, Portland wasn't a dry town yet, nor even a so-called "closed" one. Saloons were still open on Sundays, and suddenly, Lucky found himself in need of a drink. Or several.

He moved to the door, then hesitated.

No. He was not his father. He did not *need* to drink.

An image of Solace rose before him. Kind, intelligent, *extraordinary* Solace Grey. He could still smell the spicy rose scent of her silky honey-brown hair, see the budding awareness in those clear hazel eyes, feel the soft shape of her body branded on his, from the agonizingly brief times he had touched her.

He shoved open the door and walked into the saloon.

Chapter Thirty-One

Fall 1904 – Portland, Oregon

"Brooks, next in importance to Creffield managed to secure some linseed oil, with which he removed the tar and feathers from himself and Creffield. Brooks has never been seen since, and it is believed he went into the woods and died…" —*The Oregon Daily Journal*

The pretty girl with the blonde ringlets stepped off the sidewalk and crossed the street. He followed her.

He really ought to leave Portland and go somewhere else. That police detective had nearly ruined things, *poisoning* and *stabbing* a whore, attempting to make it look like part and parcel of his own work. Stabbing was so…violent. And poison! It wasn't even intentional, merely an amateurish mistake.

But strangulation…at the very moment of copulation…watching the life fade from his Angel's eyes as he saved her and sent her up to Heaven. *That* fulfilled his godly purpose in ways an upstart policeman could never comprehend.

Besides, *he* had never chosen a dark-haired girl, not once. How could anyone be so stupid as to think he would deviate from God's given plan? And after his first taste of saving a ripe young virgin, he would never, ever regress to killing whores.

That was too easy, and too unregarded. No one cared if a whore died.

But a virgin, a sweet, golden-haired angel…

Like…this girl.

He *would* stay in Portland after all. The police weren't even looking for him, as they believed he'd died nine months ago. All he had to do was stay in the shadows and no one would be the wiser.

Besides, there was that *other* woman to keep an eye on: Mrs. Baldwin. Not to mention the women she had roped into helping her. They could complicate his existence with their night patrols and rescue missions. For instance, there was that woman he'd seen at the Baldwin residence a few weeks back, and then later at the police station, also in Mrs. Baldwin's company.

Was Mrs. Baldwin expanding her reach, pushing her nose even farther into Portland's social welfare business? And was this woman her new second in command? But they were mere females, so perhaps he needn't worry about their inferior intellects after all.

He nodded decisively. Unless they got in his way, he'd ignore them. But if one *did* interfere, he knew what to do.

He straightened his Salvation Army uniform coat, polishing the badge above the left breast with his gloved fingers, then adjusted the cap until it sat straight on his head. Whistling, he stepped into the street and trotted quickly across, catching up to his Golden Angel just in time to offer her a hand up onto the sidewalk.

"Please, allow me," he said.

And she did.

Historical Notes

At the dawn of the 20th century in the United States, there was little understanding of mental health issues or dementia. Individuals deemed "feebleminded" were treated as criminals and could be forcibly committed to state insane asylums, institutions that were generally overcrowded, underfunded, and often more brutal than a jail. German psychiatrist and neurologist Alois Alzheimer had just begun researching the pathology of the brain, and his first paper on the subject was not published until 1906. So, while Lola might have known new research into "diseases of the brain" was being conducted, it would not yet have been widely accepted by the medical community. Solace's fear for Allen's fate, should his condition become known, was a very real and heartbreaking issue for families of the time.

The bizarre story of Edmund Creffield is also real. An itinerant preacher, he formed the Bride of Christ church in Oregon, and his followers' practice of rolling and screaming on the floor during services spawned the term "Holy Roller," which now describes anyone expressing religious fervor. Additionally, Creffield lived polygamously with over twenty women, many of whom were later sent to the Oregon Insane Asylum on grounds that their sexual practices proved their "insanity."

Several other key figures in this novel were also real people who shaped Portland's history. Lola Greene Baldwin, who eventually became the nation's first female police officer, and Chief of Police Charles Hunt and Mayor George Williams were all active during this period. I have diligently attempted to maintain historical accuracy regarding their public roles, documented actions, and known personalities within the novel's narrative. Naturally, the dialogue, internal thoughts, and private interactions have been crafted through my own imagination to bring these dynamic figures to life on the page.

Finally, for readers who may wonder why Ellie's cause of death is not questioned sooner: The ability to detect hemlock poisoning post-mortem was very limited at this time. It would have required witnessing pre-death symptoms and using extremely basic chemical testing, which could take days or weeks to complete, and which would still only suggest a general category of toxins, not any single plant specifically. Therefore, with no one besides her killer present at her death, the police and the coroner would likely have looked only to her external wounds. During the autopsy, the coroner might have noticed hemlock's mousey odor coming from her stomach if she had died more recently. But as she had been dead several days by then, it's unlikely the smell would still be present. And since she was a known prostitute, it's also unlikely anyone would have dug further into her death than necessary.

Thank you for reading *A Lamentation of Swans*. I hope having some historical context has added depth to your experience. To learn more about me or my books, or to be notified when the next in this series will be released, please see **About the Author** below.

A Quick Favor Please?

Before you go, would you please leave this book an honest review online? Reviews are so important for authors, as they help us reach more readers. Please take a minute to visit one or two retailer/review sites, such as Amazon, BookBub, or Goodreads, and leave this book a review. I promise it doesn't take long, but it would mean the world to me! This Book Riot article breaks it down into six easy steps, if you need tips: http://bit.ly/BookReviewTips.

Thank you for reading, and thank you so much for being part of this amazing journey!

~ Kerry

About the Author

Kerry Blaisdell is the bestselling and award-winning author of the acclaimed Dead Series, including *Debriefing the Dead* and its sequels, which InD'tale Magazine recommends for "fans of shows like 'Constantine' or 'Supernatural.'" She also writes award-winning Romantic Suspense (*The Princess Shoppe* and *Publish or Perish*, both Publishers Weekly BookLife Prize Semi/Quarter Finalists) and Historical Mystery.

She earned her Bachelor of Arts from U.C. Berkeley in Comparative Literature (French and Medieval English), and a Master's in Teaching English and Advanced Mathematics from University of Portland. Kerry lives in the gorgeous Pacific Northwest with her family, assorted animals, and more hot pepper plants than anyone could reasonably consume.

To connect with Kerry, scan the QR code or visit https://linktr.ee/kerryblaisdell to join her reader group, follow her on social media, or subscribe to her Very Occasional Mailing List for freebies, news, and more!

Psst! Turn the page for a sneak peek at Debriefing the Dead (Book One of The Dead Series)...

Sneak Peek: *Debriefing the Dead (Book One of The Dead Series)*

Chapter One

"Be sober, be vigilant; because your adversary the devil, as a roaring lion, walketh about, seeking whom he may devour." ~The Bible, 1 Peter 5:8

I smelled Death on the two men who walked into my shop that day. I should have listened to my nose.

Of course, death is an everyday part of my life, which is probably why I ignored it. I'm a dealer in rare artifacts, particularly those that haven't been acquired through, um, *normal* channels. Okay, I'm a fence, and before that, I robbed graves. But only those already being robbed, by "professional" archaeologists. And frankly, I know as much or more as they do about the care and preservation of ancient relics.

In any case, my shop, *Hyacinth Finch's Boutique des Antiquités,* now stocks items that are either stolen, or are being stolen back, by one or another of my usual clients, members of the Marseille elite who enjoy stabbing each other in the back, art-collection-wise. They pay well, and leave me to live my life the rest of the time, so I guess you'd call it a symbiotic relationship.

But these guys weren't from my client base. Until they arrived unannounced in my office above the shop, and sat, uninvited, in the chairs in front of my desk, I'd never seen them before. Which made their interest in this *exact* batch of goods even more suspect.

"Who are you again?" I asked, more to buy time than anything else.

The one on the left smiled genially. He was larger than his companion, not exactly fat, but taller and more…spread out, for lack of a better description. His dark blue eyes were rimmed with thick lashes, and his hair was oiled into a slick black shell. His tanned skin cracked and peeled in places, like he'd had one too many sunburns, and he had a heavy French accent, but as it was late August, and we were in southern France, neither was exactly remarkable. I myself spoke fluent French, but he'd begun in Franglish, and I hadn't corrected him.

"Mademoiselle Finch." He leaned forward, the flimsy wooden chair legs groaning and spreading under his bulk, making it look as if he had six legs instead of the usual two. "*Je vous assure,* nothing would please me more than to provide our *bona fides*. But the time, it is lacking." He glanced at his companion, equally dark and oily, but not as talkative. Oily Two smiled, close-mouthed, and gave a Gallic shrug. *We're all pals here, right?*

Yeah, right.

"Look," I said, suppressing a shiver of unease, despite the heat, "even if I wanted to, I'm not sure I could find this particular lot." I pretended to check a leather-covered log book I had open on my desk. "Where did you say it originated?"

"Turkey." Oily One's smile said he knew I knew that, his yellowed teeth big and sharp behind his dry, cracked lips.

I ran a finger down a column on the page. Look at

me—organized, professional, absolutely-*not*-lying business woman extraordinaire. "Nope. Nothing's come in from Turkey."

His gaze flicked to the log, then around my office. Books filled wood-and-glass cases along the walls, and papers crowded the floor. The window stood open behind me, letting in the Mediterranean breeze and the slanted late afternoon sunlight. Also, *un fourmilion*—an antlion—a long, thin-bodied insect with lacy wings, that my seven-year-old nephew, Geordi, would have been fascinated by. He loves bugs. Me, not so much, but I'm a vegetarian, and a live-and-let-live kinda gal, and this guy wasn't doing anything besides buzzing lazily around my office, looking for ants to trap. At least, that's what Geordi says they do. I hate ants, so if there were any to chow on, more power to him.

Oily One and Two didn't seem bothered by him, but I rather wished they were, so we could hurry this along. The bell on the downstairs door had only rung once since lunch—when these two entered—and it seemed like a good day to close early. One of the perks of being an independent "art dealer" such as myself. The downside is, I can't afford to alienate potential clients. I have my regulars, but business ebbs and flows, and extra cash is always handy. Especially now.

I forced a smile of my own. "I want to help you—I do. But I have no idea where to find…something like this." Technically, this was true. I'm a big believer in technicalities.

Oily One leaned in closer, waistband straining, hands on his knees, palms up. Open. Friendly. I didn't buy it, but apparently, the antlion did. It landed on his shoulder, black body silhouetted crisply as it crawled unnoticed over the expensive white of his suit.

He smiled again. "Surely a businesswoman of your reputation…?"

"*Messieurs.* I'm not sure what you've heard"—*or from whom*—"but I am merely a dealer. I buy. I sell. I don't find."

"*Vous me surprenez.* It is said you are *très accomplie* at these things."

I tilted back in my chair. "You flatter me. I've had good luck. And good clients. I can only sell what they bring in. Speaking of which—who did you say referred you?"

Touché. Point à moi. But he wasn't giving up. "A shipment from Colossae, in southwestern Turkey—*près de la rivière* Lycus. A region in which you specialize, *non?* Perhaps you have contacts. You will make some calls. We will, of course, reward your efforts."

He took out a business card and wrote on the back, the movement causing the antlion to take flight, hovering between him and his companion. Oily Two waved it away, then caught my eye and lifted a hand, as though asking if he should squash it. His full-lipped, sharp-toothed grin was creepier even than his friend's, and I shook my head hastily, noting that the insect—no dummy—was already out of reach.

His friend passed the card to me, and though our fingers never touched, I suddenly felt…*heat*…burning off him in sharp waves. I jerked my hand away, taking the card with me. It was as cool as paper usually is, and I gave a mental shake and glanced at the number he'd written, then had to hide my shock. This would be enough for me to take a year off—or pay for Geordi and his mother, my sister Lily, to get *really* far away from her ex. Some place where he could *never* hurt them, ever again.

I flipped the card over. *Les Rousseaux* was printed on it in plain type, with a cell number below. When I looked up, he smiled. Again.

"Claude Rousseau." He indicated Oily Two, who gave a slight bow. *"Mon frère,* Jacques. We are most pleased to make your acquaintance. If you hear of anything, you will call. Yes?"

"Yes," I said, the interview's end finally in sight. "Of course."

They rose to go, their tread surprisingly silent on the stairs, given their combined bulk. I waited until I heard the bell on the front door tinkle one last time. Then I ran down and shot the bolt. I flipped the sign in the window to read *Fermé,* then pulled down the shade. Next, I went to the back door and locked it as well. Only when I was alone in the dark store, so familiar and comforting in its clutter, did I take a deep breath and blow it out.

The whole experience bothered me on a number of levels, not the least of which was the timing. You see, I wasn't exactly upfront with the Rousseaux. Not only would I be able to locate the lot they wanted, I already had it—in storage, where it'd been for several months. The thing is, only two people should have known its origins.

One of them was me.

And the other was dead.

~:~:~

An hour later, I'd left the shop, wandering home via my usual circuitous route, past various markets, *plein air* or otherwise, where I picked up the parts of my dinner. One of the reasons I prefer Europe to the States is the whole notion of buying your food the day you cook it.

I'm not exactly a health nut, but I am a vegetarian, and a sucker for anything fresh.

Walking and shopping also gives me a chance to process my day. And today, I had a lot to process. It occurred to me the Rousseaux could be cops. La Boutique has been investigated a time or two, but I always come away clean. The thing is, if they were *les flics*, asking after *this* lot, then they already knew it was stolen. But it came from Colossae, a site which has never officially been excavated, so how could anyone know part of it was gone?

I'd "inherited" the catch from my business partner, Vadim, after he died in a boating accident. A lump rose in my throat, hot and sharp, and I swallowed it back down. Though we weren't "together" romantically, Vadim was more than a partner, he was my friend. His death was so unexpected; even half a year later, I still couldn't believe he was gone. I'd never even opened the crates he left me, just locked them up to deal with later. But…was my reluctance now because of my grief? Or were my instincts right and something was off?

Unlocking the iron gate leading to my building's interior stairwell, I saw my neighbor on his way down. Jason Jones is a little younger than me and a lot taller— at least a foot, and I'm five-five. He tends bar at one of the gay cabarets in Marseille, so he's frequently on his way out when I'm coming home. In theory, he moved here to pursue a theater career, but in practice, I think he likes the bar better. Rehearsals would mess too much with his "party all night, sleep all day" schedule.

"Hyacinth!"

He broke into a grin and finished coming down the steps, then gave a low theatrical bow and pretended to kiss my hand. He wore a black dress shirt, gray slacks, Italian leather shoes, and ridiculously large sunglasses that made him look like a very large insect hovering over my wrist. He can rock a pair of jeans, too, but today he was the perfect image of the playboy bartender, a look he cultivates with great care and uses to great advantage—and he has the tips to prove it. He's not actually gay, but he doesn't advertise the fact. However, he's never once tried to hit on me, which is not as insulting as you might think. I don't have the best track record with relationships, and with Lily and everything else, I had no desire to start one now.

As soon as I had the thought, I realized he was lingering over my wrist, turning it up and inhaling deeply. The heat of his breath tickled my skin, his fingers caressed my palm, and my knees wobbled. Apparently, I'm not immune to his charms after all.

He let go and straightened, examining my face. I couldn't read his expression behind the shiny glasses, but he must have seen something in mine that made him ask, "What's up? Something wrong at the shop?"

"It's nothing. Not really. Some new clients came in and wanted to chat. Actually…they might be a good fit for Vadim's last shipment."

He flipped the sunglasses up, blue eyes wide. He's never asked how I acquire my goods, and I've never asked what happens when he disappears for days with some girl he's met on the metro. He's entitled to his secrets, too. But he moved in right after Lily left her creepazoid husband and just before Vadim died. I couldn't burden Lily with my grief, and our parents died more than twenty years ago. If we have other family, I've never met them. I don't trust easily, but it turns out Jason has a strong, relatively safe shoulder to cry on, for which I'm eternally grateful.

That doesn't stop him from being opinionated about what I should do with my life. He gave a low whistle. "Are you going to sell it to them?"

"I…don't know." I moved up the steps, so I could look him in the eye without needing a chiropractor.

"You *have* to sell it. It's what Vadim wanted—why he *brought* it to you, for God's sake."

"I know. You're right. It's just—do I have to sell it to *these* guys?"

He planted his hands on his hips, glaring. "Hyacinth. It. Is. Time. *Let go.*"

His face was close, his breath warm, and despite it all, I found his earnestness vaguely attractive. He filled the narrow stairwell with his long, lean body, and I resisted the urge to back up another step.

"Okay, fine. I'll call them." He stood, unmoving, and I sighed. "What? I said I'd do it. Is something wrong?"

His gaze dropped to my sandals, then moved slowly up my legs, lingering on my hips, and from there over my chest and the sleeveless blouse that was all I could tolerate in this heat. By the time his gaze travelled up my throat to linger again at my mouth, before finally meeting my eyes, I had goose bumps in several inappropriate places, and was hoping the dark stairwell hid my blush.

His eyes flashed dark for a moment—almost black—then he gave an odd little shake of his head and took a step back himself. He dropped the sunglasses over his eyes, and when he spoke, his tone was light and friendly as ever. "Just checking it's really you. You never agree with me in under five minutes."

Before I could gather my wits for a decent retort, he

gave a mock salute, then buzzed the gate open and vanished up the block. I blew out a breath and finished the climb to my third-floor apartment—second, if you count European style.

Jason's only a little younger than me—late twenties or so—but I think he gets that whole *joie de vivre* thing better than I do. He's a hard worker, don't get me wrong. But he also plays hard, and flits from one activity to the next with an easy metamorphosis I admire. I didn't know what to make of his sudden inexplicable interest, but he had helped me feel better. And he was right. Holding onto Vadim's last catch wouldn't bring him back. It would only hold *me* back.

The apartment stairs lead to a short breezeway, open on both ends. There's one apartment on each corner, and mine's the first on the left. I unlocked the door and stepped in. My place is tiny, but less cluttered than the shop. In a complete reversal of the stereotypical antiques dealer, I am not a pack rat. Give me open space and tidy end tables and I'm a happy camper. Wood floors, throw rugs, small table and chairs in the dining nook. A kitchen that used to be a closet, as near as I can tell—only one person can stand in it at a time, and if the oven's open, nobody can. One window in the main room, another in the bedroom, and finally, a bathroom that's bigger than the kitchen, but not by much.

I have pretty basic needs, possibly due to growing up in foster care. But that's a whole other story, and I'm well-adjusted enough to know I can't blame all my idiosyncrasies on my parentless childhood. Some, but not all. The bottom line is I don't need a lot of junk to be happy. I do need a certain amount of cash, though. Lily's custody battle over Geordi wasn't only with her ex, Nick.

It was with his entire family. And I do mean Family—as in organized, with a capital F. The Sicilian Mob. Which Lily swears she didn't know until after they were married, though how either of us were naïve enough to believe Nick was just "a" Dioguardi, and not one of *the* Dioguardis, is beyond me.

Worse, since Geordi's the first son of an *only* son, Nick's family weren't about to let him go, even if Lily found the one judge in Paris brave enough to side with her. It took serious guts for her to leave, and if I had any say in it, neither she nor Geordi would ever go back.

So, if the Oily Brothers' money could facilitate that, who was I to quibble?

~:~:~

The next day was Sunday, and not only is my shop closed, most of the other shops in my area are as well. I figured the Rousseaux could wait another day before I told them of the shipment. For one thing, it would lend credibility to my claim of needing to find it first. For another, as noted, I wasn't exactly anxious to call them.

But first thing Monday, I dragged myself out of bed, showered, and drove to the warehouse I rent at the docks, near the Bassin d'Arenc. I use it to store unsorted catches or big items I can't cram into the shop. Or, let's be honest, things I don't want out in plain sight.

Ordinarily I'd walk—it's only twenty blocks—but I had to move Vadim's stuff to the shop before calling the Rousseaux. Unfortunately, my car's a Peapod prototype, and about the size of a mini-Mini Cooper. It was a gift from a grateful client, and tops out at forty-five kilometers per hour, so no *autobahn* for me. But it's electric, costs around two cents a kilometer for gas, and is perfect for getting around town.

Not so perfect for hauling stuff.

I could've asked Claude and Jacques to meet me with a truck. Since the catch was currently in three large shipping crates, this would save tons of time and effort. But though I'd decided to unload the stuff, showing these guys where I kept my stock—or what I still had on hand—might not be the smartest idea. Besides, I was curious about the contents. Vadim had never told me what he'd found, and in our line of work, it could be anything from thousands-of-years-old "junk" to priceless relics. I was guessing at least some of the latter, or why would the Rousseaux care?

In order to find out, I'd have to move everything to smaller boxes, cart it to the store, go back to the warehouse, rinse, repeat. Part of me wondered if I should just hand it over as-is and be done.

I suppressed yet another twinge at the memory of yesterday's interview. Especially Jacques, sitting still and spider-like across from me. I had a feeling he didn't miss much and wondered what I might have unconsciously revealed while Claude distracted me.

I pulled into a parking space near my unit, and my cell rang, the cheery notes of Beethoven's *Für Élise* telling me Lily was calling for our weekly chat. For a second, I thought about answering. Lily might be Geordi's mother, but I have to say, he's pretty much the light of my life. Certainly, the best male relationship I've had, even counting Jason and Vadim. Who wouldn't love a guy who brings you dead bugs he's found in someone *else's* yard, then offers to split the last éclair because you're his "favoritest *tata* ever"? He's a smart kid, too. I'm his *only* auntie, and the flattery still works.

I sent the call to voicemail. It almost killed me, but

it'd be hard enough opening the crates, knowing how excited Vadim was when he landed this catch. You can't get much fresher than an unexcavated site. If I spent even a half hour catching up with Lily and Geordi, I'd chicken out. And I had to know what was in those crates, or I'd never be able to let them, or Vadim, go.

I screwed up my courage, got out of the car, and unlocked the unit's roll door. Yep. Three large crates.

Very large.

I went back to the Peapod, opened the hatch, and extracted the paltry pile of produce boxes I'd scrounged from my favorite markets. I'd have to empty them again at the store for subsequent trips, or else go beg more boxes. This was ridiculous. But necessary.

Must let go. Must move on.

~:~:~

As is so often the case, once I got going, it wasn't so bad. Opening the first crate was tough, and I won't say I didn't cry at all. Vadim was a good partner, and a better friend. At least he'd died doing what he loved—sailing the Mediterranean, with a drink in his hand and two beautiful women at his side. He was a devout atheist, but if there's any kind of afterlife, I'd like to think he's still sailing and drinking, and looking for the next big catch.

I found a roll of paper towels on a shelf and blew my nose, then metaphorically rolled up my non-existent sleeves and dug in.

The more valuable items were wrapped in acid-free paper and sealed in airtight containers, which I didn't bother to open, because Vadim had helpfully labeled them. His clear, bold printing noted statuary and relics, both Pagan and Christian, from the ancient Phrygian city of Colossae, near what is now Denizli, in southwestern

Turkey. The general period was the first century, so any Christian items were very early. While this fascinated me intellectually, and I did have some experience with artifacts from Turkey, it was mainly because Vadim brought them to me. My own interests lie more in the Egyptians, one of the reasons we'd complemented each other professionally. But it meant I had little personal experience with anything of this kind.

It took several trips to move the best items, and a few more for the midlevel stuff, plus getting more boxes. By the time I got to the third crate, the sun was well past its zenith, but I'd reached the dregs. Items down here were either unwrapped, loose in the packing straw, or else carelessly covered with rough cloth to prevent scratching.

This crate wasn't as full as the others, and it looked like I was on my final trip. Thank God. I'd had a quick lunch—veggies, hummus, cheese, and bread—but otherwise worked straight through. Lily'd called twice more, but I didn't pick up. I'd call her back over dinner, when we'd have time to chat, and I could tell her of my sudden windfall.

I plopped my last empty box on the warehouse floor, then hung over the side of the crate to excavate the bottom. I found a few more canvas bundles and pulled them out, setting them in the box, then went back once more.

I thought I'd gotten everything, until my fingers brushed against something hard, wrapped in cloth, and oddly warm to the touch. I grabbed it and heaved myself out of the crate, then examined the bundle. It felt like a rock, heavy and solid. Most of the items in this crate were broken pottery shards, from vases and the like. Hard, maybe, but not heavy. Careful not to touch the item's surface, in case it was valuable after all, I turned it over and shook the covering loose.

Sure enough, it was a rock. Plain, gray, ordinary. About half the size of an American football, shaped like an irregular pyramid, with jagged edges and flat-but-rough surfaces. The only unusual thing about it was its warmth. Like Claude Rousseau. Which is maybe why, against my better judgment, I reached out and touched the very tip of the rock's pyramid.

And then it *shrieked* at me, the agony of centuries piercing my ears till I thought my skull would burst, electric shocks searing through my fingers, hand, arm, ripping through my whole body, gripping my lungs and squeezing until I couldn't breathe. I flung the rock away, covering my ears and dropping to the floor, shaking, gasping for air, while still it screamed, on and on and on and on, until I lay huddled on the concrete, red fire burning in my head, blackness filling my soul.

Then everything went silent.

Ready for more? Find all Kerry's books at
https://books2read.com/kerryblaisdell!

Praise for Kerry Blaisdell

"From the first moments that readers meet Allie—in the men's room, stewing about unfair treatment at work—her tenacity, temperament, and life circumstances are palpably wrought. Her will-they-won't-they rapport with Matt enlivens the already-dynamic story, and Blaisdell shows, through Allie's story, that women can have it all: a successful career, romance, and a future of their own choosing." ~ *Publishers Weekly BookLife Prize*

"Blaisdell is an incredibly gifted author and is now my favorite rom-com writer. The vivid imagery of the scenes colorfully brings them to life, making it feel like watching a Hollywood rom-com. Blaisdell effortlessly switches between introspection and drama, bringing out intricate emotions." ~ *Reader's Favorite*

"Ms. Blaisdell is a master storyteller...So many twists and turns will have you sitting on the edge of your seat!" ~ *Still Moments Magazine*

"The supernatural mystery and suspense elements drive the fast-paced plot forward, combined with enough romance to add sentimental flair between the characters. Balanced with a sense of fun and quirky situations, *Debriefing the Dead* is excellently imaginative and hard to put down." ~ *Reader's Favorite*

"Fans of television shows like 'Constantine' or 'Supernatural' will absolutely love [*Waking the Dead*]... Hyacinth is phenomenal and develops so much in this book." ~ *InD'tale Magazine*

The room was cold and flickered with shadows.

Dirt floor, poorly framed wooden walls, smells of dying plants and mold. How had she gotten here? Ellie shivered and hugged herself. Her eyes wouldn't stay open, but inside her lids or out, everything swam and shifted. Something tickled her consciousness, a memory. A *good* memory. Something had happened, something that gave her hope. She was supposed to be somewhere, or—or meet someone. Or…something.

A steady drumbeat throbbed in her skull, making it hard to think. Or maybe it was the sickly-sweet smell. She knew that smell. It pulsed in her veins with a need stronger than anything. Stronger even than the thread of life reaching out from her womb.

"*Kūdikis*," she whispered through dry, cracked lips.

A man loomed over her, dressed in a dark coat and trousers, and she recognized him as he caught her wrist. "Stay still and this will be over soon."

He held a syringe, and memory flooded back—he had grabbed her from behind. She'd struggled, then felt the stinging pinch in her neck, the sweet drug entering her veins, then blessed blackness.

"No," she whispered. Her heavy body wouldn't move, and besides, where would she go? Tears burned her eyes and the life in her womb fluttered then stilled. "*Kūdikis*…baby…"